LOT'S
RETURN TO
SODOM

LOT'S RETURN TO SODOM

A LIV BERGEN MYSTERY

SANDRA BRANNAN

GREENLEAF
BOOK GROUP PRESS

Published by Greenleaf Book Group Press
Austin, Texas
www.gbgpress.com

Copyright ©2011 Sandra Brannan

Distributed by Greenleaf Book Group LLC

For ordering information or special discounts for bulk purchases, please contact Greenleaf Book Group LLC at PO Box 91869, Austin, TX 78709, 512.891.6100.

Design and composition by Greenleaf Book Group LLC and Alex Head
Cover design by Greenleaf Book Group LLC

Publisher's Cataloging-In-Publication Data
(Prepared by The Donohue Group, Inc.)
Brannan, Sandra.
Lot's return to Sodom / Sandra Brannan. — 1st ed.
p. ; cm. — (A Liv Bergen mystery)
Sequel to: In the belly of Jonah.
ISBN: 978-1-60832-119-3
1. Murder--Investigation--Black Hills (S.D. and Wyo.)—Fiction. 2. Motorcycle gangs—Fiction. 3. Black Hills (S.D. and Wyo.)—Fiction. 4. Suspense fiction. I. Title.
PS3602.R366 L68 2011
813/.6   2011921041

Part of the Tree Neutral® program, which offsets the number of trees consumed in the production and printing of this book by taking proactive steps, such as planting trees in direct proportion to the number of trees used: www.treeneutral.com

TreeNeutral®

Printed in the United States of America on acid-free paper

11 12 13 14 15 16   10 9 8 7 6 5 4 3 2 1

First Edition

If everyone had parents as great as mine are,
the world would be a much better place.

This book is dedicated to
Dad and Mom
for allowing me to have the best childhood imaginable.
Just like you rewarded Scotch
with a scratch behind his ears when he'd
drop dead mice on your doorstep,
I hope you understand this dedication doesn't mean
you have to read the story.
A pat on the head will do.

And to Mick,
my dear friend,
who convinced me to take off my rose-colored glasses
for just a minute
to see what it was like in his world as
an FBI agent.
Thank you for helping me write a better story.

CHAPTER 1

"CAN YOU STAY?" HE asked her.

"Jens is picking me up at eight," Michelle explained.

"Forget about him. I'll give you a ride home," Roy offered.

"I'm tired," she protested, tilting her head from side to side to stretch her weary neck and shoulders. "Not that I don't appreciate what you're doing for me, Roy, letting me work extra hours so I can afford to pay off the last of my college loans, and I only have—"

"Two weeks left before graduation," he interrupted. "I know, I know. You've always wanted to be a doctor and you're one step closer. It's great that you're following your dream."

"My dream right now is to go home and get some sleep. You have me scheduled to be back here at six o'clock tomorrow morning. Or did you forget?"

"I never forget," he said, staring at her through his glasses. "You punched in at exactly five fifty-eight, two minutes ahead of time. You probably arrived at five forty-five, drank your first cup of coffee, and put your lunch in the employee break room refrigerator."

She glanced sideways at him and said, "Okay, that's weird, Roy."

It was as if he hadn't heard her. "You took your morning break at nine ten until nine twenty, shorting yourself five minutes."

Ever since they'd first met in high school, Michelle had known he was a bit off. She had felt sorry for him and he'd had a crush on her. Maybe that's why they became quick friends. Somewhere in the back of her mind she wondered if he'd ever truly outgrown that schoolboy crush. But after almost fifteen years of deflecting his advances, she hoped he had moved on and was only an attentive friend. His account of her every move didn't give her confidence in that assumption.

"You took a lunch break from eleven thirty-five to noon, again shorting yourself five minutes. You ate your lunch while reading a book, probably a mystery," Roy recited mechanically, handing can after can of fruits and vegetables to Michelle to shelve.

"Stop!" Michelle felt her breath catch as she realized Roy Barker was not kidding.

Her mind flashed to all the times in recent months when she and Jens had seen Roy around town when they went out. He just happened by their table at the Millstone, hinting that he should join them for brunch. And they caught a glimpse of him at Canyon Lake Park when they were feeding the ducks, as though he'd stood watching them before he jogged away on the bike path. Maybe Jens had been right about Roy's obsession with her, Michelle thought.

"You took a ten-minute afternoon break at four fifteen and haven't taken a break since. You expertly averted the advances of that wannabe biker dude shortly after, even though he was putting a full-court press on you to become his lady."

"His lady?" Michelle shot back, disturbed that his creepy mania was spiraling out of control. "Roy, what are you talking about?"

Just as her mind raced to find an excuse to end this conversation, Michelle saw Roy's eyes narrow as he stared past her shoulder and down the aisle. She turned slowly to see what had distracted him from his bizarre fixation on the minutiae of her life.

Three bikers were walking toward them. These were motorcycle club bikers, the real deal, the kind who were known for illegal activities like selling drugs. The outlaw bikers who often started trouble—mostly with other such bikers, but trouble nonetheless. The police watched them closely during the rally; authorities by the hundreds were flown in from all over the country for the week. And because Jens had pointed it out to her last year, Michelle knew what it meant to be flying colors, and that the authorities generally prohibited it during the rally to help prevent knife fights and shootings. These three bikers, however, were most definitely flying their colors.

The well-worn black leather jackets were decorated with patches and badges, and the skinny biker on the right was wearing a red and silver skullcap with the Lucifer's Lot logo stitched neatly across the front. The scary-looking guy in the middle was staring directly at her.

The Lucifer's Lot was one of the motorcycle gangs that were banned now and again from crossing South Dakota state lines because of the trouble they caused with the Inferno Force. Michelle had read about them in the newspapers years ago and tried to recall niggling details about a gunfight or ambush that involved the two gangs near Stockade Lake in Custer State Park. A drug deal gone wrong or something.

Roy stepped between Michelle and the men to shield her while she scuttled to her feet. Watching Roy draw in air to inflate his chest, Michelle thought he looked more like a puffer fish than the friend she'd known for so long and wondered why she had been loyal to him all these years.

She barely recognized his tone when he barked, "What do you want?"

The scary biker in the middle, who wore a black-and-gray ponytail and a black mustache, ignored Roy's question, never taking his eyes off Michelle. With a velvet Trace Adkins voice, he said, "Excuse me, ma'am. Can you help us find a few things?"

"Sure," Michelle said, relieved by the interruption. She definitely preferred a hardcore biker's attentions to Roy's disturbing interest in her at that moment.

"Michelle, no," Roy said, grabbing her elbow as she stepped around him.

The two bikers flanking the ominous one growled like two guard dogs. Michelle turned to Roy, removing his hand from her arm, and whispered, "It's okay. Really. They just want a little help finding things."

Roy scowled.

Michelle turned toward the bikers. "The customer's always right, Roy."

"My name's Mully," the biker said, cutting his eyes at Roy and walking alongside Michelle down the aisle, the two other bikers falling in behind them. She could almost feel Roy's glare burning a hole through her as she turned the corner with the strangers. She imagined his disappointment that she didn't wither or faint from the fear of it all, allowing him to protect her as the hero he was meant to be.

Lord, he was getting to be so annoying. Hang in there, she told herself. Money is freedom.

"My name's Michelle. What do you need help finding?"

One of the guard dogs handed her a short list. She glanced at it: needles, thread, matches, and rubbing alcohol. Curiously, the handwriting looked more like a woman's than one of these guys'. She wondered if they planned on sewing up a buddy's knife wound or something. And was smart enough not to ask.

Michelle walked briskly toward the aisle of miscellaneous housewares with the three bikers in tow, Mully falling in step beside her once again. She scanned the shelves for the items, Mully standing so close beside her they were almost touching shoulders and arms. The other two bikers stood behind them. By the scruffy looks of them, she had imagined the three of them would stink. But the scent emanating from Mully was actually quite pleasant, suggesting a dash of decent cologne.

"Where did they relocate the Harley-Davidson dealership?" he asked.

"So, you've been here before? To Rapid City?" she replied, handing the scrawny biker his list, and pointing to the shelf where sewing items were displayed. She watched him double-check the list while one of the other bikers gathered items.

"Lots of times. The dealership moved, though. I forget where."

"It's out on the corner of Deadwood Avenue and I-90 by the Windmill Truck Stop. Hard to miss. Do you know where that is?"

Mully nodded. "I do. I take the back roads to Sturgis when I'm here, not I-90."

They had moved over to the aisle where camping items were displayed, and the two minions were off to find the matches. She hadn't noticed before, but the youngest biker had the word "Prospect" printed on the back of his jacket just below the logo. Once again, Mully stood shoulder to shoulder with her, his eyes never once straying from her face. Michelle pretended not to notice. She glanced over toward the checkout lanes and realized Roy was nowhere in sight, which made her more nervous than having this gang leader stare at her. She saw the two grab a packet of wooden matches and snatch some light fishing line while they were at it, holding it up for Mully to see. He nodded an approval.

Michelle stole a quick glance up to the manager's loft. Through the tinted window she could just detect the light inside his office shining behind Roy's silhouette. She could feel his eyes on her and a shiver skipped down her spine. Feeling safer, with Mully standing beside her, knowing what he represented, underscored her deeper concern about Roy.

The last of the items, the rubbing alcohol, was over with the first aid supplies, and Michelle led the trio to the aisle farthest from the manager's loft. Watching the young biker retrieve not one, but several bottles, Michelle knew her suspicion that a wound was involved was probably accurate. Mully watching them from beside her, she marveled at how difficult it had been for the two to decide who would carry what, squabbling like little boys on a playground. She wasn't sure why Mully's silence made her more uncomfortable than their conversation did, so she decided to break it with more small talk.

"So, are you here for the rally?"

He nodded once and said, "Starts tomorrow. Officially."

Before she knew what was happening, he had turned to face her, smiling. She felt his groomed fingernails lightly drag across her left cheek as he brushed a strand of hair from her face, and she detected the faint smell of cloves on his breath when he asked, "Want to join me?"

Michelle took a step back, pushed the loose strand of hair behind her ear, and said, "No, thanks, but I'm sure you guys will have a great time up there."

The biker turned away with a shrug. Michelle wrapped her arms around herself and glanced over her shoulder toward the loft, surprised to see Jens waiting for her, pretending to be interested in the bandages until she was finished with the customer. He gave her a wink and she stood on her tiptoes to hug his neck and said, "Hi, hon."

Michelle sensed Jens's tension, then connected it to Mully and his friends nearby.

"Jens, I was just helping some tourists find their way around the store. You should meet—"

When she turned back toward them to introduce Jens, Michelle saw Mully walking away with the other bikers without even acknowledging his arrival and without saying another word to her. She suspected Jens was reading the Lucifer's Lot rocker above the familiar gang emblem on all three jackets as they ambled toward the checkout registers. Roy Barker, heir apparent to Barker Market, came scrambling down the stairs from the manager's loft to stand guard by *his* checkers, paying particular attention that Michelle, *his* bookkeeper and favorite employee, was nowhere near them as they completed their purchase.

"How long have you been waiting?"

"Long enough to hear him ask you to go to the rally with him."

Michelle shrugged and rolled her eyes. "As if."

"You have to be more careful."

"I know, thanks for the tip. By the way, why did you bring Char?"

"I didn't—"

Char was charging down the aisle toward them, fooling no one that she was old enough to carry off the platform sandals with the short shorts that might have been described as adorable on her the previous summer and if not for her obvious attempt to appear sexier than her youth could possibly allow.

Stopping in front of Michelle, nose to nose, she fumed, "We need to talk."

"Now?"

"Now. Let's go for a drive."

Michelle frowned. "Wait for me in your car. I'll be out in five minutes."

Char stomped off, the bikers at the checkout lane ogling her as she walked by them and out the door.

Turning to Jens with a sigh, Michelle asked, "Rain check on dinner?"

"Sure. Come by my house later, if that's okay." After a quick kiss he headed for the front of the store.

Before she could answer, Roy stormed toward Michelle and jabbed a finger at her nose.

"What the hell were you thinking?"

CHAPTER 2

JENS PULLED UP SHORT, noting Roy's tone.

"I was helping some customers," Michelle answered matter-of-factly, relieved that Jens had overheard.

"Why didn't you let me handle it, Michelle?" Spittle flew from Roy's lips. "Why did you deliberately disobey me?"

"Hey, calm down, Roy," Jens warned, approaching from behind and laying his large hand on Roy's shoulder.

Roy batted Jens's hand away and glared up at him. "Back off, Bergen. She works for me." He turned back to Michelle.

"Roy, come on. I'm your bookkeeper, not a galley slave. You said yourself I should spend more time on the floor with customers this time of year. When it's this busy people don't always pay for what they take. I thought it would be better to keep an eye on them, you know."

"That wasn't why. You treated them like honored guests. They're criminals, Michelle. The Lucifer's Lot, no less—they don't come any worse."

Unfazed by Roy's temper, Michelle shook her head and said, "Good night, Roy. See you tomorrow."

When she turned away, Roy grabbed her arm again.

Jens intervened, "Hey, hey, Roy. I said calm down."

"What's gotten into you?" Michelle wrestled quickly out of Roy's grip and checked her watch. "I have to go. Charlene's waiting for me."

Roy followed behind as she headed toward the back of the store. "The Lucifer's Lot is a dangerous motorcycle gang, Michelle. Not nice. Killing machines."

"I know, Roy. But all they wanted was a little help with their grocery shopping."

"You let him touch you."

Michelle ignored him and pushed open the swinging door that led to the cool storage and the employee break room. Roy turned and held out his hand like a traffic cop to stop Jens just outside the door marked "Employees Only." Jens shook his head in disbelief as Roy followed Michelle to the time clock.

Certain that he was alone with Michelle, Roy became a different person. His anger quickly dissipated and he almost pleaded, "How could you?"

"How could I what, Roy?" Her anger mounting, Michelle spun on her heels to find him directly behind her, too close. She felt trapped between the wall and Roy. His breath smelled of mouthwash.

"Touch you like that," he said, dragging his fingers across her cheek as Mully had.

With a shudder, she shoved at his chest, making him step back from her, and slammed her fists on her hips, hoping to snap him out of the hypnosis he seemed to have fallen under.

"What's it to you?"

Roy blinked. "He . . . he's nothing more than a filthy criminal."

"Haven't you ever heard of not judging a book by its cover?" Michelle argued, grabbing her time card. "You don't know he's a criminal. And I didn't let him touch me."

Roy didn't seem to hear her. He watched as she slid the card into the time clock. She was careful not to turn her back on him.

He cleared his throat and pointed to the small pile of belongings she was gathering. "Speaking of judging books, you're reading the newest John B. McDonald. It came in last week, right?"

Michelle scooped the items into her arms and said, "Not that it's any of your business."

Foolishly ignoring her indignation and warning, Roy continued. "On your ten-minute lunch break at four fifteen, you read this book in the employee lunchroom. Then you came back to work and relieved Sarah so she could take ten."

Michelle spun around and held up her hand. "Stop, Roy. Just knock it off, will you? You really are scaring me."

She studied the manager's large hands and bulked-up forearms showing from his rolled white shirtsleeves and felt a small wave of fear. But Roy looked back at her almost meekly. "I care about you. I've always cared about you. You're my friend."

She opted for being compassionate, yet truthful, by saying, "You're my friend, too, Roy, but I don't make it my business to know every move you make every minute of your day. It's creepy, like I'm being watched or something. Do you understand?"

She had avoided the word "stalker" so as not to further anger him, but it was definitely the word for him.

"Creepy? That's harsh, Michelle. I want only the best for you. I know how hard you've worked to get where you are."

"You don't know the half. Sorry, Roy, but I really have to go now. Oh! *Nightmare in Pink*."

"What?"

"*Nightmare in Pink*," she repeated, holding up the paperback and offering him a conciliatory smile. "That's the book I'm reading."

He stared at her and she recognized the gratitude in his expression.

Casually, she added, "And yes, it's a John D. McDonald. D as in dog, not B as in boy. And it's not a new one. It first came out in the sixties, I think; this is a new reprint."

"I'll have to read it, then." Roy's smile was unsettling. "Again."

"Again?" she said, taking a step back toward him.

"I've read everything you've read. Everything. I watch everything you do. Know everything about you."

"Roy, stop, please." She stepped backward toward the door, relieved to know Jens was nearby. But Roy's mood had changed.

"I even know your dirty little secret."

Michelle stopped dead still.

"What . . . secret?"

"What really happened in high school," he hissed, slowly snaking toward her. "Your three months' absence just after Thanksgiving. Everything about you coming down with 'mono.'" He had made air quotes around the last word then leaned in closer to repeat, "Everything!"

Michelle was stunned. Only her parents and Dr. Morgan knew about that. How in the world could Roy know?

He leaned toward her ear and said, "Was it someone filthy like that Lucifer's Lot stud? Is that why you're so attracted to him?"

Michelle was still deep in thought about her freshman year in high school, wondering how she'd slipped up and how many others might know.

"Doesn't matter," Roy said quietly, pressing his lips against her ear and placing his hands on her hips. "I still love you."

"What?" Michelle asked, snapping out of her reverie, aghast by what she thought she heard him say.

"I . . . I love you," he repeated with less confidence, his hands dropping limply to his sides. "I thought you knew."

"Are you crazy?" Michelle gaped, taking a step back from him.

She wondered what had possessed her to take pity on him just now. Her decision to show him a little kindness only inspired him to go deeper into his fantasy about her. She had made a terrible mistake.

"No, I didn't know. I have never given you any reason to believe we were anything more than friends, Roy. At least, we used to be friends until you started obsessing over every little thing I do, stalking me wherever I went this summer. Don't you understand? I'm in love with Jens. Not you. You know that. You've always known that. You are crazy, Roy. Crazy!"

Roy's sad smile faded. The anger rose to his cheeks, an anger that touched his eyes in a way she had never seen before. She was used to his childish tantrums, but she'd never seen Roy like this.

His voice was nearly unrecognizable when he demanded, "Don't ever call me that."

"Roy, this isn't—"

"You listen to me," he interrupted, closing the distance between them instantly, gripping her arms and shaking her. "Never say that word again.

Ever. Or you will pay for it. Do you hear me, Michelle Freeburg? You will regret it for the rest of your life."

His grip was painful. A shiver ran down Michelle's spine and she forced a whimper back down her throat and a smile to her face. "Roy, calm down. I didn't mean anything by it."

The door swung open and Jens was filling the space with his six-foot four-inch, two-hundred-twenty-pound frame. He had overheard Roy and she was glad of it.

"You want to step outside and pick on someone your own size?" he said, nostrils flaring.

Roy froze.

Michelle shook free from Roy's grip and clung to Jens's arm. "Jens, listen to me. This isn't worth it."

Roy and Jens squared off in the small space, and Michelle was finding it harder and harder to breathe with every passing second of mounting tension. She had never seen Roy so angry before, and she had never seen Jens angry at all. And to top it all off, Charlene was waiting in the parking lot for her, pissed about some life-shattering tragedy that only a fourteen-year-old mind could make out of trivial matters, her dinner date with Jens ruined.

This was turning into a disastrous night.

"Jens, please," she pleaded, pulling on his muscular arm, trying to make him follow her out the door and away from the store.

Through clenched teeth, he issued Roy a warning. "Stay away from Michelle, Roy Barker, or *you* will be the one who regrets it for the rest of *your* life."

CHAPTER 3

AS WE DROVE, MY mind was a bit too fuzzy to take in all the strange things I was seeing on the streets of Sturgis.

The Brain Pain Killers—aptly named and unfortunately for all of us, my sister Agatha's drink of choice—we had just shared with Dad and two of our sisters at Gunners Lounge had affected me far more than they had my brother, probably because he is at least six inches taller and eighty pounds heavier. Plus, I hadn't had a drink in over a month. Plus he opted to chase it with a cup of coffee rather than to sneak Barbara's drink and quaff it for her as I had. My head spun from the double shot of vodka and tequila. I leaned back against the headrest and questioned my flawed logic, wondering if this was a lingering symptom of the alcohol I'd just pounded or the continuing saga of bad choices I seemed to be making lately, not the least of which was my decision a month ago to pursue the De Milo murderer. I had questioned my logic a hundred times while I lay recovering in a hospital bed and in physical therapy, wondering what it was that compelled me to impose myself in the investigation of my employee's murder when it was in the capable hands of the FBI. Illogical decisions weren't something I was accustomed to.

How did I let Agatha and Barbara talk me into rolling out of bed, skipping breakfast, and schlepping into a bar in Sturgis on one of the busiest days of the year? The answer was simple. It wasn't flawed logic. It was because I loved my family. I was here at Dad's request, just as Agatha and Barbara informed me at the crack of ten this morning when they dragged me out of my deep sleep.

I had a big problem with "Honor Thy Father and Mother," drilled into my head by the nuns in grade school. My parents raised me to be independent, maybe a bit too much so for my own good, but I struggled with that fine definitional line of honor. I had clearly allowed myself creative license.

So it would be no surprise to anyone who knew me, Liv Bergen, that at my mom's insistence and despite being nearly thirty years old, I had come home for my last week of physical therapy before heading back to work in Colorado. I admit she was right, considering the sound night of sleep I had in my childhood home last night. It sure beat the noises and unavoidable interruptions at Poudre Hospital, and there's no comparison when it comes to home cookin'. Most of all, it was that elixir of my mother's healing hug at the airport that made me straighten up and hasten my steps down the walkway. Home again in Rapid City, South Dakota, in the Black Hills.

But since I fell asleep before Dad got home last night, I was only too eager to get a much-needed hug from him, too, even if it meant having to be kidnapped by my sisters, escorted in Agatha's death trap of a truck twenty miles north to Sturgis, and imbibe in alcohol before noon.

"How awesome was that?" said Jens cheerily. "Dad inviting us to accompany him on his annual trek to Gunners to toast the official first day of the Sturgis Motorcycle Rally."

For better than fifty years, Dad has always made the pilgrimage to Gunners on the first day of the rally just to have one beer. But I've never asked him if it was in celebration of the tourism dollars the throngs of bikers brought to the area every year or if it was more like remembering the Alamo, holding down the fort and showing solidarity with the locals as the horde of total strangers invaded their town. Either way, he never missed it, even with raising nine kids, running his mining company, and winning the election to the sole U.S. Congress seat for South Dakota eighteen years ago.

"I bet his buddies aren't real pleased he chose a few of his kids over them this year," I mused.

Jens shot me a look. "Not many of those friends are left, Boots."

Boots. Only my siblings call me that. I ferociously rejected that nickname and became Liv when I discovered boys, along about puberty, but I've always loved the steel-toed boots that I first associated, with childish awe, with my father's. They still get my tender toes around a quarry. And I've noticed that the boys don't seem to mind them at all.

My brother added, "You knew Joe Pike died last month, didn't you? Nate Fischer has dementia. And Harold Bolter has prostrate cancer."

"That doesn't leave many of the old gang, does it?"

"He still has all his constituents who love him."

"All seven hundred thousand of them," I said, grinning.

"I doubt if everyone in the state of South Dakota loves Congressman Bergen."

"Oh, yeah. There are the two in Oneida who didn't vote for him. I couldn't believe how many people recognized him at Gunners."

"Life with Dad in public," Jens said, powering down the windows of the truck as we maneuvered around streams of bikers.

With the rumble of Harleys filling my ears, I inhaled. The blended aroma of exhaust, human flesh, and a plethora of steaming foods cooked along the streets by eager vendors that encircled my nose was a bad omen. The redhead in the black leather thong and chaps lifted her skimpy tank top for a passing biker, who laughed in appreciation as he feasted his hungry eyes. The young cop in the gray T-shirt and dark shades several paces behind moved quickly to issue the woman what I imagined was probably an indecent exposure citation, but he couldn't conceal the smile on his own face.

When I looked down Main Street, in all its chrome-and-leather glory, mostly what I saw were overage, overweight, under-toned men and women scantily dressed in black clothing, frantically shopping for more of the scantier and shockingly revealing black clothing. Anything to uphold the Sturgis rally credo of "I shock, therefore I am."

Jens jabbed me in the ribs and pointed to a woman the size of a small car whose pendulous breasts would have outweighed two adult dachshunds. She was standing on the opposite corner wearing nothing but a smile and a black string bikini, which was difficult to discern for sure considering the strings were all but lost in the gross folds of fat.

"Yikes," was all I could manage.

Tonight there would be standing room only in the bars, people would be crushed elbow to elbow on the sidewalks, and there would be no parking for any bikes, let alone a huge truck the size of Jens's.

The smells and sounds and heat outside were blending miserably with the vodka and tequila and whatever else my tongue couldn't identify that was in that Brain Pain Killer. My experience told me that I'd consumed on an empty stomach a concoction that would only lead to vomiting.

I cranked up the A/C and rested my head against the dashboard, squeezing my eyes closed.

Jens laughed. "Want me to stop?"

"No, just give me a minute."

At times like this, when I struggle with keeping everything together, I escape to happy memories and I never know quite where my mind will lead me. My youngest sister, Ida, is a serious soprano, even studied in Italy, teaches voice in Rapid City now when she's not traversing the country on a modeling gig. She gave us all a treasure of melodies (with complete orchestral backup) to carry around in our heads. It's a reserve of beauty and passion that I can call on whenever I need a distraction from whatever is in front of me, like the rumble of motorcycles, the revolting smells, the heat, the vulgarity triumphant, that we were mired in at that moment. Click! I'm raising a glass with Violetta while everybody belts out the Drinking Song from Verdi's *La Traviata*. I'm a hoop-skirted vision with decorous décolletage, carefree in this happy paradise. *Libiamo*, Liv!

Within a few minutes, we were on the west side of Main Street and had pulled off the main drag back into the industrial block near the railroad tracks, free at last of everything assaulting my senses. I felt good again, leaning back and enjoying the view.

"You okay?"

I nodded.

Jens pulled his truck off of Sherman Street onto our industrial lot, and drove me around the ready mix concrete plant, pointing through the windshield of his truck. "See how they enclosed the plant? They installed a new boiler and heating system for winter pours."

"No way. I bet your guys love that," I said, feeling the familiar joy of work returning to my gut.

"They will this winter."

"What's that?" I pointed to concrete blocks that looked like ginormous Legos.

"That's Build-a-Block, our newest product that Matt and Travis are making. They use the returns and pour it in the mold."

Jens's smile warmed my heart. "So cool, Jens. No waste concrete to get rid of."

"No waste ever again. Just product we can sell. They're mostly used for retaining walls."

"Amazing!"

As he was pulling out of the lot to head back up the street, he saw it before I did. Face red with frustration, Travis was bolting from the small office beside the batch room and heading for a pickup.

Jens crossed the single-lane traffic, pulled the pickup alongside the curb on the left, the wrong way on the two-lane Sherman Street, jerked the stick into park, and said, "Wait here. I'll be right back."

As he jumped out of the truck, I stared after him and shouted out his driver's window, "No problem."

With long strides, he hurried past the cement silo, walked across the ready mix yard, and reached Travis's pickup before he pulled away from the office. I saw Travis motion for Jens to get in, and Jens rounded the truck, shrugging his shoulders at me and pointing to his watch. I could see him mouth that he'd be right back. I waved him off like it was no big deal to wait for him.

And it wasn't.

I sat in Jens's truck, facing the oncoming lane of traffic, like I was at a drive-in movie. I couldn't see the batch room on my left from this position because of the cement silo that blocked my view of it and thought about crawling over to the driver's side so I could ease Jens's truck forward to see the entire plant. But instead, I sat back and enjoyed watching the periodic arrival of ready mix trucks round the street corner ahead, coming in and out of the yard with fresh concrete being batched for every load. It felt good to be here, to watch everyone working so hard, knowing how difficult it must be to maneuver huge concrete trucks around all those bikes on the streets and highways throughout town.

Seeing this plant up close put me in mind of the quarry north of Fort Collins, in Livermore, Colorado, that I managed. Although my angst was subsiding, I nonetheless appreciated my older brother Ole's willingness to let me take another week of R&R here at our parents' home before returning to work. But my real fear, a secret I hadn't shared with anyone yet, was of entering my own home again. The fear of being alone in the house where my friend and FBI agent Lisa Henry had been killed. I would have to figure out how to get through that by myself, somehow.

But for now, I was enjoying the downtime in Sturgis.

A month of therapy had put me back together again, but I still relished the comfort and safety that I found, metaphorically now, as I once had for real, in that cozy sliver of bed between my Norwegian bear of a father and my Irish leprechaun of a mother. Remembering that safety zone and filling it with glorious music had brought me through flashbacks and nightmares to something near normalcy. They were the only drug I needed—although I supposed a heroin-induced stupor might be useful over ten days of a biker rally. I chuckled to myself as something in the side mirror caught the corner of my eye.

The familiar rumble echoed in my ears as six motorcycle gang members pulled to a stop by the abandoned grain silos near the railroad tracks behind me and across the street from where Jens had parked. The colors they were flying looked familiar to me, but they weren't the notorious Inferno Force. They had come from the narrow alleyway to the west of our plant that barely saved Sherman Street from a dead-end designation. Most people who used this street accessed it from the east, where I had been watching the ready mix trucks come and go. Instinct and the fact that they snuck up from behind using the alleyway told me to resist the urge to twist in my seat to get a better view of what these guys were up to. Instead, I studied the motley crew in the side mirror, trying to judge the degree of distortion that existed in the warning "Objects Are Closer Than They Appear" so I could calculate the actual distance from me to them.

My guess was that they were within about ten yards of the truck's back bumper.

The rumble stopped and all the bikers dismounted, including a woman wearing one of the bikers' leather jackets. She looked awkward in her black leather boots with spike heels, reminding me again of how my sisters looked in our mom's evening gowns and shoes playing dress-up.

"You wanted to pull a train, baby? Well, here we are at the railroad tracks. Whoo-whoo!" the old, bearded biker without his jacket bellowed.

The railroad track that he was referring to was actually a siding for the grain silo, which hadn't been used in years. And the house across the street from them, directly behind me on my left, had a "For Sale" sign in the yard and looked deserted. People in the houses down the block in front of me both on the left and right wouldn't have seen these guys unless they stepped out into their front yards. I glanced out of the driver's side window to see if anyone from our plant could see or hear these guys and realized that the cement silo obstructed the view.

A perfect cover for the bikers.

The bikers could see up and down the deserted side street, but no one from the industrial sites or from the few houses down the street could see them. They had scoped out this place ahead of time and the thought made my skin crawl.

I looked back in the side mirror and noticed the bikers looking around, making sure they were alone, just as I had done. I shrank down on the seat so they couldn't see the back of my head through the rear window and watched them in the mirror. I was glad Jens and I had lowered the windows during the tour or I would have roasted like a turkey, considering it was over a hundred degrees.

One of the straggly ones said, "Shit, Noodles, hurry up. We ain't got all day."

Noodles returned to his bike. Ah, I thought, they're leaving now. Thank God! I let out a long breath I hadn't even realized I'd held. Noodles motioned the girl to join him and she did, only not the way I was expecting. I thought she would jump on the back of the bike and they'd ride off before I ever had to see how this horrible story would end. Instead, she had stripped off the leather jacket, discarded it on the asphalt, and straddled Noodle's bike on the front, draping her long, white legs around his waist. Except for one, the other bikers hooted and chuckled as she leaned back against the handlebars and hooked the spike-heeled black boots around his waist. Now wearing nothing more than a red string bikini and a black leather dog collar with spikes, the girl rode Noodles to a climax, her head covered in black ringlets bobbing everywhere. I turned away and stared over at the plant. I wanted to bolt and run but for some reason thought better of it.

Fixing my gaze past the cement silos to the spot where I last saw Jens climb into Travis's truck, I willed him to return, willed a ready mix truck to round the corner, willed an employee to step outside the batch room and notice me or the commotion behind me and call the police. But as much as I wanted them to, I knew they couldn't see or hear what was happening in the rail yard across the street.

I was on my own.

By the time I looked back, Noodles was zipping up and retrieving his jacket. Four other bikers had remounted their rides and encircled the girl, each soliciting her to do him the next favor. Her curly hair was mussed and covering most of her face other than her lips, which were brightly covered in lipstick as vermillion as her bikini. She looked completely out of it. Too young, too lost. I felt so sorry for her, even though she was clearly participating voluntarily in this nightmare.

"My turn," one of them called.

"Wait your turn, asshole," another growled.

"How was she?" one called to Noodles, who gave a thumbs-up.

The girl smiled triumphantly.

The sixth biker, who stayed ready to ride at all times, never moved, never spoke, and never smiled. He appeared to be looking around for something, making sure no one crashed the party. My hunch was that he was the smartest of the bunch, the leader. Smart, because he didn't seem to lose focus as the watchman despite the X-rated show that was unfolding only a few yards away. He was too far away from me in the side mirror to make out any details, so I studied those closest to me instead.

Noodles put his jacket on and I noticed the crazy character decal stitched to the back of it. The pudgy man in the tight devil's costume sitting cross-legged, one hand on a pitchfork, the other holding an Uzi, was familiar. Although it read backward in the mirror, I could see the letters on the rocker and finally sounded out the Lucifer's Lot. His soiled, tattered jacket was riddled with stains and badges of all sorts, whereas two younger men had what appeared to be new jackets, same kind, but with a different rocker that said "Prospect." The fourth man, the straggly one facing the truck, was now pushing the girl down onto her knees. He didn't even have the decency to take off his jacket, which was also stained and covered in badges of some sort, and spread it on the hot asphalt for the girl to kneel on. How could I have imagined that decency and these hoodlums should even appear in the same thought?

I had to look away. I did a hundred Hail Marys once for curiosity about a male's equipment—and all for nought; the sketch that was going around Sister Delilah's class was quite incorrect from a physiological standpoint—and had eventually, some years later, cleared up the details. I didn't need Straggly to refresh my memory.

I willed Ida to sing "Ave Maria" in duet with Luciano in my head and squeezed my eyes shut, focusing hard on their amazing talents. Their climatic "Benedictus fructus ventris tui," spilling in powerful volumes, morphed into a horrible screech.

I hit my knee hard on the dashboard when Straggly let out a blood-curdling scream. My eyes shot to the side mirror and I saw the girl crash, sideways, onto the ground, taking with her Straggly's privates between her teeth. Her head bounced off the asphalt as her mouth snapped free of him at the exact moment when Straggly was dragged to the ground beside her. The sound sickened me, and I was afraid I was going to upchuck the Brain Pain Killers after all.

"What the—" Noodles growled.

"Jimmy Bones!" one of the younger bikers yelled.

"Shit!" the straggly one yelped. "Fucking bitch!"

As he sprawled beside her in the parking lot, he gave her a swift kick, her body barely moving, as if she were nothing but a sack of wet cement.

CHAPTER 4

SHE MUST BE OUT cold, I thought, from hitting her head on the asphalt. She needs an ambulance.

Just as I was about to bolt from the truck and run to the office, two motorcycles roared around the corner in front of me and I instinctively threw myself down on the floorboard of the truck. I heard them rumble by my open window toward the other bikers and I started to push myself back up onto the bench seat when I noticed Jens's cell phone on the floor still attached to the charger. I snatched it open and dialed 911, whispering for help into the phone and asking for an ambulance. They told me it might be a while because all the emergency personnel were busy.

I felt naked without my Sig Sauer, which I had vowed to carry again since my last brush with death, once I was moving about in the world of the living.

Where was Mom's Mary Poppins purse when I needed it?

No matter how dire the situation or what was needed, my mom could likely and magically produce it from that purse of hers. Hungry? No doubt she had Tootsie Rolls or granola bars. Stuck in a waiting room at a doctor's office? Playing cards came out with a flick of a wrist and we were playing gin rummy or slapjack. Weather turned at a football game? A collapsible umbrella, a polar fleece blanket, or perhaps sunshine in a can. One time when I tore my pinafore on the way to school, she whipped out a sewing kit and had me repaired and out the door within two minutes, averting an inevitable visit to the principal's office for a scolding by Sister Marie for slovenliness.

If I ever decide to carry a purse, I'm going to find out where Mom shops for that Mary Poppins version. Because right now, I sure needed that loaded Smith & Wesson she likely had neatly tucked in one of the pockets of that thing.

The rumble of the two new bikes had stopped and everything was quiet. I pushed myself off the floor slowly, praying I hadn't drawn attention to myself with my whispering. I slithered back onto the seat and stole a peek in the side mirror. Again, I let out a long breath, relieved that the attention seemed to be on the two new bikers, who had already dismounted their bikes and joined the circle around the girl and Straggly, who was hefting himself to his feet and fastening his jeans.

One of the new guys spoke first. "How appropriate. Armed soldiers standing guard over their prey."

"Mully, it wasn't my fault," the screamer whined.

As the intimidating one called Mully closed in on Straggly, he put his hands on his hips, allowing me to see the gun holstered underneath his colors. It was a formidable black pistol—a Sig like mine or maybe a Glock—but I wasn't sure. I then noticed that all of the bikers had heavy black flashlights slung from their hips, the only "weapon" allowed in plain view when walking on the streets during the rally. The hundreds of plain-clothes cops who were working undercover probably wouldn't spy con-cealed weapons, but bikers would earn themselves instant incarceration if they were caught.

"What happened?" Mully demanded.

"Please, Mully," Straggly pleaded, looking scared shitless. "It was an accident. Just an accident. I didn't do nothin'."

I saw Mully glare at the young biker next to Straggly.

"I don't know what happened," the young prospect answered quickly, heaving his scrawny shoulders to his oversized ears.

"What happened with Jimmy Bones, Creed?" Mully repeated.

So the straggly one's name is Jimmy Bones. I should be writing this down. My eyes darted around the pickup and landed on a pen tucked in the seat cushion and some discarded receipts on the floor. I started scribbling.

A man's voice I hadn't heard before spoke. "He's right, boss. It was kind of a freak accident. A fluke."

I glanced up from my note scribbling and saw the smart biker farthest away dismount his bike and approach the group. His jacket read "Enforcer" and his arms were as wide as Jimmy Bones's waist, his teeth discolored with age, tobacco, and lack of hygiene.

Mully nodded as if satisfied with Creed's confirmation. "Is she dead?"

Creed bent to feel for a pulse. His thick fingers probed around the spiked collar, and I could see his frustration mounting the longer he felt for the girl's pulse, her head lolling to unnatural angles because of the spikes propping up her neck. The men stood around the girl lying at their feet. The hot noonday sun beat off the asphalt parking lot like an unending, silent scream, and I imagined the girl's musky perfume and the body odors of recent activities rising in nauseating waves like the smell of a freshly squashed skunk on the highway. The bikers stood poised above her like Boy Scouts, albeit errant ones, around a campfire. And all I could do was sit here, helplessly, as I waited for Creed's answer and for God to answer my prayer.

"Yep," Creed said.

Not the answer I was hoping for. Not another one dead. Each year too many bikers died in accidents and at least one young girl ended up missing or dead this time of year. Years ago, they thought there was a serial killer going around killing folks in the Black Hills around the time of the rally. It was probably accidents like this, I supposed. But it was all too surreal for me. After all, the girl was kneeling when she fell. Her head couldn't possibly have hit the ground so hard from that distance to have crushed her skull or caused that much brain swell. Maybe she was unconscious, but not dead.

Before I could be mad at God for ignoring my prayer to keep the girl safe, I realized I should be doing something. I grabbed Jens's phone and tried to recall Travis's number. I fiddled with buttons looking for speed dials, the address book, anything, and stumbled across a camera function. I gave up on calling for help and started snapping shots in the side mirror. I decided to flip around, creep to my knees, and peek over the seat, taking direct pictures of the motley crew and risking my discovery. I made sure the supposed dead girl was in the pictures as well as the bikes and the license plates.

"From the beginning," Mully said softly. How incongruous Mully's demeanor was compared to the others. He was so controlled and focused. Almost . . . polite.

"Cheetah was doing his thing," Creed explained. "He found her up on Main Street. She didn't need any encouragement."

The quieter of the two young prospects lowered his eyes and swiped at a rock with the toe of his boot. I wrote Cheetah's name down and snapped a picture of him.

"She wanted to pull a train. She had started on old Noodles. He wanted it while he sat on his bike. She did him right there," Creed pointed to the handlebars on his bike.

Beneath his gray beard, Noodles grinned. "Good lay, too, Mully."

I grimaced. What a bunch of lowlifes. I noticed Mully wince in disgust at Noodle's crude comment as well. It appeared all the bikers noticed, based on the change in their expressions. I offered up another quick prayer that the ambulance would soon be here so the poor girl could, thankfully, be taken away from these scum buckets. Creed had to be wrong about not feeling her pulse, which would be easy to miss given the spiked collar.

"Then it was Jimmy Bones's turn," Creed explained.

Jimmy Bones stammered, "She was happy to do it. Really. She was real eager and all. It's not like we had to convince her of anything. Really."

Mully frowned and coolly coerced a validation. "Creed."

Creed looked down at her smooth skin baking in the late afternoon heat. "She went down on him, squatting right where you're standing. Then she just sort of . . . fell over."

"Fell over? That's it?" Mully asked.

"Just before you and Weasel pulled up," Creed explained.

I wrote down the name Weasel as the second biker to arrive later with Mully. Just in case this was important, I noted the time.

Jimmy Bones whined, "She almost bit my fucking dick off. Bitch."

He spat at her dead body.

Mully sighed, taking a slow look around to see if his motorcycle club had drawn any attention. They were all wearing their colors, which happened to be both a blessing and a curse. People would stay clear of them, thanks to their widespread reputation, but would also take notice of them.

Jimmy Bones wouldn't give up. "Mully, I swear, it was an accident."

The other young prospect blubbered, "Really, it wasn't Jimmy Bones's fault. Or ours. She didn't look like she was on anything. She was willing. None of us had to hit her or force her or nothing."

"I'm sorry, sir," Cheetah, the quiet prospect, offered.

"Don't apologize," Mully said. His impassive manner unnerved me. I reassessed my earlier impression of him as intimidating, thinking now the word was more like *imposing*. I snapped some more pictures, zooming in on his face. "We'll deal with your class later. Did she make any noise? Scream? Anything?"

They all looked at one another, searching each other's eyes for an answer. Weasel stood solidly behind Mully, his arms folded across his chest, staring down the street watching for unwelcome motorists or bikers.

"She kind of . . . hiccupped," Creed described.

Jimmy Bones nodded and looked at the biker next to Creed. "Tell him, Teddy."

I wrote down the name Teddy and snapped another picture, studying his face. He was the biker in line for the girl after Jimmy Bones, the next highest on the pecking order, I supposed.

"Hiccupped, my ass," Teddy added gruffly, sounding like he'd gargled with fire for breakfast. "It was more of a cough."

"She damn near chomped it clean off," Jimmy Bones repeated.

Mully studied the two. Looking back at Cheetah, he asked, "Hooking?" Cheetah shrugged.

Mully frowned, nudging the girl's bare shoulder with the toe of his boot. Her body flopped backward on the pavement. "Relax. We're not in any trouble here. Coroner's going to find this young lady died of heat stroke or an aneurysm. Maybe even a heart attack or something. Even if she overdosed, it wasn't us who supplied."

The other men started to relax, smile, slapping each other on the back.

Jimmy Bones grinned, "Probably died of suffocation, my dick's so big."

This brought laughs from everyone except Mully, who stood stone-faced, which made each man regret that he had. I about puked. I could hear sirens in the distance. God, please let it be for the girl.

Mully asked, "Citizens, Weasel?"

Weasel shook his head. "Clear, boss."

"Cops?"

"Clear."

"Main Street, huh, Cheetah?" Mully gave him a half smile.

Cheetah nodded.

"Based on this weekend, the Rally's going to be good for us this year, gentlemen," Mully said, walking around the girl's body as if sizing up the situation. "Made some profit and haven't agitated the Inferno Force yet for taking any of their territory. Made more contacts this year than ever before. Our chapter will be prosperous all year. Probably more than Bomber's or Striker's best years combined, may those great mentors of mine rest in peace."

The other bikers' cheers were guttural.

"Best year our chapter's ever had," Mully added.

The bikers mumbled happily.

"Maybe we should celebrate," Mully said. "I was anticipating Cheetah would find a volunteer for us to earn wings on, and we'd be eager to have them on our colors. But I never dreamed we'd have this."

I heard the sirens approaching.

Mully's velvet voice commanded, "Time to earn a pair of purple wings."

I wasn't sure what all the men were doing, but they quickly fell in line behind Mully, and one by one they dropped to their knees between her thighs, each Lot member lowering his head to her crotch.

God help me, no more pictures, mental or otherwise. I buried my head in my hands.

"Hurry," I heard Creed say.

As the last of them finished with the woman, the sirens grew close enough for them to take note. All the bikers looked down the street past me as an ambulance rounded the corner. They scrambled toward their bikes and headed in the other direction toward the alleyway.

All but Mully.

He squinted and trained his stare in my direction. I snapped a final picture and ducked behind the seat just as the ambulance completed the corner. I doubt that Mully saw me, but if he did he couldn't have seen much of me since I was mostly covered by the seatback and the cell phone was pressed against my face. I popped out the memory stick from Jens's phone and wrapped it in the receipt on which I'd written all the names, stuffing it deep into my jeans pocket. When I flipped around on the seat and looked in the side mirror, I saw Mully mounting his bike and stealing a glance my way before heading off behind the others, leaving the girl alone in the middle of the street.

CHAPTER 5

"MOM?" I CALLED OUT as I entered the front door.

The house was cool and dark and inviting after the rough day I'd had so far.

I hadn't had the heart to burden Jens with the awful scene I had witnessed before he came back to the truck to get me. I hadn't even processed it. If he hadn't noticed that I was a little quiet, it was only because he was too absorbed in his own thoughts. He was driving on autopilot.

"Mom," I called again, heading toward the garage to see if her car was gone.

Jens had dropped me off and was heading back to work. Dad had told us he was heading to Pierre for a meeting. And with no Subaru in the garage, which left only the spare pickup, otherwise known as "the Gray Ghost," I speculated that Mom must be out running errands, which meant I had the house to myself. A Monday afternoon with nothing to do. This was such a rare moment for me, I wasn't sure if I should be sad, mad, or glad about the predicament. I knew Mom had insisted I see Dr. James tomorrow at nine and that I had to do my physical therapy exercises as outlined by my doctors in Fort Collins, but other than that, I was left with nothing to do but dawdle.

After standing in the garage for several minutes contemplating my next move, I decided to retreat to the kitchen, grab a bite to eat, treat myself to a hot bath, and take a long nap. Mom's refrigerator and pantry were both still stocked for the army she raised, even though all of us had left home, so I had no trouble finding a snack. After thoroughly checking out the main floor and upstairs bedrooms one more time to make sure I was alone, I grabbed my snack and disappeared downstairs to the guest bedroom suite to draw a bath. Balancing my tuna sandwich on a plate and a glass of milk, I nearly dropped the entire quarry as the peal of the phone startled me. I carefully turned around in the circular staircase and trotted up the stairs and around the corner, setting my feast aside on the kitchen table to answer the nearby phone.

"Bergen residence. This is Liv speaking," I said. Clearly I never answered the phone at my house with such formality, but it was habitual to do so in my parents' house. Sometimes I didn't show it, but I was raised with impeccable manners.

"Liv, this is Clint White."

Not counting all the summers I worked while I was a student, my very first real job with the family business was working for Clint at our Nemo Quarry, crushing, shoveling, and sampling the iron ore we were producing at that site. I loved my work there, not least because Clint had shown an infinite amount of patience teaching me how to weld, load trucks, drill, and blast.

"Hi, Clint. How are you? Gosh, it's been too long since I've seen or talked with you. I missed you at the Christmas party last year," I gushed.

"Belinda was sick. We had to miss it." His voice was uncharacteristically stilted. "Listen, Liv, is Garth there by any chance?"

Then I realized something was wrong. "No, he had to go to Pierre."

"And Ole's in Fort Collins, right?"

A pang of guilt twisted my gut. "Yeah. He's still covering for me. What's the matter? Is there something I can do for you?"

Clint paused.

I knew that either someone was badly hurt at work or Clint was facing a more challenging situation than usual. "Really, Clint, I'm fine. No matter what you've heard. What's happening?"

"I tried reaching Ed and had to leave a message for him."

Ed Meyer was my counterpart at the Rapid City area mining operations.

"And I wasn't sure who else to call."

"Is someone hurt?"

"Well, no, not really. Someone's dead."

"Dead? Oh no, who? What happened? Are you okay?"

"Not one of our employees. And not quite on our property. Tommy Jasper, the guy who has the grazing lease on our land and on the neighbor's land to the southeast, found a body near the creek late this morning."

My gut twisted again. "Dead?"

"Yeah," he said. "The place is crawling with police and emergency technicians, and none of them seems to give a darn about the MSHA rules we have to abide by. I just don't know what to do, you know?"

"What have you done so far?" I asked, checking my watch. It was nearly two.

"I sent the crew back to Rapid City and told them to sit tight until this place clears out. I told them to report to Lenny in Rapid City tomorrow morning if they don't hear from me, and I gave Lenny a heads-up to find extra work for them. But I have my hands full up here, if you know what I mean."

I detected an unfamiliar quiver in his voice and imagined he'd been dealing with this for hours while I was off enjoying myself at Gunners. Another pang of guilt.

"Look. I can be up there in twenty minutes. I suppose you're still load-ing out trucks, too?"

"I didn't see any other choice."

"You've done great, Clint. I'll be up in twenty and I'll bring you a sand-wich. I bet you haven't eaten."

"Thanks. Bring two. Tommy's been up here since he found the body and he looks like he's about to pass out."

It took me less than a minute to slap a batch of sandwiches together, throw a jar of pickles, a bag of chips, and a box of cookies into a sack, and head out the door, my bath and nap long forgotten. The old Gray Ghost started up on the first turn and I let her run while I ran back inside to leave my mother a note.

As always, the drive up Nemo Road west of Rapid City was breathtaking and I wondered if my overwhelming sense of contentment arose from returning to the Black Hills or to work. Probably both. I was enjoying my euphoria, forgetting all about the young girl and the bikers I'd witnessed earlier. The two-lane highway snaked through the pine-covered hills with occasional views of Boxelder Creek along and under the road, and my smile grew wider than the stretches of acreage between the occasional small clusters of houses.

About fifteen miles into the drive, I had just polished off my tuna sandwich and was popping a piece of mint gum to combat my fishy breath, when I noted that Steamboat Campground was nearly full with tents and campers. Just beyond that, I could see that Bill Pulman's field had been freshly cut and his airstrip exposed, and I wondered if Tommy Jasper was responsible for that acreage as well, since it was adjacent to Broken Peaks and Bergen Construction Materials acreage that he grazed and hayed.

As I rounded the bend near the Lazy S—the tiny spot of acreage on the right that someone a while back had turned into a private campground between Pulman's and Broken Peaks—I noted that it, too, was fully occupied. I gasped at the long line of vehicles parked along Nemo Road and the crowd in the valley to my right. I had never seen so many people gathered in this sleepy little valley, even during the rally, because most of the acreage was held by a handful of private owners, like our mining company. The estimated twelve hundred acres of valley, surrounded by National Forest Service property and with the Boxelder lazily twisting and turning down the center, were rarely graced with anything but herds of resident deer or cows and an occasional curious elk or fox.

I slowed as I eased past the line of vehicles precariously parked along the nearly nonexistent shoulder of Nemo Road, hugging the double yellow line more closely than I cared to do. The entrance to Broken Peaks was barricaded by two police cars and staffed by half a dozen officers. The entrance to our property was protected by a metal swing gate, which was always chained shut to deter anyone who wasn't properly trained and shouldn't be there from entering our mining site. I pulled off Nemo Road onto our entrance road and up to the gate a few yards off the highway. I could see the loader up on the hillside about half a mile farther expertly scooping up a few buckets of iron ore and carefully distributing the load into the trailer and pup of a Williams Transport truck. I spun the combination, unchained the gate, and swung one side of it open wide. As I did, three vehicles turned onto our entrance road and tried to dart around my truck through the gate.

"Hey, hey there," I shouted, swinging the gate into place just in the nick of time, nearly clipping the first vehicle's grill. "What are you doing?"

The man behind the wheel flashed a toothy smile and jerked a thumb back toward the white van and car that trailed him. "We're with KDSD."

"So?"

"The television station?" he added, stunned that I was unaware of how many doors, or gates, swung wide with that simple proclamation.

"Aren't you lucky," I quipped.

"We're trying to get a closer vantage point to the crime scene. And that spot right there will be perfect for us," he said, extending a long, manicured finger toward an area just below where I could see Clint was working the loader back and forth from the pile to the truck, the job he had asked me to help with since all of his guys had been sent back to town.

I decided to swallow the words I wanted to say and opted instead for the more diplomatic approach. "Well, I greatly appreciate your interest, but we have rules to follow, so unless you can show me a current MSHA certification, I'm going to have to ask you to leave."

"Em what?"

"MSHA. Mine Safety and Health Administration. One of the many federal bureaucracies that outline the rules for us to follow in the mining industry. So again, if you would please turn around, I need to let that truck out, and since his load weighs a heck of a lot more than your car does, I suggest you take my advice."

It was my turn to jerk my thumb over my shoulder at the loaded truck bearing down on me from behind, headed directly toward the KDSD convoy.

The reporter's eyes widened and he whipped his car around in a U-turn and led his entourage back to Nemo Road. I once again swung the gate wide and waved at the driver as the truck pulled out along the road and fell in behind the entourage. I jumped in my pickup, pulled through the gate, and chained the gate behind me.

Maybe it was because I'd just been assaulted with a television camera, but I was suddenly aware of how neglectful I'd become with my appearance. I stole a glance at myself in the rearview mirror, curious about the outcome. Paleness had all but disappeared and my faintly olive skin tone had returned to normal. My freckle-spattered nose sported a new bump where it'd been broken. No more bags, bruises, or sickly dark circles under my green eyes, the whites, clear and bright. Hell, even with my hair pulled back in a ponytail and without an ounce of makeup, I didn't look half bad. Nowhere near the athletic supermodel comparison one mooning boyfriend suggested. We had argued over the connotation of "big boned gal" that I called myself in response; me, suggesting that it best described my healthy, athletic Scandinavian frame and he, suggesting that it was to "the girl with a great personality" as fat was to ugly. I deflected any acknowledgment of the word "supermodel" because it might lead me to divorce from my love of food to keep up the image.

As I stared at myself, assured that I had neither lost nor gained weight over the years since playing college basketball nor in the past month in my neglectfulness, I had to admit, I could do better. It probably wasn't appropriate for me to dress like a college coed anymore, and it was entirely my fault how often I got carded in bars. But at least I didn't look sick or emaciated.

By the time I had driven up the hill to the parking area and donned my personal protective gear, hard hat, safety glasses, and leather gloves that I knew Dad stored behind the bench seat of the Gray Ghost, Clint had already parked the loader in the shade and had crawled down the ladder.

I gave him a quick hug. "How are you holding up?"

"Better now," he said, a weary smile spreading across his lined face. Handsome and rugged, like the timeless Marlboro Man, he was aged beyond his years from too much sun and too many smokes. "Thanks for coming up so quickly. And I'm glad to see you're all right. I heard some pretty nasty things about what had happened to you down there."

Nasty. I'd have to grill him later about that.

I turned toward the road I just came in on and the field below and gazed at the circus to our left. "What's all this about?"

He started walking down the hill along the road and detoured right, toward the small trailer we used for our lunchroom and office. "I'll let you hear it firsthand from Tommy. You said something about bringing some sandwiches?"

I held up the paper sack filled with goodies.

"Thanks for coming, Liv."

"No problem."

"I was starting to panic when I couldn't rouse Ed, Garth, or Jens. I even saw Jens this morning, but it was before Tommy found the woman."

"Woman? The dead body was of a woman?" The news of this hit me like a fist for some reason. I wondered about the girl I had seen earlier and what might have happened to her if I hadn't called 911.

"Yup," he said, flipping a cigarette between his lips and shakily lighting up.

I thought I'd better avoid the subject for the moment and have him focus on something more benign. The crime scene technicians were arguing over some procedure, and considering that most of them were huddled near the corner next to our property, we were a stone's throw from and within earshot of them.

"You saw Jens this morning?" I whispered. I couldn't imagine how early that must have been, considering I met Jens and Dad around ten thirty or so up at Gunners in Sturgis. Maybe Clint and Jens both had a meeting to go to or something in Rapid.

"At the Nemo General Store," he said.

"Jens was here? In Nemo? When?"

"Yup. Early, around six or so."

"But that's impossible," I said, thinking that I had been with Jens for hours today, and he never mentioned it.

CHAPTER 6

WE DUCKED INTO THE small trailer, which opened up into the large lunchroom I remembered. To most it wouldn't be much, sparse and unappealing as it was. But to those of us who worked in the elements year-round, it was an oasis.

I took off my hard hat, stuffed my gloves and safety glasses in the overturned hat, and skidded it across the table. I slid onto the bench against the wall before I noticed a tall, older man laying flat on his back, his cowboy boots touching my thigh, his lanky arm draped over his eyes as he slept.

"Oh, hi," I said, extending my hand as he raised his sleepy head.

"What time is it?" he stammered, offering me a limp-fish hand. Not very cowboy-like, I thought.

"Two thirty," I answered.

A horn sounded and Clint put on his hard hat and headed toward the door. "This is Tommy Jasper. He's waiting for the authorities to stop over and talk with him. They wanted to see both of us and told us not to go anywhere, to stay here until they had time to come meet with us here."

"Oh," was all I managed.

"Tommy's the one who found the body late this morning," Clint continued, lowering his chin and giving me a look that I understood quite clearly. "Tommy, this is my friend Liv Bergen. She's here to keep you company until they arrive. I'll be back as soon as I finish loading this truck and when they get freed up to talk with us, okay?"

He nodded again, looking quite puny.

Clint was halfway through the door when he turned back, saying, "Liv, you know where to find the pop. Help yourself and make sure Tommy eats something. Been at work since the crack of dawn, I suppose."

I managed to toss a sandwich to Clint before he hurried back to the loader.

I smiled at Tommy, who lifted his aged eyes warily at me and struggled to lift his lanky body off the bench, hesitating as each joint moved. Arthritis, I thought. Or lots of rodeos. I slid off the bench and stepped into the kitchen area to give him privacy as he worked through his aches.

"They have the coldest pop," I said, sure Tommy must have thought I was crazy.

It felt good to be back in this corner of the world. Sitting at a desk in a controlled environment solving engineering problems for Boeing was not for me. Some might think I was totally crazy to give up such a prestigious, high-paying job to work in extreme temperatures shoveling material that weighed more than I did, a hundred forty pounds per cubic foot—crushed. But I've never had a moment of regret choosing instead to work at an iron ore quarry in the Black Hills of South Dakota, eventually earning my way to manage the limestone operations in Livermore, Colorado.

Although this trailer was an upgrade from the small shack we started out with as the employee lunchroom, the old-fashioned refrigerator stocked with pop and water was the same. And I was thrilled to reach inside and find the cans and bottles chilling to the perfect temperature. I handed Tommy a Coke and pulled a Diet Coke out for me.

I returned to the table and slid onto the bench across from him, pushing the Coke across the table and reaching into the sack I'd brought to retrieve a couple of sandwiches, which I also placed in front of him. I twisted off the cap of the pickle jar, opened a bag of chips, and started nibbling away at them, placing both the jar and the bag between us.

"If you don't like tuna, I bet they have some cold pizza or something." I jerked my head toward the refrigerator. "But a betting man would lay odds that the tuna salad I made an hour ago is much fresher than whatever they've got in there."

I think I earned a grin, albeit slight.

I popped open the tab of my Diet Coke and swallowed. "I'm telling you, this pop is amazing."

He looked at me with an expression that I could only describe as part annoyance, part incredulity, mixed with a healthy dose of disdain.

"Seriously," I added, tipping my can to him and wolfing down my second sandwich.

I knew guys like Tommy. He was proud. Too proud to eat other people's food, particularly from people he didn't know really well. And too proud to reveal that maybe, just maybe, he hadn't planned for this eventuality and had come ill-prepared.

Truthfully, I wasn't all that hungry since I had eaten a sandwich in the truck on the way up here, but I had the sneaking suspicion he wasn't about to eat unless he was forced. Or unless he had company who was willing to take the time to talk while eating.

Within seconds, I discovered I was right. His annoyance faded away into resignation and he lifted the sandwich to his lips, nibbles turning into gobbles. His sandwich was gone before mine and he chased it with the Coke.

He smiled.

"Good, huh?"

"Yeah," he said.

"He speaks!" I joked.

He wiped his mouth on his sleeve and looked at his watch. He reached for the second sandwich and unwrapped it, taking more time between bites.

Rubbing his knees with his free hand, he said, "Dr. Morgan tells me I'm getting old. Nothing I can do about these aches and pains. Just parts wearing out. Anymore, I'm so tired all the time, all I do is sleep."

"Sorry to wake you up a little while ago, by the way. Didn't see you lying there." I'd heard of Dr. Morgan, although I'd never had the pleasure of meeting him. His reputation preceded him as the best and most beloved family practice doc in the Hills. For some reason, I thought I'd heard he'd retired. To Tommy's insistent rubbing of his knees, I asked, "You okay?"

He shrugged.

"How long have you been waiting?"

"No idea," he said, sounding eerily similar to Eeyore. "Hours, days. A lifetime."

"Tell me about it," I said.

Tommy sighed and craned his head to look out the window to his right, my left, toward the meadow filled with uniformed men and women working the crime scene. "Ever since I can remember, I've been working these fields. Know every rock, every crevice. Run across some strange things from time to time. But nothing like this."

I didn't move, careful not to disrupt his flow of thoughts and recollections.

He took in a deep breath and thumped his head against the wall, squeezing his eyes shut. "Nothing like that."

Poor guy. I waited several beats before asking, "Want to talk about it?"

As the time ticked, I cursed myself for asking, for rushing Tommy. I was afraid I'd never get him to tell the story before either Clint returned or the authorities arrived to ask him the same questions while I waited on the other side of the door.

"You used to wear long braids," he said, his eyes still closed. "You're one of Garth's daughters."

"Yes, sir," was all I said. And I waited some more.

Eventually, he opened his eyes and sat very still.

"Haven't talked about it yet. Not even with Clint. No one's really asked except you." His eyes pierced mine, and I'm not sure if it was out of anger or gratitude. Then he added, "Don't know if I really want to put words to what I saw."

I nodded, thinking of my reluctance to put to words what I saw earlier in Sturgis. Or my ordeal last month. Or my fears of returning to my house in Fort Collins again. Alone.

He pulled out a threadbare handkerchief and honked his nose.

"Not much I can offer, but I'm happy to be your sounding board," I said.

His gaze was distant now. He looked puzzled, and I wondered if I'd lost my opportunity with my persistence. For the longest time, he didn't speak, and I figured he wasn't going to, but when he had finished the last bite of his second sandwich and drained the last of his Coke, he said, "Canadian thistle are nasty little plants. Tough to kill. Even tougher on my cattle."

I was wondering what the hell this noxious weed had to do with him finding a dead body earlier today. I contemplated grabbing his shirt collar and shaking him until he snapped out of it. Then I thought better of it. Tommy was an old-fashioned rancher somewhere around seventy, after all. And one thing I've learned as a native South Dakotan is that you don't rush a good story, particularly one told by an elder who's a rancher or a farmer. Regardless of how painfully slow it was to extract the story out of Tommy, I reminded myself not to screw up my one chance to find out what happened. And not to embarrass Clint.

Tommy took a deep breath. "I sprayed earlier this spring. Thought I got most of those little buggers. Tough to do. Even tougher to do without my wife's help. She died a little over a year ago."

I felt guilty when I recognized the discomfort that had started to roil in my belly was impatience. It dissipated quickly when I recalled that this poor man had been out here all day with nothing to eat or drink after stumbling across a dead body and having just experienced what must have been the worst year of his life.

Gently, I asked, "What did she die of?"

"Liver cancer. Dr. Morgan wasn't able to save her. Didn't even make it to the chemo phase. She passed quickly." He snapped open a lighter, flicking the igniter several times with his thumb, as if it were a nervous tic at the mention of his wife's disease.

"And did you get it?" Noting his confusion, I blushed, realizing he assumed I was asking if he had contracted cancer, too. "All the Canadian thistle, I mean," I hurriedly clarified.

He nodded and a crooked smile touched his lips. "Most of it."

"Good for you," I smiled back, observing that he had stopped flicking the lighter and had eased it back inside a pocket. "Do you feel like talking about this morning?"

He straightened and cleared his throat. "I am talking about this morning."

I blushed again at the reprimand.

"I was walking along Boxelder Creek to check on Canadian thistle, and in the distance I thought I spotted a patch of field bindweed down-stream. A big patch of it, all white and clustered. As I walked I wondered if maybe it wasn't field bindweed after all, but hoary cress or something. Eyes aren't so good these days. It was a ways off, and I had lots of time to think about it. I wondered how that particular weed came onto my fields, since normally all I see is the thistle and the occasional tansy. Then I started thinking maybe it came in on the tires of these trucks, since the patch was just south of the quarry haul road."

I could see the wheels turning as he was figuring how to solve his ficti-tious noxious weed problem, which was easier for him to stomach than the truth. He was stalling, sharing as many details as he could that led up to what he found without getting to the discovery itself.

"I walked for some time along the banks and never had another glimpse of white like I did way up the creek." He slipped the lighter out of his pocket and started flicking the wheel with his thumb again. I waited, knowing he was on the brink of sharing the moment. He spoke quietly, almost inaudibly. "I've never seen a dead person before. Not before the undertaker worked on 'em, that is. Not even Judy. She died in the hospital in the middle of the night. They didn't even call me until the next day. Had to die alone."

His voice broke, and I realized I was holding my breath.

"It wasn't hoary cress or bindweed," he said simply. "First, I saw her legs as I rounded that last bank. Then I saw. She was naked, and I covered my eyes and called out, 'Miss? You okay?'"

His thumb flicked faster across the wheel of the igniter. Flick. Flick. At first it took him awhile to push himself up from the bench, but after he rose, he walked easily toward the window, clearing his throat as he did. I fell in line behind him and stayed close. He pointed toward the massive cluster of people just past our haul road on the other side of our fence. "She was right there. On Broken Peaks ground. By the big rock. See where the man with the red bandana on his cowboy hat is standing? Right there."

Standing on my tiptoes, I peered past his shoulder to see out the small window, spotting the man with the telltale hat. I knew the spot well. We used to go down by that rock after work and throw our lines in to catch some dinner, then take turns making different barbecue recipes for fresh rainbow trout. I could see how Clint and the portable plant team missed the body when they came in to work this morning and how all the customers' truck drivers missed it as well. The big rock obstructed the view from our haul road.

"Haven't even called the Benders yet," he added, referring to the out-of-state owners who vacation for a few days at the property only once each year. "I was afraid she was dead," Tommy nearly whispered, "by how still she was and from the looks of the blood and all. But I still hoped she would answer me. I tried to find her pulse. Without touching much. You know. I couldn't find it. So I called out for help. Clint heard me. Don't know how above all the equipment noise, crushing and all. Those guys are always busy, you know?"

"I do. They work hard. Like you do," I said, trying to keep him talking.

His intake of breath was ragged. "I just stood there. Her body was crumpled on the bank of that creek."

His eyes were staring at nothing and seeing something that changed his expression to one of repugnance and fear.

"How did she look?" I whispered.

"She looked . . . dead," Tommy said, blinking once. "She was completely naked. She had a mass of dark tangles, hair everywhere, and at first I didn't see the blood that had pooled beneath her head. All I saw was the mass of blood and . . . stuff on the back of her head. It all looked like . . . like more hair, dark and . . . oh, there was so much of it. Blood, I mean. The back of her head was all smashed in, like a discarded melon. I imagine she hit it on a rock when she fell or something. She was on her left side at the bottom of that shallow bank. Her hair and the blood were caught in the creek's flow."

"You were walking with the creek downstream, right?"

He nodded.

"And her hair was caught in the creek's flow?"

He nodded again.

"So her body was in the creek?"

He shook his head. "She wasn't in the water. Just her hair. She was on her left side, her feet toward me, her head positioned downstream, but not in the water. Just her hair."

"She was on the right side of the bank as you face downstream? Opposite side of the bank from where we are, from this mining operation?"

"Yes. I called to her." He said with a nod. "She didn't answer."

Because she was dead, I thought. "You said she was completely naked?"

"Not completely naked, no. She was wearing shoes. Running shoes. That was it."

"Where were her clothes?"

He shrugged.

A shiver must have run through him by the way his shoulders shook. "God's cruel trick. Clint should have been the one to see her body when he was down by that rock earlier in the morning."

My stomach flipped. "Clint was down at the big rock? In the morning? When?"

"When I was fixing my tractor."

"I mean, what time was that?"

"Oh, I'd say sometime around six thirty or so. When all his guys were starting up the equipment."

"What was he—"

Clint White came through the door and gave me a look that told me time had run out. I nodded once, knowing the authorities had arrived to interview him and Tommy. I heard a truck honk, signaling the need to be loaded.

"Will you cover for me?" Clint asked, thumbing over his shoulder at the awaiting truck.

"Absolutely," I said, my heart racing. I imagined the naked, dead body, Clint just inches away from her, and struggled to wrap my mind around the idea that Clint White could possibly be that brutal to another human being.

He darted back outside, the door closing quickly behind him, presumably to escort the authorities into the humble office.

I did not want whoever was on the other side of that door to find me with Tommy or I'd probably be stuck here for hours. I didn't want to be caught in the wide net that was likely being cast to find clues and I certainly didn't have anything to offer. I much preferred to load the trucks while Clint was in with Tommy being interviewed, and then I'd make a quiet exit once Clint didn't need my help any longer. But I couldn't leave without asking one more burning question.

"What was Clint doing by the big rock, Tommy?"

"Smoking," he said. "Just stood there leaning against the rock, his back to the creek, and smoking a cigarette. I just wish he would have stumbled across her body rather than me having to."

I cleared the food from our lunch and asked, "Anything around her? Blanket? Weapons? Anything?"

Tommy shook his head, "No, nothing. Nothing but a pile of my vomit. Felt like stampeding buffalo in my throat, it was so violent."

"Anything about the body that struck you as odd?" I wadded up the paper towels and empty cans and tossed them in the garbage barrel.

"Just the hand."

"The hand?"

"Well, she was on her left side. Her left arm was stretched out onto the bank, away from her body, away from the creek, as if to protect it from the water. And even though her hand was still cupped, I saw the pin."

"The pin?" I asked, retrieving a cold Coke from the fridge and handing it to Tommy.

"Yeah, a pin. The kind of pin you see men wearing on caps or jackets, I guess. It was stuck in the palm of her hand, like she'd been holding it tight. Some blood dripping down her palm."

"Was there anything on the pin, Tommy? A picture? Writing?" Hearing Clint talking just outside the door, I grabbed my hardhat, leather gloves, and safety glasses and headed toward the side door.

"Yeah, letters."

I glanced at the front door as the knob turned and said, "Tommy, I have to go now. They're here to talk with you about this morning. You'll do great. Your wife would be proud of you. Stay strong."

He smiled at me, an easier smile now. I started down the steps and had the door nearly closed behind me just as Tommy called out, "The letters on the pin. FTW. Did you hear me? FTW."

Fuck the world, I thought, as I gave a nod and shut the door just in time to hear Clint introducing Tommy to the authorities. I peeked up over the ledge of the windowsill and saw a big, heavy man in a suit that Clint's muffled voice introduced as Agent Bob Shankley, and a second man, a biker dude with long, black tangles of hair and a face full of fuzzy beard, introduced as Agent Stewart Blysdorf. The FBI. The second agent, the hairy one, glanced my way and I ducked beneath the window. I didn't think he spotted me.

I crawled along the rocks and around trees until I was in the shadows and then made my way to the parked 980 Cat loader. I climbed up the ladder and into the cab. It felt good to be back in the driver's seat again, back into the comfort of a loader. My chest filled with a happiness I hadn't felt in weeks as I snapped the seat belt across my lap. I couldn't resist a hearty laugh as I released the parking brake and started working the lift and tilt levers. The impatient truck driver waiting for his load glared at me when he saw me laughing. Although I suspect he thought I was somehow making fun of him, I lingered in that happy place for several more moments before giving a flitting wave and stabbing my bucket into the iron ore pile.

CHAPTER 7

THOUGH LOCATED IN THE heart of downtown Denver, the federal building nevertheless manages to maintain an unobstructed view of the gorgeous Rocky Mountains. Standing in his boss's southwest-corner, eighteenth-floor office, Streeter Pierce was temporarily distracted by the spectacular view of the sun setting behind those mountains.

Calvin Lemley stretched out in his soft leather chair and propped his feet up on the huge mahogany desk. "Are you sure?"

"I'm sure," Streeter said with a frown. Taking a seat again at Calvin's computer, Streeter zoomed in on one of the photos that had been e-mailed to Calvin from South Dakota a few hours prior for a closer view of the skull. "Definitely."

"That was a long time ago."

With Calvin looking on, Streeter studied the electronic photos one at a time. The large man, identified as the seventy-eight-year-old landowner Ernif Hanson, was lying facedown on a rock, arms stretched over the edge and skull crushed from behind. No rocks were on the grassy hillside except for the large jutting outcrop on which the body lay. He had certainly not fallen or been bucked from a horse and smashed his skull against the rock; otherwise, he'd be on his back—unless he had been conscious and tried to crawl for help. But from the limited view of the camera lens, Streeter couldn't see any trail of blood that would indicate that. Instead, it appeared as if the body had been posed where it lay. And the wound was perfectly round.

Streeter noticed that in the background, a well-groomed trail snaked along the valley bottom, and someone from the Rapid City Bureau had marked the graveled path Mickelson Trail. Also running along the trail was a tiny creek marked North Fork Rapid Creek, where cows were gathered and drinking as the crime scene technicians took pictures. The date stamp reflected today's date.

Eyeing the close-up of the dead man's skull, Streeter studied the markings more closely.

"But it's an unsolved. Those stick with you, Cal."

"So this is definitely the work of the Crooked Man?"

Streeter nodded.

Calvin pointed to the screen. "What's the Mickelson Trail?"

"It's an old railroad bed that was abandoned and converted to a public trail in honor of the late Governor George Mickelson, who was killed in a plane crash."

"Oh, that's why the name sounded familiar. Tragic."

Streeter retrieved the other electronic file attached to the e-mail Calvin had received from Calvin's counterpart in Rapid City, Bob Shankley, Special Agent in Charge, or SAC, of the Federal Bureau of Investigation in the Black Hills. The photo of the naked woman lying along the creek bed clearly showed that her skull, too, had been crushed by a blunt object, but Streeter was sure a different perpetrator had committed this murder. This even though the bodies were both found on the same day—albeit different locations in the Black Hills—the Sturgis Motorcycle Rally within easy distance of each crime scene.

"This one was not the handiwork of the Crooked Man?" Calvin asked.

"That's what I'm saying. Shank is wrong about this."

Calvin leaned back and rubbed his eyebrows, glancing at the clock. Streeter knew Calvin had a family to go home to and felt guilty for pinning him down with questions about the photos for so long. But instinctively, Streeter knew this was important.

"How can you be so sure, Streeter? Both had the back of their skull smashed and neither died instantly; left to die slowly over time."

"Look," he said, clicking the necessary keys to make both photos appear side by side. "See here? The obvious. Our female vic is naked. The male vic is not."

"So, it could be sexually motivated and our perp wasn't interested in the old man," Calvin offered.

Streeter nodded. "The Crooked Man had killed three people by the time I turned the files over to Shank. None of them was naked. All of them had been hit on the back of the skull with a blunt object."

"The female vic clearly has been hit on the back of the skull with a blunt object," Calvin said, scowling as he did.

"But she's naked. And the wound. It's all wrong."

"All wrong? Of course it's all wrong, Streeter. The woman is dead."

Streeter shook his head. Secretly, he doubted himself as to what was conjecture and what was factual because he hadn't reviewed the Crooked Man case in nearly a decade. Three murders in the Black Hills, and he believed they were all linked.

"See how this one is almost round? It's what I remembered of the first three." Pointing to the woman's skull, he added, "This is not."

Calvin sighed. "Shank agrees with you that weapons used were not the same. We'll have to wait on the autopsy. Although the Crooked Man case has gone cold, Shank thinks both of these murders fit the modus operandi, especially because they are different weapons. He thinks the Crooked Man is on the move again after all these years."

Streeter pushed himself to his feet and walked over to the windows.

Tentatively, Calvin added, "And he wants your help."

"I know. I read the e-mail. I just don't understand why he wants me. The man can't stand me."

Calvin swung his legs off the desk and joined Streeter by the large windows, sharing the view of the stunning sunset.

"He thinks he has a solid suspect. He wants to partner with you on this because it was your case originally."

"I just don't think it's a good idea, partnering with Shank."

"He's making an effort, Streeter," Calvin argued. "And he knows that area well. He's been there a long time. Might come in handy."

"I've considered all of that," Streeter said, running his fingers through his short white hair. The military buzz cut sprang to attention the instant his fingertips trailed away. Wrapping his hands behind his neck, he added without explanation, "If I go, I want to do this one my way. I know the area too. I was assigned to that bureau as a first office agent, remember?"

Calvin nodded.

Although Calvin was only three or four years older, Streeter always considered him a father figure. His soft, fleshy face, kind as it was, was rutted with years of challenging and stressful situations that had aged him, not necessarily in appearance, but battle-earned wisdom beyond others his age. His graying hair was combed over his balding head and his rimless glasses perched delicately on his round nose.

"I don't need him as my partner on this case," Streeter concluded, padding back to an easy chair on the opposite side of his boss's desk. "I want the case assigned back to me. All the files, evidence, notes."

The Denver SAC put his hands up in surrender. "Okay. No problem. I told you it was your decision. But remember. Shank is the lead investigator on this case, and I don't have authority to assign you as the lead investigator. He does. So unless you can convince him to make you the lead, you'll have to do it his way. Do you want to take on this assignment or not?"

"He asked for my help," Streeter reminded Calvin. "And he'll get it only if we don't have to work side by side."

Calvin glowered and sunk into his leather chair across from Streeter. "Okay, cut the malarkey, Streeter. We both know you want to take this case on whether or not you're the lead investigator. When are you leaving?"

"I'm on the 6:45 am flight," Streeter answered, leaning forward in his chair and rubbing his weary eyes.

"Tomorrow morning?" Calvin said looking at the clock.

With a boyish grin and devilish look in his eye, Streeter added, "Shank's e-mail to you an hour ago indicated he wants me in the Rapid City Bureau by nine o'clock, and it's about an eight-hour drive. So I'm going to tell him to get me wheels and I'm flying up on the next flight, which is tomorrow morning."

"I saw that. He's only messing with you because he can," Calvin said with a grin. "Like I said, it's okay by me if you want to tell Bob Shankley to go to hell."

"I know," Streeter agreed, his own grin fading as quickly as it had appeared. "But you know I can't. I have to do this. I doubt if he's changed. I'll placate him for a while to see if I can get him to assign me lead on the case. If not, I'll be back in a couple of days."

"You understand the Sturgis Rally started this past weekend and their main suspect is with the Lucifer's Lot. The clock is ticking. He'll want you to go undercover immediately."

"As long as it's not with him," Streeter answered.

Calvin watched him with gentle eyes, his jowls sagging slightly as he waited for Streeter to continue. Streeter was amazed at how well Calvin knew him after all these years, knowing he indeed had more to say on the subject.

Streeter arched an eyebrow. "Dangling this unsolved case in front of me is like asking an alcoholic if he wants a drink. Knows it's the worst thing for him, but can't refuse. Of course I couldn't say no, even if it means working with Bob Shankley again."

Calvin smiled.

"Why'd you do it?" Streeter asked.

"Do what?"

"Why'd you let him reopen my case?"

"Streeter, the two murdered bodies found today reopened the case, not me."

"Not the Crooked Man case. The Glass Slipper case. You knew he didn't have any evidence on that poor woman."

Calvin looked at Streeter, dumbfounded. "That was a lifetime ago."

"Fifteen years," Streeter said.

"That's a long time to hold a grudge," Calvin said. "The Glass Slipper. I'd forgotten all about that."

"Not me."

Under Calvin Lemley's direction as the temporary SAC assigned to the Rapid City Bureau, Bob Shankley and Streeter raided and closed the Glass Slipper, the local brothel in Deadwood, South Dakota, just a few miles northwest of Sturgis.

Calvin's eyes were intensely clear, his smile nearly euphoric. "Truthfully?"

Streeter nodded.

"That woman he tried to taint in the indictments that followed was no more a prostitute than Mother Theresa. I reopened the case to see just how far Bob Shankley would go with his phony claims that she was," Calvin admitted.

"Satisfied?"

Calvin closed his eyes and shook his head. "He's what gives the bureau a bad name, Streeter. And I would never have allowed anything to happen to that woman."

Streeter scowled. "I didn't really have a choice on this case, did I?"

"Not hardly," Calvin said. "Do you really think if they asked for our help I'd send anyone but you?"

Calvin swiveled his chair around to the computer on the credenza behind him, and sent his fingers flying across the keyboard. "There. I've sent you all the electronic files that Bob scanned in from the cold cases."

"My old files? From the Crooked Man?"

He nodded. "And Bob's. He said if you accepted this challenge, you can have a copy of what's on file for these cases."

Streeter took a seat across from him at the large oak desk. "My old files. I haven't seen those in years. Well, that in and of itself is worth it, even if I can't convince Shank to assign lead investigator to me."

"All I know is that Bob Shankley asked specifically for you. I was going to tell him to take a flying leap, at first, knowing that man is up to something, but then I decided you should do this. Let's see if he'll be able to control his politically honed temper," Calvin suggested. After a beat, he added, "You know he's gunning for my job."

"I don't doubt that he's trying to kill two birds with one stone, Cal. He's setting me up for a fall, that's for sure," Streeter said, narrowing his eyes. "I just can't figure out what he's up to, and I'll have to put up with him until I find out."

"He said you'd know once you reviewed what they have on this case. You wouldn't have to take any guff from him or anyone like him if you'd take on a SAC position," Calvin reminded Streeter.

"We've been down this road before. Don't go there, my friend. You know I enjoy being a field agent."

"You'd be good at managing an office," Calvin argued. "At least consider accepting the squad leader duties, for Pete's sake."

Streeter's steely blue eyes narrowed and burned a warning to Calvin.

"Easy, friend. Just a suggestion. It's my job; you know, develop our leaders."

Streeter watched Calvin as he pushed back in his chair, comfortable with his decision.

"You think he's dirty?"

"As a SAC?" Calvin clarified. "Probably does everything by the book. As a person? You bet your sweet bippy. I think he's as crooked as they come. In this particular case? I doubt it, but I wouldn't be surprised. Knowing Shank, he has something at risk with this thing somehow or he never would have involved you."

"The Crooked Man killed this man," Streeter stabbed at the photo on the screen behind Calvin's desk.

"And that's a case that needs to be solved, whether or not the Crooked Man killed the woman too," agreed Calvin. "I have confidence you'll solve both, as long as you keep your cool working with Bob Shankley."

"Right."

"If he's into trouble somehow up there, compromised his ethics too far with something, you'll know," Calvin offered.

"How?"

"Well, the more involvement he has with a case or aspects of the case, the more likely he has a desired outcome, regardless of what's right and just. My guess is if he needs this case solved badly enough he'll assign you the lead. If he needs to cover up something that stinks, like a cat in the litter box, he'll be busy in that particular area. If he wants a desired outcome that is not likely to happen in the natural course of your investigation, he'll partner with you. He'll insist on it. Regardless of your insistence to the contrary."

Streeter grimaced as if someone had dropped a crate of rotten eggs in the middle of Calvin's desk. "Don't say that. He wouldn't. He needs me to solve this case or he wouldn't have involved me. Despite your optimism that he's making an attempt to make good and play nice after all these years."

"He'll insist," Calvin wagered. "That's how he started his request. 'I need Pierce to partner with me on this mess that's brewing up here. Fast.' If he's up to something, he'll insist on partnering with you and keep you on a tight leash. If not because he's in some kind of trouble, at least to keep you out of his business. He would never allow you the slightest opportunity to make him look bad, Streeter. Not after everything that's happened."

"I'm not going to let that happen," Streeter said, meaning every word. "I have two cases to solve. I'll be on my best behavior."

"I'd like to see that," Calvin chuckled.

Streeter rose, his six-foot frame packed with nothing but muscle, his tanned skin stretched tight and firm beneath his white button-down shirt. He cleared his throat and winked mischievously at his boss. "I'll tell Shank you'd like to treat him and his wife to dinner the next time they're in Denver."

"You wouldn't," Calvin warned.

"I would."

CHAPTER 8

IF I'D HAD ANY idea that the body they'd recovered yesterday at Broken Peaks was Jens's girlfriend, I would have told him what I was up to yesterday. As it was, I had hell to pay for worrying Mom by taking the Gray Ghost and leaving her a note that said simply that I was going for a drive. Considering the circumstances, I never did tell her that I had been helping Clint White at the Nemo Quarry. I'm glad, now, that I didn't tell her where I'd gone because she would have told Dad or Jens or both and I would have been grilled about the details rather than be freed up to help Jens today.

Dad received the call from Jens this morning at six thirty saying that he wouldn't be in to work and telling Dad they had found Michelle. Her parents had called Jens even earlier than that after identifying her body, and he had already been to the morgue since their call to see Michelle for himself. We were already up having breakfast at that hour, the Bergens all early risers thanks to Mom. When Dad shared the news, I called Jens back and insisted I stay with him, warning that if I didn't, Catherine probably would. Our sister Catherine, also known as Sister Catherine, was the most kind-hearted person who ever lived, and she seemed to have a natural homing instinct for the needy, but her motherly instinct was so powerful it

54

was smothering, not unlike her hugs, in which you found yourself engulfed by her matronly breasts.

Warning heeded, he picked me up within the hour.

All I could think of now as I was walking out to his truck was how much I hate funerals.

The mournful music, the macabre open casket, the morbid procession of pallbearers among a sea of black. The sorrow. Most of all, though, I despise my own inability to find the right words, or any words, to comfort those who are hurting. Especially when the one grieving is someone I love. I was glad I had missed Lisa Henry's funeral, unconscious as I was at the time. And I dreaded having to go to the one that would be scheduled soon for Michelle.

But I also knew this wasn't about me. It was all about Jens, and whatever he needed right now, I'd give him. I couldn't bear to see my little brother suffering, and his face showed every tortured moment he was experiencing.

"Don't look at me that way" was the only thing my brother said as we walked away from our parents' house.

I knew the look.

I'd seen it before at funerals: the pity in people's eyes as they passed the pew of bereaved family members. I prefer empathy to pity. A fine line, sure. But to me, offering pity has always seemed to put the other at a disadvantage; it implies condescension for the deprived in life, a class separation that isn't deserved. After all, we all go through losing a loved one at one point or another in life. Humans allow grief to isolate them from others for a temporary period, quarantined, like having leprosy in a nudist colony. Other primates behave like that, too. For example, Coco the gorilla cradles her dead baby for days while the rest of the clan ignores the insanity. And not one of them is stupid enough to go near the mournful mother.

Empathy, on the other hand, keeps the bereaved as an equal. Empathy builds understanding, a bridge between people. It's not an isolating gesture like pity.

I didn't think I had any pity in me, but from Jens's reaction, I must have been wrong.

"Sorry," I managed, finding it hard to relax the tension around my eyes and brows born of pity. His otherwise handsome face looked ghastly. The dark circles under his eyes, the hollow cheeks, the pale skin, the stooped shoulders on his tall, lean frame. And the emptiness in his eyes.

Having just spent the day with him yesterday, I couldn't believe how he had aged in such a short time. Although I had debated with myself at the time whether or not to say something to the EMTs or to Jens when he and Travis returned to the plant forty-five minutes after he'd left me alone in his truck, long after the biker girl had been taken away in an ambulance, in hindsight I was glad I had stayed quiet about all the commotion that had occurred behind his ready mix plant. Jens was still worked up over the customer's complaint about a job that he and Travis had gone to address. But that was nothing compared to him finding out this morning that his girlfriend had been found murdered. And looking back, telling Jens what I'd witnessed would only have added more stress and seemed so trivial by comparison.

Besides, the girl in Sturgis was probably doing fine. She must have fainted in the heat or something. Creed could have been mistaken about not finding a pulse, or maybe he lied so they would all do what they did afterwards. She couldn't be dead. She hadn't fallen that far to the ground. She was too young. And since those bikers didn't have anything to do with whatever happened to her, I didn't see the point in sticking around and sharing what I'd seen. And maybe I was a little unnerved by that final glare from the biker named Mully. No doubt, he caught the license plate on the truck. Either way, even after crouching against the floorboards of Jens's truck yesterday, working all afternoon in the loader, a rigorous walk in the woods last evening, and several trips up and down the stairs last night at Mom and Dad's house, I didn't sleep too well, and I wasn't about to pipe up about it now.

Just like I wasn't about to share what I had done yesterday afternoon at the Nemo Quarry.

"I'm really, really sorry, Moose," a term of endearment I called him from time to time. I gave him a hug before tossing my bag in the back of his truck and jumping into the passenger's side. Not eloquent, but 100 percent sincere.

He slid in behind the wheel.

We drove in silence to his house on Teepee Street. I was going to mention how green his lawn looked despite the scorching heat of August, to marvel at how well he maintained his house even with his hectic schedule, to say how glad I was to be staying with him, but opted for the appropriate silence instead. (At first, Mom had resisted the idea of me staying at Jens's house, but because I agreed to be compliant for once and go see Dr. James this morning at nine, she was willing to agree. I told her I didn't need the spare truck, the Gray Ghost, she and Dad drove; I'd ask Jens to give me a ride instead, an excuse to keep us close. She bought into my logic.)

His diesel truck rumbled to a stop as he pulled into the driveway. He sat for a long moment staring at his chiffon yellow garage, far too small for his oversized truck to fit inside. I sat staring, too, waiting for him to either go for the door handle or talk. Or not. Two minutes had passed as we sat in the truck, the warm sun warding off the chill of the brutal news.

"Funeral's in three days," he said.

I nodded, knowing there was no way the body would be released by the authorities that early in a homicide investigation. At least, I didn't think so, but what did I know?

"Freeburgs tell you that?"

He nodded. The Freeburgs probably had no clue and would have to have a memorial service rather than a funeral. At least until the authorities released the body.

I hated this.

I didn't know what to say. For the first time in my life, I was at a loss for words. Couldn't think of one word of comfort for him. Nothing. After years of Jens joking about me zipping my lip, kicking me under conference room tables to warn me when to shut up, I could not find the words when he needed them—me—most.

What an imbecile I am.

"It sucks," he added, his shoulders drooping, his head thumping against the glass behind his seat.

Jens was one of the finest orators I had ever known. His incredible command of the English language and his ability to pinpoint a description that conjured vivid images, tastes, sounds, and smells resulted in speeches that brought tears, laughs, applause, no matter what the event.

The enormity of his sorrow was evidenced in the phrase he was reduced to at this moment.

Tears welled in my eyes and I swallowed the lump that rose in my throat.

"I am so, so sorry."

Jens sat that way, his eyes closed, his hands limp in his lap, for a long time. The ping and clank of the cooling engine was the only sound on his quiet street. I sat perfectly still. Sitting still is difficult for a person like me, who can wear her clothes threadbare from the inside out. I steadied my breathing, imagining how he must have felt when he received the call after they found Michelle's body. Jens had talked to me about asking her to marry him. Then they had that terrible argument on Sunday night and he hadn't seen her since. After we relentlessly teased him yesterday at Gunner's about apologizing to Michelle, he swallowed his pride and decided to call her parents, only to discover that they hadn't seen her, either. Then he called her at work. She hadn't shown up. He must have had a horrible, sleepless night. Then there was the call early this morning.

Now, Jens is left to pick up the pieces of his shattered life, hamstrung no doubt by regrets, blame, and what-ifs that will soon follow, if they hadn't already come to haunt him.

After what seemed like hours, Jens took a deep breath, opened the door, and pulled my bag from the back of his truck without saying a word. I followed him into his house in silence and sat down on the couch. He tossed my bag into the spare bedroom and pulled two beers from the refrigerator, handing me one. We twisted off the caps and guzzled. I was not about to point out it was seven thirty in the morning. I had sunk to a new low after breaking my own record of lows yesterday for drinking at inappropriate times of the day. Ah, whatever.

"So where do you go from here?"

He shook his head and took a swig. "I'll figure that out later. I've got to get through the next three days."

"What happens in three days?"

"I already told you, the funeral. And the reception at Mom and Dad's after the interment."

I was getting on his nerves already and I wasn't used to seeing Jens this surly. I needed to steer clear of any argument or the details and snatched the first thing that came to mind. "What the hell does that mean, anyway? Internment? I thought internment meant incarceration or something. Why do they call a burial and imprisonment the same thing?"

A hint of a smile played at the corners of Jens's lips. "Interment. Not internment."

"What?"

"Internment means imprisonment. Interment means burial, you boob." A smile, weak as it was, crept to his lips before he drained the rest of his beer. I knew he'd get through this. He was still in there somewhere. He retrieved a second beer for himself. "I gave you the first because you're a guest. We're over the pleasantries, though, and you're going to have to serve yourself from here on out."

"Got it," I said, tipping my beer and stretching out on the couch.

He stretched out in the recliner and kicked off his shoes.

"How are Char and the rest of the family taking this?" I braved.

His face tightened. "Char is still missing."

"What?" I nearly choked on my beer.

Jens had told us that the argument he and Michelle had gotten into Sunday night was over Michelle's little sister Char, who had run away. Again.

"Michelle never found her," Jens said. "At least, not that I know of."

"And the Freeburgs?"

He shrugged again.

"They weren't all that surprised when Char disappeared. They still think she just ran off somewhere. They're pissed as hell that their oldest daughter is dead and Char doesn't even know it because of her selfishness. Their words, not mine."

"She's just a teenager," I said. "What if something happened to her, too?"

"I don't think anything's happened to her."

"How can you be so sure?"

Jens shrugged again. "She was difficult."

"What fifteen-year-old isn't?"

"Fourteen," Jens said.

"Why'd she run away, Jens? Did Michelle ever tell you that?"

Jens stared out his picture window to the hushed street beyond. I could see he was watching the little old man across the street who was weeding his yard in his slacks and a button-down shirt, his work clothes nicer than most people's dress clothes these days. Hell, nicer than I'm dressed today, I thought, looking at my jeans and light jacket.

"Liv, I don't know if I should be telling you anything," he said, staring at his neighbor.

I could probably count on two hands the number of times he had called me this, so its significance now was not lost on me. "Why not?"

"Because I haven't even talked to the FBI yet."

"And?"

"And Mom says we're supposed to be gentle with you."

"Gentle?"

"Because of what happened in Fort Collins. With your trauma and all."

I scoffed and drained my beer, rolling off the couch to retrieve a second one. "It's nothing more than getting my muscles back into normal conditioning, my nervous system back in sync. I'm not the delicate flower she's made me out to be, Jens. You can talk about this with me. Really."

"And you won't freak?"

"Why would I freak?" I asked, standing over him as he slumped.

He folded himself into a sitting position in the recliner and stood up beside me. I laser-locked my eyes on him, having to crane my neck to stare him down, to prove I was strong enough, even though I felt like a dwarf next to him, hence his nickname Moose. He draped his hands on my shoulders and answered quietly, "They consider me a suspect."

"Bullshit!"

He nodded.

"Well, that sucks," I added, stomping off to the couch and flinging myself onto it. So much for not freaking.

"No, the fact that Michelle is gone forever sucks. The rest is all just noise." He sank back into the recliner.

"Have you hired an attorney?"

He shook his head and buried it in his hands. "When would I have had time to hire an attorney? It's not even eight o'clock in the morning.

I just found out about all this a few hours ago. The police questioned me from the instant I showed up at the morgue at five thirty in the morning at the Freeburgs' request. They told me I'd be hearing from the FBI soon and to stay close to home. I hope they didn't stop by while I was up at Mom and Dad's to get you."

I remembered Clint White telling me that he saw Jens at the Nemo General Store yesterday morning. Michelle was found only a few miles from there, right next to our family's iron ore quarry.

Jens had opportunity.

I bolted upright, ignoring the scream of sore muscles, and knelt beside his chair. "I'm sorry about Michelle. I'm sorry it had to end this way. I'm sorry you're hurting. I'm sorry about you having to plan for the funeral and me not being able to help comfort you. But you can't minimize the fact that the authorities consider you a suspect. You need to protect yourself. You were the last one to see her?"

"No, whoever murdered her was the last one to see her." His look said, "Are you stupid or something?"

"I mean were you the last one to see her besides her killer?"

"How would I know?"

"Hubert Jens, listen to me." He dropped his hands and stared at me. Full names were reserved for Mom when we were in trouble for something. "I'll stay with you as long as you like. I planned on going back to work in Fort Collins next week. It's going to be crazy around here between now and then. I'll stay as long as you need me, but you must hire an attorney. A good one. Protect yourself. Do you hear me?"

A long silence passed. Jens's eyes narrowed. "I do need you. I need you to find out what happened. Find Char."

I shook my head. "The police are all over this. Dozens of them."

"How do you know that?" he queried.

I almost gave it away and quickly moved on. "I don't. I can only imagine. And if, as you say, the FBI is involved, this is serious shit. You don't need me. You need a damn attorney."

I was rewarded with an unexpected gleam in his eyes. "That New Year's resolution to stop swearing continues to work magic for you, huh?"

"Shut up, this isn't funny," I said. His smile was only fleeting. I found my way back to the couch, sinking into a deeper funk.

Jens stared at the floor. "I won't be able to do anything, especially now that the FBI has named me a 'person of interest.' You have to help me."

I stared at the ceiling. "How? What can I do? I'm not a cop. I don't know anything about what's happened to Michelle."

A loud rapping on the door gave us both a start. The familiar voice at the door hollered through the screen, "Yoo-hoo. Jens? Boots? Are you there?"

Jens shot me a glance and started talking quickly. "Start with Clint. Today. Before they get to him and force him to stay quiet about this."

"Clint who?" I pretended.

"Clint White. Our Nemo Quarry supervisor."

"What does Clint have to do with—"

"Jens?" Catherine's voice called again.

"That's where they found Michelle's body."

"At our Nemo Quarry?" I acted as if this was news to me.

"Nearby. On Bender's place. That's why they think I'm a suspect."

Another long silence passed. Jens took a deep breath and steeled himself. He looked me in the eye and shook his head before calling, "We're in here, Catherine." Then he offered quietly, "I'll find an attorney if you find out what happened."

I nodded. "Only if you tell me everything. Like why you were at the Nemo General Store yesterday morning."

"How did you—"

"Just give me the keys to your truck," I hissed. "I don't have time for you to take me back to Mom's for the Gray Ghost and I don't even want to think about the consequences of stealing Sister Catherine's Cadillac Seville."

He nodded and tossed me his keys.

"I'll go up there under one condition."

"I said I'd find an attorney," he barked.

"Okay, two conditions. That, and you break the news to Mom that I wasn't able to keep my promise about that doctor's appointment this morning."

He grimaced.

We both rose to our feet to give our sister a hug. Although I rarely saw her wear the tunic, scapular and wimple, Catherine was never seen in public without her veil, despite the Vatican suggesting that wearing habits was no longer a requirement of nuns. Spreading my arms wide, barely able to touch my fingertips across her back, I rushed in for the first hug because I knew if I didn't, I'd get lost in her ample bosom for too long, losing too much precious time. Better Jens than me, stuck to her like a tiny magnet, hugging a refrigerator, unable to resist the magnetic pull. After a few long moments of squashing against her massiveness, me unable to catch my breath, she released me and cradled Jens in her embrace instead. I excused myself and scuttled out the door, glad that for once Catherine's timing was spot on, because I wouldn't have left him alone and I would have never made it to Nemo in time to catch Clint as Jens had asked me to do.

And Sister Catherine would have a rosary buddy for the next few hours.

CHAPTER 9

"HER NAME IS MICHELLE Arlene Freeburg," Bob Shankley announced, clicking to the next slide in the projector.

The debriefing started precisely at nine, three minutes before Streeter arrived. The aide who had greeted him at the airport had phoned Shankley to tell him Streeter would be delayed because of a ruckus a canine had caused in the airport baggage claim area and that they were on their way, yet Shank made his point by starting without him. A small squad of eight men was seated in the conference room listening to their boss present the current status of the Freeburg murder case.

A young woman with straight, dark hair and tired eyes stared at the camera yielding little more than a sad smile. With an ounce of effort, the woman in the picture could be quite beautiful, even remarkable. With the right haircut, a touch of lipstick, and self-confidence, Michelle Freeburg would have been striking. As it was, she seemingly had intentionally uglified herself, trying to appear unappealing, unattractive.

"She was twenty-eight, was killed sometime between late Sunday evening and early Monday. Autopsy is being conducted as we speak and will further pinpoint time of death," Shankley continued, scowling at Streeter as he found an empty seat in the back. The slide changed to a graphic picture of how Michelle Freeburg's body was found. "She was reported missing late yesterday morning by her boss, was last seen by her boyfriend Sunday night before being murdered. Michelle Freeburg was a loner, independent, quiet. Early yesterday morning, her body was found at the banks of Boxelder Creek about three miles southeast of Nemo on private ground known as the Broken Peaks, a summer home for the owners of Tasty Treats, the national burger chain. The Benders haven't been to the place since October of last year and were just contacted this morning about the activities. A rancher and caretaker for the Benders stumbled across her body while walking the creek bed. His name is Tom Jasper, a seventy-two-year-old who leases ground in that area for grazing cattle and for baling hay. We questioned him late yesterday afternoon and he is not a suspect. Had absolutely nothing to do with this other than to be the unfortunate bastard who discovered the body."

Shankley advanced the presentation from the digital photo of an aged Tom Jasper, with the previous day's stamp date, to the next photo, which was of a man with a gray and black beard and mustache, neatly trimmed, wearing a red and silver bandana tied into a skullcap on the top of his head. The photo was a close-up from the chest up, and the subject was looking to his left, seemingly unaware of the camera. He was wearing a dingy, black leather vest with nothing underneath, exposing gray and black chest hair and a tattoo on his right arm. From the near-frontal angle of the photo, the tattoo appeared to be of a man carrying a gun, pointing forward, and wearing an oversized devil's suit. The letters "cifer's Lot" were clearly visible above the figure in black ink, and some indistinguishable letters could be seen to their left.

Shankley pointed to the symbols on the black vest and said, "This is why we're involved." He slammed his pointer against the screen on the emblem sewn to the bearded man's vest. "The 'one percenters' means this guy is a member of an outlaw motorcycle club. See the '1%' above the letters 'M.C.' right here?" He pointed to the abbreviation on the other side of the vest. "Law-abiding citizens comprise 99 percent of all motorcycle riders; these people are proud to be the one percent who are not law abiding, the criminals."

Someone in the front asked, "What does the pin mean?"

Shankley pointed at the small metal pin attached to the vest. "FTW stands for 'fuck the world.' This picture was taken at last year's rally. Carl J. Muldando, a.k.a. Mully, leads a chapter in Northern Colorado and attends the rally annually just to make some money for their club. We have dozens of photos taken of him over the years with the FTW pin proudly displayed on the lapel of his black leather jacket, his colors. We have a witness, who would like to remain anonymous, who told us yesterday that the pin is no longer on Mully's jacket and that he, and several of the bikers he rides with, have new wings on their jackets."

Streeter knew all about wings, but couldn't remember exactly which color wings signified which acts and would ask later.

The SAC continued. "By the way, he's also lost the beard and sports only a mustache the last we know. Looking a little more clean-cut lately. Don't let the filthy colors fool you. They're forbidden to clean their soiled jackets and vests. Never forget that these guys are professionals. Back to the FTW question. Ms. Freeburg was found clutching the pin in her left hand, maybe ripped from her attacker, her murderer. The pin was the same type FTW that Mully used to wear on his colors."

The room was silent.

"We also have a witness who can place Mully near the Broken Peaks crime scene area Sunday evening around supper time," he added, flashing an arrogant smile at Streeter.

All of this seemed a bit too neat, in too short a time frame, for Streeter's taste, reminding him anew of Shank's tendency to make an emotional and vindictive decision rather than a professional one. He wondered what beef Shank had with Carl J. Muldando to have made him the prime suspect already.

"How did this guy become a suspect?" Streeter asked, noting a hint of disdain in Shank's expression. All heads turned around to Streeter.

"Been keeping my eye on him for some time. Ever since you left nearly ten years ago. I happen to believe he is our key suspect as the Crooked Man."

The room erupted in nervous whispers.

Shankley shouted over the noise. "And we have enough evidence already to put this guy away for the murder of Michelle Freeburg. There's hard evidence and he had motive and opportunity."

"What was the motive?" Streeter asked.

"Rejection. Vic's boss, Roy Barker, who first reported Freeburg missing when she didn't show up to work on Monday morning, described three motorcycle gang members approaching Michelle Sunday night at the grocery store where she worked. He told the officer that he was worried the bikers had taken her. Mentioned the lead biker by name, saying he was standing near Freeburg when the biker told her his name was Mully, and Barker later overheard her rebuff Muldando's advances."

"Photo confirmation?" Streeter asked.

"Not yet," Shankley said. "Prefer an actual lineup and have the vic's boss pick him out. We have to go by the book on this one or he'll slip away on a technicality."

He pointed at the tattoo and added, "Mully's a member of the Lucifer's Lot, the only known outlaw motorcycle gang to have officially established a chapter in South Dakota. Keep in mind, Mully's chapter is from Colorado and they only attend the rally each year to make some extra money, money which is likely coming out of the South Dakota chapter's pockets. So we not only have a constant powder keg amongst the motorcycle clubs, we also have a situation brewing within the Lucifer's Lot club between the local chapter and Mully. Immediately after the initial investigation of the dead body yesterday, Leonard, the Lawrence County Sheriff, who recognized the FTW as a Lucifer's Lot pin, checked with other counties and learned about the death in Sturgis of a teenager yesterday, also a vic last seen with a Lucifer's Lot prospect on Monday morning. The sheriff became concerned that this was an act of serial killing by the motorcycle gangs. Serials and gang activity both call for FBI jurisdiction. The rumor is that Mully's Northern Colorado chapter has two prospective members riding with them during this rally.

"Prospects generally have to commit heinous crimes in order to be accepted into an outlaw motorcycle club. Therefore, it's logical to conclude that Mully or the Lucifer's Lot prospects are primary suspects in the murder of Michelle Freeburg and the Jane Doe teenager at Sturgis."

Streeter asked, "How does Sheriff Leonard know so much about this Muldando character?"

Even in the darkened room, Shankley's frown was unmistakably one of irritation. "Sheriff Leonard has been keeping a close eye on this thug for years, watches his gang daily during the rally since they set up camp just a few miles from the sheriff's house. He drives by their camp each day on his way to his Deadwood office. The campground is adjacent to Broken Peaks, where Freeburg's body was found. He's been dreading the day that something like this might happen but couldn't do anything about it since Mully and his gang are on their best behavior each year at the campground."

"Regular altar boys," someone growled. The room filled with snickers.

Streeter heard a low growl from the man sitting next to him.

Shankley added, "As I mentioned, the campground is a stone's throw from Broken Peaks property. Once Leonard was notified that Ernif Hanson's body had been found Monday on his ranch, also with a blunt force trauma injury to the back of the skull, just as the previous Crooked Man murder victims had, he called us in on it. Plus, as I mentioned, a Jane Doe was killed in Sturgis, which the Sturgis Police Department reported, also indicating a connection with the Lucifer's Lot. All three discovered dead on Monday. Killed."

The SAC flashed a picture of a large man lying face down on some jutting rocks on a hillside, the back of his skull bloodied and mangled. Streeter had seen the picture last night on Calvin's computer and had reviewed the electronic files on the Crooked Man case. But he had never seen the second picture Shank was showing, the young teenager in the red bikini heaped on the asphalt. He leaned forward, studying the details from his back row vantage point.

"Killed? All three confirmed?" Streeter had irritated Shankley once again.

"Autopsies aren't done on any of the three yet. But considering they speculate the female vic's a teenager, I highly doubt she died of natural causes. These guys are tough bastards. By merely insinuating that one of them is suspected in a murder investigation, you may as well get your affairs in order, because the next death certificate signed may be your own. Which is why I asked our Denver Bureau to send us one of their best. Someone who knows this area, has worked this area, was initially involved in the Crooked Man case, and has worked the Sturgis Motorcycle Rally many times. Maybe some of you have heard of Special Agent Streeter Pierce."

Streeter sat uncomfortably erect in his chair as all eyes turned toward him in the dark.

Someone asked, "Didn't you nab a top tenner?"

Another said, "The best field agent in the country."

"A legend," a third one announced. "All those high-profile cases."

Streeter didn't respond to any of them. The scruffy man with the long hair and beard sitting next to him sat up in his chair and gave Streeter the once-over.

Shankley cleared his throat.

These men had done their homework on Streeter Pierce. He had indeed been responsible for arresting a Top Ten fugitive, a "top tenner," an achievement the bureau recognizes as one of the highest honors an agent can receive. But he knew they were warming him up for something.

"Pierce will be the agent in charge on this case," Shankley announced. "Any and all files that we have received over the last twenty-one hours on all three murders from the Lawrence County and Meade County authorities will be turned over to him immediately. I have told him you will all be at his disposal if he needs your help. The rally started yesterday, four days ago unofficially, and will start winding down this weekend. It's Tuesday, so we don't have a lot of time. Mully's pattern is for his gang to pull up stakes on Sunday morning and head south, but they've been known to pull out much sooner."

"Why don't they stay at the Lucifer's Lot hideout on the east side of Rapid?" someone in the front row asked.

The man sitting next to Streeter answered, "They just might, but Mully's chapter would have to kill every one of the local chapter members, first. Didn't you hear, boss man? The two chapters' leaders aren't so fond of one another."

Shank grimaced. "Don't call me boss man. It's Special Agent in Charge Shankley, to you." He cleared his throat and continued, "As usual, we've got agents who flew in from all over the country, each one eager to work that circus for top tenners. Pierce will focus on Mully, the Lucifer's Lot biker suspected of killing Hanson early Sunday night, the Freeburg young woman sometime late Sunday night or early Monday morning, and the unidentified teenager yesterday just after noon. The ambulance driver and EMT saw the Lucifer's Lot bikers drive away as they arrived to attend our female vic in Sturgis, one identifying Mully from photos. Pierce, during investigations, you will be accompanied by me."

Bingo, Streeter thought.

CHAPTER 10

CALVIN HAD BEEN SPOT ON.

Shank was imposing himself on Streeter as a partner to keep tabs on him. He'd be standing in the wings in case there were bows to be taken or in the event a body—namely Streeter—needed to be thrown under the bus if everything fell apart. It had to be one or the other. At least Shank had publicly named Streeter agent in charge, which meant he could find ways to direct Shank's activities elsewhere.

"During the undercover work, Streeter, you will be assisted by Special Agent Stewart Blysdorf," Shankley said as the meeting wound down.

"Our expert on outlaw motorcycle gangs? I've heard of him."

Shank flicked the lights on and everyone's eyes blinked in adjustment to the change. "Good. Now you know him."

The hirsute man sitting next to Streeter extended his hand. "I'm Bly. Nice to meet you."

Streeter noted Bly's piercing steel-gray eyes as he shook his hand in greeting. "Streeter. Pleasure meeting you, partner."

Bly reached up and apologetically rubbed the hair on his chin. "My cover. The Sturgis Motorcycle Rally started over a month ago for me, and I have to look and live the part if I'm going to get any intelligence."

"Do you own a Harley?"

Bly nodded with pride.

"Sweet."

Shankley ended the meeting. "Pierce and Blysdorf, in my office for the rest of the debriefing."

The two men followed Shankley's broad shoulders and even broader girth to his office. Though a few years younger than Streeter, Bob Shankley looked older. Fifty at least. Before the agents had a chance to sit down, Shank ordered Bly to get coffee. Streeter knew it was because Shank wanted a few moments alone.

As the door closed behind Bly, Shank stuck a large finger accusingly at Streeter and growled, "Look, Pierce. I've worked my ass off to get where I am. I don't need you fucking it up for me, you understand? I've got these guys' attention and that matters when you're in charge. Don't start any stories circulating about me or, damn you, I will breathe life into the old rumors about Paula so fast your head will be spinning."

Streeter winced at the mention of his late wife's name.

He felt more anger and hatred than he had felt in years. And he didn't like what it was doing to him. He managed to stay calm, however, despite being unnerved by Shank's emotional and unexpected assault, and to answer, "I have no intention of saying anything about you, Shank. Not good or bad. I came up here because I have a job to do. Because you asked for me. I'm not any happier to have to come back here than you are to have me. But we're stuck with each other because of the Crooked Man."

Shank's beady eyes leveled on Streeter's, and moisture was gathering on his upper lip.

It was Streeter's turn to threaten. In a harsh whisper he added, "And my wife is off limits to you or anyone else involved in this investigation. No one mentions her name. You understand me?"

Shank shrank back in his chair. "Just wanted to make sure we were clear on these things."

"We're clear," Streeter replied in a cool, low voice.

"Good, because I'm going to be your fucking shadow for the next week, watching every fucking move you make in these interviews," Shank spat as he spoke. "And you sure as hell better not fuck up, Pierce."

Bly returned with three cups of coffee, two precariously balanced in his right hand. Streeter took both cups and handed one to Shank with a warning stare to back off. Shank's glare was equally threatening, and the two settled into the business at hand under a forced truce.

"Blysdorf and I interviewed Tom Jasper yesterday afternoon and Helma Hanson, widow of Ernif, last evening," Shank began. He pushed two thick files toward Bly and spoke to no one in particular when he said, "It's all in there. Plus what we have from the Lawrence County Sheriff's department and the scant information we have from the Sturgis Police Department, because they're just too busy to do much at all for us on Jane Doe. Sheriff Leonard only worked the Freeburg case for a couple of hours, but they've had years to gather surveillance on these thugs. The minute the sheriff saw the FTW pin stuck in the vic's palm, he knew the trail led straight to Mully or one of his gang, and he quickly called us."

"What's everyone got against this guy Mully?" Streeter asked looking at the pictures in the file that Bly had handed him.

"What we've got is the fact that Carl Muldando is a murderous bastard who likes messing around with young girls."

"Allegedly or factually?" Streeter pressed.

Shank ignored him. "And he's from your neck of the woods."

"Denver?"

"North of there. Longmont area," Bly corrected. "Colorado has some established branches of the Lucifer's Lot as well as Serpents and Renegades. We don't see much of the Renegades up here. Occasionally we've had some visits by Serpents, but we don't get much in the way of many gangs anymore. The Inferno Force guys see to that."

"I thought you said in your debriefing that the Lucifer's Lot were still the only known outlaw gang with an official presence in South Dakota."

"I did," Shank said, running his fat fingers through his slick, thinning red hair. "But the Sturgis Motorcycle Rally in large part is primarily run and policed by the Inferno Force, many of whom are from San Bernardino, California. At least the traditional places at the rally like the Chopper Campground and the beer tents at the Cattle Jump Campground. They don't mind other gangs attending the rally, but they won't tolerate any fights or trouble of any kind that would draw the police. A couple of bikers were knifed outside of the Full Throttle last year in a fight, and the Inferno Force allegedly told that group they couldn't return this year."

Streeter whistled. "Is Cattle Jump Campground still *the* place to be for rally goers? If I remember correctly, they always had live bands, big names, lots of beer, and plenty of adult entertainment."

"You remember exactly right," Bly answered. "Miss Cattle Jump won last year in nothing but white boots. If you call that adult . . . entertainment."

Streeter sensed Shank's irritation with Bly and instantly liked the man.

Shank frowned. "Christ, Blysdorf. And we pay you for this? If it wasn't for the information you seem to extract from that trash, I'd have half a mind to send your sorry ass to the reservation this year."

"Why Mully?" Streeter asked again, holding up the photo of the man from the file. "I've studied the reports, Shank, and with all due respect, I see no connection between this guy and the Crooked Man cases. None."

"Other than the fact that the three cases you were investigating, plus the two I have since added to the file, all involved people having their heads bashed in and that all five murders occurred during or around the time of the Sturgis Motorcycle Rally," Shank countered.

"I'll concede on those points," Streeter admitted. "And I'll even go so far as admitting that this Mully character appears to be a prime suspect for the Freeburg murder and potentially even with Jane Doe's death. But what I don't see is the connection of the Freeburg murder with Hanson and the Crooked Man cases. First and foremost, Freeburg was naked. And a woman. The five earlier Crooked Man cases were men and none of them were undressed. Plus, as you said, Freeburg had a motorcycle gang's pin stuck in her palm. None of the others offered up any such evidence."

"And there's no way any legitimate member of a one-percent motor-cycle gang would be so hubristic as to declare their guilt by leaving a gang pin in a vic's hand," Bly added, picking at his teeth.

Streeter gawked at Bly. "Hubristic?"

Bly gave him a wink, still picking at his teeth.

Staying focused on Streeter, Shank coaxed, "But Hanson appears to be a victim of the Crooked Man, in your estimation?"

Streeter answered honestly, having studied the scant information about Ernif Hanson's murder and related the facts to the Crooked Man cases. "Strong possibility."

"Maybe the Crooked Man is slipping, by leaving evidence behind.

Maybe he's bored with killing men." Shank waved his thoughts aside and added, "Then let's focus on the Freeburg murder, flush it out first and see what comes of the evidence. If we nail Mully on the Freeburg case, possibly even the unidentified female in Sturgis, maybe he'll be willing to plea bargain with information about the Crooked Man cases for a reduced sentence on Freeburg and Jane Doe."

"Let's not jump ahead of ourselves," Streeter warned. "Back to Mully and the Freeburg murder—don't most of the gang members have the FTW pin? Couldn't any one of them have lost it?"

"That's what you're going to have to find out. Go to the rally, find Mully and his gang, confirm they have the new wings, and bring him in here for questioning and a lineup for Roy Barker. Pronto, before someone else gets killed. Any interviews you conduct, I want to be there with you. Starting with Lawrence County Sheriff Leonard Leonard, who happens to be waiting for us in the next room. And understand, Pierce, the sole purpose of these interviews is to confirm what we already know, got it?"

"What is it that we know?" Streeter challenged.

"That the Lucifer's Lot is behind these murders. At the very least, Freeburg and Jane Doe. That Carl Muldando is responsible." Shank leaned back in his chair. Streeter observed his oddly anchored stubbornness on this yet unproven allegation. "Even if Mully himself is not directly behind these murders, all signs point to one of those dirty bastards murdering those poor women just to earn their wings."

"Yeah, you mentioned that during the briefing. Which wings are the Lucifer's Lot bikers supposedly wearing now? And remind me again the color scheme for the wings?"

Shank nodded at Bly to answer.

"You probably remember that wings are bragging rights for performing oral sex on women. Black wings for a black woman. White wings, white woman. Yellow wings, Asian woman. They even have color variations for their wing patches indicating if the woman was menstruating during the event. Black on red to indicate . . . well, you get the picture. Green wings if the woman had a venereal disease. There are even wings for performing cunnilingus on a female infant."

"Infants? It's just gotten worse," was all Streeter could manage.

"These people are sick," Bly confirmed.

Shank added, "And even sicker when you think about the fact that all wings must be earned with witnesses present."

"What wings are you speculating Mully or someone from his chapter to be wearing? White?" Streeter asked.

Bly and Shank exchanged a wary glance.

Bly shook his head. "Purple."

Bly stared directly into Streeter's questioning eyes and answered, "A dead woman."

CHAPTER 11

"**THANK YOU FOR COMING** back, Liv," Clint said as he rushed toward me. He offered me a hand as I stepped down from Jens's truck, which was something he'd never done before yesterday, and the gesture made me feel more fragile than I was.

I just couldn't imagine that this man would ever strike a woman, the whole idea of him being involved in Michelle's death, insane, even if he was seen lingering near the big rock yesterday morning.

"No problem," I said, glancing around at the growing number of people in the field nearby and the handful of tents that had been erected since last night. "You mentioned yesterday that you sent your crew to Rapid City, and I thought you might need a hand again today."

"Sure do. There's nobody here to help. I'm constantly jumping on the loader for the trucks. Could you cover for me there while I finish this report for the agents Tommy and I talked with yesterday?" he asked.

"Absolutely. That's why I'm here."

"Come on and wait inside the trailer until the next truck arrives. I just made a fresh pot of coffee."

"Thanks, but I picked up a big one on the way over. That's why I'm so late." I turned my wrist to check the time and noticed it was later than I'd hoped. Nearly 8:40 a.m.

"Late? I'm just glad you're here."

"How long do you need me?"

"An hour or two should do. Sure you don't want to come inside to wait?"

"I'd prefer to play Gladys Kravitz and scope out the activities next door."

He chuckled as he retreated to his office, and I once again donned all the necessary personal protective equipment. This time, though, the hat, gloves, and so forth, which belonged to Jens, were also stored behind the seat of his truck. I retrieved my supersized Styrofoam coffee cup and meandered over to the corner of the property and leaned casually against a fence post as I eavesdropped on the busy team, who barely noticed me. I pulled my hard hat low on my forehead and adjusted my shaded safety glasses.

Although the line of vehicles parked along Nemo Road had drastically diminished since yesterday, the media types who remained were diehards, craning and finagling to get a telescopic photo or even a glimpse of the crime scene—most of which was blocked by the fabric-covered buildings—from two hundred yards away. Most were likely quite envious of my position; the newsman I'd chased off was probably wishing he had run me over when he had the chance.

For what must have been three hours, I slouched against the fence post near the clustered birch, watching the criminalists working the banks along the creek and the surrounding meadow. Now and again I had to pry myself away and load a truck, but I was back in a flash, glued with fascination and genuine interest in the process. My perch, slightly uphill from the creek, offered me a unique bird's-eye view of the activities.

The criminalists were all clustered within twenty or thirty yards of me, but they never once acknowledged my voyeuristic presence. As I dashed to and from the loader, my breathing sounded like a bellowing seal with its tail caught in a whale's teeth, yet they still took no notice of me. How long it takes to get into shape and how quickly we get out of it. Physical therapy wasn't working fast enough for me.

As I watched the busy bees below, I wondered what percentage of the aches, pains, and strains were the result of being hospitalized for four weeks or from leaning against a post for the past three hours, standing in one position. Without a doubt, my weakness was the result of the entire cocktail, regardless of the proportions.

My mind drifted, and the movements of the criminalists took on a familiar rhythm. I found myself comparing them to those who had worked in my home after my friend Lisa was killed there, and I toyed with the idea of taking seriously her comment about me joining the FBI. I had a knack for being inquisitive, I loved investigating (more like poking my nose into other people's business, really), and I was talented at solving problems in creative manners. But it still didn't feel like the right fit to me, somehow. Glancing over my shoulder at the purplish-red iron ore highwall, a quarry we'd been mining for nearly half a century, I sighed. The FBI would be too distant from this, too far from my love for mining. Despite my fascination with the crime solvers' dedication, brilliance, and industriousness, I couldn't imagine leaving this world behind.

No crime in being an interested third party and student of the criminalists, though, so I got back to my studies. The yellow crime-scene tape to cordon off the area was primarily strung across the Broken Peaks entrance road, about ten degrees to my left and half a mile away. The entrance road paralleled our haul road, which lay directly in front of me and saw steady truck traffic. To my right ahead of me was the office trailer, and to my immediate left in front of me was the big rock, the crime scene. The Benders' lodge on Broken Peaks was about a quarter of a mile to my far left, down the creek.

From time to time it was so quiet that I could even hear a bit of chatter from the people parked along Nemo Road when I strained to listen. I was most afraid of someone using the telescopic lens of an expensive camera to zoom in on my face, the photo appearing on tomorrow's front page below the headline: "Suspected Killer Had Sister Stand Guard" or something damaging like that. As long as I limited my movements and kept my hard hat pulled low across my eyes, I should remain anonymous.

I hoped.

The noonday sun was approaching, and I felt its rays beating down on me. Sweat dripped down my back. I decided to find a place to sit down and let my achy muscles rest. This grassy knoll midway up the slope with its stand of birch trees is perfect habitat for bighorn sheep and mountain goats, so I sat perfectly still, half expecting one to nuzzle my ear at any moment. This, of course, would cause me to scream or wet my pants or both, an embarrassing scene any way you looked at it. So periodically I glanced back over my shoulder, just to make sure, and prayed my sweaty self would scare them away before they ever made it too close.

I had been watching the team gather whatever evidence they could from the area, crime scene photographers snapping a constant stream of photos, but I never saw any major pieces of evidence like clothes or weapons being bagged and tagged. I did see two technicians bag a few rocks from above the banks, and although I couldn't hear their exact words, I could hear them mumbling to one another about a fine spray of blood, high velocity or something. Another technician, a slim woman with blond hair, combed the meadow floor on that same bank's edge through the tall grass, using what looked like magnifying goggles and tweezers to find and pluck small items, bagging each piece carefully. Her voice was so soft I couldn't distinguish a word she said, but I did hear "flashlight lens" spoken by one of the young men nearby. A technician who was working the creek bank had a loud and distinct voice, and I heard him declare, "Probably the kind the gangs carry when they can't carry weapons. You know, those heavy-duty flashlights with the long handles?"

The mumbling continued, as did the tedious and meticulous work. I watched and learned. Michelle's body had been found right here. A few miles from where Jens had been earlier that same morning. No wonder he was a suspect. My stomach lurched at the thought of how Jens must have felt when he first learned where Michelle's body had been discovered. It must be eating away at him that he was so close, yet couldn't help her one bit.

I wiped my brow and checked my watch. It was nearly noon. About an hour earlier, when I had gone inside the trailer to retrieve a Diet Coke, Clint apologized for needing me longer and said he hoped to be done in an hour, so I would likely be going back to Rapid City soon. Clint told me two agents, Blysdorf and a new guy, had been by half an hour prior to pick up his statement and to peruse the crime scene. I had been loading a steady stream of trucks about that time, but I never saw either man cross the fence or walk among the criminalists.

As I studied the movements in the valley, I eased up to my feet to stretch my legs and realized that my fear of making things worse for Jens had cooled a bit in the warmth of the summer day. I slowly sank back down to my knees in the grass.

Suddenly, I heard someone shout, "Hey!"

I didn't dare move, thinking I'd been spotted. I held my breath and froze, squeezing my eyes shut and hoping the man, if he'd seen something move in this little grove of trees, would take me for a rabbit, or at least not Jens's sister. The air was still and hot and unforgiving. The muffled voices nearby, the chatter that began to grow, and the scuffling of shoes on rocks and pine needles surely meant they were headed my way. I kept my eyes closed and forced myself to hold my breath a little longer, kneeling in the tall grass amid the thin shadows of the birch trees.

"Look!" the same man shouted.

More muted voices, more movement. But this time the movement sounded slightly different: it was not closer, as I expected, and it was not the sound of rocks sliding beneath hurried footsteps on the gentle slope in front of me; rather, it was farther to my far left, and steadier.

As slowly as my lungs could stand, I released my breath and inched my head sideways in their direction, raising my eyelids and expecting to see the criminalists standing in front of me, hands on hips awaiting an explanation. I drew in a deep breath of relief when I saw a small group huddled on my side of the creek, but much further down the tree line to my left and well east of where they all had been working. I caught their murmurs and nods, and I saw them pointing at something in the woods to my left. My eye scanned where they were pointing and I could barely make out off in the distance down the road toward Rapid City the tops of what looked like a row of tents and the bodies of campers moving about in the trees and the clearings. It was the campground between Broken Peaks and Pulman's place.

I rocked to my feet and walked the fence line, scuttling between the trees until I closed the distance between where I had perched all day and where the criminalists had moved into the tree line. I stopped behind a large pine tree when I came within earshot and strained to hear them.

"Boot prints," one of the younger men said. "Leading along the tree line on the Broken Peaks side of the fence."

The man with the loud voice took charge. "Those are hiking boot treads or something similar. Not the same print as the tennis shoes our vic was wearing. Cast the prints before we lose them completely."

Another voice said, "I've got two sets of prints by the creek bank; one set heads back down this fence line. Toward the Broken Peaks place."

"We searched that place yesterday. Higher-ups say the Benders confirmed they hadn't been anywhere near the place since last October, and the dust that had gathered suggested no one had been hiding out or staying at the place."

"Then where is this person headed?"

The loud man answered, "Let's follow the tracks. My guess is they will lead us to where the killer took off in a vehicle or something."

"See this? Two sets of tracks coming this way, one set returning. The killer made our vic walk in on her own volition. She was alive until he hit her over the head."

"Like I said, based on the shards of plastic that McMillan found, I would guess they were from the lens of an industrial flashlight."

Then I thought I heard, "Lucifer's Lot. Those treads are probably from biker boots, not hiking boots. Hope they all burn in hell."

"The boyfriend's with the Lucifer's Lot?"

"No. Shank said the suspect is some guy named Mully."

At the name, my breath caught in my throat.

I heard two of the techs fall away from where I stood, following the tracks along the tree line downstream. I heard the other retreat back across Boxelder Creek, sloshing through the shallow water, and call out to someone to help with a cast.

I darted quickly back from tree to tree until I was near the loader. I crawled into Jens's pickup, hoping I wouldn't hurl all over his seat. I cranked the engine and turned the fan to high on the coldest setting in an attempt to stave off the nausea.

Lucifer's Lot. Mully.

The same bunch that I had seen the day before with that poor girl at Sturgis on the deserted street near our concrete plant. The one the EMTs were trying to revive and whisked away in the ambulance before I ever got a chance to find courage enough to crawl out of Jens's pickup and tell them what I saw. Why hadn't I told someone yesterday about this? What happened to the girl? That certainly wasn't Michelle, although it did look a little like her, only younger. I worried now if the girl had died. I assumed she'd lived because I waited for Jens for at least forty-five minutes after the ambulance left and no policemen or FBI agents ever returned. If I had witnessed a crime, they would have returned to the scene on Sherman Street to canvass the neighborhood, surely. I was prepared to say something, tell them my story if they had, but they never came back. So I assumed she'd lived. What if she was dead, too? And how did Michelle fit in to all this?

I had to talk to Jens. Now.

I took a deep breath and stepped down out of Jens's idling truck. Making my way to the trailer, I poked my head in the door and called out to Clint that I had to go in for an appointment in town. He thanked me for my help and I hurried off to the pickup, dropped the stick into drive, and spat gravel with my tires as the pickup jumped forward out of the lot.

I told myself to calm down and not draw attention to myself. I drove the long stretch of road exiting our quarry, opened the gate enough for me to squeeze the truck through, then swung the chain back around the gate and locked it tight. Jumping back in behind the wheel, I noticed the clock read 12:10 pm. I hooked a left onto Nemo Road and craned my neck to locate the two criminalists who had decided to follow the boot prints. I spotted the two young men emerging beyond the Broken Peaks lodge on the far end of the property and cutting across the meadow toward the campground. I drove slowly, hugging the shoulder to find out where they ended up. The pair followed the boot prints to the tents and campers sandwiched between the open spaces of Broken Peaks acreage and Pulman's land.

As I followed their progress, I saw the campground on the left and slowed. About to round the bend to my right away from the campground, I crept along the curve in the road, stealing a glimpse over my shoulder at the criminalists nearing the lot.

Just as I was about to signal a left to turn into the campground, I saw the line of motorcycles pulling around the rear of the lone building and toward the parking lot exit. There were indeed several tents pitched in the campground, as well as one camper and two vans. The Lazy S Campground sign above the door caught my eye, as did the man who exited the front door, waving at the line of motorcyclists. I had nearly slowed the pickup truck to a complete stop on the shoulder so I could get a better look at the familiar-looking man.

It was Mr. Schilling, the PE teacher from my junior high school. Though obviously older, he still looked very much the same, still wearing a tank top and shorts and sporting a tan. His attention was on the gang of bikers leaving his place, as though he wanted to make sure they were gone. I was about to pull in and ask him if he knew anything about what was going on over at Broken Peaks, or if he knew anything about Michelle Freeburg, when I noticed the two criminalists approach Mr. Schilling. I also noticed that the motorcycles had rumbled to a stop at the campground's entrance, waiting to turn onto Nemo Road.

My eyes darted from Schilling to the bikers and suddenly I realized that they were the Lucifer's Lot members. I scanned the group, skipping from face to face and finding some familiar ones. My eyes landed on the biker in the lead. Sure enough, there was Mully. And he was staring back at me. Grinning.

I hoped the spray of gravel from the truck tires didn't shower any biker because I'd heard how important bikes are to them, and they were already mad enough at me for witnessing something I shouldn't have. I just hoped they would choose to turn right and head to Sturgis through Nemo rather than fall in behind me.

In my rearview mirror, I saw Mully pull out. Turning left. Going my way.

CHAPTER 12

"SHANK, I TOLD YOU yesterday that I was washing my hands of this thing," Sheriff Leonard insisted. "So why don't you boys get on with your business and leave me out of it."

The name tag pinned to his uniform above his badge read Sheriff Leonard L. Leonard. Streeter couldn't help wondering if Leonard's parents had been cruel enough to give their baby boy the middle name of Leonard as well. Wasn't their sense of humor warped enough, to name a boy Leonard Leonard?

Shank leaned across his desk, beefy elbows spread wide, and said, "You handed this off to me like a hot potato because the trail leads directly to Mully, and you guys don't want to have to be the ones to break the news to him that he's a suspect."

"Right," the sheriff affirmed simply.

Bly murmured, "Can't say as I blame them, boss."

"Shut up, Blysdorf."

"Where can we find Mully now?" Streeter asked, cutting across Shank.

Sheriff Leonard shrugged. "Can't say. But he'll show up at their campground tonight sometime. More like in the early morning, around three, four. To sleep for a couple of hours, just like he always does. His boys set up camp at the Lazy S every year and they stay about a week or two."

"The Lazy S?"

"Yeah," Leonard said with a tobacco-stained grin. "It's Schilling's idea of a joke. You know, like lazy ass?"

Streeter smiled. "I suppose the S in Lazy S has something to do with the man named Schilling?"

"Yep, he's the owner. Name's Eddie Schilling. He bought that land and opens it up for camping during the tourist season. Memorial Day through Labor Day. But I think he makes his steadiest money during the rally. He reserves the entire place for the Lucifer's Lot every year. Won't let anyone else camp there. So they have privacy."

"And so the owner doesn't have to keep peace among other campers," Bly added.

"The Lazy S is just down the road a stretch from Nemo, adjacent to Broken Peaks," Sheriff Leonard explained. "It has some areas where people with tents or campers can pull in, build a campfire, and share the bathrooms and shower facilities in the common area. But nothing too fancy. Primitive, you might say."

"You know him?" Streeter asked Shank.

"Mully?"

"No, Schilling," Streeter asked, noting Shank's evasiveness.

"I suppose everyone in this area knows him or knows of him. He's a coach at a Rapid City high school."

Streeter turned back toward Sheriff Leonard. "And you're convinced Mully killed Michelle Freeburg?"

The sheriff shrugged, looked cautiously around as if to make sure no one was listening, then nodded slowly. "I'm not convinced of anything, if you're asking for the record. Off the record, you bet your sweet ass I'm convinced. I sent a guy over to the Lazy S yesterday right after we found the girl and had him shoot the shit with Eddie, the owner. I told him to pretend to be a buddy, look around, keep his eyes open. He saw three of the guys crawl out of their tents and head for the shower. One of them was Mully, who was wearing his colors. But Mully wasn't wearing an FTW pin. I asked my deputy to check all of them and report on who was not wearing a pin. Mully was the only one not wearing the pin, as far as he could see. And we've never seen him without that pin. Ever. Got dozens of surveillance photos over the years to prove it too."

He slid a stack of photos toward Streeter. Bly peering over his shoulder, Streeter flipped through the stack and noticed the date and time stamp on every photo, spanning the last five years. He also clearly saw the FTW pin on each of Mully's photos where the angle was right. He wished Shank's files on the Crooked Man were as complete and as thorough as Sheriff Leonard's on the Lucifer's Lot.

"When was this? When your informant noticed that Mully wasn't wearing his pin?" Streeter asked.

"Oh, I'd say between noon, one o'clock. Yesterday."

Bly asked, "Any of them with new wings, particularly purple?"

Sheriff Leonard buckled his brow and shook his head slowly. "Don't know. Never asked. Why?"

"No reason, just wondering," Bly said, cleaning his fingernails with an eight-inch buck knife.

Shank asked, "Anything else you want to share with us?"

Leonard leaned forward and whispered, "Just one more thing. Rumor around here is that one of the old ladies works for Pennington County in the licensing department."

"Old lady, you mean the equivalent of a biker's wife? For a local Lucifer's Lot biker?" Streeter asked.

Leonard and Bly both nodded.

Rubbing his sagging chin, Shank speculated, "Probably how they're getting their stolen bikes and cars registered. Using falsified titles."

"That's the story," confirmed the Lawrence County Sheriff.

"Anything else?"

Sheriff Leonard leaned back, glanced over at Streeter and Bly, and squinted skeptically at them. "I don't know who your friends are, Shank, but I don't want any trouble. Like I told you yesterday morning, my department found nothing except for the body along Boxelder Creek. You understand me? I'll be the first to deny anything else you say about me or about anyone from my department. Do I make myself clear?"

He glared at all three men, pointing a warning finger at Shank. "I'm serious, now. Our investigation wasn't even an investigation. It was your investigation. Right from the very beginning. We were just assisting, containing the crime scene until you boys got there. Who you investigate is your business, but we did not in any way suggest that Mully or anyone from the Lucifer's Lot had anything to do with this. That's our story."

Streeter met his distrustful glance and leveled his own unsettling stare at Leonard. "What about this Mully character scares you so badly?"

Sheriff Leonard folded his arms tightly across his scrawny chest and looked down his narrow nose at Streeter. "You have any kids?"

Streeter shook his head.

"You?" he asked Bly, who also shook his head.

"I do. My oldest daughter is seventeen, works as a clerk in the grocery store in Deadwood. A family-owned grocery store, just like the one where Michelle Freeburg worked. My youngest is sixteen. Works with her sister bagging groceries sometimes." Leonard sat forward in his chair and crossed his arms on the corner of Shank's desk. "These men are nasty. They find their sheep, their mammas, at places like the Deadwood grocery store. You know what sheep are, Agent Pierce?"

Streeter nodded, but the sheriff explained anyway.

"They're the young girls the gangs pass around among each other. They're the playthings. The old ladies are not to be passed around; they're dedicated to one biker, like a wife, but the old ladies turn a blind eye to the sheep. These young women are eager to please these scumbags and even more eager to anger their parents with a little rebellion, turned on by the macho image of the bad boy bikers. Only problem is, once they start, they can't get out."

Bly nodded in agreement.

Streeter watched the hard, angry lines around Leonard's eyes and mouth dissolve into the softness of fatherly concern.

"Oddly, despite the abuse these women receive, there's never a shortage of volunteers ready to jump on the next bike that comes their way. Pretty women. Young women. Vulnerable women."

Sheriff Leonard lowered his head.

Bly completed painting Leonard's picture for Streeter. "Usually these women are victimized, abused, passed around in the gang, performing sexual acts for them in which anything goes. They often become their prostitutes or drug peddlers on the streets, bringing in extra income for the gang. These women mean nothing to the bikers. They are bought, sold, traded,

and even given away like unwanted trash, becoming another biker's treasure, at least for the moment. In a word, they're expendable."

Shank sighed heavily. "Michelle Freeburg was expendable. Probably
passed around the gang, doped up on drugs, used and abused, and eventually became worthless to them."

"Did the autopsy show up yet?"

Shank plucked a file from the top of his pile and slid it across the desk
to Streeter. He read it quickly as the other men sat quietly.

Bly asked, "Any signs of drugs? Penetration? Sexual abuse? Multiple
partners?"

Sheriff Leonard tilted his head thoughtfully toward Streeter. Shank
scowled.

"Actually, no. These are just preliminary results. More to follow."
Streeter was scanning and finding the pertinent facts to read. "No detect-
able level of drugs or alcohol was in Miss Freeburg's blood. She died from
a blow to the back of her head. Body temp indicated she died about the
time she was found."

"I didn't know that," Sheriff Leonard said, his face puckering with
disgust. "She was alive when Tommy Jasper found her?"

Shank grimaced.

Knowing that someone had delivered a brutal blow to the back of
Michelle Freeburg's head and left her for dead, yet she had survived over-
night in what were likely chilly temperatures, Streeter could only hope she
hadn't suffered too much. He said, "Not for long."

"And they are sure about this?" Bly asked.

"As I said, these are just preliminary findings. Official autopsy to follow soon," Streeter read, still scanning. "Dried blood was found along her
neck, but mostly across her skull into and around her left ear and under
her head, which meant she likely bled through the night. Hard to tell how
much blood she had lost, since only a small amount pooled around her on
the ground and some washed away into the creek. Early results indicate
she'd been there eleven, twelve hours."

"All night," Bly said.

A long silence passed.

Streeter didn't want to imagine how that must have been for Michelle
and hoped she was unconscious the entire time.

Abruptly he asked, "And how does Ernif Hanson fit into all this?"

Shank shrugged. "He may not, but what kind of a person would club an old man like that and leave him for dead in his own field?"

Bly answered, "Probably someone who got caught with a meth lab in the woods or something."

Shank added, "Or someone who was as mean as a snake and killed him for no reason. As an initiation. Someone like Mully or one of the Lucifer's Lot."

Sheriff Leonard rubbed his tired, saggy eyes with his spindly fingers and pushed his wavy brown hair away from his face. Streeter sensed he was sincere about his concern for his daughters, not easily intimidated by motorcyclists.

"I'm just tired of dealing with these outlaws," Leonard admitted. "Tired of dealing with all the riffraff that the gambling has brought to our sleepy little town. I preferred the gold miners."

"The mines have been slowing to a trickle for almost two decades," Shank said.

"I know. I just wish the hands of time would rewind to when we had nothing but gold miners to deal with. Those were happier times."

"Maybe it's time to retire," Streeter offered, recognizing the signs of when a man's usefulness is spent.

With heaviness and sincerity the sheriff replied, "Maybe so. That's why I don't want to have anything to do with this case. Too much at stake here. I know it doesn't sound rational, but it just hits too close to home. I won't take a chance with my girls. Not with someone as vile as Mully. Those people are bad to the bone and proud of it."

———

After Sheriff Leonard left, the mood remained somber.

Bly asked, "So you still think Mully killed Michelle to earn his purple wings?"

Bly shot Streeter a sideways glance that Shank didn't catch. Streeter assumed that meant Bly didn't think so.

"It's all theory," Shank said waving his hands dismissively. "But, yes, I'm sure of it. Only way to confirm the theory is for you to check him out when he makes himself at home at the Lazy S Campground tonight or sometime over the next few days. He's never had purple wings before, so if he has them now, it's probably a pretty good indication he had something to do with this."

"We can't just arrest him because he's wearing purple wings. That's not exactly evidence of a murder. We have no proof he killed anyone," Streeter argued.

"That's right," Shank said. "You'll need proof."

"Wearing a badge of honor for performing cunnilingus on a dead woman doesn't mean he killed the woman. It doesn't even mean the woman was murdered at all, Shank. It just means the woman was dead and that he did the vile act in front of witnesses. Unfortunately, there's no law against that."

"Defiling a corpse," Shank argued.

"Even if there was a law, with their code of silence, we couldn't get any witnesses to testify," Bly said.

Shank said, "You saw how Sheriff Leonard reacted. That's why you'll need indisputable evidence. You'll figure out how to nail the guy. You're clever enough."

The pause that followed allowed Streeter to organize his thoughts. He hated to admit it, but Shank was right about following up with the strongest lead suspect, Carl Muldando. Not because Mully was likely the Crooked Man, but because regarding Michelle's death he appeared to have had opportunity on Sunday night and possibly motive, rejection, which was left to be determined. No, the reason Streeter had to chase this lead, even if it was a dead end, was that the Lucifer's Lot were accessible for a short time and would be leaving as soon as the rally was over. And if he didn't pursue Mully, the handwriting was on the wall that Shank would ride his ass every inch along the way of investigating the Crooked Man cold cases until he did.

"After your meeting, I asked your aide to ship the pin on the next flight down to Denver. I'm asking Jack Linwood from the Bureau's Investigative Control Operations down there to work on identifying striations in the pin found in Michelle Freeburg's palm and comparing them with those on the pin from Mully's lapel in early photos," Streeter said.

Shank looked truly shocked by this news. Streeter wasn't sure if it was because he was happy that Streeter was finally following the thread that might lead back to Mully or if it was because he was angry that the visiting legend, without telling Shank, had directed his own staff to do Streeter's bidding for him.

Streeter didn't wait to find out.

He turned to Bly. "So, what you and I are going to do is find out what this Carl Muldando is all about and chase this lead aggressively as it relates to Michelle Freeburg and possibly the unidentified female victim in Sturgis, although we'll need the autopsy first. I don't want us to get bogged down in the connection between the cold cases and the Freeburg murder. It will only cost us time. Time we don't have. And the Crooked Man cases have remained cold for over a decade. We'll let the team work the scene up there. We can get back to that case in a few days once the rally is over."

Although his eyes remained focused on Bly, from his peripheral vision, Streeter could see Shank's wide grin and the obvious satisfaction with the plan.

"Tell me," Streeter continued, "I've heard that the Lucifer's Lot believe that you can share a secret with another person only as long as that person is dead. Is that an outdated concept or a widely embraced ideology with these guys?"

"Still true. A philosophy held by most biker clubs. Their loyalty is one of the reasons they remain untouchable by the law," Bly answered.

"Then dividing to conquer the Lucifer's Lot from within is not an option."

"So what's your plan of attack? With Mully?" Shank asked with excitement.

"Bly will help me prepare for our undercover work tonight in Sturgis. I want to talk with the people at Broken Peaks and at the Lazy S today, assuming the motorcycle gang is nowhere to be seen. Once we get back into Rapid, we interview those on the short list, those who were closest to Michelle and saw her last. The grocer, the parents, the sister, and the boyfriend."

"The sister's still missing," Shank answered flatly. "And we already met with the people at Broken Peaks and at the Lazy S, so that won't be necessary."

Bly cocked his head. "We never went to the Lazy S today."

"Oh, that's right, we didn't. Sheriff Leonard and I went over there yesterday. You'd just be wasting time. You should focus on finding Mully and on proof to nail him with these two murders. Besides, you might blow your covers if you go to the Lazy S where the Lucifer's Lot are camping. Right?"

Streeter could see this was going nowhere fast. He had a method of investigating crimes and Shank had another. Shank would greatly impede progress unless he could get out from under his watchful eye. And the only way to do that was to agree with him.

"You're right. Time is wasting. Bly and I should be focused on preparing to go undercover and on finding the Lucifer's Lot bikers."

Bly cut his eyes at Streeter, not understanding that Streeter was merely trying to get Shank redirected and out of their way. "I'm going to need your help, Shank. It's imperative that we have a source here in the office working the phones, coordinating the information that comes in from all the departments and especially our people. I need you to get hourly updates on findings from the crime scene technicians out at Broken Peaks. Call us with those reports. Keep us abreast of what's happening out there and keep good records on the Crooked Man case from the murder on the property near Rochford, too, only don't call us about that. Just keep really good notes on everything about Ernif Hanson. I don't want to be distracted," Streeter lied, happy to earn a wider smile on Shank's contented face.

The truth was Streeter wanted to turn this case over to Bly while he focused on the Crooked Man. "Check occasionally with the Sturgis PD at least a few times a day on the unidentified young lady and see if there is anyone reported missing. Call me immediately if you get the official autopsy report on either Michelle Freeburg or the Sturgis vic. Get updates on the missing sister from whichever department is following up on this. The Rapid City Police Department, Pennington County Sheriff's Department, Highway Patrol, whoever is responsible for looking for her. Stay by this phone and coordinate everything that's coming in, including our reports from the field."

Shank nodded, jotting down the last of Streeter's instructions. "Got it."

"If we need to later, we can always talk to all those other guys, like the grocer, the parents, the boyfriend . . . what're their names again?"

"Roy Barker is the grocery store manager who filed the missing persons report on Michelle Freeburg. Frank and Arlene Freeburg are the parents. Charlene, Char, is the missing sister. Jens Bergen is the boyfriend," Shank enumerated.

"Who? Bergen, did you say?" Streeter asked, barely able to form the words. His throat was suddenly dry, probably from being overcrowded by his heart, which had just leapt into it.

"The boyfriend. Jens Bergen," Shank repeated.

Streeter couldn't believe his ears. He had heard Shank correctly. What were the chances this would be the same family as Liv Bergen from Fort Collins? He cleared his throat and asked, "Bergen? As in the mining family Bergen?"

CHAPTER 13

I DON'T THINK I'VE ever driven so fast in all my life. And considering my impressive string of speeding tickets earned from here to southern Colorado, that's saying a lot. I kept checking my rearview mirrors and sure as hell, Mully and his buddies were still following me. With this highway so curvy and narrow, I was convinced either one of them or I would end up in a ditch soon enough. And I was bound and determined not to let it be me. On the other hand, if one of them took a spill, I was convinced Mully would show no mercy.

Why hadn't I told someone about what I had seen yesterday? I would have to find my jeans and root through the pockets to find my notes.

If I had told someone, at least they'd know to look for Mully and the Lucifer's Lot if I ended up dead somewhere. If I flip this truck, I thought, they'll write my death off to speeding or a deer in the road or just a string of bad luck for me. Worse, at this rate and with my luck, they'd somehow blame this all on Jens, making his life doubly troubled. Damn if I didn't think about how this might affect him. And Mom and Dad. The whole Bergen family. I'd never be able to nuzzle my nephew Noah's cheek again, a horrible thought.

I had to do something.

I was coming up fast on a lumbering camper. Like most highways that meandered through the National Forest known as the Black Hills, most of this highway was striped with solid double yellow lines. Summers in this area meant tourists taking in the spectacular sights, driving significantly under the speed limit to soak in the breathtaking views, the wildlife that dotted the rocky hillsides and green meadows. I had been lucky so far not to get behind one of these tourists and my luck had just run out.

I slammed on the brakes and glued my eyes on my rearview mirror, praying Mully wouldn't slam into the back of me, tip his bike, and slide underneath Jens's truck. Sporting a new road rash from head to toe would really piss him off. I saw him grip his handlebars and hold on for dear life, as did the other dozen bikers with him. For an instant, I envisioned myself slammed into the camper ahead and them crashing into me, like magnets stacked up on my crumpled tailgate.

At the very last possible instant, I swerved into the oncoming lane and whipped around the camper, thankful that the approaching cars were far enough away that I could squeeze through the opening without incident. The woman in the camper flipped me the bird and leaned on her horn as I righted the wheel of the pickup and drove off in front of her. The old man in the lead car of oncoming traffic did the same. I didn't hear any metal scraping or see any bodies scattering behind the camper. My eyes darted back and forth from the road ahead to my rearview mirror, waiting to see cars stop for scattered bikes and bikers. But no one did. The camper was getting smaller and smaller in my side mirror, as was the long line of cars, motorcycles, and campers headed in the opposite direction.

I sped past the intersection of Norris Peak Road, careful not to let any merging traffic pull in front of me, and whipped through the S-curve that followed, taking a sharp left and doubling back up the hill on Wide View Drive to the Sun Ridge Road development on the outskirts of Rapid City. I speculated that Mully would assume I'd stayed on Nemo Road and prayed that he and his followers hadn't closed the distance in the last harrowing seven or eight miles since my Norris Peak Road maneuver. I turned right onto Sun Ridge Road and pulled into the first driveway I saw that had a camper, pulling my truck around it so I couldn't be seen easily. I left the truck idling just in case and I recited the only thing that came to mind to calm my nerves. After nearly twenty minutes and taking down my eighty-eighth of ninety-nine bottles of beer on the wall, my breathing had slowed and my shaking hands steadied. Wiping my brow on my sleeve, I took down and passed around the last of the bottles in my mind, then slowly pulled out from behind the camper, thankful that the homeowner either hadn't been home or hadn't noticed my use of his space.

I never saw Mully or the Lucifer's Lot bikers again in my rearview or on the streets of Rapid City, and I slowed to a more manageable speed as I headed back to Jens's house. Just to make sure I had lost them for good, however, I turned left on Canyon Lake Road and backtracked in a circuitous route onto Jackson Boulevard. I took a deep breath when I glanced to my left and saw that Teepee Street was free of any motorcycles.

The clock on the dashboard read nearly one thirty. No garage for me to hide Jens's truck in, so I just left it in the small driveway. I stepped down out of his truck and made my way to the front door, which was unlocked.

Jens was sitting in the living room, his head cradled in his hands. No music, no television, nobody else with him.

"Jens? You okay?"

"What's there to be okay about?" he asked, never lifting his head.

"Where's Catherine?"

"She just left."

"Have the authorities been by to question you?"

"No," he mumbled. "Where've you been?"

"Kinda busy," I said, helping myself to a beer to calm my nerves. I took a seat in the living room where I could look out the picture window down the street, misbelieving my good fortune in having shaken free of the Lucifer's Lot. I twisted off the cap and asked, "Want one?"

He finally lifted his head, leaving his elbows propped on his knees but dropping his hands, wrists limp and long fingers dangling down, as if all his energy had been zapped with the simple movement. His eyes and nose were rimmed in red.

"You look like crap," I said, taking a long draw from the bottle.

This brought a hint of a smile to his parched lips. "Been doing a thousand Hail Marys with Catherine."

"Did it help?"

"A little."

I tilted my beer toward him, raising my brows inquisitively. His smile grew. A little. "Haven't had one since breakfast."

I pushed myself out of the chair and felt every muscle rebel at once. It had been a long morning of breaking nearly every rule of trauma recovery in the book, not to mention every rule of the road. I retrieved a beer, opened it, and handed it to him, saying, "Pray for us sinners."

"Now and at the hour of our death." The smile Jens had worn quickly faded and he guzzled the whole bottle in one long draw.

"What the hell! Didn't Catherine feed you or anything?"

"She tried," he said, slumping back onto the couch. "After each decade in between every single mystery."

"Every mystery?"

He nodded. "She'd whip out a snack after every 'Glory Be' and told me it was part of the deal, had to keep up her energy."

I had to think about this. It had been a while since I had said a rosary, and, I admit, I missed the cadence and trance-like peacefulness unique to it. I knew the rosary was intended to help people focus on certain events in the history of salvation, or what Catholics call "mysteries." And I remembered there were four categories of mysteries, each with five events, and a decade, which consists of one Lord's Prayer, ten Hail Marys, and a Glory Be To The Father. Doing the math, that meant Catherine and Jens did something like four complete rosaries, pausing to eat twenty times.

No wonder as I was going to St. Ives I passed my sister with forty chins.

"And you didn't eat? Not one of those times?"

He shook his head.

"Well, I'm glad she at least stayed with you this whole time."

"I tried to get rid of her," Jens admitted. "Just wanted to be alone."

"Yeah, sure," I said. "That's not going to happen. You're a Bergen. Eighth of nine. You don't even know what alone is."

I was rewarded with another brief smile before it disappeared. His eyelids drooped. I thought I was going to lose him to sleep brought on by hefty doses of grief, adrenaline, and cold beer.

"Did you call an attorney?"

The long fingers of his right hand shot up to his forehead and raked through his short, brown hair, then falling to linger on the back of his head. "I haven't showered yet today."

"Call Jason Stone. He's your friend. He can find someone for you."

I was rewarded with a nod. "I'll do that. What'd you learn about Michelle? Did you find Char?"

There was no way I was going to share anything with Jens before the authorities talked with him. In his condition, he might not be discreet or able to distinguish what I told him from what he already knew before all this happened.

"Jens, listen. I need to ask you something."

He tipped his bottle and drank the other half of his beer. I did the same.

"Okay. Ask."

"What were you doing up at Nemo General Store yesterday morning?"

He cut his eyes at me and dropped his arm back on his knee. "Ironic, huh, Boots? Michelle only a couple miles away and I never knew."

"What were you doing?"

"This is bad. Really bad. They're going to think I killed her. But you know what? That's not the worst part. The worst thing is maybe if I knew, I could have saved her, helped her somehow. Maybe she was still alive. But I didn't know."

Leaning forward, head bowed, elbows to knees, limp wrists, he twirled the lip of the empty bottle with his fingers just inches from the floor.

"Jens, Clint said he saw you. Early. What were you doing?"

He let the empty bottle drop and watched it teeter on the carpet, tumbling sideways with a soft bump. He took a deep breath and straightened his posture. "I was helping Brody. We brought up trucks from Rapid City for a small pour on a foundation for the new addition to that restaurant behind the store. Brody said the owner wanted to make sure the fewest number of guests were disturbed by the construction and by our large trucks driving in and out of there. So he wanted the work done while bikers slept. He said he'd rather have guests pissed off from being awakened than one wrapped around our ready mix truck axles. But everyone was tied up on projects yesterday morning, being Monday and all. He asked if I was willing to oversee the pour, since one of the two drivers was a new hire. I told him I'd help."

"And you got there at what time?"

"Five o'clock, when the trucks started arriving. I left by seven or so."

"Clint said he saw you around six," I said.

Jens nodded. "I went into the Nemo General Store to get a cup of coffee between loads. Clint was getting a pack of cigarettes." He sighed again. "They said a guy found her about five hours later."

I grew still, emulating Jens. The silence whistled in my ears as loud as death.

"It was cold yesterday morning. Cold, Boots. You know how cold it gets in the Hills at night in the summer. And Michelle must have been freezing and scared and lonely and . . . so cold."

He buried his head in his hands. I moved beside him on the couch, glancing out the window as I did. No Mully. No bikers. No police. No FBI. Just my brother and me. I gave him a hug and rubbed his back.

"Jens, there was nothing you could have done for her. Nothing. She was dead. Someone killed her and it wasn't your fault."

"Wasn't it?" he said, snapping his head upright and looking at me accusingly. "The last thing I said to her was that she needed to see a psychiatrist. A psychiatrist, for God's sake!"

"Why'd you say that?"

"Oh, I was just fed up with her obsession over Char. It's unnatural. Even as a sister."

I thought about how vested I was with my siblings and wondered if he was right.

"She stormed out of here so fast I couldn't do a thing to stop her. Didn't do a thing to stop her. I should have. Don't you understand? I should have stopped her and if I had, she'd be alive."

He pushed up from the couch and started pacing. I glanced over my shoulder out the window again, retrieved his empty beer bottle, and retreated into the kitchen. There was nothing I could say that would help him get through his grief. He had to take that lonely journey on this own. But one thing I could do was to honor his request of me and figure out what happened to Michelle and Char. I started a pot of coffee and looked in the refrigerator to see what I could feed him, finding the plate Catherine had made: some kind of pasta dish, a salad, and four fudge brownies, all neatly covered with plastic wrap. Thank you, Catherine.

"Eat," I said shoving the plate toward him along with a fork.

He stopped pacing and stared at me, like I was handing him a two-headed snake or something.

"I said eat. Catherine went to a lot of trouble. Plus, if you don't, I'm going to fix you up some of that famous goulash those lunch ladies used to make for us in grade school. It's the only thing I know how to cook. And I'm going to force feed it to you."

Talk about a motivator, for sure, but it didn't earn me a smile.

He took the plate and fork from me and settled back onto the couch. I picked up my beer, drained it while I stole another quick look out the window, and went back to the kitchen for two cups of coffee. Back in the living room, I handed him a cup.

"Thank you."

"You're welcome," I said, taking a seat across from him. "Now let's talk. I have places to go. You told me I have work to do, so I've got to get it done."

He nodded.

I sipped my coffee as I watched him shovel the food into his mouth and turn on his CD player. Out floated the soothing sounds of Rachmaninoff. Jens flipped on the ceiling fan and settled back onto the couch with his cup of coffee.

I hadn't noticed how still the summer air had been until it was stirred by the fan blades above me. The smell of afternoon barbecues drifted in through the screened windows of Jens's kitchen, and my stomach growled; it was wishing now that Jens had saved a little bit of that plate of food for me. I'd eat something later.

The roar of distant motorcycles, hundreds of thousands visiting the annual Sturgis Motorcycle Classic Rally, rumbled in the background, its tempo incongruous with the orchestra's magic. But with each glance out the front window, I assured myself that Mully had not found me.

"Tell me what happened. From the beginning. Start on Sunday and take me through every step until this morning when you got the call from the Freeburgs."

He did.

Jens told me about going to work for a few hours Sunday afternoon, driving around to different job sites to see what the status would be for the upcoming week, stalling until Michelle got off work at eight. He told me about being impatient, waiting in the truck for Michelle to go to dinner with him, and how he'd wondered what prompted him to be so impulsive as to go inside Barker's Market to see her at work, which was totally out of character. He told me about finding Michelle busy helping some bikers find stuff, and that he overheard one of them inviting her to join them at the Sturgis Rally. He explained how Michelle graciously avoided the question but that her boss was infuriated with her. He described what happened when Michelle tried to clock out and how he'd overheard Roy Barker threaten her. He told me how he'd lost his temper, which was uncharacteristic for Jens, and how he'd threatened the boss. After what had happened at the grocery store, Michelle had told him she was in no mood for dinner and would meet him at his house later because she had to talk with her sister, Char, who had dropped by Barker's Market as Michelle was getting off shift.

"Originally, Michelle had planned to go to dinner with me," Jens said. "But then after what had happened with the biker and with Roy Barker, she felt less like having dinner with me and more compelled to impart some sisterly advice to Char. Her words, not mine."

"Who's Roy Barker?" I asked.

"Michelle's boss at the grocery store. He's the manager there," Jens said, curling his lip as he spoke.

"The one you threatened to kill?"

Jens looked a bit sheepish. "I didn't threaten to kill him. I just threatened him by saying he'd regret it if he did anything to Michelle. Something like that. I know I was wrong, but I'd had it with that jerk."

"Had it? You mean you two have a history or something?"

"The guy's a total stalker, Boots. Has a creepy obsession with Michelle. Had an obsession, I mean. We go to dinner, he shows up at the same restaurant. We go to the movies, he's sitting behind us. We take in a play, a concert, or a hockey game at the Civic Center, he's there."

I heard more rumbling of bikes and stole a look out the window. No Mully.

"And you said that Roy threatened Michelle? You're sure about that?"

"Definitely," Jens said.

"Did she ever tell you why he threatened her?"

"Uh-uh," Jens answered. "Later that night, when she came by after dropping off Char at home, Michelle was agitated, not about what happened at the grocery store, but because she and Char had been in an argument. It took me a while to get her calmed down. She never sat still, not for a minute, and she must have been here for at least an hour or so."

"What time was that?"

"I don't know. Maybe ten o'clock or so? Anyway, I asked her what happened in the employee lunchroom while I was waiting, and she said he got all weird again, talking about how he knew what she was doing every minute, at lunch, what she was reading. Then he said he loved her and she told him he was crazy. It set him off."

"And you heard all this? Because this might be really important, Jens. Try to remember the words exactly. Roy Barker might have killed Michelle, and what you tell the authorities when they interview you today might help them a lot."

"You mean interrogate me," Jens said. "I'm their main suspect, remember?"

"Maybe not, or they would have already been here by now." I wasn't about to tell him what I overheard at the crime scene: Agent Bob Shankley had indicated their prime suspect was Mully, the same Mully who was after me. My eyes shot up to the window again. Nothing but a quiet, small town neighborhood in Middle America.

"Besides, the only thing I heard was Roy yelling at her, telling her to never call him crazy ever again or he'd make her pay the rest of her life. Those were the words," Jens said, finishing off his cup of coffee.

I wondered if Roy Barker had made good on his promise; if he owned a pair of hiking boots and a large flashlight that was missing a lens.

"If you only saw the way he would look at her," Jens said. "But she called him a friend anyway and tried to keep him at a distance, saying she felt sorry for him. This time, it spooked her. A lot. He went too far. I asked her to quit her job early, forget about the last two weeks, and move in with me if it was about money for medical school. I told her she should tell Roy Barker where to go."

"And?"

"And she was seriously considering it. She said she needed to think about it but that she was leaning toward reporting to work the next morning and telling Roy it was her last day. She had already given him a month's notice out of courtesy so he could find a new bookkeeper."

"So why did you two get in a fight? You told me that the last thing you said to her was she needed to see a psychiatrist. So far, it sounds like you two were largely in agreement," I pointed out to Jens.

"We were. Except about Char," he said.

"What about Char made you think Michelle needed to see a psychiatrist?"

He unfolded his long legs, stood up, and went to the kitchen to get more coffee. I could tell this was a subject he was avoiding and plainly didn't want to talk about. Jens was a very private person, and revealing any detail about a personal relationship was difficult enough for him, but this seemed to hit a more inflamed nerve than usual. I stared out the window, willing Mully to drive by just once so I could throw my coffee cup at him. Just having this thought made me realize the fear had dissipated and my heartbeat was back to normal.

Jens padded over to the couch, his back to me as he, too, stared out onto the street. "Michelle and Char got into another argument. They did that a lot. Sunday night it was over a guy. Someone she was seeing who was way too old for her."

"How old is too old?" I asked, wondering if it would help me narrow in on the guy so I could see if he knew where Char was. "Sixteen, seventeen?"

"Forty or fifty," Jens said.

I gasped. "Didn't you say Char was only fourteen?"

"Mm hmm. That's why Michelle was so angry with Char and needed to talk to her. Char ignored her warnings and went out with him anyway. Michelle said the guy came and picked her up at the Freeburgs', parking way down the block so the family wouldn't see him. Michelle decided to follow them, and the guy drove up Dinosaur Hill and parked with Char. Michelle said she was so mad, she decided to confront the guy." Jens looked down into his coffee cup for a long moment.

I couldn't ignore the tension that paralleled the haunting second movement of Rachmaninoff's Piano Concerto No. 2 , which hung softly in the warm summer air. Unaffected, Jens took a sip.

"And did she?"

He had been in a daze. "Hmm? Oh, yeah. She said the man and Char were about to make out in the front seat, and she was prepared to give him a piece of her mind, but then she realized she knew the guy. She panicked, grabbed Char, and made her come with her. Liv, I have never seen Michelle so agitated."

I would be, too, if my little sister was necking in a car with a fifty-year-old man. I thought about Clint White. He was at least forty-eight. Maybe older. Then I instantly dismissed the idea.

"She didn't tell you who it was?"

"Refused. Said I knew him, probably everyone around here did, and that I would probably kill him with my bare hands if she told me," Jens said, lifting his face and driving home his point by locking his gaze with me.

"Roy Barker? After all, you threatened him earlier that night."

Jens shook his head. "I asked her the same thing for the same reason, thinking she said forty or fifty just to throw me off. See, Roy's our age. She assured me it was not Roy Barker with Char. I believed her."

Doesn't mean Roy wasn't the one who murdered Michelle, I thought. My mind went to Michelle's panic and I thought of Mully. He was probably forty or fifty, and that would really shake me up if my little sister were kissing and messing around with a biker from the Lucifer's Lot. Speaking of panic, my eyes darted back to the windows.

"Was it the guy from the grocery store? The biker who asked her out?" I asked. "Had he met Char in the parking lot that night or something?"

"I don't think so," Jens said, furrowing his brow as he thought about it. "Did I mention that the bikers were with the Lucifer's Lot motorcycle club?"

My heart nearly stopped. This was all too coincidental. It couldn't possibly be the same bikers, but I had to know. I stammered, "Any names ever mentioned?"

"Who? The bikers?"

I nodded, swallowing hard.

"Michelle introduced one guy to me as Mully. But he walked away before I could shake his hand," he said, rubbing his chin as he thought about it. "I don't think I heard any other names."

I felt like an elephant had just decided to lounge on my chest. I could barely breathe. This was unbelievably bad luck.

"Anyway, those guys were long gone by the time Michelle and I left Barker's Market, and I think Michelle would have told me if it was one of those bikers. She did say I knew the guy, but I got the impression it was someone I knew from around town or had known all my life."

Shaking off the willies that crept along the back of my neck and down my spine, I stuttered, "Well, it would have helped to know who the old guy up at Dinosaur Hill was because it would have made my search for Char a little easier. But back to Michelle. Why did you and she get in a fight? There's something you're not telling me, Moose."

Jens's shoulders sagged.

"If you want me to help, you have to tell me what I need to know." I had no idea what it was I needed to know, but I was counting on the fact that he did.

"Michelle was . . ." he started to say. "Michelle and I . . ."

I could see this was excruciating for Jens, but I was losing patience— and daylight. "Michelle and you what?"

Lips pursed, he set his empty coffee cup on the table. "I overheard Roy tell Michelle that he'd been stalking her for years. Since high school."

"A creeper."

"But that's not the worst part. He said he knew all about Michelle's 'dirty little secret'—his words, not mine." Jens's hands were clutching and unclutching as he struggled to get the story out. "So I pushed her to tell me what he meant, and she told me. Over a period of months in the eighth grade, she was repeatedly raped by one man—a grown man—and got pregnant by him. Then it stopped."

I hadn't seen that coming; I wanted to throw up. Michelle's whole life suddenly looked tragic, a bleak trail with a terrible ending. I threw my arms around Jens for the comfort of it, his and mine.

"But you know, she got past it. She was tough," he said, turning me loose. "She wasn't going to let one awful year ruin her life. Look what she did, Liv. She got herself enough training to become a decently paid bookkeeper. She put herself through college and was going on to medical school this fall. She always looked good—a little conservative, I guess you'd call it, but good—and her eyes were on the future. The future that she never got."

"Jens, the guy should still be in jail. Didn't she tell her parents?"

Jens shook his head. "You'd have to know Arlene and Frank to know why telling them would have been useless. Brain dead, both of them. She was always the only grownup in the family, and that includes those idiot brothers of hers."

I thought that was a little hard on them, but then I'd never met them and he had. But I could see now why Michelle had felt the need to protect Char at close range, if she didn't trust her parents to guide Char any better than they'd guided her.

"I think she was lying to me," Jens confessed. "She never lied to me."

"About the rape?"

He shook his head.

"About what?"

He buried his face in his hands. "I don't know for sure. She told me the guy left her alone once he found out she was pregnant and when I asked her what happened to the baby, she told me it was all a false alarm. But I think she was lying to me."

"Do you think she had the baby? At thirteen?" I couldn't imagine it. "Oh, no. Not an abortion. Maybe she miscarried?"

"Boots, I don't know!" Jens barked, removing his hands from his face and glaring at me. His shoulders slumped. "I'm sorry. It's just that I've run it back in my mind a hundred times, and I can't pinpoint why I think Michelle was lying to me, but I do."

My mind raced. Someone knew something. A false alarm or miscarriage would be the only explanation for no one knowing anything. And according to Jens, Michelle indicated that Roy knew something about all the shit she was going through during high school. But if Michelle had had an abortion or went full term with the baby, a doctor would have been involved. Or someone.

"All I know is that on Sunday night, Michelle lost it completely. Told Char a thing or two and dropped her off at home, warning her not to step one foot out of the house or she'd see to it she would never date again, or something like that. She drove over here to calm down, told me what had happened, and said she was going to fix this once and for all."

"Fix this? What did she mean by that?" I asked.

Jens shrugged. "Michelle said she wouldn't be surprised if Char ran off with the guy that same night and she could not let that happen. I told her she had already done the best she could and was bordering on meddling. I told her she was obsessed with Char and that she couldn't keep torturing herself like this. That she had to live life. *Her* life. Not Char's. I suggested she needed to put some effort into fixing her own life rather than to continue to live vicariously through Char."

I couldn't bear to see the torture that was etched on his face. "Jens, you didn't cause this. You're not to blame."

He looked at me with pleading eyes, needing to finish what he had to say. "We had argued up until then, Boots. Argued hard. But when I mentioned something about it being a parent's job to handle issues like Char's, noting how numb Arlene and Frank were to the world of parenting, the argumentativeness disappeared. An eerie peacefulness came over her, like a shroud. Like she was in a trance or something. It was so weird. It shook me up. I told Michelle I thought she should see a psychiatrist—to help her through the unaddressed emotions concerning the rape, her lost childhood. Michelle placed her hands on my cheeks and said she loved me. And she walked calmly out of here, vowing again to fix things once and for all, to make it right."

"Think back, Jens," I said, a niggling feeling starting to form amidst all the facts I had gathered today. "What were her exact words? Her last words to you before she left?"

I could see him thinking hard. He rubbed his chin and worked through the discussion in his head. He looked up at me and his facial features had softened. On the verge of tears, Jens answered, "She said, 'I love you and have loved you long before I met you. But you're right. I know what I have to do. I have to learn how to love me. I have to end this. Once and for all.'"

CHAPTER 14

AFTER SETTLING INTO THE safe house—rented for federal agents working the rally and looking for top tenners, a place with a view down Sturgis's infamous Main Street—Bly and Streeter left in the bureau car for their first interview. They had scheduled their afternoon interviews carefully so they'd be back in time for the rally's nighttime activities. After poring over both crime scenes, Streeter was convinced more than ever that the Crooked Man had killed Ernif Hanson but not Michelle Freeburg. They were two completely different cases. Because the Lucifer's Lot would be leaving town after the rally and because of his desire to work the Crooked Man case, Streeter abandoned the idea of assigning one to Bly and working both cases simultaneously. Instead, he decided to focus on investigating Michelle Freeburg's case first, then dedicating all his time to the Crooked Man's latest murder. Of course, choosing the Freeburg case as the more urgent one to solve had nothing to do with the Bergens' involvement.

"You asked if there were any comments in the report about penetration, multiple partners, sexual abuse. I saw the look on your face," Streeter said, looking over at Bly, who was weaving expertly along the winding roads through the Black Hills. "You don't believe the Lucifer's Lot murdered Michelle Freeburg, do you?"

"Nope," Bly said.

"And it really bothered you when you heard she had probably been lying out there for at least eleven or twelve hours, maybe more, and died about the time she was found," Streeter continued, never taking his eyes off Bly.

"Yep."

After a long silence, Streeter said, "No biker from any outlaw gang, the Lucifer's Lot or otherwise, killed Michelle Freeburg in your mind. Am I right?"

Bly nodded and said, "And no, I'm not some biker-loving undercover agent gone bad who protects the one percenters at any cost. I cannot be bought, bribed, or blown."

Streeter grinned. "Didn't think so. But you are smart. And let me guess; you've done enough work with these lowlifes to know they wouldn't just kill a woman without having left some sign—mutilation, sperm, something on her dead naked body, particularly if it was some sheep they picked up at a bar, who would likely have drugs in her system or a whole lot of alcohol. Right so far?"

"Sort of."

"And last but not least, they would not, under any circumstance, bash a woman in the back of the head and leave her for dead without making darn sure she was indeed dead," Streeter guessed.

"Exactly," Bly said, a smile twitching near the corner of his lips. "Unless it was a prospect who seriously fucked up."

"Which would mean we would be dealing with four dead bodies, not three."

"Quick study. You're good at this. And Shank said you couldn't find your ass with your own two hands." Bly reached behind the seat and whipped out a small bag of candy, opening it one-handed. "This is a setup, Streeter. Mully is getting framed. The location, the FTW pin. Someone wants him out of the picture."

"Another gang?"

"Maybe," Bly mumbled, "or someone within the Lucifer's Lot."

The attention Bly was giving his snack annoyed Streeter. "Are you watching the road?"

Bly popped another chunk of hard candy in his mouth before handing the open bag over to Streeter, "Want some?"

"Peanut brittle?"

"From Wheeler Farms," Bly said, returning the bag to his lap and picking out two more pieces to munch. "Yeah, it's that good."

Streeter shook his head. Bly grinned, crunching away at another piece.

Streeter admitted, "I worked more rallies than I care to admit. Thousands of businessmen and doctors and lawyers and white-collar professionals come to the annual Sturgis Motorcycle Rally from all over the country to let their hair down for a week. Upright, model citizens in their communities the other fifty-one weeks of the year. Party one week out of the year. And no one will chastise or criticize them for their bad behavior. It's Sturgis. It's expected."

Bly nodded. "Only difference between them and me is I don't dress up like a wannabe biker as if this is nothing more than a blue-collar Mardi Gras, a place to behave badly, to get polluted on tequila and whiskey, to whistle at naked women or get a twenty-dollar hand job. I dress up to become one of them for a short time each year so I can learn as much as I can about the sons-of-bitches from the outlaw motorcycle clubs and their covert operations, hoping someday to see their sorry faces behind bars. Talk about sophisticated networks."

Streeter saw anger flash in Bly's eyes.

"They murder, rape, burglarize, steal, assault, intimidate, victimize, you name it. They traffic narcotics, force their women into prostitution, commit any number of weapon offenses, launder money, and evade taxes."

"The bureau used to think the biker clubs were Public Enemy No. 1."

"Not since 9/11, they don't. International terrorism is a bigger perceived threat—not that the bikers' tactics can't be a form of terrorism. They're pros with weapons and intelligence gathering, and that keeps the FBI kind of interested in them, you might say."

"What I remember is that the clubs actually appoint one of the members as an intelligence officer. He's assigned duties of collecting and documenting intelligence, like pictures and information about rival clubs and their members in case a war erupts. Gang war."

"Exactly," Bly affirmed with a quick nod. He eased the car left off Vanocker Canyon Road onto Nemo Road.

"What starts the wars these days?" Streeter asked.

"Same as when you were here. Mostly when one gang crosses another's territory," Bly answered, heaving one shoulder toward his ear. "Methamphetamine is the biggest money maker now for those that traffic drugs. The gangs control everything from manufacturing to distribution of meth in this country. Other motorcycle clubs traffic guns, women, murder for hire. It's all about money and power. When one club starts infringing on another's territory, wars erupt."

"Just like the Mafia," Streeter said, glancing out the window from time to time.

"Only damn near more organized. The clubs have structures, with presidents, vice presidents, secretary/treasurers, enforcers, sergeants at arms, at both the national level and the local-chapter level. Many of the members in the local chapters don't hold what we would consider a steady job. Instead, they manage the business, like the drug trafficking, stripping down or reselling stolen bikes, trafficking of illegal weapons, and of course keeping tabs on the prostitution."

"What's Mully?"

"President of his chapter," Bly answered. "And a hell of a businessman. Smart."

"How do they launder their money?"

"The usual," Bly said. "Ice cream parlors, bike repair shops, bars, hotels, campgrounds, apartment buildings. Some of the members run these businesses, but most of the time they hire nonmembers to run them so that they look legitimate."

"You think Eddie Schilling is one of these guys? A nonmember hired by the Lucifer's Lot to launder money?"

"I doubt it. Not enough income from that little piece of shit campground. I'm talking more like owning the beer tents at the Cattle Jump Campground, where tens of thousands of dollars are made each year."

"Is this part of their intelligence network?" Streeter ventured. "Keeping an ear to the ground and an eye on the community for changes, gossip, rumor, etc.?"

"Sure." Bly looked in his rearview mirror as he slowed through the tiny town of Nemo. "But their biggest source of intelligence is from the old ladies."

"The biker women who are like wives, the ones not passed around the club?"

"Right. The ones who usually hold down regular jobs at the county courthouses, in the jails, at the police departments, in city offices. Wherever they could overhear what may be coming down the pike, whether it be a change in laws, regulations, procedures, an arrest, subpoenas, whatever. The motorcycle clubs are the first to know and are prepared before anything ever comes their way."

"Like the one Leonard mentioned to Shank who's working at Pennington County in the titles department. The impact that probably has on policing such activities must be significant."

"They're untouchable," Bly said.

"It's how they've always gotten away with trafficking stolen vehicles and weapons. They get their old ladies to lift a few blank titles or licenses from the counties."

"Exactly."

"Which makes it all appear very legitimate," Streeter figured, "and nearly impossible to prove otherwise."

"Correct again," Bly said, his eyes scanning the small town. "And compounding the problem of busting these guys up is that loyalty to the club we talked about earlier. Allegiance is one of the highest regarded philosophies among any of these clubs."

Streeter stared out his window as they passed the Nemo General Store. He rubbed his short, white hair and said, "Hasn't changed all that much. It's just gotten a lot more sophisticated. We had a lot of volunteers throughout the country back then to work the rally in the hope of apprehending a Top Ten fugitive. That meant I could focus on the dead bodies left behind each year. Or the reservation work," Streeter said, clearing his throat when something rose in it.

The sooner Streeter could get this present business done here, the sooner he could escape the flood of memories of his last case on the reservation and return to his sanctuary in Colorado.

Bly reached above his visor and handed Streeter a photo. "This is why I do it. The most recent photo we have of Michelle Freeburg. It was taken a few weeks ago by her boyfriend at a Fourth of July celebration near Mount Rushmore."

"It's a good one," Streeter remarked. "Nice smile that actually reaches her eyes. Very relaxed and genuine."

"She didn't know the photo was being taken."

Michelle's smile in the photo was easy and wide, her dark eyes soft with laughter. Her face glowed with beauty and femininity, unlike all the other photos he'd seen in the files. She had tied her thick dark brown hair in a knot at the back of her head, loose strands curling delicately around her face. She was a vision. Streeter's intuition had been confirmed. Michelle Freeburg worked to downplay her loveliness, and it took great effort.

"Tell me about the boyfriend," Streeter asked in his low, gravelly voice, hoping not to seem too anxious to learn everything he could about Liv Bergen's brother.

"That's the difficult part." Bly spoke slowly, shifting uncomfortably. "No one has questioned the boyfriend yet. Don't think Shank wanted to touch that one."

"Why not?"

"Because Jens Bergen's father is pretty well known around here. He's a U.S. congressman."

"Garth Bergen is a congressman?"

"You know him? Great guy. That's why everyone's a bit hesitant to bring his kid in for questioning. But the son was most likely one of the last people to see Michelle alive."

"How about we interview him today? He must be terribly anxious."

"Sure," Bly said, slowing as they passed the Broken Peaks property on the left. "Shank will want to go."

Streeter ignored the warning. "Tell me about Garth Bergen. Why is he so popular?"

"Congressman Bergen is friendly, outgoing. Honest."

"Not a phony bone in his body," had been Streeter's own assessment of Garth after he'd explained to the man what had happened to his daughter while they waited together in Poudre Hospital for the doctor's report. That had been a little more than a month ago.

Streeter had liked Garth Bergen immediately. Not to mention his wife, Jeanne, who stood vigil—and guard—constantly by Liv's bedside. Streeter admired her commitment to her daughter and eventually gave up his attempted visits, thinking she would consider him inappropriately attentive if he persisted.

Aiming for nonchalant but willing to accept simply curious, Streeter asked, "What do you know about Garth Bergen's other children?"

A cloud of dust enveloped the car immediately after Bly turned onto the dirt road entrance to the Lazy S Campground.

Bly parked in front of the office but left the engine running while he continued to debrief the interview he and Streeter had just left. "Well, that was helpful. Either Clint White is an innocent, to-the-point, sharp, and honest man or he's the coldest and cleverest murderer I've run across."

"His distress seemed genuine," Streeter agreed. "He showed concern primarily for the woman herself, the terrible fate she endured, and for Tommy Jasper having to find her body. But I didn't like that he was reluctant to admit he was down by the big rock earlier that day and probably would never have told us that if Tommy hadn't mentioned it. White acted nervous."

"Still on the list," Bly said.

Streeter nodded.

"And when we said we were going to meet with Eddie Schilling next, I sensed Clint wasn't a fan of the man," Bly continued.

"Agreed. Helps to know Eddie eats lunch up at the Nemo Guest Ranch frequently. If we need to talk with him again after this first meeting, that's the first place we'll look."

When Bly turned off the car's engine, the pinging under the hood underscored the isolation of the campground. "Here we go," he said.

"I'm not sure we want to risk this. Having you spotted by Mully and his boys, blowing years of your undercover work."

Bly grinned, turning the rearview mirror toward himself so he could see the button-down shirt he was wearing and the fedora hiding his long locks. "I'd look just like a regular preppie if it wasn't for this nasty beard. Correction: just like Jason Mraz." Bly tucked a loose strand of hair up under the hat and smoothed out his beard.

Streeter growled, "Even so, let's make it quick just to be sure."

Before the agents were out of the car, a man approached them with hand extended, smile wide. He was wearing an aqua muscle shirt, tight gym shorts, and white low-cut crew socks under his white-and-black Nikes. Though his skin was smooth and tan and taut, Streeter guessed that Schilling was in his late forties after studying his eyes, his neck, and his hands. Schilling's tousled dark curls spilled boyishly over his faintly wrinkled forehead. His eyes twinkled mischievously.

"Hi," he said, a cheerful welcome. "I'm Eddie Schilling, owner of the Lazy S Campground. Sorry to disappoint you two, but the campground is full. You'll have to find a different place to pitch a tent tonight, boys."

Bly gripped Schilling's hand, feigning a smile and squeezing tight, judging from the look of discomfort on Schilling's face. "I'm Agent Stewart Blysdorf and this is my partner, Agent Streeter Pierce."

The expression on Schilling's face collapsed.

Streeter, too, shook the Lazy S owner's strong, welcoming hand, squeezing a bit harder than was necessary. "Hello."

"Hi, Streeter," Schilling said, showing a pearly white, albeit forced, grin. "You don't mind if I call you Streeter, do you?"

"Not at all," Streeter answered, not really meaning it. "Whatever makes you comfortable, Mr. Schilling."

"Eddie, please," Schilling corrected Streeter. Turning to Bly, he said, "And you? Can I call you Stewart?"

"No," Bly said, plain and simple.

Schilling's composure wavered; his eyes darted nervously toward the highway. "Follow me into the office, guys, and we can have a pop and cool off."

As they followed him into a small office building, Streeter turned to see Broken Peaks and the crowd of professionals who had gathered near the fabric-covered buildings that had been erected for the criminalists working the crime scene. "You can see the iron ore quarry from here?"

"Sure can. Tourists eat that up. Think they're in the Wild West or something," Schilling said with a wink.

Streeter sat down at a small metal table that seated four. Clint was a good judge of character, Streeter thought, taking an instant dislike to Schilling.

Bly stood by the door, keeping watch.

The business counter and cash drawer were to the right in the small front room. A bathroom was to the left, and in the back of the house was a small room, presumably Schilling's private living quarters.

"Clever old goat," Eddie added.

"Pardon?" Streeter asked, not sure that he had heard him correctly.

"Old man Bergen. Owns that quarry. Starts by staking a few mining claims, then slowly buys up all the private ground around him, growing his empire."

Streeter felt the muscle in his jaw tighten when he countered, "You mean Congressman Bergen? The man who built his company from the ground up, from a lot of hard work and even more sweat equity? The hard-working man who now supports dozens of communities and hundreds of employees? The man who has invested a couple of decades of his life to public service as a way of repaying his state? You mean that old goat?"

Bly's eyes widened as he mumbled, "Impressive."

Schilling's boyish grin waned as he flicked a loose curl of hair from his forehead. "Easy, Streeter. I'm on your side. The Bergen family works hard. Didn't mean anything by that."

Streeter reminded himself to relax. Something about Eddie Schilling made him uneasy despite his easy charm. He moved on. "We were hoping to ask you a few questions—"

"Seems to me you know all you need to know about the Bergens," Schilling said with a chuckle, an attempt to clear the air.

Streeter cut in, "About the dead woman found nearby."

"Sheriff Leonard has asked all the questions I could answer," Eddie said, taking a chair beside the agent and facing the door. "Before we get started, let me buy you boys a pop. I've got Coke, Pepsi, 7UP, Mountain Dew, Dr. Pepper."

"Diet Coke," Streeter said when Eddie pointed at him.

Bly ignored Schilling.

"Is he always this friendly?" Schilling asked, jerking his thumb toward Bly.

"No," Streeter said simply, confusing Schilling.

Motioning to Streeter, Schilling said, "You don't look like you need to watch your weight." Putting in the quarters, he punched the Diet Coke button twice and handed the agent a can. Schilling sat in his chair, leaning forward against the table on his strong, hairy arms, eager to start the interview.

"I know about the dead body that was found just up the creek a ways," Schilling blurted, not waiting to be asked. "Rumors spread fast in small towns. Paper didn't say much today, but the rumors flying around said she had a chunk missing from the back of her skull. Heard she was found naked except for her shoes and socks."

Streeter was surprised by the detail and accuracy of Schilling's account of rumors. Sheriff Leonard's department didn't seem so small-town that they wouldn't understand the importance of holding back details of the crime scene as a way of helping solve the crime. But maybe Streeter misjudged Leonard. Or maybe Schilling had heard rumors from the Lucifer's Lot.

"Did you know the woman?" Streeter asked.

"Personally?" he asked. "Not really. I mean at first I didn't recognize the name. But then as the story came out in today's newspaper, I think I recognized her name from where I teach. I'm a physical education teacher for one of the public high schools in Rapid City."

Streeter's eyebrows arched. "Really? Which one?"

"Central High School," Schilling said, popping the tab on his own can of Diet Pepsi and taking a sip. "Dang, that tastes so good when it's this hot out."

"So you work the campground in the summer months only?" Streeter asked.

"Uh-huh. Memorial Day to Labor Day. The rest of the time the campground is closed. Sometimes I open during weekends just before and after tourist season, but only during the busy summers. We judge it by the weather and the gas prices. When the temperatures are high and the gas prices are low, we open early and close late. Just a summertime hobby, really, to kill time until my regular day job kicks in." Back came his smile—easy, wide, and boyishly innocent.

"As a PE teacher," Streeter repeated.

"Right."

"So you say you knew Michelle Freeburg?" Streeter pressed, trying to stay on task. Schilling was not nearly as busy with tourists as he let on and much more hungry for conversation. Probably out of boredom.

"Well, I can't say that I knew her, but her name sounds familiar," he said, scratching his head and screwing up his face as if thinking too hard might cause some permanent damage. "I might have had her in my PE class in junior high school. Seems to be about the right age for that. Hired on to the high school ten years ago. I've been teaching for nearly twenty. Can you believe that?"

"No," Streeter said flatly. His instincts warned him that this guy was a phony. He was more than the dumb jock persona he was so desperately trying to portray.

For the first time since they'd arrived, Bly chimed in. "You're being modest. Aren't you the volleyball coach, and haven't you won coach of the year for the umpteenth time? In the South Dakota Sports Hall of Fame? Bunch of records for the most wins or something?" Never taking his eyes off the highway beyond, Bly turned his head to the side and spat tobacco juice through the open door.

"That's me," Schilling said. Streeter noticed how his chest had puffed up like a bantam rooster's. "I like to coach. I love being around kids. Especially when they work so hard and have such great attitudes."

"Eddie Schilling, All-American receiver for Auburn," Bly added, wiping his lip with the back of his hand.

"Yeah, can you believe that? Small world that me and Shank end up out here in the Black Hills, him playing for the Crimson Tide and all. Rib him about it all the time."

Streeter tried to keep the surprise off his face. Shank gave the impression that he'd never met Schilling before, only knew him by reputation. Yet here was Eddie Schilling making them out to be old pals. Streeter saw the blood suddenly drain from Schilling's face; he had made a mistake.

To keep him talking, Streeter lied, "Shank told us all about that, didn't he, Agent Blysdorf?"

Without missing a beat, Bly added, "Said you were a pain in his ass and that if you didn't play for the Bear, you weren't worth a piece of shit. Something like, 'Who bleeds orange and blue anyway?'"

"Really," Schilling said, tilting his head and studying Bly in the doorway, the fear visibly subsiding and relief washing over his rugged face. "He said that? Well, linemen are always so full of shit their eyes are brown, right?"

Schilling laughed. Streeter smiled. Bly shot a glance toward Streeter, then back out the door toward Nemo Road.

"He told us you two were tight and that you could help us out," Streeter lied again.

"Hey, no problem. Anything for a friend. Makes it easier. And now you understand my problem. And why Shank's so willing to help me, owing me a favor and all. I asked him to help me get rid of these guys. They're bad news. I don't want these guys renting my place anymore, but I can't very well tell them, can I?" Schilling swiped a hand across his brow. "Doesn't mean the interview's over, does it? Now that you know."

He mouthed the words, in the slightest of whispers, and pointed at his chest. "I'm the mole. The one who told Leonard about Mully's missing pin and new purple wings."

Streeter realized he was afraid of being overheard. Paranoid.

Then Schilling spoke loudly again. "I mean it gets kinda lonely out here all day. The first part of the summer it's nice being away from the students and their parents, the cameras and journalists. But round about now, I'm starting to get antsy to get back to the grind. I hate to sound cocky or something, but I kinda like all the press, the hoopla, the accolades. I just need a break once in a while."

"School must be starting soon," Streeter stated, eager to get back to the interview.

"In a few weeks. My wife comes up during the last weeks of the season and starts preparing the place for the winter shutdown. She's a kindergarten teacher. Kids love her. We don't have kids, so she gives all her motherly love to them kids at school. And then we both run this place up here in the summer. When I'm not here, she covers for me. She's a jewel."

As if his words were an incantation, a thin woman emerged from the back room.

"Well, here she is now," Schilling announced with a stupid grin, standing up to kiss her pursed lips. Streeter easily read the wary expression on her face, a facade of practiced pleasantries and greetings. "This is my wife, Samantha."

During introductions, Streeter was surprised at how firm Samantha's grip was, given her otherwise petite stature and prudish demeanor. She carried herself like an heir to an ancient fortune and looked like an aged cheerleader, forever in the mode of playing too hard to get and too good for most. Her hair was bleached blond and styled with puffy bangs and cut to one length just below chin level. Her eyes were large and dominated her still striking face. Given her standoffishness, Streeter was even more surprised to learn that Samantha Schilling was a kindergarten teacher.

Streeter guessed the sour lines around her weary eyes and mouth were born of enduring Eddie's perpetually grating "dumb jock" routine. She must have tired long ago of having married a man who would forever remain a boy. She would be what his late wife would have described as a hardened woman, a kinder choice of words than those he would have chosen.

Streeter noted how stiff and uncomfortable Samantha appeared to be when her husband introduced her to Bly.

"Have you been here this entire time?" Streeter asked, nodding toward the living quarters and trying not to sound as irritated by her as he felt.

"I've been napping," she said, defensively.

"Hope we didn't wake you," Streeter added, returning to his uncomfortable perch on the folding chair. He turned to face Schilling. "You were saying you start the school year soon?"

Streeter could see peripherally that Samantha made no move to join them.

"Samantha starts right after Labor Day. Not much prep needed for snot-nosed five-year-olds." His wife's grimace deepened at Eddie's chuckle. "I'll go back the last week of August to get ready. Like to get a jump on things even though school doesn't start until after Labor Day."

"And you coach the girls' volleyball team?"

"Uh-huh," Eddie replied, straightening his shoulders a bit more than he needed to. "State champions four years in a row."

"Did Michelle Freeburg play volleyball for you at Central High School?" Streeter pressed.

"Now that would be kind of hard to do," Eddie said with a slight chuckle that bordered on mockery. He turned to his wife and winked playfully. She feigned enjoyment of his humor by offering a cool smile. "There wasn't a volleyball program at Central until two years after Michelle graduated."

"For someone who said he only vaguely recalls Michelle's name, you sure know the dates pertaining to her pretty darn well," Streeter said, spinning the can of Diet Coke slowly between the tips of his fingers. He decided to clamp the screws a little tighter on Eddie Schilling. "You know the year she graduated, the exact year the volleyball program started—"

"Now wait here a minute, Streeter," Schilling said, a bit more nervous than before.

With a sigh, Samantha pulled up a chair beside her husband and gripped his thigh, stating calmly, "Michelle Freeburg's history and bios have been plastered all over the newspaper today. She's a common house-hold topic. It's all we've talked about since they found the body yesterday. It's all anyone has talked about."

"We?" Streeter asked.

"The locals." Schilling supported Samantha, more relaxed than with the prior question. "Rapid City, Nemo, Sturgis, all over the Hills. Everyone has a theory on how the poor girl got to that creek bank."

"And what's your theory?"

Schilling's eyes looked away from Streeter for a second. Then he returned his stare, eyes boring directly into Streeter's, the smile appearing once again on his tanned, good-looking face. Samantha's gaze drifted toward the open door, in the general direction of the passing cars on the highway.

"You really want to know my theory?"

Streeter nodded slowly, not releasing Schilling from his icy stare.

Schilling rolled his eyes to the ceiling as if this kind of pontificating required such concentration. "I think I know who killed that girl, but I don't have any proof. I also think that if I breathe a word of it to you two fellows, I'd be the next body you'd find at the bottom of that creek."

Streeter asked, "Who?"

Schilling exchanged a glance with his wife then mouthed the word. "Mully."

Streeter calmly asked in a normal voice, "And what would make you think Mully killed Michelle Freeburg?"

Schilling's eyes sprang open, wide with surprise. His eyes darted around the room like a wild pinball, seeking the ears he must have thought the walls had. "I didn't say that," he said hurriedly, adjusting his shorts. He reached for some paper and wrote, "This place could be bugged."

"Relax," Streeter said, conjuring up his biggest lie yet. "This place isn't bugged. Agent Blysdorf over there has a mechanical apparatus to detect listening devices. You're safe. Nothing, right, Agent Blysdorf?"

Bly looked over his shoulder at Schilling, patted his pants pocket, and flashed an affirming smile.

Schilling closed his eyes and breathed a heavy sigh of relief, wiping the sweat from his brow as he did. His hands were like paws on a big grizzly bear, oversized compared to every other feature of his body. Perfect for playing sports like football and volleyball, Streeter thought.

Samantha seemed disinterested in the entire topic, to judge by the slouched position she'd settled into.

Schilling leaned closer and whispered, "Look, I don't want any trouble. I never said anything about Mully and that girl. Nothing. You understand? Shank told me not to worry. That you would put these guys behind bars. Leonard told me to keep quiet and you guys would get this all taken care of. That's the only reason I ratted Mully out, told Leonard that Mully wasn't wearing his pin anymore and that now he was wearing purple wings. Purple wings. You know what that means?"

Before Streeter could answer Schilling plunged ahead. "I'd love to help you guys out on this, but you have to figure this one out on your own. Mully and his guys might be back any minute, and I don't need them hearing any rumors that aren't true, like the FBI were here and I fingered the bastard. He'll kill me."

"You mean that?" Streeter said, leaning toward his nervous host.

Samantha interjected blandly, her pink lips moving imperceptibly with every word. "Eddie gets a little melodramatic sometimes."

Her husband leaned back and took a long drink of his pop. "It's a figure of speech; didn't mean anything by it. But you understand why this is so important, don't you?"

The only thing Streeter understood was that everyone was trying really hard to give the impression they never suspected Mully of hurting anybody, while pointing every finger and toe in his direction on the sly.

"And Shank and Leonard told you to keep quiet, did they?" Streeter asked.

"Well, yeah. They said you'd take care of all this for me." His searching eyes volleyed from Streeter to Bly. "You will, won't you?"

Streeter said reassuringly, "Don't you worry about a thing. As long as you tell us what you know, we'll take care of the rest. Does either of you remember seeing or hearing anything unusual Sunday night or Monday morning while the Lucifer's Lot bikers were camping here?"

Schilling shrugged and grinned stupidly. Samantha grimaced as she turned away from him toward Streeter and said, "Everything these people do seems strange. They are not the cream of the societal crop, if you understand what I mean."

Streeter nodded.

"Eddie worked up here on Sunday from around three in the afternoon until Monday around two or two thirty when I came up. Wouldn't you say, dear?"

"Yep," he admitted.

Streeter asked Schilling, "So you were up here all night?"

"Uh-huh."

Streeter didn't think his answer was as convincing as the first affirmation. "Alone?"

Schilling licked his lips as he glanced at his wife.

"Don't look at me," she said. "I was at home all night, doing laundry."

Samantha stood up and tilted her head slightly, saying to Streeter, "You asked if anything unusual happened. Last night one of the prospects—a prospective member of the club—was being teased by another member about 'licking a stiff.' I didn't really understand what they had meant, but they completely stopped their conversations when they noticed me returning from one of my walks."

Schilling was staring up at her with his mouth stupidly agape. She reached over and, without reservation, pushed his chin up with the tip of her index finger, closing it.

Samantha explained. "That's not very intelligent looking, dear."

"You never told me that before," Schilling said, surprised by the information.

"You never asked," she answered simply. "Besides, you didn't get here last night until after ten thirty. And they left hours before that. But quite frankly, those loathsome creatures say all sorts of things that don't bear repeating. I didn't think about their comment regarding 'a stiff' until this morning, during my walk, when I put it in the context of the conversation we had with Sheriff Leonard and Bob Shankley yesterday afternoon. And once I had read the paper about the details of Michelle's body being found, I thought it might be of importance."

"And you think they were referring to the prospect having oral sex with Michelle's dead body?" Streeter asked.

"Who knows what they were referring to? I was just repeating what I heard as I walked by their campsite." Her wary eyes landed on Streeter's.

Thinking of Shank's call when they were pulling out of the Nemo quarry, telling them about how the crime scene technicians found a set of boot prints headed back in this direction, Streeter turned to Schilling and asked, "Are you also a hiker, Eddie? Is that how you stay in such good shape?"

Schilling shook his head and grinned. "No, lots of free weights and playing volleyball with my girls. That's my secret."

Samantha looked impatiently at her watch. "I've got to go grocery shopping before it gets too late. Good-bye, dear." She bussed Schilling's cheek and turned toward the door.

"Can we talk again, Mrs. Schilling?" Streeter asked, rising from the table as she made to leave.

"Any time, Agent Pierce," she said, her smile softening for the first time. "Am I on your list of suspects, too?"

Streeter could see in that smile how lovely she once was, could have been, if not for the bitterness. He speculated it was because she had married Peter Pan. Returning the smile, Streeter said, "Just gathering the facts."

She chortled. "You sound like Sergeant Joe Friday."

Streeter had no idea what she was talking about, but he liked how amusement made her less tense. "Who?"

This made Bly snicker, and Streeter wondered what inside joke the two were sharing.

Schilling smiled awkwardly. "I can talk with you again, too, of course. But once Mully returns, I'd prefer we meet somewhere else or while he's up at Sturgis doing his business. Okay? I'll help you as much as I can, but I don't want to die."

CHAPTER 15

I REMEMBERED WHEN BARKER'S Market used to be a Piggly Wiggly. It must have been quite a feat for Mom to keep all nine of us little ones in line while grocery shopping to feed her army. I recalled the fun we had piled high in and dancing around that cart. And that Mom was always one hell of a cook.

I could feel the heat rising from the asphalt as I walked through the parking lot toward the grocery store. It brought to mind the image of the girl in the red bikini at Sturgis, and I thought how hot she must have been lying on the asphalt. I made a mental note to call the Sturgis hospital to see how she was doing, refusing to believe Creed's prognosis.

I made my way through the automated doors and approached the closest checkout clerk.

"Do you know where I can find Roy Barker?"

The clerk pointed up to the mirrored windows of the small, elevated room perched on the left overlooking the store. I pushed through the swinging door by the public restrooms near the front of the store and made my way up the narrow staircase where a sign with an arrow marked "Manager" pointing to a single door on my right.

A man with dirty blond hair was sitting with his back to me at a desk pushed against the opposite, northeast corner of the windowed manager's loft, tallying up numbers on a large tabletop calculator. I could see the logic in this layout, an ability for whoever was supervising to work the paper side of the business while having the ability to simply lift the eyes and view the entire grocery store below out the mirrored window, looking right, toward the checkout lanes or to the left, into the produce section and to the back of the store farther back.

"Roy Barker?" I called through the open door.

"Uh-huh," the man hunched over the desk grunted as he wildly punched the keypad. "Give me a sec."

I did, taking the opportunity to snoop around the office. I read the plaques on the walls to the right of the door and studied the collage of photos that were on an organization chart on the other side, the manager, Roy Barker, perched at the top.

The young man who swung around in his desk chair to greet me was definitely the same man in the picture below Roy Barker's stenciled name. I could detect under his thin white polyester shirt wide, bony shoulders and a long, lean body, layered in sinewy muscles. His face had angular features, his skin had an orangey hue that could only have come from a bottle of Mystic Tan, and his eyes had the benefit of the expensive designer glasses that were perched on the bridge of his narrow nose. He didn't look much older than a senior in high school.

Roy extended his hand and I shook it, feeling as if the bones in his frail hand—incongruously weak compared to the rest of his buffed body—would break. "I'm Roy. How can I help you?"

"I'm here to ask some questions about Michelle Freeburg," I said, not really wanting to tell him I was Jens Bergen's sister. "Do you have a minute?"

"The FBI agents just left. Who are you?"

I didn't want to lie to Roy, but here he'd gone and offered me the perfect opportunity to do so. "I'm Agent Genevieve." I'd always heard that sticking as close to the truth as possible makes the lie more believable. And since Genevieve was my baptismal name—not Liv, which is technically my middle name—and I was acting as an agent for Jens, I figured I was kinda telling the truth. Okay, I'd say my ten Hail Marys later. Maybe even call Catherine and ask her to say a few for my sorry soul in her official capacity.

"Agent Stewart Blysdorf asked me to conduct a follow-up interview with you, if you have a minute." I used his name because he seemed to be the common denominator among all of the FBI's interviews so far.

"Look, I'm already way behind because of their visit. I can't imagine what I can tell you that I haven't already told them. Is this absolutely necessary?"

His annoyance with them was genuine. The irritation showing on his narrow face was mirrored in his arms, tightly folded—deliberately so, I suspected—across his chest. Other than that, he was a nice enough guy. And he looked really familiar to me somehow.

"Just a few minutes. Please." I flashed him my most sincere smile, stopping short of batting my eyelashes at him.

Roy was unimpressed. Charm had never been one of my strong suits. He didn't offer me one of the four plastic chairs that were stacked in the corner, which made me wonder if the agents who came before me had been met with the same discourtesy.

"I don't have a lot of time," Roy announced.

I started pacing, hands slammed to hips, in the expansive space between the door and the window beside his desk, bobbing along the wall with all the glossy photos in the makeshift giant org chart. His eyes went wide when I stopped, towering over him where he sat, nothing between us but my angry huffs. Unsympathetic toward Roy's workload, I practically shouted, "Not for the murder investigation concerning one of your employees?"

After wearing a few more paths in the linoleum in his small office, I cooled down and yanked one of the plastic chairs down from the stack and slammed it on the floor behind Roy's desk without being invited to sit.

"Get on with it," Roy said.

"How old are you?"

"What's that got to do with anything?"

I said nothing.

"I'm about to turn twenty-eight."

Two years younger than me. Jens's age.

"Wow, kinda young to have earned a manager's slot, wouldn't you say?"

This earned me a cocky smile. "Kinda young to be an FBI agent, wouldn't you say?" He shot back.

"Touché. Are you from here originally?"

"Yeah, why?"

"Small talk sometimes relaxes people," I said, knowing it was a load of crock.

"It annoys me," he countered, refolding his arms across his chest.

"Me, too," I said honestly. That earned me a bigger (albeit brief) smile. "How long have you managed this store?"

"Two years," Roy said, contempt in his pale eyes. He rubbed his long, bony fingers through his dishwater blond hair, pushing the strands into place again with habitual strokes.

"Impressive. And before that?"

"Before that I was assistant manager for three years and worked my way up from bag boy. I've worked here for twelve years, full-time for ten."

"Straight out of high school? Damn, that was ambitious."

I noted the muscles along his strong jaw bulging. "I'm saving up to go to college."

"To do what?" I asked with genuine interest.

"I was . . ." His words trailed off, but his eyes widened slightly. He cleared his throat and quickly added, "Business."

I nodded but would have guessed he'd have been more interested in computers.

"Did you know Michelle Freeburg?" I had years of practice interviewing job candidates, but not a single experience with interrogations. I was probably making a total fool out of myself for sure.

Roy blinked several times before answering, "Of course. She worked for me."

"How long had you known her?"

"For about fifteen years." Roy stared at his hands fidgeting in his lap, averting his eyes. "We met in high school. As freshmen."

Now I knew why I had thought him familiar. He had been in Jens's class at Central High School. But he looked like a scrawny little boy back then. Not nearly the man he'd grown to be today. Got teased a lot, if I remember correctly. I think the kids called him Playboy Roy, but for the life of me, I don't remember why. I prayed he wouldn't suddenly recognize me, hoping I'd changed enough for him not to make the connection between Agent Genevieve and Liv Bergen—or think Agent Genevieve had facial features eerily similar to those of Jens Bergen, like the strong, tall frame, the long legs, and the friendly smile.

I'd always laughed off the stories of my swan-like transformation in college from a grungy looking jock to an athletically built model, but I never quite believed everyone until now. Roy Barker had no idea who I was. And I wasn't going to let this golden opportunity pass without using it to my advantage.

"I told her about an opening here in the store her senior year. She had moved into her own apartment and needed to find work that would fit around her classes. Didn't take her long to earn the key position as book-keeper. My father promoted her almost immediately. She worked directly for him until he retired two years ago."

And yet, his dad didn't place the same confidence in his own son until two years ago. I asked, "And she's worked here ever since?"

Roy had a far-off look in his pale eyes, his smile a bit eerie. "Ever since. Paid for her college, even though it took twice as long as if she'd gone to school full time."

I sensed I was getting somewhere. His cool veneer was starting to melt a degree or two. "A good worker?"

"The best," came his retort, as if Roy was offended that anyone would think otherwise. "She was my best worker. Never late, always working hard. Never complained about anything. Covered for anyone else's shift whenever I needed her, as long as it didn't interfere with her classes."

"Dream employee?"

"Yeah, she was a dream all right," he conceded, a slight blush befalling his hollowed cheeks. He turned his back to me and stared out the window above his desk overlooking the checkout lanes, intending to give the impression he was watching for something. I wasn't buying it.

"A dream, huh? Interesting choice of words."

Roy jerked his head around and snapped, "Your word, not mine."

"Easy, Roy," I said, holding my hands up in surrender, tipping my chair back on its hind legs as I did. Roy had responded exactly as I would have expected, given how Jens described him. There was definitely something more to Roy's relationship with Michelle than he cared for me to know. "Tell me about the last time you saw Michelle Freeburg."

Roy let out a ragged breath, turning his chair to face me. "Sunday night, 8:11 pm."

Amazing. The guy actually remembered to the minute the last time Michelle Freeburg had walked out of this store.

"During the rally, I'm always short-handed and Michelle was always willing to fill in for people. She liked having the money to pay off her student loans. I needed her to work the six-to-two shift the next day and she said she would come in. But she didn't. By six fifteen, I tried calling her cell. She didn't answer. I called her parents' house. Her mom told me she wasn't there and told me to try Jens's house." The condescension as he spoke Jens's name was clear. "Jens Bergen's her boyfriend. No answer there either. By nine, I was worried. One of the girls said she thought she saw Michelle's car in the parking lot. I went out to check, and sure enough, it was parked out there. But not in her usual parking spot."

Again he turned in his chair to stare out the office window to the aisles below, probably imagining Michelle walking among the rows and rows of food and staples.

"I tried to get her to stay that night, but she wouldn't. Said she had other plans, which I assumed meant she was going somewhere with her boyfriend."

The corners of his mouth turned down at every mention of Jens. Contempt, disgust.

He rose from his chair, and stood by the window. Roy placed his long, bony fingers on his thin hips.

"I sense you're not a fan."

"He was mean to her."

I forced the anger down, knowing my brother wouldn't hurt a fly, the nicest, most cooperative and compatible man I knew. Seeing now that the contempt might really be jealousy, I braced myself for what I believed would be Roy spinning a yarn, but I encouraged it anyway, telling myself to appear neutral and unfazed. "Mean? Like as in he beat her or something?"

"No, nothing like that. I saw how they were together. In the store. At the mall. In restaurants. At the park. He didn't treat her or love her the way he should. The way she deserved."

"What did he do specifically?" I asked, trying to understand more fully Roy's sense of reason.

"He would tease her and hurt her feelings," Roy countered, screwing up his face.

"He hurt her feelings? How so?" Oh, this was going to be good.

"Well, like one time, he made her carry their lunch all the way to a picnic table in the park while he stayed in the car on his cell phone," he mumbled. "And another time, he ordered for her at a restaurant while she was in the restroom, treating her like she was his possession or something."

Seemed like fairly normal dating behaviors in my book. I just wasn't getting where the real envy or contempt was coming from with Roy.

I said, "But she loved him."

"I suppose," he said. "One day she said something about loving him, which I just didn't understand."

"All wrong for her, I suppose?"

"Definitely," Roy said, not seeing the trap I'd carefully laid for him. "He was a jerk. Didn't know anything about Michelle or what she was all about."

"But you did?"

"Well, yeah," he said without hesitation. "She was warm and funny, smart and self-confident. She had everything going for her."

"Sounds like a special person," I coaxed.

"That's an understatement. She was incredible. She was the kind of girl . . ." Roy dropped his chin to his chest, hanging his head low and shaking it from side to side. He had no idea that I knew he had told Michelle on Sunday night that he loved her, starting the argument between him and Michelle, between him and Jens. He turned toward me, leaning his back against the window, and proclaimed, "I loved her."

"But she didn't love you back," I added. A strong motive for murder, I thought. Rejected by a woman he'd loved for more than a decade.

Roy stood staring at the movements of the shoppers and employees below.

"She loved Jens Bergen, didn't she?" I taunted, hoping to find him slipping me more information out of anger than this practiced calm.

"She thought she did," he said evenly, turning back to the window.

"What do you think happened to Michelle Sunday night, Roy?" I moved to my feet so I would be level with him when he turned back toward me again, which he would.

"I think Jens Bergen killed her," he said coldly.

My stomach flipped. Those words were just too hard for me to hear. I dropped back into my chair. I started to speak but the words lodged in my throat.

Before I could respond, he added, "She was fine until the end of the day when he showed up. Then she seemed a little edgy."

I recovered enough to counter, "Don't you think that might have had something to do with the biker gang showing up?"

Roy shook his head. "That's what those other agents said. But if I had to guess, I'd say you should question that pretty boy, Jens. He said some ugly things to Michelle that night. She was shook up about that."

"Such as?"

"Ask him," Roy said, collapsing into his chair and turning to face me.

"I have, and he told me he said some ugly things to you, not Michelle."

His face crumpled. "He said I'd better not piss him off or I'd regret it the rest of my life."

"Right after you told Michelle not to piss you off or she'd regret it the rest of her life," I countered. "And did she? Regret it for the rest of her short life, Roy?"

His eyes drifted, his shoulders and face sagged. He pushed the expensive frames up the bridge of his nose.

"It wasn't like that. She called me crazy. I was just telling her to knock it off and that big bruiser boyfriend of hers got all huffy."

"And did you tell that part of the story to the other agents? How you threatened Michelle first before her boyfriend threatened you? Or did you just tell them the part about the big bruiser boyfriend threatening you?"

He shook his head. "I told them he threatened me."

"Well, that might end up problematic for you, don't you think?" I said in my best authoritative cop-like voice. "You neglect to tell the other agents that you got a little hot under the collar, hot enough to threaten that you'd make Michelle have regrets for the rest of her life and then she shows up dead the next day."

His eyes widened. "It wasn't like that. I swear."

"What bothers you so much about the word 'crazy'?" I asked bluntly, seeing how the muscles twitched around the corners of his mouth every time the word came up. He stared at his hands, pushed his glasses up again even though they hadn't slipped from seconds earlier, then flipped around in his chair to face the desk, and for a moment, I thought he was going to whip out a pistol from a drawer he opened and shoot me. Instead, he grabbed a piece of paper, spun around in his chair, and shoved the strip of paper toward me.

"Here," he said, "take it to them."

"To whom?" I looked at the strip of paper in my hand and realized it was a cash register receipt dated Sunday. The few things listed on it didn't make any sense to me: Housewares—Needles (1), Housewares—Thread (1), Outdoors—Fishing wire (1), Outdoors—Matches (1), and Pharmacy—Rubbing Alcohol (4).

"Your friends. The other agents. They asked me to find out from the clerk that night if she remembered what they bought. That's it, the list. We found it on the computer and printed a duplicate."

It had looked like a scavenger hunt list, but now that I knew Mully and his gang had bought the items on it, I guessed that one of them was sporting a new tattoo and wanted to ward off any infections with the rubbing alcohol. I stuffed the list in my pocket and suddenly realized that because of my decision to impersonate a federal agent, the investigation was compromised; the agents would never see this list. I felt horrible, both for interfering with Agent Blysdorf and for bullying Roy Barker.

I stood up and walked over to the right of his desk by the window, staring down at the customers at the checkout registers as Roy had done off and on during our interview. I had to either come clean with Roy or continue to do the best I could harvesting as many details as I could about Michelle Freeburg's last night on this earth.

"When did you leave the store Sunday night, Roy?"

"I don't remember exactly," he replied, shaken. His pale eyes were flat and lifeless.

"Did you work all night?"

"Of course not," he said, understanding the sarcasm I had intended. "The other supervisor came in around ten."

"But you stayed at least until ten, right?" He nodded. "It seems odd that you remember such an exact time for Michelle's departure from the store, Roy—8:11 pm—but you don't have a clue when you left the store."

"It was about ten fifteen," Roy said, eyes to the floor.

"And was Michelle's car in the parking lot at ten fifteen?"

"No."

"Was it there when you came to work the next day?"

"It was dark. I really don't know. It wasn't parked where she normally parks."

I believed him. But I wasn't convinced he was innocent.

"But it could have been in the parking lot when you got there?"

"Yes."

"Did you follow Michelle into the parking lot when she left at eight eleven?"

Roy said nothing, folding his hands and raising them to his pursed lips.

"Did you ask her out again? Reconsider your proclamation of love? Take advantage of the opportunity when she made Jens leave? Maybe Char saw the whole thing, and now she's gone too?"

The muscles in Roy's jawbone flexed and bulged. He repositioned the tips of his fingers to slide the designer frames into place then rested them back against his lips.

"Did she reject you for the last time, Roy?"

I was trying to hit a nerve and finally did.

Slamming his hands against the edge of his desk, Roy barked, "I loved Michelle!"

After a long moment, listening to the echo from his words fade and the muffled sound of voices on the intercom requesting price checks, I said, "Interesting." I noted he didn't proclaim he hadn't killed her, just that he loved her. To death? I speculated there was more to this story than he was willing to share. "You went over to the Freeburg house to see if she was there, didn't you? When you didn't see her car, you went over to Jens Bergen's house. Am I right?"

His worried eyes studied me. He wiped the tears from his cheeks. "And then what, Roy?"

"Nothing, I swear!" he shouted, spittle flying again from his mouth. He wiped his face with his sleeve and glared at me. "Michelle was with Jens. I could see them in the living room. I wanted to talk with her about what I'd said, to explain. So I waited outside for half an hour, thinking she'd go home soon. She had to work at six the next morning, and it was about a quarter to eleven by this time."

He sniffled and sighed.

"Go on," I said.

"But when she walked over to Bergen and gave him a hug and a long kiss, him rubbing her back, I just snapped."

I held my breath, waiting to learn what "snapped" entailed.

He leveled his gaze at me and said, "I drove home and told myself to forget about Michelle Freeburg. She didn't belong to me. She belonged to Bergen."

Well, that was a letdown. And hard to believe. "Do you have an alibi as to your whereabouts from ten forty-five until you reported to work yesterday morning?"

"I live alone," he said, not discomfited in the least by my implication. "But to answer your question, I was on my computer from about eleven until two. I couldn't sleep after that. I was playing X-Box Live, so I'm sure there are records to prove what I was doing, players who could verify I was there. I was home while Jens was off somewhere killing Michelle. Check his alibi."

"I have," I said. Then, something Jens told me came to mind; something about Michelle possibly quitting her job earlier than the target date she'd mentioned when she gave her four-week notice. "Did Michelle come back here, Roy? Sunday night?"

Something in Roy's face changed. He shook his head, a little too quickly. "No. Like I said. She left at 8:11 pm and didn't show up for her shift the next morning."

"Did she call in?"

"No, I filed the missing persons report, remember?"

"Did she quit?"

Roy winced. He turned back to the glass and stared off for a long moment. Finally he said, "Well, of course she had. Michelle turned in her notice at the beginning of the month. She told me that August 30 would be her last day."

"But did she quit on Sunday night, after you two argued?"

"No," he practically shouted, "but I thought she would."

If Michelle had told Roy she was quitting immediately, there was no doubt in my mind that he might have "snapped" at the news. But I didn't see him having the ability to hastily concoct a viable plan that would lead the FBI to a Lucifer's Lot member.

Unless he simply got lucky.

"You're not telling me something," I said.

His mouth opened and closed like a guppy's.

"Are you going to tell me or do I have to beat it out of you?"

He stared for a long moment, weighing his options. Something behind his eyes hardened and he said, "I've told you everything."

"Tell me about the secret."

He furrowed his eyebrows. "What secret?"

"You told her you knew about her secret from high school," I explained, noting how his face collapsed along with the brows. "What was Michelle's secret?"

He sagged in his chair, removed his glasses, and buried his face in his oversized hands.

I waited.

"She was going to be a doctor. She could have been anything she wanted." He wasn't crying, but his words were sloppy. "She was wasting her talent. I told her that. I told her again and again."

"How was she wasting her talent?"

"Here! She was wasting her talent working here," he mumbled. "She wouldn't leave."

"Because she couldn't afford it?"

"She could have gotten a scholarship anywhere she wanted to go and finished her undergraduate in four years. She could have been doing her internship by now, rather than just starting off into medical school. She was wasting her talent because of Charlene."

"The secret?" I pressed.

I watched as he lowered one hand, smoothing his face and hair with the other, replaced his glasses, and straightened his back. He sat still for a long moment, his back to the desk and windows, staring longingly at the yawning office door, as if he was about to bolt and run.

Eventually he said, "She was pregnant. As a freshman. No one knew. No one."

"Except you?"

His eyes landed on mine. "She hid it well. First with baggy jeans and shirts, then with sweats. She started wearing her brothers' clothes. Then, just before Thanksgiving, she contracted 'mononucleosis.'" His fingers made air quotes when he spoke of the illness. "Took all her tests that semester from home. Didn't come in until the end of February. She was smart. Kept up with studies at home and never missed a beat. Teachers liked her, helped her."

"How did you know she was pregnant?"

His face reddened.

"You're a peeper, aren't you, Roy?"

His embarrassment morphed into indignation. "I am not a Peeping Tom. I loved her."

"Let me rephrase the question, then. You loved her enough to keep an eye on her at night when she undressed, bathed, and slept and to follow her movements by day?"

"Well, no. I mean, I cared for her, so yes, I kept an eye on her. At first, it was because I liked her, but then I realized she was in trouble, being forced against her will to have sex," he said, flustered by the ancient thoughts, his fingers flying to his face to adjust the position of his eyeglasses.

"And why didn't you do anything about it?"

"I tried," he said, red blooming on his cheeks again. "But I couldn't."

"Because you were too scared?"

"I was just a boy, then," he argued. "The guy looked like a man, not a boy. But I couldn't be sure. Anyway, he was big, strong."

"Who was he?"

"I don't know," he mumbled, staring down at his shoes. "I only saw him with her twice, and both times he surprised her when she was walking home. He holed up in a house that was being constructed. Always hiding."

I thought about the horror Michelle must have felt at age thirteen, leery of every shadow.

"Who was he?"

"I don't know," he said, ringing his hands. "He always wore a hoodie that covered his head. Like I said, he tended to ambush her so fast and pull her into the construction before I really knew what was happening. I tried to peep the second time, but I could never get close enough without getting caught. After the second time, Michelle walked home from so many different directions, I could never keep up. I kind of lost track of her."

"So you started peeping in her windows instead?" He cradled his head in his hands. "Why didn't you call the police?"

He shrugged, his eyes cast to the floor. "My father said if I was ever caught peeping again, I'd never get to work at the store again."

"So let me get this straight. You know the woman you claim to love was enduring rape repeatedly and you did nothing to help because you were afraid the police would realize you learned all this by peeping, a crime you'd been caught committing in the past? You threw her under the bus for a job?"

"It wasn't like that. I tried to talk to her about it once, but before I ever got to explain myself, she told me to leave her alone."

He sighed.

"What happened with the baby?" I asked.

He shrugged.

"Did she have an abortion? Or did she go full term?"

"I don't know. Her curtains were always drawn in those last few months."

I went through the timeline in my head, thinking that she would have started showing around six months; Thanksgiving to the end of February—the period when she had "mono"—would have been her third trimester. She almost certainly carried the baby to term. I wondered if a doctor was involved. Or a midwife. Or if Michelle gave birth to the baby by herself and left the child on someone's doorstep. Or in a dumpster.

Then I realized the baby would be fourteen. Char's age.

"And you think Michelle gave up all her dreams, wasted her talent, to keep an eye on Charlene because that's her child, not her sister?"

He scowled. "Where the hell did you come up with that idea? Char's her sister, not her child. I told you, I don't know what happened to that baby."

Could it be that Michelle's mother was pregnant at the same time as Michelle? I wondered. Clearly if she wasn't, wouldn't someone close to Mrs. Freeburg question how she ended up with a baby if she had not appeared to be pregnant at the time? Could she have been so plump as to never appear to be pregnant?

Roy continued, "I assume Michelle had a late-term abortion, maybe even got an infection or something and lost it. Maybe she almost died herself. Or she put the thing up for adoption. Or it died at birth. Who knows? What I was saying is that Michelle could have been a doctor by now. But she decided to stick around here, take her time getting her undergraduate degree, put all her dreams on hold; she was wasting her talents just to make sure Char stayed safe. Kept watch over her like a pit bull on a pork chop."

"Okay, then who else knew? Her parents must have known. Her brothers?"

He heaved his left shoulder toward his big left ear. "No one. I told you. She kept all that a secret. She was great at keeping secrets."

"Roy, did you ever see her go to a doctor's office?"

"I saw her go to the Black Hills Medical Clinic on Fifth Street a couple of times during that winter, and even afterwards that spring and summer, but I don't know about any doctor."

A doctor would have been involved in the mono cover-up, or, at the very least, her parents would have suspected something. Unless they truly were brain dead, as Jens suggested, but I found it hard to believe they would be so numb as not to notice a pregnant teen. But it happens.

Leaning toward him, putting on the best menacing expression I could affect, I asked, "And tell me again how you knew all this about Michelle, about her secret?"

"I . . . I followed her," he admitted.

I pushed back in my chair and stomped to the door, leaving him with his mouth agape. Standing on the threshold, I turned and demanded, "Pick up that phone and give those agents a call. You still have their business cards, don't you?" He nodded. "Tell them you forgot to share with them how you threatened Michelle, which is why Jens Bergen threatened you, and about the spying you did Sunday night at the Bergen house. Then tell them about the secret and her visits to the Black Hills Medical Clinic."

"But—"

"But nothing. Do it, Roy. And if you do as I say, I won't report this to headquarters and this visit never happened. No obstruction of justice charges filed against you." Or me, I thought.

I waited by the door while he made the call. He was smart enough to preface all of this by saying he had been thinking about their visit with him and realized these memories might be useful to their investigation. I listened as Roy told Agent Blysdorf all about the threat to Michelle and why Jens returned the threat and about how Roy went to the Bergen house out of concern for Michelle. I heard him retell the story about Michelle's secret and what he knew about the three missing months and her visits to the medical clinic.

I handed him back the list and mouthed, "Read this." He did, adding the story about him waiting outside Jens's house to talk with Michelle until ten forty-five, then returning home to play video games. He told them to call his Internet provider and listed all the live gamers he engaged to confirm his story.

To assure he never mentioned our visit and offered to the real federal agents to send the list of grocery items back with Agent Genevieve, I slipped out the door and down the stairs.

CHAPTER 16

"WELL, THAT WAS WEIRD," Bly said, closing his cell phone. He told Streeter about Roy Barker's call, and just as they pulled to the curb outside the Freeburg house, his cell phone rang again. He answered, "Yo."

Streeter could hear Shankley shouting through the phone, something about "disrespect" and "written warning." Bly smiled and handed the phone to Streeter without saying another word.

"Yes?"

"Pierce, why don't you join the rest of us in the twenty-first century and invest in a cell phone that works," Shank snarled.

"My phone works. I just keep it turned off."

Streeter tilted Bly's phone toward him so he could share in the experience of choice words and expletives. Bly turned to him and grinned, adjusting his fedora in the rearview mirror as he waited for Shank to report his hourly update to Streeter.

"What do you have for me, Shankley? We're kind of busy here."

"The crime scene technicians have finished and pulled out of there already. Nothing from Sturgis PD on Jane Doe. Nothing from RCPD on Charlene Freeburg. And nothing on either autopsy yet."

"Then we'll talk in an hour," Streeter said, ending the call abruptly, unable to shake the disturbing idea that a young Michelle had been raped and impregnated and had kept it a secret all these years. The suspect list grew longer.

As they walked up the narrow sidewalk to the front door, Bly chided Streeter, "Don't know why you're wasting so much time interviewing all these people when you know the killer is Mully. Seems like such a waste."

Streeter grinned, rapping his knuckles against the door. "Your boss's goal is to get me out of here as fast as humanly possible, back to Denver where I belong."

"Far, far away," Bly added. "But only after you take care of his Carl Muldando problem, which is why he asked you to come up here."

The door opened. The woman who peered anxiously through the screen was short and pudgy, wearing high, perfectly coiffed, and unnaturally yellow hair. Her fleshy smile was tentative as she suggested they come in.

When she pushed the screen door open, Streeter entered first, introducing the two of them. "I'm Special Agent Streeter Pierce."

"Yes."

"This is Special Agent Stewart Blysdorf. Please, allow us to offer our condolences about your daughter, Michelle."

"Sure," she said, dismissing the gesture, and instead regarded Blysdorf cautiously at first, then her eyes widened with recognition. "Oh, I've seen you before at Ken Vincent's mayoral inauguration party when you first arrived to Rapid City. It was quite an event."

Streeter was amazed at how emotionless she seemed to be about her daughter being murdered. Upon his mention of Michelle's death, she seemed to be too easily distracted in connecting dots from Bly to all the names she could drop.

"Nice to meet you," Bly said, frowning and extending his hand to her.

She shook it and folded her hands across her wide belly. "Pleased to meet you. You know I already talked with Bob Shankley. Did he send you over here?"

"Not exactly," Streeter said.

"Well, any friend of Bob's is a friend of mine. You see, we're all great friends with Ken."

Streeter wasn't making the connection.

"Ken and Bob play poker together. We see them up at Deadwood in the casinos from time to time." She motioned them toward the floral patterned couch. Streeter and Bly exchanged glances.

"Poker buddies, huh?" Bly asked. He leaned into Streeter and whispered, "The mayor, the coach, the sheriff, and the SAC. All they need to round out the party is a butcher, a baker, or a candlestick maker."

"Why, yes. I understand from Ken they're very good friends."

Streeter was annoyed to learn Shank was friendly with the mayor, but he wasn't sure how or even if the information was pertinent to the case. But he was sure that Shank intentionally forgot to mention being friends with Eddie Schilling, and this made Streeter even more aware that every unknown tidbit he learned might come in useful.

Before easing herself into the worn recliner, once a match for some of the roses all over the couch, she asked, "Would either of you gentlemen like some iced tea or water? Frank isn't home yet. I expected him ten minutes ago, but he must be running late. You see, his boss at the post office is somewhat of a tyrant, and Frank really doesn't get along well with him. It could be that—"

Her unwarranted explanation was interrupted by the sound of the garage door opening.

"There he is now." She sat back, more at ease in her chair, knowing he would soon join them.

"Tea would be great," Bly told Arlene Freeburg.

She pushed herself from the recliner, attempting to hide her embarrassment that she had made the offer only to forget it seconds later. "And for you, Agent . . . uh, what was it again?"

"Pierce," Streeter said with a tender smile. "Water, please."

The door from the garage to the kitchen closed with a creak and heavy footsteps pounded across the linoleum. The house was small, and Streeter imagined that every sound could be heard from anywhere in the house, even with the thin doors shut.

Arlene didn't seem to remember this as she whispered, "We have company, Frank. In the living room."

Frank did not respond, choosing instead to pad his way directly toward the room. Both men rose from the couch and extended their hands.

"Agent Pierce. And this is Agent Blysdorf," Streeter said, gripping hands with the spectacled man.

"Frank Freeburg. Arlene, bring me tea." To Bly, he added, "I think I saw you earlier this morning at the morgue, didn't I? With Shank?"

Bly nodded.

She handed the tea intended for Bly to Frank and the water to Streeter. Retreating to the kitchen, she returned with two more teas and handed one to Bly.

Settling into their recliners, the Freeburgs regarded the agents cautiously. Streeter sensed their reluctance and decided to play off of it from the beginning.

"Look, I'm sure you have just about had it with all the questions, the probing, the insensitive nature of investigations. I'm sure you would both like to get on with your lives and grieve in peace for your daughter's tragic death. I'm sure there is nothing positive you can see coming from another round of questions posed by us." Streeter leaned forward on the couch, resting his elbows on his knees and twirling the glass of water between his hands. Looking directly at Michelle's father, who sat rigidly in the recliner, he added, "We appreciate your being willing to take the time."

"Agent Blysdorf and I are the primary investigators assigned to this case."

"Bob told us he was the primary investigator," Arlene said.

Streeter looked at Bly.

Bly offered, "He was. But he made Agent Pierce the agent in charge today and turned over the field investigation to us. We are responsible for finding Michelle's killer and bringing him or her to justice. We will do absolutely everything we can to do that, but we'll need your help."

Streeter stared earnestly from Arlene to Frank, making sure he had their attention. "We have read everything in the files about conversations you had with Bob Shankley earlier, and we thank you for being so helpful up to this point. Agent Blysdorf and I want to make sure we aren't missing anything. No stone unturned."

He let his words sink in as they sat silently, the only sound the over-head fan beating its unbalanced rhythmic hum above them.

"Will you help us?"

Arlene glanced over at Frank. She said, "I will."

Frank nodded once, his eyes appearing sad and tired, his mouth relaxing as he lifted the glass to his lips.

"Thank you. We'll make this as quick and painless as possible and try hard not to make you repeat yourself."

Without taking his eyes from theirs, Streeter could see peripherally the picture of the Freeburg family hanging on one wall, a crucifix on another.

"Did Michelle live here with you?"

The mother was the first to answer. "In the basement."

"Mind if we take a look?"

Without another word, she led them downstairs. The contents of the room could only be described as scant: A twin bed. No pictures on the walls. One tiny window. One small dresser with four drawers, only two of which held items of clothing. A small closet with less than a dozen items hanging on neatly spaced hangers—two skirts, four blouses, three pairs of jeans, one pair of slacks, and a coat. Nothing in the pockets. Nothing under the bed, pillow, or mattress. Few toiletries in the tiny half bath. Absolutely nothing that would suggest Michelle lived any other life than the one everyone had observed.

When they returned to the living room, Streeter nodded at Frank and took a seat on the couch.

As if by way of explanation, Arlene said, "She didn't spend much on clothes. She was trying to save her money for school."

"What was she going to go to school for?"

"Nursing," Arlene beamed proudly, settling back in her recliner and drinking her tea. "She wanted to help others. She was a good girl that way."

Streeter was glad he had managed to loosen her up a bit so quickly. He sipped his water.

"Nursing is a great profession," he added casually.

"And Michelle would have been good at it. She was a quiet girl, a worrier, always caring about everyone else." Arlene's mouth turned down a bit at this thought.

"To the point of self-neglect?" Streeter asked.

Arlene regarded him curiously as if it had never occurred to her until now. "Yes, I suppose. I guess I never really thought of it that way, though."

"She was a lovely girl, but from the photos, she seemed to put little effort into her appearance."

Arlene primped her hairdo with brightly colored fingernails. "I never understood that girl. She could have been so lovely if she just tried even the slightest. It was as if she was embarrassed by her looks. She was always the most delightful, spirited child, popular with everyone. A bit of a tomboy, but not to the point of concern."

The mother settled her weight deeper into the recliner as her thoughts drifted to earlier times. "She would try so hard to keep up with her older brothers, playing football with them, basketball, even wrestled with them. She liked to win."

With a heavy sigh, she added, "We both so hoped she would grow out of all that."

Frank nodded in agreement when she looked over at him. He lifted the glass of tea to his lips and drank, swallowing hard.

Streeter had observed a wide variety of grieving loved ones. Grief had not yet settled in with these two yet, but it would. And when it did, the devastation would be profound. He sensed they were uncomfortable about something, choosing their words a bit too carefully, but he wanted to be gentle with them, considering their fragile emotional state.

"Did she? Grow out of it?" Streeter continued.

"Very suddenly," she said, looking again at Frank for confirmation. "I don't recall exactly when, but it was sometime around eighth, maybe ninth grade. She was in all the sports she could be in and did quite well. Then, she dropped out of basketball, volleyball, and track. She continued with softball, but only because it had nothing to do with the school. It was a city league. She refused to participate in any extracurricular activities at school after that year."

Frank nodded in agreement again and looked at Streeter with confidence. He was beginning to get more comfortable, too, although content to let Arlene do all the talking.

"She had been involved in so many different things. Could have earned a scholarship if she'd continued with track. But she dropped out."

"Did you ever ask her why?"

"Countless times," Arlene said defensively. "Of course we asked her. But she just clammed up, saying she was simply no longer interested. Frank and I speculated that maybe someone at school had teased her about being a tomboy or made fun of her somehow. Who knows why teenagers do the things they do?"

Frank finally contributed his first word to the conversation. "Puberty."

Streeter nodded in understanding. "Was it then that she started to . . . work hard at looking plain?"

"That's a very kind way of putting it, Agent Pierce," Arlene said, offering a grateful smile. "I tried everything to get her interested in makeup, curlers, dresses, but the more I tried, the worse she got. Baggy clothes, bad haircuts, aversion to makeup. For some time, we were concerned she might be . . . well, a lesbian." She quickly covered her lips as if she had never spoken the word aloud. Then she just as quickly discounted the thought by adding, "Until she . . . well, we knew she wasn't gay. She couldn't be."

"Until she what?" Streeter asked.

Arlene looked at Frank, whose lips were unmistakably drawn into a warning. She answered, "Until she started dating and such. You know how teenage girls are."

Frank seemed pleased with her answer. He sipped his tea.

"Did she ever have any serious boyfriends?" Streeter asked, drinking from his water.

"Not really," Arlene said, looking at Frank. "Maybe her latest one was the closest thing to being serious, but she was never really serious about anybody. She was pretty independent."

"The latest one being Jens Bergen?"

"Yes."

"Hadn't they dated for a year or so?"

Arlene hiked her shoulders and looked at Frank, who also shrugged. "I don't think so, but maybe. We didn't know much about the Bergen boy until this spring. We only called him this morning because we thought he might want to know."

"Why is it you wouldn't know about the man your daughter had been dating for a year?"

Arlene pursed her lips in disdain. "There were many things Michelle kept secret from us. She wasn't the type of daughter who confided in her parents. We knew precious little about her and only knew about the Bergen boy because he would come by for her after she moved in with us."

Streeter wondered how much they hadn't known about Michelle's pregnancy after all, considering her resourcefulness and strength as a thirteen-year-old.

"As I said, Michelle had only moved in this spring. She had lived on her own in a dingy little apartment in north Rapid City ever since she was eighteen."

"Seventeen," Frank corrected her.

"Like I said, she was very independent."

"Yet, she moved back in with you at age twenty-eight?" Streeter asked. "That seems strange, considering she had put herself through college, lived on her own all this time. Wasn't she about to graduate?"

"Michelle wasn't very predictable that way," explained the mother. "She never did anything we would expect. I'm not sure exactly why she moved into the basement. She told Frank and me that she moved in because her lease expired and rather than get a sublease over the summer, she opted to move in here so she had enough to go on to nursing school."

"Medical school," Bly mumbled.

Oblivious, Arlene continued, "That's what she said, although we can't help but think it had something to do with Charlene."

Frank drank his tea, shifting his gaze between both agents as he did.

"Your youngest daughter?" Streeter asked.

Frank nodded.

"Have you heard from her, by the way?" Streeter inquired.

Frank lowered his glass and looked down at his tea. "No."

"And you're not concerned?"

Arlene ignored the question. "Those girls were always at each other's throats. Girls are just too much to handle. One refuses to have anything to do with makeup and curlers and pretty clothes, the other uses everything she could to make herself look older."

"Like a floozy," Frank said, tightening his lips in reproach, suddenly embarrassed that he had spoken his thoughts aloud. His cheeks flushed red.

"Why did she run away from home Sunday night?" asked Streeter.

"Who, Charlene? We don't know exactly." Arlene looked to Frank for support. "It happens all the time."

"Both of your daughters turned up missing within a few hours of one another. Michelle was found murdered. Yet you don't seem concerned about Charlene being gone," Streeter stated, hoping for an explanation.

"You'd have to know these two," Arlene added, defensively, as if she were speaking to a child who had difficulties understanding.

Streeter shot a glance Bly's way and said, "That's why we're here. You know and we don't. Help us understand who these two young women are."

"We had little control. They were impossible to manage."

"And why do you say that?"

Neither spoke.

Bly prodded, "Skip school? Steal cars? Spit in your face?"

Arlene's lips pursed again and she refused to look at Bly. "Of course nothing like that."

Streeter urged, "Then what?"

"Well, Charlene runs away a lot. And Michelle . . . well—"

"Well what?" Streeter encouraged.

"Well, she is just so stubborn."

He could not get her to talk about the alleged pregnancy. "So you think Michelle moved back home after all these years to save money?"

"And to try to exert some influence on Charlene."

"And did it work? The influence?"

"It only drove Charlene away."

"So you're telling us that Charlene ran away more often when Michelle lived with you than when she lived apart from you?"

Arlene and Frank exchanged a look.

"Forgive me, but I'm trying to reconcile what you two consider girls who are difficult to manage. Because so far, from what I've heard from others, they both seemed to be good people in their teens and, for Michelle, into adulthood."

Frank harrumphed. Then silence.

Trying to spark some reaction to measure their response, Streeter asked bluntly, "Is it at all possible that Char would be capable of killing her sister?"

To Streeter's surprise, Frank answered, "It's possible."

Streeter wasn't sure which concerned him more, the fact that a father would think his daughter capable of murder or how little nonplussed he was by the question posed.

"No, it's not," his wife protested. "They were close. They loved each other, Agent Pierce."

Streeter was convinced that these two were completely in shock. Or clueless. No parent could possibly be this cool about discussing their murdered daughter and the likelihood that a second daughter might be the murderer.

"Char will return home on her own terms and in her own time. And as for Michelle . . ." Arlene's eyes filled with tears, her chubby cheeks turning blotchy red.

Streeter watched Frank pull out a well-used cotton handkerchief from his pocket and blow his nose, pretending he wasn't crying.

"Do you think Jens Bergen had anything to do with Michelle's disappearance or death?"

Arlene's brows netted and Frank frowned. They had obviously never thought about this, either.

"I don't know," was all Arlene could say.

"Can you think of anyone who would want to harm your daughter?" Streeter coaxed.

Impassively, they both shook their heads as if it had never occurred to them that anyone would have killed their daughter. Denial, Streeter thought. Frank and Arlene Freeburg couldn't handle the thought that either Michelle or Charlene could be murdered or dead, even though they had already identified one at the morgue.

"Tell us about your sons."

Frank, who had been stingy with his words about his daughters, barely took time for breaths between the bounties of praise he showered on his boys. The two proud parents shared every detail about Frankie Junior and Brian. The eldest had advanced by four promotions after enlisting in the Navy. Streeter's question about whether or not either son had ever been in trouble with the law or in a fight was answered with another long-winded session about how Brian had finished college and was the top real estate salesman of the month in July. They briefly mentioned Brian's children, their grandkids, but spent most of their time bragging about both sons' accomplishments. Arlene just watched while her husband did most of the talking, nodding in all the right places, contributing little else to the conversation.

As Streeter listened, a situation came to mind where he and Blackstone, another Marine Recon specialist, were in a hot zone. Blackstone froze, never having been pinned down by gunfire before. Despite the screaming and tugging Streeter did to get Blackstone to move, to seek cover, he remained fixed, like a statue. Streeter finally removed his tactical ballistics helmet and slammed it against Blackstone's helmet, jarring him from his fear. Both men scrambled to safety behind a chunk of ratty concrete left from an earlier explosion.

Knowing that time was of the essence in catching Michelle's killer, Streeter decided it was time to clock the Freeburgs with his helmet.

At the first natural break, Streeter asked, "Did you ever witness any trouble between your sons and your daughters?"

"Well, of course all kids scuffle," Arlene said dismissively.

"I'm talking about serious trouble between them."

The Freeburgs stared at one another, blank expressions whitewashing their already bland faces.

Arlene spoke for herself and her husband when she said, "We're not sure what you're asking, Agent Pierce."

"Did either of your sons ever give you reason to be concerned for your daughters' well-being?" Streeter asked as tactfully as he knew how. He was dancing all around the issue he really wanted to address—Michelle's pregnancy. And he was using these questions to decide whether her parents were ready for such a direct approach or whether they truly never knew at all about their daughter's condition in high school. At this point, his instincts told him to retreat and come at the subject from a different angle.

"Did my boys strike or swear at their sisters? Is that what you mean?" asked an indignant Arlene Freeburg.

Bly beat Streeter to the punch, slamming his own helmet to wake up the Freeburgs. "Did you ever suspect one or both of your sons of diddling on, experimenting with, or otherwise playing doctor on Michelle or Char?"

CHAPTER 17

I HAD DONE THE unthinkable.

I pulled up to the Freeburg house with good intentions, but when I saw two men through the window sitting in the living room with what must have been Michelle's parents, I decided to sneak around the neighbor's house through their backyard, slide along the side of the Freeburg house, and dive into the hedge that lined the front of the house, just under an open window.

What had I become?

I never even eavesdropped on my own brothers and sisters, and believe me, I had had plenty of opportunities to do so, considering we were packed like sardines in those tiny rooms. Even though I am no longer a practicing Catholic, I had the sudden urge to close my eyes and bow my head: "Bless me, Father, for I have sinned. It's been FOREVER since my last confession . . . and this time it's a biggy. I'm eavesdropping on total strangers."

My heart was pounding so hard I kept looking up to see if the people inside the house were all staring down at me, wondering what all the racket was about.

From what Jens had told me about Michelle having two brothers, I assumed the men were Frankie Jr. and Brian Freeburg.

I listened intently as I heard Mrs. Freeburg—unmistakably Michelle's mom, who Jens told me wore her blond hair in a beehive hairdo—say, "Did my boys strike or swear at their sisters? Is that what you mean?"

I heard one of the men ask, "Did your ever suspect one or both of your sons of diddling on, experimenting with, or otherwise playing doctor on Michelle or Char?"

That was hitting below the belt, I thought. These two men were certainly not Michelle's brothers. But I was thrilled that, whoever he was, he had asked the question so directly because then I wouldn't have to. After all, maybe it was a brother or the father who had ruined Michelle's life when she was thirteen. And these two must have followed the same supposition. I doubted it, but I needed to rule out as many presumptions as possible. It appeared I had arrived just in time. I closed my eyes a second time: "And Father, the bigger sin is that I'm so glad I decided eavesdropping would be a good idea."

A garbled and pissed voice sounded, "I don't know what kind of filthy gutter you crawled out of, but our boys wouldn't lay a hand on either of those girls. And if you want to know the truth, it was those girls who caused most of our problems."

I concluded that Garbled must be Michelle's dad.

"Problems?" I heard the third man ask. His voice sounded like he gargled with gasoline every morning. And lit a match when he did. I so badly wanted to check out what this man looked like. I turned and slithered my body up the brick wall like a slug. My eyes instantly landed on him. Tall, strong, rugged looks, shock of white hair, and buff. A hotty. What came instantly to mind was the line from the Disney song where the crooning princess is singing about a dream being a wish your heart makes. Oh my, this man was dreamy! Stunning, like the Greek Adonis.

Definitely not Agent Bob Shankley, the man I'd seen yesterday with Clint and Tommy. It took a lot to peel my eyes from Agent Adonis, but I managed and saw that Agent Blysdorf was the other man, for sure. Only today he had all his hair tucked up under a fedora. He was sitting nearest me, by the window across from Michelle's mother, whose hair looked like a fresh butter-colored swirl from a cotton candy machine.

"Trouble, more like," Michelle's dad answered.

"What do you mean by trouble?"

"Like Arlene mentioned to you earlier, one or the other of them was always sassing back to her or me. They were always doing whatever the hell they pleased. They didn't ever seem to mind any rules. Only wanted to bust them all."

"Kind of girls who needed a lot of discipline?" Agent Adonis asked. His tone had changed, as if to squelch Mr. Freeburg's anger and get him talking again.

Just then it dawned on me that I was no better than Roy the Peeping Tom. Only I was eavesdropping on federal agents. Holy crap! There must be a law against that. Surely I was not going to get out of this with an easy penance of three Our Fathers and two Hail Marys. More like three years in the pokey.

"That's putting it mildly," Michelle's dad replied, obviously calmed down and willing to participate in the conversation again.

But then Agent Blysdorf asked the granddaddy of them all. "Were you ever concerned for your daughters' safety when your husband was disciplining them, Mrs. Freeburg?"

"Now that's enough. You get your ass out of my house. Arlene, call Shank and tell him these assholes have gone too far," hollered Frank Freeburg.

I could hear the squeaking of chairs and the sound of a recliner folding back up with a fabric-muffled metallic thump, a scuttle of feet, and someone's heavy breathing. I desperately wanted to peek in the window but didn't dare. Instead, I tucked myself deeper in the hedge.

Then I heard Agent Adonis say in a commanding tone, "Mr. Freeburg, it's our job to ask the difficult questions. If you have nothing to hide, your wife should simply answer our questions. Put the phone down, Mrs. Freeburg."

I assumed the Shank the Freeburgs referred to was Agent Bob Shankley. I heard the phone being returned to the cradle and Michelle's mom say, "I was never concerned about Michelle and Char's safety as far as Frank is concerned. Or as far as Brian and Frankie Jr. were concerned. My husband didn't beat, rape, or abuse those girls. Ever. If anything, maybe he should have been heavier handed, because the good Lord knows nothing else worked."

"Heavy handed enough to bash your daughter's head in?" the feisty Agent Blysdorf asked.

"You don't have to answer any more questions, Arlene. Call Shank," Michelle's dad said.

"Not necessary. We're leaving now," Agent Adonis said.

I ducked deeper behind the hedge to make sure I wasn't seen. The two agents left. I heard their footfalls on the concrete and two car doors slam shut. I peeked up over the hedge and saw Agent Blysdorf behind the wheel. I couldn't see Agent Adonis with the sun's glare on the window, but I assumed he was in the passenger seat.

As they pulled away from the curb, I eased up to glance in the living room. The Freeburgs were gone. I could hear noises from the kitchen, and the sound of water running came from down the hall to what looked like the bathroom and bedrooms. As I quickly glanced around the living room before making my escape, my eyes landed on the various pictures arranged on the mantel above the gas fireplace. I saw a large photograph of one son in a military uniform and of another son dressed in a suit surrounded by little children. I saw an old wedding picture of the Freeburgs and a second picture of the happy couple in recent years.

There were also several candid photos in which Coach Vincent, my childhood softball coach, stood out. In the first he was draping his arms over the shoulders of the boys as they stood with their parents; in the second he was wrapping his arm around Michelle's waist; and in a third photo, he was standing beside a young girl with tousled black curls. The girl in the photo looked familiar, and I assumed it was Charlene. She looked enough like Michelle to confirm my suspicion that she had the baby and Michelle's parents raised Charlene as their own. But something else about the young girl looked familiar in a different way. From this distance, it was hard to tell. A thread of the story's fabric tugged in the back of my mind, but I wasn't quite able to get a grip on it.

I heard a toilet flush and ducked down from the window, sneaking along the hedge and popping out between the houses. As I was making my way back to Jens's truck, trespassing through strangers' yards a different way than I had come, I realized I needed to see Coach Vincent, hopefully before the federal agents got to him first. I was about to hop my last fence and break for the pickup truck when I heard the window slide open and a woman call, "Liv? Is that you?"

I turned, embarrassed, and said, "Hi, Mrs. McKinney."

The mother of my high school buddy Pam had not changed one bit in the past decade. But I couldn't believe she recognized me and wondered how long she'd had a bead on me.

"What are you doing in our backyard, dear?"

———

I had been afraid that my unexpected but necessary stop at Mrs. McKinney's house for a fresh baked brownie and a glass of milk was going to throw my timing off with Coach Vincent. But after I spilled the truth, Pam's mom let me off the hook. And she confirmed the idea that I shouldn't worry about Char, that she was always running away from time to time and that she would return home soon. Mrs. McKinney also promised not to tell the Freeburgs about me spying on them if I promised not to do it again. Ever.

I spotted him instantly when I came into the retro diner. Coach Vincent was sitting in one of the back booths, grinning and waving at me. He was shorter than I remembered, thinner. In his late forties or early fifties, he had a lot less hair than I recalled, and the blond was more ash gray, swept over his scalp in the same style he had worn when I was a teen. His baby blue eyes were no less penetrating than they used to be.

"Hi, Coach," I greeted him.

Coach rose to his feet and we embraced. "Liv, you're getting around better than what I expected."

His wide, friendly smile was disarmingly charming and as genuine as always, more handsome than I remembered.

"What were you expecting?"

"Have a seat," he said, motioning to the other side of the booth.

I slid in slowly and repeated, "No, really, Coach, what have you heard about me? Are you disappointed that I'm not on crutches?"

Coach Vincent laughed. "Oh Liv. You could always make me laugh. No, I'm glad you're ambulatory."

I wasn't trying to be funny. I really wanted to know what he'd heard. But before I could say so, he added, "I'm so sorry to hear about Michelle Freeburg. I knew your brother was dating her. How's he taking all this?"

I nodded. "He's pretty broken up about it. How'd you know they were dating?"

"Well, I saw her down at the courthouse about three weeks ago. She was excited about graduating and being accepted into medical school. She told me she was serious about the guy she was dating. Even talked marriage. But I didn't know it was Jens until a friend of mine told me yesterday. Bob Shankley. He's the agent working this case. Works for the FBI," he said.

The waitress interrupted us and said, "What can I get you, Chief?"

He ordered a slice of pie and a cup of coffee. I ordered the belly buster burger with a side of fries and a Diet Coke. The brownie just didn't satiate.

"Chief?" I asked, as the waitress scooted toward the kitchen. "I thought it was Mayor Vincent now."

He grinned. "Former chief of police. Old habits die hard, you know. Like you calling me Coach, right?"

Coach Vincent didn't look like a chief. Or a mayor. Or a local hero. He looked like a normal guy. He could have passed for a former track star in his youth, small and strong. Or maybe even a semiprofessional baseball player. But he didn't seem to be big enough, strong enough, stereotypically man enough to be a chief of police or mayor. I knew better than anyone that generalizations were just that, and there were exceptions to every rule. The size wasn't what made the person in the job, but for some reason, Coach Vincent had always been so kind, tender, that it was difficult for me to reconcile his manner with his job of either managing a police force or running a city. Although I had to admit, Ken Vincent had that one characteristic so many wanted and too few possessed from birth: likeability.

His easy smile revealed the signature gold-capped tooth that, rather than giving him the appearance of being shamelessly wealthy, made him appear fragile and human somehow.

"Thanks for meeting me on such short notice, Coach. My brother Jens asked me to help him find Char. I'm hoping you can help me."

Coach Vincent laughed. "Char is a free spirit. No telling where that girl might be."

"You don't seem surprised to hear she's missing."

"The FBI told me."

"Agent Shankley again?"

"Like I said, we're friends. Good friend of mine, actually," Coach Vincent said, sipping the coffee the waitress had just poured him. "I'm the one Shank called late yesterday afternoon to confirm Michelle's identity."

"But I thought the Freeburgs did that this morning?"

"Officially," he said. "I was the one who told Shank to let them sleep, to go over there this morning around four because Frank's shift at the post office is from six to two and they'd be up at four. No point in waking them up to deliver such horrible news."

"Incredible," I thought aloud. "I would have wanted to know immediately if I had been Michelle's parents. I wouldn't care about sleep or work schedules or anything if my daughter was found murdered."

"But that's you," he said, thanking the waitress as she laid the heap of fries and monster burger before me and a tiny slice of pie in front of Coach Vincent. I can see why he stayed so thin. "I've been doing this sort of thing for many years, Liv, and the one thing I've learned is patience. When death is involved, so are a myriad of emotions, personalities, reactions, and surprises. I have never been in a rush to deliver bad news; that's why I told Shank to wait."

My eagerness to learn what he knew about Michelle's teen pregnancy was shadowed by my raging hunger, and I could hardly open my mouth wide enough to take my first bite. I could feel the nourishment instantly, each succeeding bite coming slower than the one before. Wondering why I felt so famished, I realized it was almost four and I hadn't eaten since dinner the night before, Mom's awesome barley and pot roast. Oh, except for the couple of beers at Jens's house. Breakfast of champions. Oh, and a brownie at Mrs. McKinney's house. It was way past lunchtime, closer to dinner anyway. My mind was beginning to clear and my ears perked up to hear his story.

"So it's easier for the victim's family if you approach the situation with patience and calmness. It makes them feel that at least someone is in control in an otherwise out-of-control situation."

"Hmm," I grunted, stuffing a fistful of fries into my mouth as a chaser to my belly buster. Coach Vincent stared at me, unblinking, which made me painfully aware of the pig I was being. With cheeks full, I attempted a smile, slowed my feeding frenzy, and dabbed my mouth with the napkin from my lap. He returned the smile and picked up his fork to take a bite of his pie.

I swallowed. "How did you become such close friends with the Freeburgs, Coach?"

He touched the corners of his mouth with a napkin. I'd never noticed how slender his fingers were and how well manicured he kept his nails. I did find his cologne familiar and still a bit overpowering, though, just like the olden days.

"That's a long story," he said, smoothing the lines of his light tan suit coat.

"I have time if you do," I said, taking another bite of what was left of my burger.

"I would like to help you, but I'm supposed to meet more federal agents in a half hour. I want to help those guys any way I possibly can in this murder investigation. Michelle meant the world to me."

Were those actually tears that were pooling in his baby blue eyes, I wondered?

Jens's words drifted to my mind about Michelle refusing to tell him about the man she saw with Char, a man in his forties or fifties, someone everyone knew and trusted.

Someone like Coach Vincent.

CHAPTER 18

AS QUICKLY AS THE thought came to mind that Coach Vincent might have been the man responsible for preying on Charlene's innocence, I dismissed the idea. But not entirely. Not any more than I had dismissed the idea that maybe Clint White—who was also the right age and somewhat known around town—had something to do with Michelle's death. Jens certainly knew Mayor Ken Vincent and fellow employee Clint White, but the idea of either one of them being such a heinous predator seemed so foreign to me.

I had to remind myself that everyone was a suspect. Everyone, that is, except Jens.

I cleared my throat. "That's exactly what I wanted to know. Why did she mean the world to you?"

He studied his coffee cup, his slight hands wrapped around the warm ceramic. "I was still coaching the junior league, twelve- and thirteen-year-olds."

"I remember. You were talking about moving up with us to senior ball, but you decided to stay, right?"

Coach nodded. "My daughter and Michelle were in the same class, and she had come to tryouts at Brittany's encouragement. Michelle was a little reluctant because she had never played softball before. Several had come up from little league, so we coaches had already gotten a good look at most of the girls' playing abilities."

I was familiar with Coach Vincent's dedication to the sport and to excellence. He had an eye for talent.

"I remember Michelle very well because she looked so scared, nervous, yet so intent on proving, as an unknown, what she could do." He laughed, and his eyes glazed over with far-off thoughts. "I swear the first ball she swung at was still rising when it cleared the left center field fence."

Eating another bite of pie, he waved off the waitress from refilling his coffee. "Thanks, but I need to get going soon. I'll take the check."

The waitress smiled, "Okay, Chief."

I knew I'd better hurry up or I was going to lose my opportunity.

Coach Vincent added, "I was lucky enough to be the all-star coach for both of her years in that league and Michelle was chosen every year. She played third base."

"So that's how you knew Michelle?"

"That, and Brittany became close friends with her," he said, his brows knitting. "My daughter wasn't really very skilled at the game, but she thought she was. At first, Brittany thought I was favoring Michelle over the other girls, which I suppose I was. I sensed she needed the extra attention."

"How so?" I asked, intercepting the check from the waitress and handing her a twenty.

Coach's light blond eyebrows buckled. He sipped his coffee before answering. "I can't put my finger on it, really. All teenage girls are difficult. I've had three, Brittany being my oldest. But Michelle changed from the little girl I saw drive the ball out of the park when she was twelve. By the end of her second year, at thirteen, she was . . . troubled."

"Troubled? In what way?"

"I've been around kids all my adult life, particularly around kids who come from challenging backgrounds, broken homes, abusive relatives. I went to college to pursue a counseling degree, focused on children, but I dropped out halfway through my junior year when my dad died. My family had a ranch east of town here. As the oldest son I had no time for luxuries like finishing college." Coach Vincent smiled almost apologetically at me.

"Sorry, I kind of got lost in my thoughts. Forgot for a minute that you were one of the kids I relied on to help with some of these at-risk kids. You've seen firsthand how troubled some of them were. You were one of the lucky ones. Amazing parents. Not the least bit troubled, but you understand."

I nodded. "I remember a few of them, how you helped them. Remember Rhonda? You used to bring her food and sneak it into her backpack when you thought none of us was looking."

The former coach blushed. "She needed to eat. Anyway, from what I learned and from what I've experienced, Michelle was troubled. I tried to study her home life from a distance to see if I could detect any abuse or molestation or something. Eventually, I got to know the whole family."

Coach Vincent's suspicions that Michelle was troubled somehow lined up with the timing of Roy's story about Michelle getting pregnant and with what Michelle confirmed to Jens.

"Classic signs. Bright, energetic, full of life one minute, withdrawn, quiet, introverted the next. She was covered in so many emotional layers that it would take years and the best experts to peel away all those protective layers and get to the core of the problem."

"Were you successful?"

"In peeling away the layers?"

I nodded.

"Only a little, I think. She wasn't much for talking if others were around, yet she almost refused to be alone with me. Internal struggle there, too."

"When was that, Coach? That she changed?" I urged. I saw him glance at his watch. I would have to speed this up. "Look, my brother said she was raped when she was thirteen. Does that fit?"

Coach squeezed his eyes shut. "It fits. That's what I was afraid of. My guess about Michelle Freeburg was that someone molested her in some fashion, probably pretty significantly, but as I got to know the Freeburgs, I knew it wasn't one of her family members."

"Jens said she got pregnant," I added, watching as his body stiffened with the news.

Coach Vincent dropped his head in his hands. "Oh, no. I didn't know that. When?"

"He said Michelle told him she was raped when she was thirteen, the guy continued his abuse for a year until she got pregnant. So that would have been when she was fourteen."

"But she played all seven years, twelve through eighteen, on my city league teams, Liv. I didn't see her pregnant. Although, I have to admit, I didn't see much of her or her family during the winter months. When did your brother say she got pregnant?"

"I thought he said when she was fourteen, a freshman in high school," I answered. Remembering what Roy Barker had told me, I added, "Probably got pregnant by my guess sometime in late May or early June. Likely had a late-term abortion sometime between November and January or carried the baby full term to February sometime."

"When she was fourteen, you say?"

I nodded.

"I just don't remember her being pregnant then. Let me see. Was that the year before Charlene was born?"

"Same year, by my calculations," I answered, not filling in the blanks with my assumptions.

His eyes widened. He stared at me, reaching the same conclusion I had.

"Holy manhole! What a coincidence."

"Isn't it?" I raised my eyebrows and sipped on my soda, letting him do the math and his own speculation. "Would she have had an abortion?"

Coach shook his head. "No way. Not Michelle. She was adamantly against abortion. Loved life. Chose life. She helped me counsel kids from time to time to help them get through suicidal thoughts. She was amazingly strong, Liv."

"My brother said that Michelle told him the pregnancy was a false alarm. He also thought she was lying about that. And she told him that it emboldened her to stand up to the guy. What people think they might do in certain circumstances is not always the same as when they are actually tested."

He shook his head. "So, so sad. My memory tells me she was helping other girls even when she was on the junior league team, twelve- to thirteen-year-olds. She must have been doing that while dealing with some very scary personal issues." He rubbed his eyebrows, deep in thought.

"Do you remember seeing Mrs. Freeburg pregnant?" I prodded.

His crimson face told it all. "I'm not so good recognizing whether a woman is pregnant or just a bit plump."

Arlene Freeburg is as wide as she is tall. I understood his embarrassment and his inability to decipher the difference if she looked anything fifteen years ago like the way she does now.

He suddenly added, "Have you met the Freeburgs?"

"Not exactly. Why?"

"Well, if you had, you'd understand when I describe them as . . . well, let's just say I'm not quite sure where Michelle's brains and ambition came from."

"Jens mentioned that Arlene and Frank were somewhat brain dead."

"Not the sharpest knives in the drawer. But also, not the most in tune with reality, either," Coach said. "Arlene works hard at appearing lovely. And Frank, well . . . Frank is Frank. They both loved their kids dearly in their own way. But neither one was equipped to deal with Michelle's issues, if you understand what I'm saying."

He glanced at his watch again. "I need to leave in about five minutes, Liv. But let me ask you this: Did Michelle ever tell your brother who did this to her?"

Deep concern etched his face. And it gave me pause; was he afraid that his name had been mentioned?

I shook my head. "I was hoping you would know. She told Jens it was an authority figure. Someone everyone probably knew. Wouldn't tell my brother because she said he knew the guy and was afraid of what Jens would do to him. She swore it wasn't her father or brothers, though, just like you said."

Coach Vincent let out a long breath.

He cradled his head in his hands. He had a sunken, lost look in his eyes. For the first time, I thought his pain of losing Michelle was genuine.

"I could have helped her work through that fear."

"How could you have known?" I comforted him. "The last thing she said Sunday night to Jens was that she had to 'end this, once and for all.' What do you think she might have meant by that?"

He straightened in his chair and cleared his throat. "Strikes me that she was finally ready to face her demon," he replied without pause. "What little I knew about her then, she was extremely responsible, bright, ambitious. At thirteen, I suspect she probably thought the grown-up way to handle her situation was to keep quiet, forget about it. Shove all those feelings down deep. Maybe too traumatized by the whole event, she blocked out the entire moment from her mind as if it never happened. Until she was ready to face that demon."

"Until Sunday," I concluded.

Coach Vincent rubbed his eyes, and when he opened them, his age was more apparent than ever. "My wife fusses at me all the time, Liv, because I tend to 'adopt' kids like Michelle all over town, like they were stray animals needing shelter. I adopted Michelle. She needed my help. And I failed her."

"It sounds to me like Michelle relied on you when she couldn't rely on her parents," I said with a smile. "I wouldn't call that failing her."

He smiled softly. "Well, I felt so damned inadequate as protection. Whatever the storm was, it seemed to have had hurricane force."

"You were a cop. You were around. She was safe when you were around. The person who traumatized her was still around her, though," I concluded.

Coach Vincent stared at me, his forehead wrinkling slightly with his thoughts. "Are you a budding psychologist?" Now it was my turn to blush. He touched my hand. "Among all your other talents, that might be one of your strongest. And by the way, your brother made Michelle the happiest she'd been in a very long time."

"Thank you for saying that. I will definitely share that with Jens. He needs the assurance. Tell me, do you think Michelle could be vindictive? Facing her demon by punishing whoever did this to her? Was that what she meant Sunday night by ending this once and for all?"

"No, never," he said, shaking his head adamantly. "She wasn't like that."

"And what about Charlene? Why would she go missing?"

"Oh, that's Char," he said, batting the air like the idea was crazy. "She's very melodramatic. Does this all the time. Disappears for a few days just to make everyone worry, then shows up after hiding at a friend's house."

"But Michelle is dead. You're not worried that Char might be dead, too?" I asked, finding this belief universal with those who knew the allegedly rebellious teenager.

"Have you ever met Char?"

I shook my head.

The former coach opened his wallet and fished for a picture. "I brought this for the agents. She would have you believe she's a wild child, but despite her facade, which she has carefully crafted to annoy, she is just a child inside. She wants to give the world the impression she is an invincible, sexual woman rather than the awkward, innocent fourteen-year-old she actually is."

He slid a picture of himself with Char and Michelle, the first picture I'd seen of Char other than my peek at one from her childhood through the Freeburg's window. I recognized the young Michelle, her eyes haunting, and Coach Vincent with his easy smile.

An icy chill skipped along my spine as I stared at the girl with the black curls, a girl who looked a bit too much like the one I saw teetering on high heels Monday wearing a red bikini. I gasped and brought the picture closer, trying to determine if the girls were one in the same.

Coach Vincent touched my wrist. "Liv? What?"

I swallowed hard and laid the photograph on the table between us. "Nothing. It's just hard for me to accept that Michelle is gone. Nice picture. Can I keep it?"

Shaking his head as he slid the photo back in his wallet, he answered wearily, "No, sorry. The agents asked me to bring any photos I might have."

"One more thing before you go," I said, clearing my mind of the image of the girl with Noodles. "How would I go about finding Char? Who are the friends that help her hide?"

Coach Vincent slid out of the booth and smoothed out his suit jacket. "If I were you, I'd start with all the girls on her volleyball team. They've been working together the entire summer so they can be ready for junior varsity."

Another piece fell into place. A common link. "As freshmen in high school? On Mr. Schilling's team?"

CHAPTER 19

"COME ON IN," SAID the man with a smile as wide and perfect as Liv's. Streeter instantly recognized the family resemblance.

After introductions, Jens offered, "Do you gentlemen need anything to drink? Water, pop? Gosh, it's almost five. Would you rather have a beer?"

Bly waved his hands. Streeter said, "Thanks, we're good."

Jens offered them a seat in his living room. "Agent Shankley said he'd be sending someone over today to talk with me. Told me not to go anywhere, but I went up to my mom's this morning on the way back from the morgue and picked up my sister."

"Your sister? Is she here?" Streeter said a bit too eagerly, wondering if the sister was Liv.

"No, she's on the loose with my truck. Probably because she would be concerned I'd take off and miss you guys. Agent Shankley told me that I was under suspicion and not to do anything stupid." Jens's grin was sad. "So here I am, not doing anything stupid."

"All day?" Bly said, shaking his head and cutting his eyes toward Streeter.

Streeter detected resentment behind Jens's solemn face. "I'm sorry about that. We didn't know. And let me ease your mind. You are not our primary suspect." Streeter glanced at Bly, who was arching an eyebrow. "But we do have to ask you some questions, to be thorough."

"I understand," Jens said, staring at his folded hands. "Everyone's a suspect."

Streeter studied the room of the house, which was old and small, but smelled fresh and breezy. The space was clean, neat, not the least bit pretentious for a congressman's son. Humble. Jens's resemblance to Liv, the easy smile, the strong, lean body, and the mischievous eyes, made it difficult for Streeter to think of him as a potential suspect, despite Roy Barker's accusation. Knowing his objectivity had, on occasion, faltered when his personal life was involved, Streeter had to concede that Jens Bergen was still a suspect.

"Starting with Sunday evening, tell us from your perspective what you know," Streeter began.

Jens told the agents what happened at Barker's Market, which matched up with the story Roy Barker had told them earlier plus the information Roy called to tell Bly about as an afterthought. Jens also described his time at the morgue with the Freeburgs and Agent Bob Shankley earlier that morning. He volunteered that, in their investigation, they would learn he was at the Nemo General Store on Monday morning from five until seven, supervising a small concrete pour, and no, it was not typical for the manager of the ready mix division to perform such a task, but because they were so busy, the dispatch supervisor requested his help, which he did from time to time.

As Jens told his story, Streeter not only listened, he watched. He was looking for telltale signs of tension and deceit, nervousness and omission. His instincts were usually correct. And his instincts told him that Jens as murderer was only a remote possibility.

Streeter flashed back to Liv's home near Fort Collins, Colorado, the one he and Lisa Henry converted to a makeshift headquarters during the De Milo murder case. He couldn't shake the image of the rocks that Liv had collected and neatly placed by the photo of her family atop her dresser, racking his brain to recall which rock represented Jens. Jens Bergen appeared to be straightforward, honest, and genuinely kindhearted, just like his parents. He was even a bit soft-spoken, which surprised Streeter, given Jens's imposing stature. Streeter would later convince himself that his assessment of Jens had nothing to do with his opinion of the Bergens in general, or Liv in particular. He could certainly be objective, impartial. No problem.

Jens was saying in a voice as soothing as warm milk on an icy evening, "She told her parents she wanted to move back in with them because her lease expired and to save money for college, but that wasn't the whole story."

"She didn't plan to go on to medical school?" Bly asked.

"No," Jens said, shaking his head a little and pushing his long, lean fingers through his short brown hair. "I mean, yes and no. Michelle was about to complete her degree in premed. But she had lived like a church mouse and saved up every extra penny she earned since she moved out of the house her senior year. She had paid off nearly all her student loans as well as saved up enough money to get started at medical school." His smile seemed empty and waned as quickly as it had appeared. "She had more money than most of us. Michelle got by on very little, rarely pampered herself. She saved and invested with a purpose. She was going to make a difference."

"Ambitious," Streeter concluded, watching as Jens's chest filled with pride.

"She is," Jens said, sporting a proud smile, which quickly dissolved into a sorrowful frown. "Was."

Streeter hadn't seen the pain in Jens's eyes until that moment when he lifted his chin from his chest.

Jens added, "I just can't get used to the fact that she's gone."

"It isn't easy, Jens. I know. My wife was murdered," Streeter said, offering him a nod of reassurance. Bly rubbernecked at the comment and Streeter realized that this was the first time he had ever said the words aloud. He cleared his throat and added, "Would you consider Michelle responsible?"

"Very responsible and very remarkable," he answered, regaining his wide-eyed optimism. His eyes were not the unusual sea green of Liv's, but blue, and brilliant nonetheless. "She is much older than her years. Very mature. Almost hauntingly so. She cares so much about others. Sorry, cared."

Streeter knew how difficult it could be for a loved one to refer to the deceased in any other way but present tense. A rather convincing sign that the person had nothing to do with the death.

"Did she ever go out partying on a whim, just to let her hair down?" Bly asked gingerly.

Jens furrowed his brow. "Not at all. She never indulges herself that way. She's too practical. The only impetuous act I know of that Michelle ever committed was when she left home before she graduated. She had not told me as much, but hinted that her parents were not at all pleased with her decision to move out on her own. She was only seventeen at the time."

"Why did she move out?"

"She said she and her mom were arguing a lot. Char was just three, and Michelle felt she had to give her mom space."

"Interesting. Most seventeen-year-olds want space for themselves, not to give space to others," Streeter said. "Then why did she move back in with them after being on her own for nearly a decade?"

"She was serious about saving money and she was worried about Char. Her sister is fourteen going on twenty-one, which bothered Michelle a lot. Char occasionally spent the night at her older sister's apartment, sometimes the whole weekend. Classic teenager, yes. But you've met the Freeburgs—I can't say that I blamed Char. Those people are totally vacant. Michelle's apartment a safe haven from her parents. For Char, too, which I never quite understood."

"What didn't you understand?" Streeter pressed.

Jens glanced warily at him before explaining, "Why would Michelle ever move back home to help Char, when Char had used Michelle's apartment as a getaway? I don't know. I tried to talk to Michelle about her obsession with Char, but she was relentless in trying to protect her."

"Would you say she was overly protective of Char?" Streeter urged.

Jens became studious, staring at his hands and flicking at one of his fingernails. He hummed in a low, monotonous note as he thought. Streeter suspected Jens wasn't so much searching his mind for possibilities as searching his heart for the right decision about sharing with him and Bly what he knew.

"I'd say she was," he finally answered.

"You mentioned they would argue," Streeter said, deciding to give Jens more time to volunteer whatever information he was withholding. "Would Char's visits have been upsetting enough to Michelle that she would behave irrationally herself?"

"What do you mean?"

"Would she scream, yell, throw things, fight with her sister—slap, pull hair, cuss, that sort of thing?" Bly asked.

Jens's face collapsed into repulsion. "No, not at all. Michelle wasn't at all like that. She would never fight. She was more of a 'flight' type person when it came to conflict."

"Have you ever seen Michelle react violently?" Streeter asked.

"Never," Jens said quickly. "Even when she and Char would argue, Michelle was always calm, cool, totally in control of her emotions. The only time I'd ever see her get worked up was against an injustice done to someone. She wouldn't hurt a fly. When I said she'd argue with Char, it was more like debating, discussing, explaining another viewpoint. She would never have been physical with Char. The closest I ever saw her come to losing control of her temper was Sunday night."

"What was that about?" Streeter asked.

"It was about a guy Char was dating, but again, Michelle didn't share much with me."

"What did she tell you?"

Jens recounted, "Michelle was angry about Char dating an older guy. Someone their parents didn't know about and wouldn't approve of."

"Was it common for Char or Michelle to argue with their parents?" Streeter asked, still trying to figure out how the Freeburgs concluded their girls were "trouble" or "problems."

"I'd say Michelle often disagreed with them, but was respectful. Frank and Arlene saw Michelle's disagreement with them as synonymous with being a difficult child. Michelle was just honest about her opinions. When Char disagreed, she was not respectful about it. Not in the least."

"I sense you don't like Char all that much," Streeter pressed.

"It's not that. And I don't blame her for reacting the way she does with the Freeburgs, considering their total disconnection from reality. From her. But sometimes she can be a bit . . . spoiled. And she has so much more going for her than to grow up to be like her parents," Jens said unapologetically.

"So, Michelle would argue with Char about being spoiled?"

"No, she would try to convince Char to be more respectful to her parents. They would argue about Char's willful independence leading her too far into wild ways with her friends, Michelle trying to teach Char the difference."

"What kind of wild and who were the friends she'd spend time with? Do you have names?"

Jens shook his head. "I don't know names. But it would be easy to figure out. They all play volleyball together. Char would brag about them trying marijuana for the first time, cigarettes, beer. She was only twelve when she started hanging with the wrong crowd, feeling the peer pressure."

"Normally, school sports teams are considered the good crowd," Streeter observed.

"True, but in this case, I think a few bad apples spoiled the whole bunch. Michelle tried to keep her cool about it but warned Char about the trouble she could bring on if she wasn't more careful. Michelle told me she was concerned that her parents couldn't . . . or wouldn't handle Char. I think those were the words she chose."

"What do you think she meant by 'wouldn't'?"

Jens wilted against the couch, his long lean legs bent at a prefect right angle with his feet planted firmly on the carpet beneath him. To Streeter, Jens resembled JFK Jr. only taller and with a much handsomer face, if that were possible.

He buckled his brow and answered, "I guess I really can't say, other than to couple my observations with speculation from the things she told me about her parents. Frank and Arlene adore their sons. Odd, considering their total disregard—my observation, not Michelle's—for their daughters. But not so odd when you consider that Arlene will do anything and everything to please Frank. And Frank—again my opinion—feels threatened by strong women." He chuckled. "I can't even imagine either of those women living their lives conceding to Frank's every whim like Arlene does. Maybe it's a generational thing. I wouldn't know, since my parents were nothing like them. Brian and Frankie Jr. can do no wrong. But when it comes to the daughters, they give up before anything is started. I've only met Brian and Frank Jr. a couple of times, always around their parents. They're nice men. Just a bit too eager to please ol' mom and dad."

Bly's eyebrows arched. Streeter suppressed a grin.

Jens's cheeks flushed. "Okay, not that being eager to please parents is a bad thing. I'm just overly protective of Michelle." His bright eyes dimmed and he lowered them toward the carpet.

"How so?" Streeter encouraged him to continue.

"I remember one family barbecue this spring when I first met them. Michelle and I were out back by the grill where Frank, Arlene, and Brian were sitting. Frankie Jr. had excused himself to go to the bathroom. A little while later Michelle said she was going to the car to get some sunglasses, and when she returned, Frankie Jr. was with her, looking guilty as hell. So plain to me, a complete stranger, I thought the whole family would be asking what had happened. They didn't. I could tell Michelle wasn't happy. Arlene asked them if they'd seen Char. Frankie Jr. said he hadn't. Michelle said she had seen her out front. Arlene went out to the front porch and found Char drinking a beer and blamed Michelle for it."

"Had she given it to her?"

"No, Frankie Jr. had, along with some weed he'd been smoking. Michelle jumped on both of them, but mostly Bubba—that's what she called her oldest brother—for being a bad influence on his baby sister. Arlene went to her room crying, and when Frank came back from checking on her, he asked us to leave. Michelle and me. Apparently, her mom thought Michelle was responsible for Char's behavior. Frankie Jr. flashed us an apologetic smile when we left, offering no explanation or defense for Michelle. After all, how could he be culpable? He was their shining star. Their precious son, the naval hero. The good boy."

"Sounds like there's some serious sibling rivalry going on in that family," Bly concluded, easing back in his chair.

"Not really," Jens said. "Oddly, that was right after Michelle had decided to move in with them. Michelle thought her dad had asked her to leave the house, but while she was downstairs packing up her things, he came down and told her that she should just get out of the house for a couple of hours until her mother calmed down. I don't know why Michelle put herself through all that. I guess for Char's sake. She was hoping to get her straightened out. So I don't know if I would call it sibling rivalry."

"At least not on Michelle's part?" Streeter asked.

"Where the rest of the family was concerned, there was always some tension when it came to Michelle and Char. I can kind of see Char's side of things a little bit. It was like she had two mothers and three fathers, being as young as she was."

"You think that's why she has a tendency to run away?"

"Michelle wouldn't say why Char ran away this time, but I'd guess it's for the same reason she always runs away. Michelle believed it was her fault on Sunday night. All she said was that she and Char had a big falling out over one of Char's boyfriends."

"Were you there?" Streeter asked.

"No," Jens said, shaking his head. "But keep in mind, Char's always doing this, running away from time to time. She's never gone for more than a few days."

"So the argument between Char and Michelle was Sunday night?"

"Yes. Between eight and ten."

"What did this boyfriend do or not do that bothered Michelle so much?"

"Michelle said she followed them when Char took off with the guy. He pulled up to a drive-through liquor store, bought beer, then drove up to Dinosaur Hill—kind of the local make-out spot. If that didn't set her off, you could imagine how cool Michelle was. What really got under her skin was that this guy was old, in his forties or fifties, and Michelle knew him."

"Who was he?" Streeter asked.

"She wouldn't say. Said he's known around here and was afraid of what I might do. I told my sister to ask Char. She'd know who."

"Your sister? What does she have to do with this?"

Streeter's expression must have signaled something because Jens's eyes visibly shifted into a deeper sadness. "Oh no. I asked her to find Char for me, so I could know what happened to Michelle that night. I've put Liv in some kind of danger, haven't I?"

Streeter's stomach fluttered at the mention of Liv's name. So she was the sister staying with Jens.

Jens buried his face in his hands, preventing the agents from either confirming or alleviating his concern. After a minute, he lifted his head and added, "On the surface, Michelle appears to be a very serious person. Just the opposite of Char, who is fun-loving, always laughing and flirting." Jens's eyes narrowed as he spoke, the contrast he'd drawn between the two sisters poignant to Streeter. "But it was really just an act, sort of. Michelle had a tough exterior, a shell, but once you got to know her, she was rather tender. Maybe even too tender."

Jens excused himself from the room when Bly's cell phone buzzed.

"It's Shank," Bly said, stepping out the front door onto the tiny porch.

Streeter turned on his cell and checked a text message from Jack Linwood, then waited for Bly to end his call and for Jens to return. He scanned the room again quickly, absorbing every detail. Jens lived the way Streeter expected a man from a very wealthy family to live, despite his age and occupation. He had surrounded himself with solidly good furniture and expensive art but not too much of it and not too venturesome. Surprisingly hospitable for a bachelor's hangout, the house had huge windows and generous proportions. Streeter, browsing the living room's contents, could tell that the sound equipment was outstanding, and towers of CDs, classics mostly, proved that Jens enjoyed it. Brahms, Rachmaninoff, Chopin, Tchaikovsky, nothing radical. If he didn't fit the miner stereotype, that just showed what stereotypes are worth.

Bly snapped the cell phone shut as he stepped back through the door, chuckling. "Haven't heard him this angry before. Said he just got done talking with the Freeburgs. And Roy Barker. Said if we interview one more person without his permission, he'll personally fire me and force you into early retirement."

"Really," Streeter said, amused. "We must have hit a nerve."

"Said if we don't get our asses up to the Sturgis Rally and find our primary suspect, he'll reassign the case."

"Pretty upset, then?"

"Livid."

"Hmm," Streeter said, settling back in his easy chair to wait for Jens. "Imagine how he'd feel if he knew we were here. I could make Shank happy and tell him the analysis from the Investigative Control Operation

in Denver is complete on the FTW pin. It's definitely Mully's. But we better do as Shank says and get up to Sturgis, huh, partner?"

Bly grinned.

When he returned, Jens appeared refreshed, as if he had splashed cold
water on his face. "Did you get your business taken care of?"

Bly nodded and tucked the cell phone in his pocket.

Jens sat back down and said, "Michelle's gone. It really hasn't sunk in
yet. And I'm not really sure if I want it to."

Streeter said, "That's okay, Jens. We'll wrap this up. But before we go,
we need to know what it is that you're so reluctant to tell us about Michelle.
Might it have something to do with teen pregnancy?"

Jens's eyes widened. "How did you—"

Suddenly the front door flew open and Liv Bergen marched into the
room as if ready for a fight. She pulled up short, however, when she saw
the two FBI agents, and her eyes settled on Streeter Pierce. He thought
he detected a faint smile tug on the set line of her mouth when she said,
"Oh, it's you."

CHAPTER 20

BEFORE THEY COULD INTRODUCE themselves, I decided to give them a piece of my mind. "What in God's name are you doing here interviewing my brother without his lawyer present?"

Both men gaped.

I took advantage of the silence. "Did they Mirandize you, Jens? Did they?"

He gaped as well. I took that to mean they hadn't. "Jens ought to sue you two for not reading him his rights and not allowing him to make a phone call."

"You watch too much television," Agent Blysdorf deadpanned.

"I do not," I said, only then noticing Jens had come to my side and put an arm around me. I shrugged it off and turned to him. "Jens, please. I beg you. Don't talk to these men. They're only trying to hurt you. They're trying to get you to incriminate yourself."

"Listen," Agent Adonis said, his voice rough and tender all at the same time. "We appreciate your help and everything you've done so far. But we're not here to hurt your brother. We're trying to help him."

"Right," I said, trying not to get lost in those steely-blue eyes of his that were pinning me into submission. I hated him for that and hated myself even more for allowing me to lose focus. "That's why he was told not to go anywhere because he was a suspect."

Agent Adonis held his hands up in surrender. "Okay, I admit we didn't handle that as well as we should have this morning, but I—"

"But nothing. Get out!" I said pointing to the door.

"Boots, stop," Jens said.

"Out!" I shouted, treating the two agents like dogs.

"Listen, Liv," Agent Adonis started.

I walked over to the door and held it open. "Until my brother has an attorney present, he doesn't need to talk with you. Got that?"

Then I realized Agent Adonis had called me Liv. I wondered how he knew my name, knew who I was. Now I wished I hadn't been so hasty to kick him out. Agent Blysdorf exited and said nothing to me. As Agent Adonis passed by me, I thought I smelled Old Spice, yet it smelled amazingly better on his skin than on any other man I'd known to use it. I refused to look at him as he stopped right next to me.

"Liv, stay out of this one. We're talking about some dangerous people here, and we don't want you getting hurt again," he said in a low, concerned tone, slipping what I could feel was his business card into my hand.

Then he was gone.

On wobbly legs, I made my way back to the couch, trying to gather the boomerang of random thoughts that were ricocheting in my skull. I stuffed his card in the back pocket of my jeans before tossing myself down on the cushions.

How did he know my name? What did he know about me getting hurt again? Did he know about the broken nose? The black eyes? The scraped up knees and hands from the scuffle on the highwall? Did he know about my brush with death from DeMilo's injecting me with heroin? Oh, no. What had I done?

Jens sulked. "You were wrong to do that."

I said nothing. The sinking feeling in my gut said I had been very wrong. I tried to dismiss everything except my thoughts on how much to tell Jens about what I had learned from my research and what I suspected. I was so upset when Coach Vincent showed me the picture of Char, which looked so much like the girl I'd seen at Sturgis, I immediately went to the library to find more information. My grief, fear, and anger, not only because Michelle was dead but possibly that her little sister was, too, had seriously clouded my judgment.

"I'm sorry, Jens." My voice was so small I'm not even sure he heard me.

He was punching in numbers on his cell. "Jason? Jens. I need your help."

I watched as he walked out the door onto his front lawn. At least he was calling an attorney. I saw him fish something out of his pocket and make another call. Within minutes, a flashy silver sports car pulled up to the curb, Jason Stone behind the wheel waving at Jens. Closing the cell phone, Jens said something to Jason and headed back into the house.

"Where are you going?" I asked, knowing the answer before he said it.

"I'm meeting the agents you just kicked out of here."

"I'm sorry, Jens," I repeated. "I was only trying to protect you."

"I know," he said, giving me a crooked smile. "Thanks. I know what I need to do now. They're right. They're trying to help me, not hurt me, and I need to tell them everything I know. We're meeting them at Jason's office down the street."

"Can I come?"

His grin widened. "Hell, no."

I grinned back. "Was that them you were calling?"

"Yep. See you later. I need to get this over with. Wish me luck."

"Luck," I called after him as he headed down his walkway. I watched through the open doorway as he folded himself up into Jason's sporty car and sped off.

I was so mad at myself I pushed myself off the couch and started pacing. After wearing out a small portion of Jens's carpet, I decided it was more urgent than ever that I get to work on finding Char.

While I was at the library before my little temper tantrum with the federal agents, I had found a photo in the Rapid City Journal archives of Char spiking a ball in a game late last fall. The volleyball net somewhat obscured her face, but I printed off several copies nevertheless. I had spent the rest of my time at the library searching for articles about the other Central High School freshmen and junior varsity volleyball team members, which was fruitful because I now had several names to check out. I had rushed home to make sure I didn't miss Jens being interrogated by the agents, but in hindsight, I wish I had checked out the volleyball players instead.

I glanced at the clock. Ten minutes past five.

I went outside and retrieved my stack of notes from Jens's truck, bumped the door shut with a swing of my hip, and made sure the front door was bolted shut.

When I dropped my stack on the kitchen table, I thought I heard some scuffling noises from the direction of Jens's bedroom and made my way down the hall.

"Jens?" I called, approaching his closed door. It dawned on me that this couldn't be Jens because I just saw him leave and certainly I would have noticed if he had come back for something. Then it further dawned on me that the only weapon in the house was on the other side of this door.

I put my ear against the door, held my breath, and heard nothing. So I turned the knob and cracked the door open, expecting to find his room empty. Instead, I saw the backside of a man crawling up onto the window-sill and crouching in the open window, an intruder who must have heard me coming.

"Hey!" I shouted.

The man sprang from the windowsill and cleared the bushes next to the house. I sprinted to the window and saw him running down the street. He never showed his face, but I recognized the clothes, the wavy blond hair, and the unique muscle-bound body type. There was no doubt in my mind it was Roy Barker.

My heart was racing, and I sat on the edge of Jens's bed to catch my breath.

My first thought was to wonder what Roy was doing in Jens's house. I looked around the room, stupidly assuming it would somehow reveal to me what had changed in it or what was missing. I wondered if Roy had set a booby trap of some sort for Jens. Then I thought of Agent Blysdorf's comment about my watching too many crime shows on TV and concluded I was being ridiculous.

Unfortunately, the very next second the image of Peter Sellers tip-toeing around his own apartment leaped into my mind. The scene in an old movie where Inspector Clouseau moves stealthily through each room saying, "Cato. I know you're in here somewhere. Where are you, Cato?" But the screwy image made me think that maybe I was on to something. Maybe Roy had been eavesdropping on my brother and the federal agents just as I had done earlier with the Freeburgs.

Worried that Roy's intention was to hurt Jens somehow, I checked to make sure Jens's loaded gun was still where he always kept it and that his secret stash of money was untouched. Everything seemed in order, although I didn't recall ever seeing the book on the nightstand before. It was an old mystery classic, *Nightmare in Pink*, considered one of the best one hundred mysteries of all time. I flipped through the pages and a small key fluttered to the floor, the tag of the key acting as a makeshift parachute. Inside the book cover was Michelle Freeburg's name in black cursive pen strokes.

I punched in Jens's cell number and it clicked over into his message center immediately.

"Jens, listen. I know you're in with the FBI agents. I need to know, were you reading *Nightmare in Pink*? Because right after you left, I caught Roy Barker in your room, and I think he left the book behind on your nightstand." As I spoke, a hunch kept growing in my gut. "I heard something, opened your door, and saw him crawling out your bedroom window. Tell the agents, will you, please? The book has Michelle's name in it. And there was a key in the book, a key with a red tag. It might mean something. I think Roy Barker's trying to set you up. Be careful."

I hung up, wondering what Roy Barker was up to. I needed time to process all the information, quiet time. Relieved that I finally had the house and my thoughts to myself, I rubbed my eyes and got to work jotting down what I knew on a legal pad from Jens's home office across the hall from his bedroom and next to the spare room where I was staying. A tiny little room with no windows, really no bigger than a closet, but it served the purpose. As I started scribbling, I realized no one could read my handwriting, which would make my notes utterly useless, so I decided to log onto Jens's computer instead and type what I remembered.

Michelle's dead. Worked from 6:00 am to 8:00 pm with Roy Barker Sunday. Michelle's last customer of the day was Lucifer's Lot. Mully. Bought thread, fishing line, needles, matches, rubbing alcohol (lots of it). Asked Michelle to attend rally with him.

Roy told Michelle he loved her. Michelle called him crazy and Roy went crazy. Jens overheard all this. Michelle told Jens later that Roy confessed he knew Michelle's secret about being pregnant as a freshman in high school. Peeper. Roy threatened Michelle. Jens threatened Roy.

8:00 pm to 10:00 pm Michelle with Char.

10:00 pm Roy leaves grocery store and looks for Michelle, first at Freeburgs, then finds at Jens's house. Peeps until 10:45.

10:00 pm to 11:00 pm, Michelle with Jens. "End this, once and for all." Jens didn't kill her. Jens thinks Roy had something to do with it. Did Roy go home at 10:45? Or lie in wait for when she left at 11:00? Find out if Internet service confirms Roy's claim that he was on computer from 11:00 pm until 2:00 am. Or did Roy kill Michelle when he "snapped"? Snapped because of rejection, kiss between Michelle and Jens, or did Michelle tell Roy she quit for good after Roy told her about knowing her secret? Roy insists Jens had something to do with it.

Tommy Jasper found Michelle's body Monday morning along Boxelder Creek just off Nemo Quarry on Broken Peaks property by big rock. Clint White seen by big rock around 6:30 that same morning. Jens at Nemo General Store between 5:00 and 7:00 same morning.

Roy broke into Jens's house until 5:15 pm Tuesday. What was he doing/ taking? Left Michelle's book and work locker key. Setting up Jens? FBI needs to know.

FBI thinks Mully and the Lucifer's Lot had something to do with Michelle's death, not Roy. FTW pin? Boot prints led toward Lazy S, Mr. Schilling's campground where Mully and Lucifer's Lot are staying.

Char is missing. What happened between 8:00 and 10:00 with Michelle and Char? Jens said fight between them over a boyfriend, forties or fifties, someone Jens knows, authority figure. Jens said when he asked about Roy Barker's 'dirty little secret' comment, Michelle confessed she was raped repeatedly at thirteen, false pregnancy by fourteen. But he thought she was lying about something. I think she had the baby and the baby is Char. Check blood tests. People who knew Michelle's mom back then agree it would be hard to notice if Arlene was pregnant, since she's always been plump. Freeburgs know. Doctor knows. Maybe Michelle successfully hid her pregnancy from everyone else but Peeping Roy. All hush-hush. Need to confirm my conclusion and find out who her doctor was at Black Hills Medical Clinic where Roy Barker said he saw Michelle go as a teen.

Char started running with bad crowd, at the same age as Michelle when she found herself in trouble. Might explain Michelle's overprotective treatment of Char. Is Char Michelle's baby or reminds her that her baby would be same age? Ask Freeburgs.

I witnessed collapse of a young girl on Monday around noon who looked a lot like Char. May be sitting on information that could help piece it all together. Mully saw me watching them that day. Been chasing me around the Hills ever since.

Purging myself of this data helped me realize I had some places to go and people to see. As I had realized right before I heard Roy in Jens's bedroom, finding Char was high on my list. Finding out what happened fourteen years ago to Michelle's baby was also high on my list, though, and could actually help me find Char. I prayed that if Char and the girl I saw yesterday with Lucifer's Lot were one and the same, she was alive.

I fetched the jeans I'd worn the day before and reached into the pocket for Jens's memory stick. I jammed it into his laptop and opened the file. Although the quality of the pictures wasn't great, I had a fairly good set of photos to work with.

As I stared at the last picture, at Mully's face, the phone rang. Startled, I nearly toppled out of my chair. Hesitantly, I answered, "Hello?"

"Oh, Boots. It's you."

"Don't sound so disappointed."

"I was looking for Jens." The voice on the line was that of Elizabeth, my sister who lives in Louisville, Colorado. At least for the time being. She's our tumbleweed. If I didn't know better, I'd have sworn she was crying. Then I realized she actually sounded slightly drunk. Neither was characteristic for Elizabeth.

"What's wrong?" I asked, assuming she had just learned about Michelle from Mom.

"It's Ernif. He's dead," was all she said.

"Mr. Hanson?"

In the warp speed of the story she proceeded to unravel, all I could make out was something about Helma calling her and asking for help.

"She needs me, Boots. I'm getting in the car now to drive up there."

"Have you been drinking?"

"No. What makes you think that?"

"Crying?"

No answer.

"It's nearly six o'clock, Elizabeth," I said, turning my wrist to verify the time. Quarter to six. "And it's at least an eight-hour drive. You won't get here until after two in the morning."

"I was calling to see if I could crash there," she said.

"Jens isn't home, but I'm sure he won't mind. I'm staying here, too. You can bunk in with me in his guest bedroom. I'll leave the spare key in that knothole on the corner post in the backyard in case neither of us is here or we're fast asleep."

Before she hung up, I could have sworn Elizabeth said that Ernif was murdered. But that just wasn't possible. My mind couldn't wrap around the concept of yet another person killed, much less anyone wanting to see Ernif dead. Everyone loved him—and his wife, Helma, for that matter. And who could kill an old man? Impossible. Elizabeth must have gotten her wires crossed somewhere, was overreacting, overly concerned about her dear friend. The two women had met and befriended each other years ago at a support group meeting for parents who'd lost children. Elizabeth and Helma shared similar stories, losing their babies to SIDS fifty years apart almost to the day. I shook it off and got back to the task at hand.

Gathering my thoughts, I read through what I had typed so far. From my notes and my memory, I pieced the story together, matching names with faces, explaining the story.

Monday, Noon: Sherman Street, Sturgis, SD

Six bikers arrived on Harleys. One biker had a girl riding with him. Girl was wearing red string bikini, black boots with spike heels, matching spiked dog collar, and a leather jacket way too big for her.

Creed, the enforcer, kept watch.

Noodles's semen would be found in the unconscious girl left for dead.

Girl looks similar to missing girl Charlene Freeburg.

Cheetah, the prospect, was the one who convinced the girl from Main Street to go with them on their bikes and to pull a train.

Another prospect whose name I never heard.

Teddy, the bald guy with the bandana.

Jimmy Bones, who almost had his penis bitten off and whose spittle could be found on her left shoulder.

Mully, the outlaw gang's leader, who succeeded Bomber and Striker, arrived later with Weasel. Best year the chapter ever had. Doing what?

The girl did seem to be there on her own volition, albeit drunk or stoned. Loopy. The Lucifer's Lot didn't seem to have anything to do with that. I could also attest that she did not die of suffocation or pass out based on what I saw of Jimmy Bones's manhood. Probably couldn't choke a fly.

After girl dropped, Mully talked about celebrating business success of rally by earning purple wings (what's a purple wing????). All men dropped to knees between her splayed legs and went down on the poor girl while she lay unconscious. Not dead? Creed thought dead, had trouble finding pulse because of spiked collar. Not dead. Unconscious. Only fell against the pavement from a kneeling position. Wasn't hit, struck, or smacked by anyone or anything. Just fell over.

Bikers left as EMTs arrived. Mully spotted me and probably got the license plate to my brother Jens's truck, where I witnessed the whole thing.

I saved my Word document with embedded pictures and toggled back to the Internet, searching for phone numbers and finding only three hospitals where the EMTs may have taken the bikini girl in and around Sturgis, including Rapid City Regional Hospital. I called all three asking for anyone brought in from Sturgis around noon the day before, a Jane Doe or a Charlene Freeburg. I got no help. If the girl was not Char and was awake and aware, she would be registered under her name, which I would never know. But I couldn't shake the image of Creed being so responsible, too responsible to miss a heartbeat, no matter how much I wished he had.

I searched for the only other agency that would know about the girl I'd seen with the Lucifer's Lot and dialed the number.

"Sturgis Police Department," a woman announced, unenthusiastically.

I couldn't imagine how crazy their jobs must be this time a year. "Hi, I was wondering if I could talk to someone about a woman who may have passed out or been hospitalized yesterday afternoon."

"Can you narrow it down? We had dozens of fainters yesterday. It peaked at a hundred and three degrees. A new record."

"Well, I just want to know if the woman that was found on Sherman Street is okay or not. Do you know which case I'm talking about?" I continued.

There was a pause. "Ma'am, what's your name?"

I ignored her request. "Who might be able to answer my question?"

Without covering the receiver, the woman shouted, "Stanley, you need to take this one."

I heard a series of clicks, assumed it was the sound of me being transferred, and elevator music started playing. I couldn't believe my ears. Elevator music on a police department line? I took a breath and jotted some more notes as I waited, organizing the list of girls' names and addresses I had compiled to find out who might be harboring Char. I refused to believe the red bikini girl and Char were one in the same, even though I was waiting to confirm my beliefs.

I stretched my legs and walked across the hall carrying the portable handset to Jens's bedroom, watching the sun as it began its descent to the west. This late in the summer, sunset wouldn't be for another two, two and a half hours, or so. I thought about Jens and wondered how he was doing with the FBI this time, glad that Jason was with him and relieved that Elizabeth was on her way. She'd keep Jens's spirits up if anyone could. And Jens could lift her mood. I was daydreaming about my siblings, listening to a song my dad used to sing to me when I was a toddler. "Would you like to fly in my beautiful balloon? Would you like to glide in—"

"Detective Stanley Hoyt." The gruff voice scattered my balloons. "Who am I talking with?"

"Listen, I just have a quick question," I said, trying to avoid explaining why the sister of Jens Bergen, a person of interest in Michelle Freeburg's murder, was calling about a Jane Doe. "The girl on Sherman Street. In the red bikini. Do you know who I'm talking about?"

Pause. "Yes."

"Can you tell me how she's doing?"

"Who is this?"

"I saw what happened. I saw the whole thing. I just need to know if she's told you her name," I pushed on, returning to Jens's desk across the hall.

"No," he said, his voice softening. "Do you know her name?"

"No, I . . . Well, I was wondering if you could check to see if she's Charlene Freeburg. Char's been missing since Sunday night and well, I thought it kinda looked a little like her."

No reply.

"Do you have Internet access, Detective Hoyt?" I volunteered.

"Yes, of course."

"She may not want you to know who she is. She may be a runaway. That's probably why she's not telling you her name. But check the *Rapid City Journal* photo on page D1 of the October twenty-seventh edition last year. See if she's Char."

I waited, my palms sweating.

Detective Hoyt returned to the line and said, "October twenty-seventh, D1. The girl spiking the ball?"

"Yep."

"I'll do that. But could you give me the rest of the story, please?"

"Do you have an e-mail address?" I asked. He gave it to me as I typed, and I promptly sent him all the notes I'd just compiled and photos I had taken from Jens's cell phone.

I waited, expecting more music but was rewarded only with silence. I waited so long I was starting to think Detective Hoyt had forgotten about me.

To ward off the boredom, I replayed my horrible behavior with the FBI agents earlier. I remembered the card in my back pocket and retrieved it, wondering what Agent Adonis's name was. My fingers started to shake when I read the embossed name on the bright white card.

Special Agent Streeter Pierce.

I could not believe my eyes.

Agent Pierce. The man who killed the De Milo murderer for me. The man who saved my life. Streeter Pierce and Agent Adonis were one in the same! My stomach flipped with excitement and dread. Excitement because I'd finally met Streeter Pierce. The man I owed my life to. Dread because

I had just made a complete ass of myself. Instead of showering him with gratitude, I had figuratively kicked him in the balls and out of my brother's house.

What in the hell could top this for bad luck!

"Impressive," Detective Hoyt eventually said. "Names, photos. Now, what's the story and how did you get these photos?"

I had just started to tell the story and explain what I knew when I heard the distinct sound of Harleys nearby. I ran across the hall, glanced out the master bedroom window, and saw Mully and three other Lucifer's Lot bikers staring at Jens's truck in the driveway. And the house. I dropped to the floor behind the bed before they could see me, phone still in my hand. My heart was pounding.

"Officer?" I croaked.

"Detective. Detective Stanley Hoyt. Is there something wrong, miss?"

Barely above a whisper I asked, "Is the girl okay? The girl from Sherman Street?"

"She's dead. What's your name, miss? Miss?"

I dropped the phone and crawled to Jens's dresser for his gun.

CHAPTER 21

"QUIT PICKING AT IT," Bly scolded.

"I'm not picking at it. I'm just looking at it," Streeter harrumphed and walked over to the mirror. He could clearly see the two tattoos on his forearms, "TCB" on his left and "Eat Shit" on his right. But he needed the mirror to spy the tattoo on his upper right arm, a snakelike creature coiled on a pillow of flames with the word "STNEPRES" in black on the arc above the spindly beast and the words "YESREJ WEN" on the rocker below.

"I'm a Serpent from Jersey? That's almost worse than being tattooed."

Bly chuckled. "Better than working the rez during the rally."

"Says you," Streeter sulked. "I've had enough of both," he said somberly.

"You ever talk about it?"

Streeter knew "it" would come up eventually. Everyone in the bureau knew about his wife, Paula. But he had never talked about her death and wasn't about to start now. He had no idea what got into him at Jens Bergen's house. In the uncomfortable silence that followed, they both scanned Main Street, eyes darting from biker to biker filling the streets.

Ignoring Bly's question, Streeter asked, "What do the letters 'TCB' stand for?"

"Taking care of business," Bly answered. "It's kind of the Serpents' motto."

Streeter barely recognized himself in the mirror: tattoos, prewashed button-fly jeans, and a black T-shirt. He'd never owned a pair of jeans in his life.

And he couldn't seem to focus on the job at hand, worried about what fool's errand Jens had sent his sister on to find Char. He secretly agreed that her whereabouts were the key to all this, and they, too, would need to find her. Tomorrow, he thought. Tonight he had to find Mully. He had comforted his mind to think that the best way to help Liv stay safe would be to have Mully behind bars. Then he chided himself. "What business is it of yours?"

As if Bly had been reading Streeter's mind about her, he said, "Wow, Liv Bergen is smokin'!"

"You think so?"

"Know so. Those fiery eyes and luscious lips. Those long legs that last for weeks, that killer body all fit and trim. Not a stitch of makeup, her hair tucked under a baseball cap, and she lit up the room the second she busted through that door. My kinda woman. What I wouldn't give for an hour alone with that bobcat."

Streeter flinched at the thought, resisting the urge to pop his partner in the mouth for some reason.

"Oh, by the way, your name," said Bly. "Our motorcycle gang name or nickname. Mine's 'Bly' and yours is 'Streeter.' Those are our legal names."

"I think I can remember that," Streeter said, tightening the knot of his black skullcap, which had the initials B.F.F.S. stenciled in white across the front. Brothers Forever, Forever Serpents.

"I am far too old to be dressing like a grungy teenager," Streeter mumbled.

He pointed at the emblem on his T-shirt. "What's this supposed to be?"

"The New York office got it for you. It's a souvenir from a smaller rally they hold up in the northeast every spring. Just so you know, you attended this year."

"Maryland's Mad Dog Rally," Streeter read upside down. "Sponsored by Harley-Davidson?"

"You got it. We're members of the Serpents, which originated in Maryland in 1959. The other clubs will be looking for clues to make sure you're legit, especially the clubs' intelligence officers, who will no doubt be trying to pump you for information. You'll spook them all at first, considering none of them has ever heard of you. You did study everything I gave you in that manila envelope, right?"

"Committed to memory. Every detail. While you were in the shower." Streeter wanted Bly to wonder if he was telling the truth or pulling his leg.

Bly asked, "What are you thinking now that we've talked with Vincent?"

"I'm thinking," Streeter groaned as he tugged on his boots, "that Vincent having mentioned Michelle was raped at thirteen confirms what Jens said Michelle told him after Roy outted her. I'm thinking that, despite my good friend Bob Shankley's insistence, that this is an open-and-shut case and Carl Muldando killed Michelle, my gut says we're looking in all the wrong places. It has since the beginning. Too neat. Shank is deceitful and can't be trusted. He's got a vested interest in the outcome of this case, and I don't know exactly what that is yet, but his motives are not entirely pure. And he's pushing hard for Mully to be the one we charge with Michelle's murder, pushing even harder for people to know I'm the one to finger Mully."

"You missed that he'll be quick to steal the credit when you solve this case, my friend," Bly added with a wink.

"A picture's worth a thousand words, and the succession of photos taken of Michelle confirms the story. Look at the way she intentionally uglified herself from the age of fourteen. Also explains why she was so overprotective of Char."

"You think Vincent knows more about this, stayed close with the family all these years because he was the one who raped Michelle?" Bly suggested.

"Maybe. But then why did he tell us he thought Michelle was raped and got pregnant when she was thirteen? If he were the rapist, why would he be so willing to redirect the investigation toward something he didn't know we already knew? He wouldn't know that Jens Bergen and Roy Barker had already told us about Michelle having been sexually abused. Why not just let us investigate her recent murder rather than distort it with her tainted past? No one else seems to know or believe anything was ever wrong in Michelle's life. What would Vincent have to gain by telling us that, if he was Michelle's killer?"

"I'm no psychologist, but if I had been raped when I was only thirteen, I would be damn sure not to let something bad like that happen to someone I love, like a wild, know-it-all little sister. Michelle playing mother hen makes sense. But she moved in with her parents to keep an eye on who? Just her baby sister, or dear old daddy, too?"

Streeter shook his head. "I don't think so. I think Frank and Arlene were and continue to be oblivious to any of this."

"Older brothers?"

"Maybe. Haven't met them yet. Could explain why Michelle got so mad about Frankie Jr. giving Charlene a beer and a toke on his weed. Who knows?"

"What does Michelle having been raped have to do with her being murdered?"

The cell phone buzzed and Bly flipped it open on speaker.

"What's up, boss?"

"The autopsy is done on Michelle Freeburg. Time of death was sometime between ten forty and eleven yesterday morning," Shank said.

"About the time Tommy found her," Streeter said.

"And the autopsy suggested she died of blunt-force trauma to the back of her skull, the murder weapon likely an industrial flashlight, based on the field work."

"When was she struck?"

"Between midnight and one o'clock Sunday night. Well, actually Monday morning. Casts taken of boot prints leading away from the murder scene toward Lazy S Campground indicate men's size ten and a half. The print is being run through the database now and we'll get a brand. But I already know it will match with whatever Mully's wearing."

Streeter still hadn't told Shank that Jack Linwood and his Investigative Control Operations team had confirmed the FTW pin found in Michelle's palm had the same striations as the pin seen in Mully's lapel.

"Thanks," Bly said, about to snap the phone shut.

"By the way," Shank added. "The Jane Doe in Sturgis is not Charlene Freeburg."

"When did we think it was?" Streeter looked at Bly. Both men shrugged.

"When the Sturgis PD got an anonymous call from someone who suggested it might be."

"When was this?"

"About an hour ago. The caller sent photos. We now have proof Mully and several more of the Lucifer's Lot were involved in Jane Doe's death. We've got the pictures to prove it. Bring him in."

Streeter was dumbfounded. Photos and proof of Mully having been involved in this girl's death on Monday afternoon, too. "Do we have any idea who called?"

"You're going to love this," Shank said. "E-mail of the photos, names, gang ranks, and field notes came from an e-mail address associated with an L. Bergen at Bergen Construction Materials."

Streeter stood at the kitchen table, staring at the picture of Michelle's naked body along the creek's bank. He couldn't help comparing this image to the one of Liv on the highwall just a month earlier and shivered at how close she'd come to dying. And how Michelle wasn't so lucky. And incredibly, somehow Liv seemed to be tangled up with the Lucifer's Lot, with Mully.

The phone call to Jens Bergen about Roy Barker leaving Michelle's book and key on Jens's nightstand had been helpful. It was also helpful, of course, that Jens had provided them with so much information about Michelle and her pregnancy. But knowing that much of the information somehow came from Liv made Streeter wonder how involved she was in this investigation. And whether she might be putting herself in harm's way again, which disturbed him to think about. Streeter had asked Bly to get someone over to Jens's house immediately to retrieve the book, the key, and Liv, but Liv was nowhere to be found. Neither was Jens's truck. Jens recognized the key and explained that it opened Michelle's locker at work. Streeter told them to bag everything in Michelle's locker into evidence and call him with the results. The fact that Jens didn't know where Liv had gone after she phoned him was unsettling.

When Streeter tried calling Liv at her parents' house, Jeanne Bergen bent over backward to be helpful. She explained that Liv had come back to town and was staying with Jens, gave Streeter Jens's home and cell numbers, then invited him for dinner while he was in Rapid City. She had no way of knowing, of course, that Streeter already knew all those details. Probably the most genuine, hospitable woman he'd ever met, he thought. For the time being, he would focus on the undercover work in Sturgis and worry tomorrow about Liv's involvement with the young girl found dead at Sturgis and with Mully. As long as he kept an eye on Mully, Liv should be safe.

"Where are you going with this?" Bly asked, studying the picture Streeter handed him.

The pale skin of Michelle's fingers and hand clearly showed the FTW pin stuck in the palm, her fingers loosely curled toward her palm, blood dripping onto her white skin and the grassy bank.

"Autopsy report indicated that Michelle didn't grab this from her murder's lapel as a clue, like Shank and Leonard suspected. No indication whatsoever that she scratched, clawed, or fought her assailant. Her fingernails weren't broken, had nothing beneath the nails. Her hands had no bruising or fight wounds of any kind. It appears the FTW pin was placed in her palm by her murderer," Streeter said. "Not consistent with gang behavior."

"Absolutely not," Bly argued, shaking his head vigorously. "They're way more sophisticated—not to say intelligent—than that."

"All motorcycle club members?"

"Well, not all," Bly retracted. "The Serpents tend to leave their calling card."

"Aren't we Serpents, supposedly?" Streeter asked.

Bly nodded.

"What's our calling card?"

Bly ignored him. "I just haven't ever heard of something like this, particularly with a Lucifer's Lot biker. It just wouldn't be smart. They brag through the patches and pins they wear on their colors, but it doesn't prove anything or become evidence in a crime. That would be suicide."

"Still think someone's trying to set him up?"

Bly nodded. "Let's get moving. It'll be dark soon."

They exited through the back door and skulked through the alley, blending into the crowds on the streets.

As if by way of explanation and before the rumble of the crowd became too much, Bly confessed, "I put up with Shank's crap because I love what I do."

"Fun job," Streeter mused, his senses stimulated by the wafting odors, the cacophony of street party noises, the visual assault of bizarreness everywhere.

"Some days it's fun," Bly admitted. "Other days are not so fun. Some of the shit you go through . . . some of the things you see . . ."

Streeter took Bly's cue to restrict their work-related conversations only to those times when they were circling one of the bikes on the street for a closer look. Or when they had privacy. "You mentioned the Lucifer's Lot being dominant in the southwest."

"Right. The gangs are kind of territorial, regionalized in a way. Inferno Force are on the West Coast; Hombres, Southeast; and Serpents, Northeast," Bly explained. "Historically, most undercover cops and agents come in as a Nomad."

"Not belonging to any specific chapter of a gang. Or any gang."

"Right again. That's what makes our undercover legals so convincing. Anyone pulling our bios would see that you and I came from a very specific chapter of the Serpents, which are nomadic and hard to pin down anyway. They aren't a big presence during the rally, like some of the other gangs. I can't pose as an Inferno Force because they do make a huge showing. Hell, it's their show. So, I have effectively convinced the other clubs that I'm with the Serpents, originally from one of the New York chapters. I'm sure their intelligence officers have had my false dossier for years. Boys over in the New York bureau made sure to slip it in so one of the intelligence officers found it."

"Are the Serpents a large group?"

"One of the four biggest, in terms of national and international importance from the perspective of criminal impact. So my cover's believable," Bly explained, winking at the passing blonde dressed in a leather corset, miniskirt, knee-high leather boots, and spiked collar.

After she and four trailing gawkers passed by, Streeter squatted down to study the detailing on the side of one motorcycle and said, "These four criminal organizations. We're involved because of Title 18?"

"They're the only four outlaw gangs of the motorcycle club world that have enough criminal impact to warrant an investigation under the federal RICO statute. Let's grab a beer," Bly said as he led Streeter across the street and ducked into Gunners on Main Street, the first bar they came to.

At first, it was quieter in the bar than it had been outside. Then the crowd inside let out a holler that sounded like the most avid sports fans expressing elation over a game-winning score. Streeter wondered what all the commotion was about and noticed everyone staring out the Main Street windows, apparently people watching. He had forgotten how overwhelming was the number of bikes and bikers, odors and oddities, that flooded the tiny town. He followed Bly through the crowds huddled around the tables to two empty stools at the end of the bar.

Bly offered Streeter the bar stool closest to the wall and said, "Sit facing me, so you can prop your back up against the wall. Better view of the door that way," he added, noting Streeter's confused expression. "I'll face away from the patrons and keep watch in the mirror behind the bar."

They were anticipating that at some point during the night Mully and his gang would patronize Gunners, one of the oldest biker bars in Sturgis. Veteran club leader that he was, Mully certainly wouldn't miss this spot if he were roaming the streets on foot. Particularly with its famous tattoo parlor in the basement that passersby could see into through the street-side windows placed at shin level.

"We'll camp here for now and if he doesn't show, we'll go to the Full Throttle later tonight," Bly said, ordering two Coors from the barmaid.

"What's Full Throttle?"

"It's a bar east of town. Built after you left for Denver. They claim to be the biggest indoor/outdoor biker saloon in the world. Home of the funniest bar stool races and midget wrestling I've ever seen."

"Bar stool races?"

The barmaid returned with two plastic cups of beer.

Bly growled, "What the hell is this?"

"You ordered draft," the young woman with the hard voice barked between choruses of Adam Lambert's "Sure Fire Winners" and over the occasional cheer from the crowd, their volume an obvious rating for how hot—and naked—the biker chick was who had just walked by the windows. The bartender was a pretty kid dressed to look available—cutoffs below, nothing but a T-shirt above, tied to show a pierced belly button— with overpainted eyes that said anything but.

"We're out of beer mugs at the moment." The whooping crowd indicated a particularly hot commodity parading along Main Street, all bar patrons' eyes glued to the windows. She sighed and jerked her head in their direction, saying, "We're kind of busy in here if you haven't noticed."

Her sarcasm was not lost on Bly.

"Then bring it in bottles next time and keep them coming." He laid a twenty on the bar, adding, "Start a tab for the beer and we'll want food, too. This is for you if you keep us happy."

She granted Bly a hint of a smile as she pocketed the bill and quickly disappeared to fill his order and attend to the other patrons.

Streeter knew the bar would be packed, but he couldn't believe it would be standing room by only seven o'clock in the evening. He could hardly imagine what it would be like later tonight, after dark, when people really started to show up, and understood why Bly had suggested leaving their Serpents leather vests at the flophouse. They would draw too much attention to both men at this point.

"What do you see?" Streeter asked quietly.

"Mostly citizens," Bly said, drinking his beer and studying the crowd's reflection.

Streeter wondered how he could see anything in the cloudy mirror on the back wall behind the bar, which stretched the length of the room, especially with the two shelves above it jammed with hundreds of different varieties of spirits and the counter working area in front of it completely cluttered.

"Citizens?"

"Garden-variety bikers," Bly explained. His arms were splayed across the bar as he hunched over like a bar stool veteran, looking comfortable in his role. "Members of the A.M.A., the American Motorcycle Association, but not part of the one percenters. They're the good guys."

"Any one percenters?"

"Not that I can tell, yet," Bly added, "but there are a few cops."

Streeter nodded and drank from his plastic cup. Two men near the restrooms were in their early twenties, fresh from the gym with what appeared to be more bulk than brain. They were both clean shaven, hair slicked back neatly. They were wearing navy blue dress pants and gray T-shirts with the word "Police" stenciled in navy blue across the chest. They were underplaying the cop role, but not so much so that someone who needed help wouldn't know whom to ask. He assumed the minimal show of police force meant there were more men in blue working undercover, as he was doing.

Streeter hadn't removed his sunglasses when he entered the bar, following Bly's lead. At first it had been difficult to even reach the empty bar stool without tripping over someone, but now his eyes had adjusted, and he was glad for the privacy the dark shades afforded so his gaze could wander freely across the patrons. And although he and Bly weren't wearing their colors, they each had their Serpent headgear on, so people would leave them alone. Anyone who would know anything would be wise enough to stay clear of the members of such a notorious club, not wanting to strike up a conversation or hassle either man. Streeter likened himself to a bristled porcupine, and he smiled at the isolation it afforded him in such a crowd.

He scanned the bar. Six people were seated at the table closest to him and Bly: four men and two women. The men were all wearing dime-store varieties of Harley-Davidson T-shirts, solid black. Two were clean-shaven; the other two had stubble from a day, two days at the most, of missed grooming.

One woman, who was much too large to be doing so, wore a turquoise leather halter with fringe, the leather expertly dipping to show a mile of cleavage. Her platinum blonde hair rose high on her head and a cigarette dangled from her ruby red lips, drawing attention to the spidery lines around them where, over time, the lipstick had bled outside their intended boundaries.

The other woman was a redhead who wore a black cotton spaghetti-strap Harley-Davidson cami that clung to her small breasts like Saran Wrap to miniature cupcakes. She had a butterfly tattoo above her right breast and a dainty little heart tattooed on her wrist. Although not as adorned in jewelry as was her friend, she, too, chain-smoked. The table was innocuously safe, all patrons engrossed in their private conversations, unaware of the two bikers who sat perched on the bar stools behind them because they, too, had turned their chairs to face the window for the show.

Streeter noted that next to Bly was a woman whose back was to them. She was focused entirely on the mangy-looking biker next to her, but he was more interested in what his buddy to his left was saying than in what she was doing. Her hands were sprawled all over his crotch, yet he didn't seem to even notice her advances. Her jet-black hair was pulled back into a scraggly ponytail to reveal parts of a large spider tattooed across her back, visible beneath the black tank top she wore. A fire could erupt in Bly's beer and those patrons wouldn't notice.

They were safe to talk.

"Are we going to interview Frankie Jr. and Brian Freeburg?" Bly asked.

"Tomorrow," Streeter answered. "And we're not telling Shank, if that's what you're thinking. And I want to go to Black Hills Medical Clinic to see what we can learn. If we're lucky, the doctor who cared for Michelle fourteen years ago for her alleged mono will still be there and remember."

Bly grinned and drained the last of his beer, which was quickly replaced with a cold bottle by the brunette bartender. Streeter finished the beer and collapsed the plastic cup with one bug-smasher stroke.

A biker filled the doorway, his shabby red beard spilling down his bare chest and his craggy face hidden partially by dark sunglasses. He was wearing a ratty leather vest with no shirt underneath, exposing the tattoo emblazoned on his belly, "L.L.E."

"Lucifer's Lot in Eternity," Bly, his eyes on the mirror, explained in answer to Streeter's unasked question.

Streeter studied the man's vest, tying to ignore the woman who followed him through the doorway. She was wearing nothing but a swimsuit consisting of a multitude of black leather strings, thicker bands strategically placed so she could avoid paying indecent exposure fines. Her long black hair was dull from lack of hygiene; her skin was white as flour, making the black lipstick she was wearing even starker. She was being led by the Lucifer's Lot biker on a leather leash attached to the studded dog collar around her neck. She was at least twenty pounds too heavy to be dressing that skimpily, the skin stretching over her buttocks and thighs looking more like plastic Baggies full of hominy.

"Big Red," Bly said, reading the tattoo on the man's arms, which were the size of the legs on a baby elephant. "Must be his legal."

Streeter focused on the man's vest. He spoke under his breath to Bly, reciting what patches he could see on the man's colors. "M.C., FTW, three sixes, and a twenty two."

"Mark of Satan and he's been in prison," Bly said, tipping his beer.

"A white fist that's clenched," Streeter added as the couple made their way past the bar toward the back.

"His belief in white supremacy. That's outdated for the Lucifer's Lot. Most chapters are not so ethnically pure anymore."

"And what looks like a white cross."

"He's done some grave robbing with witnesses present," Bly said, watching the man as he passed. "He's a Nomad."

Streeter saw "Nomad" on the bottom rocker beneath the club's logo on the back of his leather vest. On the top rocker were the familiar words "Lucifer's Lot."

"What's that mean?"

"He's an enforcer. Doesn't belong to a particular Lucifer's Lot chapter. He performs his duties for several chapters."

"Think Mully's close behind?" Streeter asked, watching the two find a table near the back of the restaurant. The table had been occupied until Big Red stood over them, glaring. The four startled tourist bikers excused themselves and hurriedly left Gunners, tossing some cash at a waitress on their way out the door.

"Not necessarily, but maybe," Bly said. "Hopefully."

Streeter watched as the woman sat obediently beside Big Red, smiling at him like a demented, freakish circus poodle.

"Did he spot you?" Bly asked.

"Not yet, but he will," Streeter answered, assuming Big Red would be clever enough to notice the B.F.F.S. on his skullcap. It was their underworld communication. The patches, pins, and emblems on their colors and their choice in tattoos were not unlike a living résumé of each gang member. They were, in essence, walking billboards of their past criminal activities.

As Big Red and the she-devil were getting cozy, Streeter noticed that the silver stud piercing one of her nostrils came with a chain that led, presumably, to a matching stud in her tongue. Streeter shivered with revulsion.

The barmaid brought out a platter of appetizers, placing it in front of Bly. On it were rows of fried shrimp, fried mozzarella sticks, fried chicken pieces, fried mushrooms, and fried zucchini. Bly smiled at her and placed another twenty on the bar.

"Thanks, sweetheart."

She smiled back and pounded two fresh beers in front of them. In bottles. Bly grinned and popped a fried mushroom in his mouth.

As he chewed, he mumbled, "I think Shank's on to something with this Sturgis girl. Photos? A witness? Probably time to bring Mully in for some questions."

Streeter frowned, worried about the connection between Liv and Mully, knowing he must find the man and bring him in for questioning if nothing more than to protect Liv. "Agreed. We need to find him ASAP."

Bly gobbled up a few more fried delicacies while Streeter once more scanned the bar. The crowd was getting noisier and more restless as the evening went on, everyone in biker garb and grunge enjoying a cold beer on this hot August evening. A lone cowboy came through the entrance. Streeter watched him ease his way patiently through the crowd and amble up to the bar near the front window, the opposite end of the bar from where Streeter and Bly sat.

Streeter imagined it was routine for this cowboy to come to the normally quiet bar for a cold beer after a long, hard day of ranching, and he wasn't about to let some tourist bikers make him change his beloved routine. Although he anticipated the cowboy being harassed for his out-of-place dress, Streeter was surprised and pleased by the maturity of the biker crowd, who seemed to ignore him altogether. Either they were more civilized than he would have anticipated or they sensed that this cowboy wasn't about to take any guff from anyone. Probably the latter, Streeter mused, as he sized up the man's rugged face and taut muscles.

Bly nudged Streeter on the knee, motioning toward the door. Streeter stiffened when he saw the four bikers enter the bar. They were all wearing their colors, and Streeter knew instantly they were the Lucifer's Lot because of the red and silver skullcap the second biker was wearing.

Streeter scanned their faces. He couldn't tell if any of the bikers was Mully because of the crowd closing in around them. They took only a moment's hesitation before making a beeline toward the back of the bar where Big Red was saving them a table.

As they passed, Streeter asked, "You see him?"

"Nah," Bly grunted, "they're from New Mexico."

Just as he spotted the state name that Bly was referring to on the bottom rocker of their colors, a beer bottle shattered against the wall inches from Streeter's face.

CHAPTER 22

MY THINKING SEEMED CLEAR at the time. I had decided to drive the circuitous route to Nemo via I-90 through Sturgis and up Vanocker Canyon. What better people to explain my story to than federal agents, dozens of crime scene techs? But when I drove past Nemo toward Broken Peaks all the tents and people were gone. No crime scene techs. No agents. No one.

I had glanced in my rearview mirror the entire way and had seen motorcycle after motorcycle behind me, the idea of running away from Mully and his Lucifer's Lot toward Nemo through Sturgis ridiculous in hindsight. But now I was finding comfort in a place I knew well. Legs trembling, hands shaking, I fumbled with the padlock and swung the gate open to our family's quarry road. I hurriedly pulled the truck inside and closed the gate behind me.

My comfort didn't last long.

Before I could wrap the chain around the swing gate and slam the padlock shut, the rumble of motorcycles turning off the highway onto our long gravel road made me jump. The bikers were less than fifty yards from me.

My hands trembled and the padlock slipped through my fingers into the gravel at my feet. My feet wouldn't move when I looked up and saw

Mully's broad grin, he and his posse heading straight for me. My steel-toed boots scrabbled across the crushed stone as I bolted for the truck. The door wasn't even shut before I yanked the stick into gear and sped toward the quarry, trapping myself against the unforgiving mountain of iron that rose in front of me. Between a rock and a hard place.

Staring in my rearview mirror the entire time, I whipped the pickup into the shadows of the trees. Just before I reached the large pieces of equipment now dormant, intending to park between them for cover, I heard the rumble of motorcycles lurch through the swing gates. I pulled a sharp left between the 980 Cat loader and the Atlas Copco drill, jammed the truck into park, and scrambled out the door, fumbling for Jens's Browning pistol and shoving it into the back waistband of my jeans. I climbed up the ladder into the cab of the loader in long, quick strides and ducked low in the seat, hoping they hadn't seen me. I whipped off the stupid sunglasses I'd been wearing and took several deep breaths, trying to calm myself.

I had tried to ditch Mully and his boobs for a second time that day. While they circled the block for the third time, I had sneaked out to Jens's truck the same way Roy Barker had sprung from the windowsill. I revved the engine, put it in reverse, and headed in the opposite direction. I had gotten a jump on them and even saw one of them spill his bike when they U-turned to chase me. I had floored it all the way here, thinking if I headed toward where they camp, toward the throngs of authorities at Broken Peaks, it might be the last place they'd look for me.

The entire time that I was fleeing for my life, all I could do was rack my brain to remember the name of the guy in the Old Testament who lost his buddy and hero, Elijah, in battle and got sent by God to Jericho to purify their drinking water only to be hassled by a bunch of young boys. I remember pudgy little Sister Delilah hopping around from foot to foot, her wimple pinching an extra three or four chins, while she imitated the teasing boys: "Get out of here, Baldy! Did you hear us? Get lost, Baldy!"

I don't know if that's really in the Bible or not, but I seriously doubt that Sister Delilah would ever lie—or had the vivid imagination creating such a story would require. For some crazy reason, though, these thugs reminded me of those young boys taunting Baldy. Only I wasn't bald. But the most engrossing part of her story was that Baldy got so pissed off, he glared at and cursed the boys in God's name, conjuring up two even more pissed-off bears that came charging from the woods and ripped forty-two boys to pieces.

A sublime story to any third grader.

And now, here I was, not fooling anyone with my clever attempt to ditch these guys by heading here, remembering those forty-two little bastards and thinking they were bearing down on me as they neared the quarry, their leader, Mully, staring directly at me. For the life of me I couldn't remember the incantation Baldy recited to summon the two indignant bears.

But I was grateful to have this Cat.

Remarkably, I felt safer inside the loader. I was a soldier inside a tank and knew I could outmaneuver half a dozen bikes with the bucket of this beast if I needed to. But I couldn't do that if I was sitting like a lame duck.

As I bolted into action, my fingers flying to the key in the ignition, I growled, "One Cat is better than two bears. Any day."

The loader quickly roared to life. I enjoyed the surprise that registered on the faces of the approaching bikers. Needing both hands, I simultaneously worked the shift and steering wheel with my left and the bucket tilt and lift with my right. I kept the gun stuffed down the back of my pants and quickly backed the loader out of its spot. Maneuvering the lift and tilt in fluid motions, I squared the loader to the road like an angry mother bear pawing at the ground, challenging the bikers to come at me. Following Mully's lead, they all slowed to a stop a few feet in front of me, unable to encircle me since my loader blocked the steep road, the only entrance to our quarry.

With no hand free to grab the pistol, I shifted the loader into drive, my foot firmly on the brake, my other on the gas, ready to lurch forward toward the line of bikes. Mully dismounted his bike and walked a few steps in my direction. I pulled the lift back with my right hand as far as I could and punched the gas. I watched the alarm register on the bikers' faces as the arm of the bucket sailed skyward high above their heads. At its peak, I let go of the lift lever and pulled my hand back to the tilt lever, pulling just enough to angle the teeth of the bucket menacingly toward the heads of my unwelcome visitors.

My heart pounded and the loader idled in the moments that followed. It was as if time and all movement stood still, other than my labored breathing and my pounding heart. If any of the bikers made a move toward a gun or released either hand from the handlebars, I was prepared to drop the jagged steel teeth and bucket on their heads, charging their bikes like one of those biblical bears and ripping them to shreds, leaving a heap of tangled chrome and mangled bones for the criminalists to sort out later.

At least that was my initial thought.

Mully remained unnervingly still, looking nothing like a taunting boy, and I remembered the Sig Sauer or Glock I had seen beneath that leather jacket yesterday when he was in Sturgis. I edged my hand to the waistband of my jeans, gripping the loaded Browning just in case. Careful not to let them see the movement of my hand from their ground-level positions, I slipped the Browning next to the tilt and lift levers and repositioned my free hand back onto the lift.

The longer the bikers remained inactive, the easier it was for my breathing to settle into a steady calm. I leveled my steely gaze directly at Mully, feeling nearly invincible with my foot stomped hard on the brake, my right hand back in position to lower the lift if necessary.

In the sliver of time that defined either the last moments of my life or theirs, I imagined myself nestled in the palm of God's hand, life coursing through the veins of red iron ore that would give the granite fingers behind me the strength to hold me steady. I felt like Elijah's prodigy who had invoked the bears, only I had a Cat and a Browning, and my ears were filled with Luciano singing the role of Calaf as he proclaimed, "Nessun dorma!"

Nobody shall sleep.

I had concocted a weird mix of Old Testament lore and operatic fable, but I was at peace. And my face must have given me away.

Incredibly, Mully lifted his hands in surrender and took two steps toward my loader, directly under the iron teeth welded to the lip of the bucket. He just stood there. Staring at me. For what seemed like . . . forever.

Nobody shall sleep because victory was eminent. The boys would either leave me at peace or were about to be ripped to pieces.

Vincero! Vincero! Vincero!

I will win!

I released my grip on the lift lever and felt for the pistol, lifting my hand and leveling the sights directly on Mully's testicles, preparing to shoot through the loader's big glass windshield, aiming low and knowing the angle of the glass would deflect the bullet for a kill shot higher than my aim.

Mully offered a shrug. Through the cab and over the idling engine, I heard him say, "I just want to talk with you, okay?"

His calm, soothing voice yanked me from my peace, unnerved me, scattered Luciano's victorious aria.

"Not okay," I shouted, my mind willing my hand not to tremble or my eyes not to show fear.

After a long moment, I saw Mully's eyes soften into amusement and a smile play in the corner of his mouth. Oddly, his charm and this entire ordeal made the unknown Prince Calaf, the man motivated by an overwhelming power of love, materialize right in front of me. And for a split second I forgot that Mully was an outlaw, the leader of the Lucifer's Lot motorcycle gang, the guy who was trying to kill me.

His smile reached his eyes just as he shrugged again and said, "Okay."

I was a bit confused and told myself to stay alert, that this was all a seductive trick to lull me out of my readiness. As he turned slowly on his heels, I discarded the Browning and slid my right hand back onto the lift lever, ready to drop it with any sudden movement.

"This ain't dawn, Calaf, and I will win. Not you," I growled at his back.

He must have heard me, because Mully drew up short for a second, turning enough so our eyes met.

I swallowed hard and prepared myself for the worst.

"Did you say . . . Calaf?"

After pinning me with his stare, eyes filled with a mischievous secret, he erupted in laughter. Not mocking, more like joy. Then he simply walked away. He swung his leg over the seat of his Harley. Before stepping his bike backward a few paces and making a U-turn, he offered me a wicked smile and a gentleman's nod that reminded me of the tight, practiced bows reserved for royalty.

As he bowed, I could have sworn he said, "Princess Turandot."

As he led his restless boys out of our quarry entrance road in a small dust cloud of rumble, the line of bikes turned right onto Nemo Road.

I hadn't noticed I was holding my breath and dripping with sweat, my leg trembling from stomping so long on the brake. I lowered the lift and tilted the bucket back as I eased the loader into its parking spot, killing the engine.

I don't know how long I sat curled up in the seat, waiting for the adrenaline to ebb, but it was enough time to reflect on what had just happened and to allow the roar in my ears to disappear. What had seemed like a good idea at the time was a disaster. All I had managed to do was wedge myself into an isolated area with nowhere to run. A kill or be killed situation, my second in a month. The stress of it all must have affected me because the fear of what might have been was overshadowed by the power Mully's charm held over me.

Just as my pounding heart started to calm, I heard a knock on my window. I think I screamed, but it came out as an unusual sound. More like a gurgle. I sat upright and found myself pointing the barrel of Jens's Browning at Tommy Jasper, who simply stared at me through the big glass window of the cab door.

"What are you doing, Liv?"

My shoulders sagged and I tossed the gun onto the seat beside me like it was a rattlesnake about to bite. I extricated myself from the cab onto the platform beside him, my legs feeling like rubber.

"Bad day?" he asked. I wrapped my arms around his neck and held tight, not thinking how, at his age, he must be precariously balanced on the ladder, too.

"Shitty day," I said, using him as my buoy until I settled my nerves. "Almost as bad as yours yesterday."

"Huh."

Apparently, Tommy Jasper was a man of few words, but he seemed completely calm about having had a loaded gun leveled at his face and a woman using him as a human crutch. I was far more discombobulated than he was. He lowered himself to the ground and waited for me to follow on wobbly legs, gripping tightly with both hands to the rungs of the ladder. The gentleman he was, Tommy offered me a hand as I stepped off the last rung onto solid ground.

I let out a long sigh, glad to reach dry land after bobbing around in that sea of confusion.

"I was just finishing up with my cutting. Baling tomorrow. Want to join me for a bite at the Nemo Guest Ranch?"

"Love to," I said. "Maybe we can talk for awhile. Have a drink."

He didn't seem surprised that I was insisting on our becoming fast friends, considering we had just met the day before. And despite the gun thing. Oh, crap. I had left the gun in the cab of the loader.

"How's your brother holding up? I heard that girl was his companion," Tommy asked, holding open the door to his 1974 IH Scout for me.

"She was and he's not doing so hot," I answered honestly, crawling in and buckling up. I'd retrieve the gun when I got back after dinner. After I was sufficiently calm not to point it at anyone else.

When we got to the restaurant, my eyes darted around the bar to make sure none of the faces belonged to a member of the Lucifer's Lot, and I asked Tommy if we could choose a table in the back corner. He obliged.

When I asked the waitress to bring me nothing but two shots of vodka and a Coors Light, Tommy asked, "Do you want to talk about it?"

I shook my head. "No, but thanks for being here."

He nodded. Later, I was grateful that Tommy had placed an order for two hamburgers, knowing I wasn't clearly thinking for myself. We ate in silence. The dinner was perfect. Once again, I hadn't realized how hungry I was. My energy bolstered and mind cleared, fear dissipated, and I was back to my almost normal self.

"How about some coffee while we talk?"

"That would be wonderful," I said, my eyes skipping from face to face around the room.

The waitress brought us two coffees, and I got right down to business and told Tommy everything that had happened yesterday and today, including the two close calls with Mully and the Lucifer's Lot bunch.

"You should call the agents and tell them everything, Liv. You know they think these people may have something to do with Michelle's death, don't you?"

I confessed about my eavesdropping on the crime scene technicians all day today at the fence post by the big rock overlooking the creek, and he laughed.

"The stories Clint told me about you are true," he managed, sipping his coffee.

"What stories?"

He just shook his head. "Now, that wasn't very smart, coming toward their campground. You know that, don't you?"

"I do now. Tell me what the agents said after I left yesterday. Do they know what happened to Michelle?"

"I spent several hours with those people yesterday and a few more with some agents today, probably while you were holding up that fence post."

His eyes were kind, more alive than they had been when I first met him. And he had a sense of humor.

"I just don't know how I can help them," he said evenly. "They gave me a photo of Carl Muldando, the man you refer to as Mully."

He fished in his denim shirt pocket and pulled up a 3 x 5 glossy of the man who had been after me since yesterday. It was indeed the man I knew as Mully.

"And they think Mully killed Michelle?"

He leveled a gaze my way. "Sheriff Leonard thought so from the git-go. I think that big dog, the one named Shankley, is pressuring the other agents into arresting Mully for that girl's death. But I didn't get the same sense from the other two agents who came up to talk with me today."

Thinking of the two I kicked out of Jens's house, I asked, "Was one of them wearing a fedora?"

He nodded. "Agent Blysdorf. Stewart. Nice young man. Could use a shave."

"And the other was Agent Pierce, right?"

He nodded. "Funny first name. Skeeter or Scooter or something."

"Streeter," I said, resisting the smile that automatically came to my lips. "Do they think Jens is the killer?"

"I don't think so. They knew he was here Monday morning. At Nemo. And Clint told him he'd known Jens most of his life and that he couldn't imagine Jens capable of such a thing."

"The big dog, Shankley. Is he the boss or something?" I said sipping my coffee and feeling the vodka leave my limbs.

"Director of the FBI office in Rapid City. Or whatever they call it."

"So Agent Blysdorf and the others work for Agent Shankley? Why did they give you the picture of Mully?"

"They wanted to know whether I'd ever seen him walking around in the forest or on Broken Peak property Sunday or Monday. I told them of course I had seen a bunch of them Lucifer's Lot hoods, but I never took much of a notice to their faces. The Schillings often tell their campers to eat here at the Nemo Guest Ranch. I told him those guys were rooting around at the campground on Sunday and ate supper here."

"Supper as in lunch?" I clarified, working the time line in my head.

"Yep. Ted's wife, Cecelia, served them. Nervous about it too."

"Nervous because they were part of the Lucifer's Lot?"

"No, nervous that Eddie would show up with them. Cecelia doesn't like Eddie Schilling. Won't let her girls near him."

This surprised me. "A problem with Mr. Schilling?"

His lips thinned with distaste. "Nothing but rumor, I suppose."

"What are the rumors?" I asked hopefully.

"I don't want to be a part of any rumors," he said. Nodding at the woman near the kitchen, he added, "Ask Cecelia yourself."

She was standing in the kitchen doorway talking with our waitress, and I excused myself to talk with her. Her wary expression only intensified with my question. "Cecelia, I'm Liv Bergen. Can I ask you a question about Eddie Schilling?"

"What about?" She was direct, to the point, her chocolate brown eyes unwavering.

"Tommy Jasper tells me you don't take a liking to the man. Can I ask you why?" Only in South Dakota, I realized, could I be so forward with a complete stranger.

"What's it to you?"

"I'm trying to find a friend. A fourteen-year-old. She's a volleyball player on his team. I'm worried about her," I answered honestly.

"Check his bed," she said, turning abruptly toward the kitchen and letting the saloon-style doors swing shut behind her.

Alrighty then. I thought I had found my answer. Some people thought Eddie Schilling had a thing for teenage girls. Or something to that effect.

I returned to the table only to find that Tommy had company. The old man had kind eyes and a wonderfully infectious smile that smoothed the wrinkles that congregated all over his face. He rose as I approached, with some difficulty, and balanced himself by gripping tightly to the big brass ball of his hickory cane. One leg appeared misshapen and I tried to check the natural tendency to look down at it. He was younger than I had thought. Maybe sixty, sixty-five, not the seventy-five I first assumed.

Tommy rose too, groaning, and introduced us. "Liv, meet Dr. Morgan."

The doctor extended his free hand to me, and beneath my firm grip, I felt strong, thin fingers.

"Dr. Morgan," I repeated. "So very good to meet you. I've heard so many great things about you over the years."

"Oh, my," he chortled. "All lies, I assure you."

Tommy took extra care in lowering himself back in his chair, clearly bothered by the pain in his knees again.

"I hear you're about to find the elixir for my friend's joint aches," I said, motioning toward Tommy.

"Well, I don't know about that," he said with a chuckle. "How are you doing with your medication, Tom?"

Tommy nodded. "Still okay. Just hate to take it because it makes my head fuzzy and makes me sleepy all the time. Can't work feeling sleepy."

"Take those pills," he said with a wink and a nod. "Nice to meet you, Liv. I just came in for a bottle of the elixir of my choosing, and I'm on my way home to enjoy a few nips." He held up a bottle of Johnny Walker and hobbled toward the door.

"Nice man," I said.

"Don't let that bastard fool you," Tommy said with a grunt. "Nice and ornery, I'd say. So what did Cecelia tell you?"

"The rumor is that Eddie Schilling messes around with high school girls," I said, looking to Tommy for confirmation.

"I suppose," he said, draining the balance of his coffee.

"Have you seen any young girls over at the campground with Mr. Schilling?"

"Nope."

"Ever?"

He shook his head.

"And you're out there every day working the fields, right?"

He nodded.

"Did you ever see Michelle over there? I mean, other than yesterday when you found her."

He shook his head again.

"Do you think Mully or one of these Lucifer's Lot bikers killed Michelle?"

He looked into my eyes and said, "I wouldn't put it past them." I sensed a "but" might follow. "But those FBI guys will do the right thing."

Translation: He believed someone else was responsible, not Mully. "And do you think I'm safe? As far as Mully is concerned?"

"Not until and unless you call those agents and tell them what you know," he scolded, pointing at the pay phone on the wall by the bar. "Now is a good time."

"I think I need more privacy, if you know what I mean. Mind giving me a ride back to my truck on your way home?" I asked, eager to be on my way.

"My pleasure, Miss Bergen."

At my truck, Tommy offered a smile and said, "Make the call."

"I will. When I find a phone."

He surprised me when he shoved his cell phone into my hand.

"And find that girl, Char. From what you've told me, she's definitely the key," he said, knowing far more than he let on.

I agreed with him wholeheartedly.

Before I shut his door, I asked, "Do you know Ernif and Helma Hanson?"

"Of course," he said. "They live by my cousin up past Rochford."

"I heard today that he died," I said, searching his face.

"On Sunday," he said, leveling his eyes on mine. "That's what Dr. Morgan was telling me before you came back to the table. He's caring for Helma in hospice, and he said she didn't take the news all that well. He was killed just like Michelle."

"Oh," I said, not sure what he meant by that.

As quickly as I had wondered, Tommy explained. "Struck from behind. On the back of his head."

My gut twisted. Elizabeth was right.

Ernif Hanson had been murdered.

CHAPTER 23

WHEN HE OPENED THE door to the bathroom, Streeter was startled by the unexpected presence on the other side.

"Quit sneaking around," Streeter scolded, holding a cold towel to his jaws.

"I was bringing you coffee, you ungrateful asshole," Bly said, extending the cup and tossing him a frozen package. "And peas. For your jaw. It will keep the swelling down."

"Thanks. Nice shiner."

"Go to hell," Bly mumbled, walking toward the little kitchen and placing another package of frozen peas to his own face.

"We're too old for this."

"Well, those idiot college kids had it coming," Bly argued, remembering how they left all three in a heap at the bar. A boyish grin snuck up on his lips. "I'm kind of glad you misinterpreted my signal to go. I meant go as in leave, not go as in go after the guy. I haven't been in a bar brawl in a long time. Kind of felt good."

"I figured if we were real Serpents, we wouldn't have done anything less," Streeter agreed, drinking the tepid coffee that Bly had just handed him.

"Really getting into your character, aren't you? I like that. At least Big Red and his boys won't question if we're really Serpents," Bly conceded.

"I'm going to have to buy some more sunglasses," Streeter said, holding up the pretzel mess of plastic and dark lenses.

"Shank sent me a diagram while you were nursing your jaw, so I marked the boot prints leading away from Michelle's body back to the Lazy S on this quadrangle map here. Two sets of footprints going up, one coming back. They confirmed that the second set matched the shoes Michelle was wearing when they found her."

Files, papers, and pictures were scattered across the big oak table in the safe house. Bly unrolled a map and placed his coffee cup on one corner to keep it from rolling up. Streeter checked his watch; 7:47 pm. Still plenty of time before the late night activities in Sturgis got rolling.

"This is Sturgis," Bly said, pointing to the map. "This is where Michelle's body was found, where Tommy Jasper found it, and where Clint White was seen early Monday morning taking a smoke. Here's the Bergen quarry. I also marked the Lazy S Campground, of course." He continued to point with his index finger to each of the dotted marks as he dictated the list of the players' homes. "Frankie Jr.'s, Brian's, Frank and Arlene's, Ken Vincent's, Eddie Schilling's, Jens Bergen's, Roy Barker's, Michelle's old apartment, and Barker's Market. Michelle's Vega was found in the grocery store parking lot right here, but Roy Barker said she always parked here."

"Someone else was driving," Streeter concluded. "Or Michelle was trying to tell us something."

"Barker and Bergen both confirmed that Michelle mentioned having car trouble. Maybe Char was driving."

Dragging his finger across the creek from the Lazy S Campground and into the tree line up the creek to where Michelle's body was found, Streeter speculated out loud, "So, Michelle walked from the Lazy S to where she was killed. How did she get to the Lazy S in the first place?"

Bly offered, "Mully or one of his crew enticed her into partying with them? She climbed on one of their bikes?"

"I don't buy it," Streeter said, shaking his head from side to side. "From everything we've learned about her, she didn't seem to be that kind of person. Too responsible to be a partier. Besides, she had declined Mully's offer in the grocery store."

"Unless she had a Sybil thing going on," Bly snorted.

"Entirely possible. But Michelle didn't appear to be like most rape victims, particularly victims of violent rape, who often deal with the emotional aftermath by using coping mechanisms, like compartmentalizing their feelings and emotions, in order to deal with the trauma, the shock of it all."

"Give it to me in English."

"Michelle was highly functioning, had moved on with her life," Streeter said, walking to the picture window and studying the night movement of the vendors, bikers, and tourists on Main Street.

The majority of them looked like boys on their way to Pinocchio's Pleasure Island, thinking they were going to have the time of their lives, not knowing they were about to turn into jackasses filled with regret.

Streeter refilled his coffee, wanting to stay sober as he rode the Harley.

"But it isn't entirely out of the question that Michelle could have hopped on Mully's bike willingly and been his sheep for the evening," Bly concluded, playing devil's advocate.

"Possible, but I doubt it," Streeter said, "but without having any psychological analysis, it would be hard to prove. And even if we could, it doesn't prove who murdered Michelle. Having information about Michelle's psychological state might be helpful to us at Mully's trial, if he really did murder Michelle. For now we need to focus on viable suspects rather than chasing any dead ends."

"Before we call it a dead end, Streeter, should we investigate whether or not Michelle was seeing a shrink?" Bly asked.

"Might not be a bad idea, although I seriously doubt if anything will turn up. Just instinct. But that would be a good way to keep Shank busy."

"What about the hypothesis that Michelle was forced onto the bike with Mully?"

"Does that fit the Lucifer's Lot style?"

"If she affronted them somehow," Bly answered, nodding. "Maybe she got lippy at the grocery store and Mully didn't like it. Or maybe she ran into his bike in the parking lot, tipped it over or something. Who the hell knows? From what Eddie says, it doesn't take a whole lot to get Mully's blood boiling."

"Or maybe she was protecting Char. Would they kill her for that?"

"Not likely," Bly said, thinking of other scenarios. "Maybe it was a class for one of the prospects and the beating got a little too rough, causing her to die."

"With no bruises, no semen, no sexual violation of any kind?" Streeter asked, incredulous. "Would they have handled a situation gone poorly by dumping the body like that?"

"Definitely," Bly answered, shoving a chunk of summer sausage into his mouth. He spoke through a mouthful. "But only if she was really dead first. And only after everyone who wanted them earned his wings, which would mean the swabs for saliva will start showing multiple DNA patterns."

"We've got to find out if Mully or any of his gang are wearing the purple wings."

"It'd be a start," Bly admitted. "We've got to find him first. By the way, they pulled Roy Barker in for questioning about the B&E at Bergen's house and found nothing out of the ordinary in Michelle's locker at work. They'll let us know what they learn from Barker."

"We're still going to the Cattle Jump Campground tonight?"

"And Main Street again. He'll be at one of those places. The Miss Cattle Jump Campground contest is in two and a half hours. If I had my guess, he'll be out there. But he won't be wearing his colors. Inferno Force don't allow it."

"That's right," Streeter said. "You mentioned they police the campground."

He remembered the last time he was at the Cattle Jump Campground, images as clear and disgusting as if it were last night. He rubbed his tender jaw, amazed at how true the saying was about nothing ever changing.

"He'll be there, though," Bly asserted. "Mully won't want to pass up that kind of entertainment. We'll have to follow him until he leaves. They'll fly their colors as soon as they leave the campground and then we'll be able to see if he's wearing any purple wings."

"If you ain't limpin', you ain't shit" was the bumper sticker slapped to the back of the wheelchair in front of him being self-propelled by the broad-shouldered biker. Streeter had forgotten how claustrophobic the Sturgis Motorcycle Rally crowd made him feel until he found himself up to his nose in elbows and greasy hair, right smack in the middle of it. Then again, he reminded himself, the attendees ten years earlier had been merely a fraction of the four to five hundred thousand participants that had streamed into this small South Dakota town for this week. He was grateful for the breathing room the wheelchair gave him as he trekked up one side of Main Street and down the other.

To parallel the thick crowds on the sidewalks, hundreds of thousands of motorcycles were parked in a row down the center of the street and along both sides, allowing two narrow lanes of traffic that provided a continuous motorcycle parade for onlookers. The bikes were an amazing display of the best, the brightest, the oldest, and the oddest. Mostly Harley-Davidsons, the bikes lining the street thus looked like obedient, stout soldiers outfitted for action. Onlookers could ogle to their heart's content, but the unspoken rule was that bikes were never to be touched. Again, Streeter was amazed by the self-discipline these bikers exercised in following such a simple rule. Either that, or the last person who touched someone's bike found himself with rearranged fingers.

Streeter searched in the sea of bikers for any sign of red and silver or Mully's salt-and-pepper mop of hair. His eyes seemed to land on everything but: beer bellies, scruffy whiskers, unkempt hair, and black T-shirts. The men weren't much better, Streeter mused, realizing it was his humor that would assure he'd keep his cool as an undercover agent rather than bolting, as instincts would have him do. Granted, some of the women were not bad looking, he admitted to himself, but most were overweight, under-dressed, overly intoxicated, and badly in need of eau de Febreze.

It was the sea of black that made Streeter feel particularly claustro-phobic. The ratty-looking T-shirts that engulfed him on the streets were adorned with Harley-Davidson logos, raging ghouls or fiery skulls, or naked or sparsely clad women. A few featured clever sayings: "If you can read this, the bitch fell off," or "Satan is my copilot," or as one woman confessed, "If it has a dick or a kickstand, I'll ride it." Still other societal outcasts wore T-shirts with messages intending to shock, such as "I fuck sheep," or "50,000 battered women and I'm eating mine plain." Along with the black T-shirts were black leather chaps, black domers, black skullcaps, black vests, and black leather jackets, despite the sweltering heat. The only thing more suffocating than the sea of black was the smell of it all.

And the smell of all that black leather was now rising in waves off distant, hot asphalt. Mixed with the hot leather was the rank odor of sweat from the street vendors who were flipping grilled pork and beef and chicken, smothered in biker-preferred grilled onions and peppers, as quickly as the throng could order them. Wafts of greasy fries, exhaust from legions of motorcycles, acres of freshly tattooed skin oozing blood, and fetid body odors sickened him, and Streeter thought if one more person with halitosis breathed the word "Serpent" in his nose as they passed by him, he might punch someone. Anyone. It wouldn't matter.

There were made-to-order shops and stands galore: hemp and halter booths, tire and tattoo experts, glow-in-the-dark nunchaku and nameplate artisans, souvenir and skullcap vendors, bra and beer tents. If a person had the mind to, anything on his or her body could be pierced, collared, painted, tattooed, or exposed.

Streeter turned his head toward the street for a moment to stop the involuntary gag that had risen in his throat. Bly moved beside him and both folded their arms across their chests as they stared out at the motorcycle parade. A speedboat mounted over a motorcycle drove by, painted with licking flames of silver and red.

Streeter pointed and scoffed, "The irony. I've been looking for red and silver all evening and this is what I see."

The next bike had two shirtless men riding on it, both in black leather chaps—period.

Bly grunted, "They're practically begging for trouble. It's a sin to have a man riding in the bitch seat, particularly with another man. When it's a man riding with a woman, they just consider him pussy whipped."

Streeter pointed at the next bike that passed by. The man driving it looked like a half-naked Santa Claus. "And you don't think he's asking for trouble?"

"He's looking for naughty girls to sit on his lap and tell them what they want for Christmas." Bly studied Streeter a moment before asking, "You okay? You're looking kind of green. Drink too much earlier tonight, bud?"

"Hell, no," Streeter growled. "It's the disgusting whiffs of BO and caramelized onions and pus-festering, oozing tattoos and stinking leather. Darned if I'm not going to puke all over the next person that breathes on me."

Bly roared with laughter.

A small crowd gathered behind them, pointing at their colors. It was rare for Serpents to attend the rally, and Streeter had quickly become accustomed to the pointing and whispering.

Streeter talked from the side of his mouth so only Bly could hear his question. "Do Serpents puke?"

"Obviously, this one does," Bly said, gesturing with his thumb toward his fellow agent.

The next motorcycle in the parade was a tricycle towing a jailhouse, a beautiful redhead in a pink bikini caged within the bars.

Bly nodded at the biker, who flashed a toothless grin his way, before turning toward Streeter, saying, "Pus-festering, oozing tattoos? Where do you come up with this shit?"

"Just take a look around you, friend."

The next biker on parade was straddling an ape hanger, the handlebars rising high above his ears on either side. He had a scraggly gray beard, a tattoo on his naked belly of one fat pig mounting another one, and a plastic pig nose covering his own.

"What did that say?" Streeter asked of the words tattooed as a rocker on the biker's belly.

"Makin' bacon," Bly chortled.

"Okay, I give up," Streeter confessed. "I just don't get this."

A woman with long blonde hair that covered all of her seemingly naked body parts rode by on the back of the next tricycle. She was waving at her adoring fans in the crowd.

"Delusional," Streeter muttered. "Absolutely delusional."

"You forgot portable potties," Bly said as the motorcycle with a canoe for a sidecar paddled by.

"What?"

"The odors," Bly explained. "You forgot the distinguishably vomit-inducing smell of the public portable potties, especially when they're over-due to be emptied."

"Geez, Bly," Streeter said, covering his mouth with his hand. "I'm picking your boots to puke on."

"Let's get you some beer," he offered. "It'll calm—"

Midsentence, Bly smacked Streeter on the arm and nodded to the other side of the street.

It was definitely Mully and his boys headed in the opposite direction.

"Can we cross here?" Streeter asked.

"Make it look like we're looking at the bikes."

The sun was setting, the moon already high and the sky every shade of orange and gray, as they made it past their first line of parked bikes. They waited until the biker and the heavy brunette on the Indian rode past before crossing the narrow lane with oncoming bikes to the center of the street where another row was parked. Pretending to be studying the artwork on one particular bike, Streeter sought Mully in the crowd and spotted him half a block away.

"He's moving pretty fast," Streeter noted.

"Come on," Bly said, walking along the line of parked bikes on the yellow striping in the center of the street, unobstructed by the crowd on the sidewalk.

They were a few paces behind Mully and his gang when they crossed the last lane of traffic and fell into the crowd. Pushing their way through the few people between them and the Lucifer's Lot, they settled into a comfortable pace only a head or two behind their target, waiting for the right opportunity to assess the wing patches on their vests.

The air was thick and warm, as though someone had just opened the oven door where a turkey was roasting. Streeter's excitement grew as he and Bly narrowed the gap between them and the Lot. He said nothing to Bly over the next several minutes, knowing that he was as focused on timing as Streeter was. He willed Mully and his minions into the next beer tent, but they didn't go.

The night crowd was even denser than the early evening crowd had been. Certainly more colors were being worn, even though it was discouraged by law enforcement; more of the gorgeous babes were out, and fewer of the heftier women; and more of those who simply didn't fit in seemed to have come out of the woodwork. Cowboys, college coeds, office clerks—the looky-loos of the rally.

A teenage hippie with dreadlocks and multiple body piercings strolled by and said to his companion, "Hey, man. Look. The Lucifer's Lot. Cool." Only to say a few steps later, "Hey, man. Look. Serpents. Way cool. Never seen one of those before."

Bly cursed the idiot punks, hoping that Mully and his gang had not heard the kid. If they had overheard the comment, they gave no indication. They paused outside the tattoo parlor, all six of the members gawking at the bikers getting fresh tattoos while seated in the eight chairs normally reserved for hair styling. One patron was leaning over a table getting his butt cheek tattooed, and Mully was pointing and laughing.

Streeter and Bly hung back just far enough not to be noticed by him, but close enough to stay in view.

"Come on, turn around," Bly mumbled. "Turn around."

He had whispered it quietly enough for just Streeter to hear, speaking his thoughts aloud and wishing the Lucifer's Lot bikers would turn toward them, even for a moment, so they could scan their colors for the purple wings.

Incredibly, they did as Bly asked, only in the wrong direction. Their backs squarely to Streeter and Bly, they continued to make their way through the stream of people.

"Damn it," Bly grumbled.

Next stop for Mully and crew was in front of a row of bikes where a heavy teenage girl was sitting on top of her biker boyfriend. She couldn't have been more than eighteen, her face pimply, braces still bracketing her teeth. He was at least forty-five, maybe fifty, Streeter guessed. The girl wore a loose, V-shaped halter, which was desperately trying to harness her pendulous breasts, too saggy for someone her age. Her cutoff shorts made Streeter recall the comment about a ten-pound sausage being shoved into a five-pound casing, and he marveled at how accurately he had envisioned that statement all these years.

The girl was sitting backward on the Harley, rocking back and forth on the old biker's crotch. A crowd was gathering, and Mully's bikers were cheering the teenager on. Mully was watching someone across the street. Streeter couldn't tell what caught his eye. The old biker leaned back on his bike and flashed a toothy grin at the crowd that encircled him, pleased to have his five minutes of fame. The young girl accommodated his fantasy, and her own, by leaning back on the handlebars and laboriously lifting her wide hips to strategically mount his raggedy face. He obliged her, encouraged by the whoops and hollers of the crowd, not the least of which was coming from Mully's gang, until the poor girl's arms and legs weakened from her own weight. She stared up the crowd and flashed a tinny, amateurishly seductive smile at the crowd as if taking bows at a curtain call.

If Streeter ever doubted the theory about young girls who were eager to jump on the back of a stranger's bike, he would only have to recall this mortifying incident to remind himself of his job to make sure the bad guys were behind bars. Then girls like this would be safe from their own naïve decisions.

Streeter and Bly angled to see the front of the Lucifer's Lot vests just as they turned away and slipped into the crowd once again.

"Damn it," Bly mumbled again, this time loud enough to startle the woman next to them. "Just when we get close enough."

He didn't finish his thought. They both watched as the red and silver bandanas of two members bobbed in the crowd ahead of them and turned into a beer tent.

"We've got them now," Streeter said.

He didn't see it coming. An arm reached around him, slamming him against the storefront. A few of the crowd scattered, but most went on streaming by as if nothing had happened. The stars dancing across his eyes had not yet cleared, but there was no mistaking the knife's edge against his neck. He squeezed his eyes shut to scatter the stars and opened them long enough to see the B.F.F.O. tattooed across the bald man's forehead. A member from Outraged, the motorcycle club that loves to torture, Streeter thought. Great.

"Fucking Serpent," he spat at Streeter. "You and your friend have a choice to make tonight. Talk or die."

CHAPTER 24

EMBOLDENED BY MY TIME with Tommy, not to mention the double shot of vodka, which set my teeth on edge, I slowed as I neared the entrance to the Lazy S Campground. I checked to make sure no bikes were in sight. I figured my luck would certainly run out on a third high-speed chase through the Hills. Lucky for me, the lights still glowed in the lone building, but all else was in darkness. There was no activity around the tents and vans parked to the right where Mully and his merry men had come from earlier today when I drove by—the first high-speed chase. I turned into the campground, my tires crunching on the gravel as I circled the building.

Two cars were parked in the rear: one a green Volvo and the other a red sports car. I've never been much into cars, so I had no clue what make and model the red one was, but I assumed since there were two cars, my chances were pretty good that one belonged to Mr. Schilling and I was glad to know he was still here. And if I was really lucky, maybe the other belonged to a teenager, a girl, and I'd catch them in a compromising situation, which would allow me to launch into a good old-fashioned western confrontation about Char. Maybe one of the cars belonged to Char, which would be the ultimate in showdowns. And, just maybe, all of this would go nowhere, the whole teen girl fetish thing nothing but rumors aimed to fuel someone's petty envy, taint a local hero.

I pulled Jens's pickup into a parking spot near the office entrance and saw Mr. Schilling standing outside the door, bare arms folded across his chest. His expression was one of concern.

Before I was fully out of the cab, Mr. Schilling called out to me. "No vacancies in this campground. Try KOA's up the road past Nemo and on into Lead/Deadwood. Sturgis campgrounds will be full," he said, squinting at me in the darkness, his eyes not adjusting fast enough after stepping out of the bright lights inside.

"Mr. Schilling. It's me, Liv Bergen. Do you remember me?"

"Come on inside where I can have a better look," he said, waving toward the door.

I followed him inside, noting the painted concrete block structure and wondering if the blocks had come from our manufacturing plant. The building was solid, but sparse, a rectangular shape of not more than eight or nine hundred square feet. The front room reminded me of a prison cafeteria: two tables, eight folding chairs around each; several vending machines along two of the bare walls; a sink and a counter in one corner, upon which sat a coffee pot that looked like it perked high-test java 24-7; and a flat screen television chattering away in one corner. A woman emerged from the doorway that led to the back rooms.

Not a teen.

"Samantha, we have a visitor," Mr. Schilling explained, brushing a thin black curl from his forehead.

"At this hour?" she turned her wrist. I had lost all sense of time and glanced around the room to spot a clock, which didn't exist. She didn't hesitate to scold me. "It's almost ten."

"Sorry for the late hour. I'm hoping you can help me," I said turning to Mr. Schilling. "I'm looking for someone and heard that you might know where I could find her."

After a quick glance Samantha's way, Mr. Schilling's eyes narrowed. "What'd you say your name was again?"

"Liv Bergen."

"Garth Bergen's daughter? The mining Bergens? Well, imagine that Samantha. Liv is our neighbor." Samantha's scowl was obvious, and Mr. Schilling's mocking tone wasn't helping my nerves.

"I was in your PE class at Dakota Junior High School a while back."

I saw a flicker of a different type of recognition in his eyes. "A long while back, actually. Like sixteen years ago or so."

The woman named Samantha pulled out a chair from beneath the table, the legs scraping across the cheap linoleum. She was the cheerleader type; thin, but fit, spent a good deal of time on her appearance, the type of woman I could learn from, if I wanted more dates. Her eyes were large but too big for her face—an image of Betty Boop flashed across my mind—and her mouth was tight and small, as if she'd been sucking on a lemon. She wore a hefty amount of makeup. Her blonde hair tumbled against her shoulders in chunky pieces, a messy, devil-may-care style that took much maintenance and upkeep. I had to hand it to her, though; she seemed to be holding her own in her battle with aging, as so few do.

"I remember you," said Mr. Schilling. "The basketball player."

I nodded, noticing Samantha roll her eyes at the mention of my athleticism.

"Quite good, if I recall. You went on to play college ball? Division I?"

I nodded again. "For a couple of years."

At least I had softened Mr. Schilling.

Samantha, on the other hand, hunkered down in her chair and pretended to watch the television. I didn't want to stay here any longer than I absolutely had to; I was worried both about finding Char tonight and about avoiding Mully. My mind danced across the list of names and addresses of all the volleyball players, which was stuffed in my back pocket. I could have visited all the addresses, but it might take me an entire day or two, whereas Mr. Schilling could easily narrow my search.

I pulled out my list and unfolded the sheet, earning attention from Samantha. "I need to find Charlene Freeburg tonight."

Mr. Schilling's eyes widened slightly and again darted toward the woman he called Samantha, who I assumed was his official girlfriend or wife.

"I have reason to believe she's staying with a friend, another volleyball player."

"What's her name again?" Mr. Schilling said, wetting his lips and altering his expression to one of confusion.

"Charlene Freeburg. She goes by Char."

Samantha stood and sidled up next to Mr. Schilling, who stood staring at me like a bastard calf at a gate.

"Can't say . . . I don't know that I . . ." he stammered.

Her eyes settling on me, Samantha elbowed him and said, "I bet she's related to Michelle Freeburg, the girl whose body was found yesterday morning up the creek. Am I right?"

I nodded. "Her little sister. She might not know about Michelle. I'm trying to find her."

Mr. Schilling flicked his tongue across his lips. He looked nervous. Really nervous. Maybe about Char, but definitely at the mention of Michelle's name. He had shifted his weight at least four or five times since I started in on this line of questioning, which to me didn't seem to warrant the nervousness or the act if he really didn't know Char or Michelle.

I pulled the rug out from beneath him so I could move on. "She's trying out for your junior varsity squad later this month; she's been practicing all summer long with the others. Oh, right, something they'd be doing without your knowledge." I winked cartoonishly at him to let him know I knew he was simply trying to cover his ass about rules that banned coaching teams outside the season. "Thin, dark curly hair."

Mr. Schilling cleared his throat. "Oh, Char. Yes. I don't spend a lot of time with the underclassmen, even if they are trying out for my junior varsity team. And I knew nothing about the summer practice squad, of course."

"Of course," I repeated.

"That would be against school sanctions. But I can't stop the girls from volunteering to get together and play on occasion."

"Yeah, whatever," I said, crossing my arms in disbelief. "I'm not here to bust your balls about rule violations. I'm here to find Char. Which of the girls on my list would she be hanging out with?" I practically shoved the crumpled paper under his nose.

Samantha folded her arms and leaned away from Mr. Schilling, eyeing him.

"What?" he said. "How should I know? I barely know the girl."

Samantha tapped her foot, annoyed as I was at his act. "Tell her, Eddie. Or you can tell Shank."

Bob Shankley's name coming up again. Interesting. "Are you Mrs. Schilling?" I asked, appreciating her help in cutting to the chase.

She nodded. "Twenty-four years."

"Wow," was all I managed. They didn't look like a happily married couple, but who was I to judge?

"Maybe she's at the rally," he grunted.

"Sturgis? She's underage."

"Don't have to be twenty-one to walk the streets of Sodom," he said with a shrug.

I gawked at him. Then I shot a glance at Mrs. Schilling, who appeared to be more confused than I was.

He furrowed his eyebrows. "You know, Sodom and Gomorrah? Sturgis and Deadwood? Sex and gambling?"

I had to get this back on track. Besides, I happened to like the quaint little towns of Sturgis, home for a VA hospital, and of Deadwood, one of the last historic Wild West towns settled during the Gold Rush and home of Black Hills gold. And the people who lived in those towns were nothing like those referred to in biblical references.

I resisted the argument and asked, "So you think Char is messing around in Sturgis or Deadwood during the rally? That's why she's missing?"

Mrs. Schilling crossed her legs, folded her arms, and glared at her husband. I was starting to like her. The silence was thick enough to smother any smoky fires of distraction that he was trying to set.

"Eddie, where's the girl?" Mrs. Schilling spat.

"Try Valerie Sanchez. Or Mandy Blunk." Mr. Schilling was flustered, consulting the list but appearing, rather, to grab at any names that seemed to pop into his mind. In the silence that followed he quickly scanned the list again. "Hope Smith. That would be my best guess."

I snatched the list from him and refolded it, placing it once more into my back pocket. "You've been so very helpful."

"What's it to you, anyway?" he called after me as I turned to go.

"Michelle was to be my sister-in-law and she was brutally murdered. I won't rest until I find out who did this to her," I said, a bit melodramatically, but honestly nonetheless. I left him standing there, his mouth gaping like that of a landed trout, his face blanched, his wife glaring at him. I suspected a marital tiff was about to erupt, and I wasn't about to be caught in the middle of such a mess.

Besides, I had tempted fate long enough and it was time for me to get the hell out of there before Mully and company returned.

I sat with the windows of the truck open, listening to the hum of the street-lights in the stillness of the dark neighborhood. A cricket's song lifted in the night, breaking my train of thought, and my hands reached for the cell phone I had borrowed from Tommy. I punched in Jens's cell for the fourth time and left another desperate message not to go home tonight, to stay with Ida. His greeting had been specifically for me, and although it was the fourth time I'd heard it, I listened carefully for any change in the message saying Ida had returned home from her latest trip and asking me to join them for dinner at the Firehouse. Any change at all would mean he'd heard my pleas. But it was the same old message. I stretched my gray matter to remember Ida's cell number and left her a message as well, hoping one of the two would intercept my warning before finding themselves face-to-face with an even angrier Mully or some other Lucifer's Lot biker. I was ready to call the agents and tell them what I had seen the previous day in Sturgis and prayed the girl who died was not Charlene Freeburg.

Surprised that Tommy had a cell phone at his age, even more surprised that he had lent it to me, and shocked that he had Internet access as well, I searched the Web for the FBI number and assumed I'd get the night answering service. As the call rang through, I watched the Smith house, lights glowing beyond the curtains. I considered checking with Valerie and Mandy, but something in the way Mr. Schilling settled on Hope Smith made me choose this house as the first place to inquire about Char. Simul-taneously with the second ring, two shapes appeared behind the curtains, both looking like young women, one looking as if she had a curly mop of hair.

Just as a woman answered the phone, "Federal Bureau of Investiga-tion," I hit the end button, terminating the call.

I bounded from the truck, sprinted up the front steps, and knocked on the door. I noticed the stack of rolled newspapers piled up on the corner of the front porch. A redhead with a ponytail answered, opening the door wide, but not so much that I could see into the living room.

"Hope Smith?" I asked her.

Her eyebrows buckled. "Maybe."

"Is Charlene Freeburg here?" I asked simply.

The girl looked over her shoulder into the living room, and I heard someone turn down the music. Hope looked back to me, a question forming in her eyes as to how to answer.

"Are your parents home?"

The door eased shut to within inches of slamming on me.

I ad-libbed a little, based on the newspapers. "Because I heard they were out of town on a trip and that Char was staying with you while they were gone. I need to talk with her."

Hope glanced again over her shoulder at someone who I assumed was Char hiding beyond.

"Char, we need to talk," I called out before Hope could close the door on me. "It's bad news, I'm afraid."

Framed in a halo of black ringlets, Char's angelic face peered around the door and stared out at me, concern in her eyes. It felt like someone had poured a bucket of warm honey onto my head, purging the chill of dread I had yoked around me since watching the bikers near the grain silo. The honey flowed all the way out through the tips of my toes and fingers in a flood of relief as my eyes verified that the girl who had died in Sturgis and Char Freeburg were definitely not one and the same. This was Char Freeburg. I definitely saw a resemblance to Michelle, particularly around her wide eyes.

Although Char was mostly tucked behind the door, I could see that both she and Hope wore tank tops and shorts, and they were barefoot and makeup free. I could smell pizza from somewhere beyond and what might have been freshly baked brownies. The transition from commercial to announcer to song told me the music had most likely been coming from the television, probably MTV or another music video channel. The girls were enjoying some summer fun, freedom from parental interference for a few days, nothing that was harmful or shameful in anyway.

"What about?" she said, her voice small.

Hope stood rigid at the door, neither swinging it open to let me in nor slamming it shut to force me out. Char studied me, gripping the door as if it was the only thing holding her up.

"I'm Jens's sister, Liv Bergen. I think you should come with me. I need to take you home," I said, leaving it for someone else to deliver the news.

Hope gripped her arm and said, "Maybe you should go, Char."

Char nodded and looked over her shoulder into the living room.

"Don't worry about it. I'll clean up," Hope added.

As Charlene Freeburg stepped from behind the door into the full light of the entranceway, brushing the curl that had spilled onto her forehead away from her face, I gasped. Everything was clear to me now. The entire story unfolded as I stared at her familiar face. To confirm what I suspected, I asked bluntly, "Who was the guy you were with Sunday night?"

She glanced back over her shoulder at her friend for reassurance and I added, "It's important, Char. Life or death."

"Life or . . ." her words trailed. She swallowed hard, looking to her friend for support and guidance. Hope nodded and Char turned to me, drawing a deep breath. "Michelle followed us. We went to buy some beer and hang out. We drove up to Dinosaur Hill to look at the city lights. I was feeling good and he was enjoying the music. We weren't doing anything much. Just having fun."

"When was this?" I asked.

"Sunday night," she said. "I don't know. When did you pick me up, Hope?"

"Around ten, I guess," the redhead answered, scooping up empty soda cans and pizza boxes, afraid she might find herself in trouble along with Char.

"What happened? With you and Michelle?"

She shrugged and looked back at Hope again, presumably to draw confidence. Hope shot a sideways glance toward her and continued her cleanup efforts. "I was . . . she had snuck up on us. Like I said, we were just having fun. I think she thought we were having sex or something, but we were just listening to some music. Just playing around, you know?"

I was tired of asking so many people so many questions, and my tone reflected my impatience. "What. Happened?"

"Michelle shone the flashlight on us, saw who I was with, and yanked me out of the car, dragging me back to hers. I was so embarrassed. We fought all the way home, and when she parked the car, I ran off. Called Hope from the corner liquor store," her eyes were starting to fill with tears. "I've never seen her so angry, so upset. She . . . she told me things. She scared me. What's this all about? Where's Michelle?"

I took a deep breath, waiting to hear the answer I already suspected but needed to hear, from Michelle through Char, when I asked, "Why was Michelle so upset? What did she tell you?"

"That the guy I was with . . ." she started sobbing.

Hope stood, wide-eyed, and came to Char's side. Clearly Char hadn't told her this part, since all pretenses of cleaning and the fear of getting into trouble herself had been completely overcome by intrigue and fascination with Char's answer.

"That the guy you were with was what?" I insisted.

"That he hooked up with her when she was my age."

"Hooked up? Or raped?"

Her eyes dropped to the floor and her fingers twisted into a worried tangle.

All the pieces slid neatly into place.

"Tell me his name, Char."

CHAPTER 25

RUBBING HIS FINGERS GENTLY across his neck and over his white whiskers, stubble he'd allowed to go unshaved for the first time since he became an operative in the field, Streeter said, "You know what, Bly?"

Through splashes of cold water against his face, Bly asked, "What?"

"Working with you hurts," was all Streeter offered, inspecting the fine beads of blood that had already coagulated along the long stretch of a superficial blade mark spanning left ear to right collar bone across his Adam's apple.

"Me?" Bly rose from his bent position over the basin, his ruddy, scraggly-bearded face dripping with water. He grabbed for a fistful of coarse paper towels from the dispenser. "It hurts working with me? Hell, I've been working this rally for years, and so far, I've been in more fights with you in five hours than I have in any other rally ever. Working with *you* hurts."

Bly was pointing a stiff finger at him.

"Holster that finger, cowboy." Streeter pushed each of the three stall doors open to make sure no one was in the bar bathroom with them. "What was that Outraged fellow all about?" Streeter asked, dabbing away the blood on his neck with a damp paper towel, leaving an angry red line.

"He was probably an intelligence officer," Bly answered, rubbing his eyes with the palms of his hands. "Only thing he could have been. He was from the Atlanta chapter and he knew too much about the Serpents' presence in Florida. He must have seen our rockers and took the opportunity to gather a little intelligence while he was partying hard up here."

"And it was my New Jersey connection that set him off, right?"

"That, or the idea of two Serpents together in public. A rarity," Bly said, groping for another fistful of the stiff paper towels. "Good thing you read all those files, Streeter. You were brilliant. Knew plenty about Operation Marlin. Enough to make him leave us alone."

"Well, how could I forget about one of my fellow freaking gang members being hired by a New York Mafia outfit to go down to the docks in Florida and stomp the life out of their enemies, literally?"

Bly shuddered. "You were brilliant, I say. Even remembered some of the names. Good job."

"Hard to shake. My fellow New Jersey Serpent, Mad Shark, wrapping up at least seven hits in newspaper and stomping them to death like they were fish," Streeter said, staring at his own ghostly reflection in the streaked mirror as he spoke. "I can't even picture what would make a guy do something like that, let alone admit to being his buddy."

"But you did admit it and you were believable," Bly said, slapping Streeter on his back. "And it's greed that motivates a guy like Mad Shark. Those guys in New York paid him a ton of money to wipe out their competition."

"So what got the Outraged so huffy about it? Were the Serpents cutting in on their territory for being the hit men for the Mafia?"

Bly shook his head and tossed the paper towels in the overfilled garbage bin. "Hiring out as hit men isn't the Outraged style. In fact, it really isn't anyone's style except the Serpents'. We're a nomadic, independent sort," Bly added mockingly, tugging on the tails of his black leather jacket. "Even though that ugly bastard kept saying he was going to kill you, and any other Serpent he could get his hands on, I just couldn't buy it. Just because we had infringed on their territory down there? I think they're scared and they're pissed. Pissed because Mad Shark's especially ingenious murders brought on a brighter focus from the feds in that area, which is Outraged territory."

"And scared because Mad Shark was so ruthless and acted alone?" Streeter surmised.

"Exactly," Bly said, leaning up against one of the sinks and crossing his arms. "Wouldn't you be? A crazy bastard like Mad Shark going around stomping Mafia thugs to death? Gives me the willies."

"Having a knife shoved up against my throat doesn't do wonders for me, either," Streeter admitted sourly, inspecting the wound in the cloudy mirror. "Looks more like an age line. Great. Can't even look macho out of the whole deal."

Bly chuckled. "Damn, you're one tough customer. You almost get killed and you're cracking jokes."

"Right."

"I'm telling you, you answered all their questions perfectly. They'll leave you alone the rest of the rally. You gave them what they wanted. They wanted to know who you were and what you knew about Mad Shark."

"But I didn't give them a thing on the thirteen," Streeter replied.

"That's okay. They really didn't expect you to know who any of the thirteen members are in the Serpents' mother chapter. Very few do. That's how they stay out of trouble and how they keep from getting snagged by the long fingers of the law," Bly explained.

"Well, he sure scared the hell out of me. I thought we were both dead when I couldn't come up with a name of one of the thirteen."

They both stared at the moldy grout between the tiles of the dank bathroom floor, eyes glazed over by the thought of what could have happened, what almost happened. They were startled into movement from their frozen positions when the door swung open, a large, beer-bellied man belching as he padded to the first stall.

"You want a beer before we roll?" Bly asked.

"Two," Streeter answered.

———

Cattle Jump Campground wasn't anything like what Streeter had expected compared to days long since gone by. It was much tamer, less raunchy, and far cleaner under the new ownership. He even spotted several teenagers and children among the crowds of interested tourists; that would never have happened years ago. What he had remembered was no longer. Hookers carrying buckets of soapy water offering blowjobs for five bucks were replaced with hired models wearing skimpy clothes selling cartons of cigarettes and offering to pose for pictures with their arm draped familiarly around any biker's neck for five bucks. Spoons and bongs for methamphetamine, cocaine, and marijuana were now spoons stuffing food into mouths of toddlers and young children. Nipples of bare-breasted woman at the campground once exposed for the bikers' enjoyment were now behind suckling babes in arms at the rally, with only an infrequent flash of the past visible. It was certainly a different campground from the one he remembered.

Nevertheless, there were still hundreds of thousands of sweaty, stinking biker bodies swilling beer and flicking lighters in appreciation of whoever was on stage performing or in an effort to light whatever was being smoked. There were still countless rows of tents and mini-campsites surrounding the stage area, bikes and people scattered throughout the acres of land. The price for admission and for anything within the campground remained astronomical, including the beer.

Spotting the Inferno Force members standing guard at both the entrance and the exit to the beer tent, Streeter deduced, "Beer gardens still owned by the Inferno Force?"

"Probably," Bly answered, weaving through the crowd and lowering his voice so no one would become too interested. "The campground has changed hands a bunch of times since you were here. It's owned now by some promotional company, but I can't remember the name. My guess, despite protests to the contrary, is that the Inferno Force still have their thumb on the money coming from those beer tents."

"Still have the Chopper to deal with?" Streeter asked, referring to the other popular campground rumored to be exclusively reserved for another motorcycle club.

Bly nodded, adding nothing more as they approached the entrance to the beer tent.

"You guys selling beer to just anyone these days?" Bly asked.

The man's bare and tattooed arms were as large as his thighs. His salt-and-pepper beard and mustache were neatly trimmed, his smile fulsome, and a thick red scar bisected his face from left temple to right jawbone. Streeter preferred his "age line" after all.

"Not just anyone," replied the gatekeeper, staring at them with dancing, piercing eyes.

Streeter tensed, wishing he could wear the shoulder holster he was accustomed to rather than the small pistol in his riding boot.

With a toothy grin, the man explained, "We only sell to guys who have money. Lots of it, so start by slipping a bill my way." He laughed a little louder than Streeter thought necessary. He didn't understand until the man slapped Bly on the back and added, "What the hell you been up to, Bly? Long time no see."

"Hey, Chomp," Bly said gripping the man's hand and shaking it vigorously. "Not much, man. Not much."

"When are you going to ditch that piece of shit jacket and start wearing one of ours?"

"When you get rid of that sissy looking wing for a logo and sport something a little more befitting," Bly answered.

Chomp laughed. "And exchange it for that stupid snake on the back of your jacket? I don't think so."

Streeter couldn't help but notice Chomp's eyes flick back toward him several times throughout the discourse. His eyes, an odd color of murky blue, as if faded by bleach, were menacing, maniacal, and merry all at the same time.

Bly added, "Meet a friend of mine, Chomp. This is Streeter."

Chomp's grip was as his name. Streeter would later swear to Bly that it was Chomp who had fractured the small bone on the underside of his right hand, not the earlier fight with the rowdy college kids at the bar on Main Street.

"Chomp saved my ass four years ago and I haven't forgotten. Can I buy you a beer?" Bly asked.

"Beer's on me," he said, still inexplicably cheerful. "Just the first one, though, Bly. Price is double for you assholes for anything after the first."

Streeter had no clue if Chomp was joking or not. He didn't care to ask for clarification, lest the seemingly drug-induced merriment give way to the avalanche of rage that lay behind his eyes. He noticed the "Road

Captain" patch at the bottom left of his vest as he passed. He also noticed Chomp eyeing him carefully, assessing everything about his dress and demeanor, just as he had Chomp. Two dogs, sniffing.

Bly joked, "That means one beer and we're out of here."

"You got it. If you want to live," Chomp agreed, his smile dissolving quickly to a menacing expression.

Streeter recognized the warning that they were not welcome to stay and that he had only been cordial to keep up appearances for the other guests. If they lingered much longer, they'd find themselves with untraceable shanks stuck in their guts, their bodies discarded behind the port-o-lets.

They drank their beers standing close to the entrance of the beer tent, assuming that if Mully and his gang were here, they would eventually gravitate this way like flies to butter, considering it was the only outlet selling adult beverages. The crowd was loud and growing as the night sky filled with stars. Bly and Streeter blended easily into the crowd because they weren't wearing their colors. Campground rule; the exception was given only to the Inferno Force. Streeter mentally noted how this rule seemed to have made the atmosphere much less confrontational than a generation ago. But it certainly made it much more difficult to find Mully, not to mention making it impossible to confirm whether or not he had purple wings as the newest patch on his lapel.

The crowd was screaming at a pitch higher than Streeter believed possible for a bunch of old, overweight bikers as the band completed their three-hour show. From Streeter's perspective as a music critic, all he could say was that he recognized the band's name and they did a good job of being loud. And the crowd went wild.

Streeter noticed a particularly rowdy group of what looked to be underage teenagers huddled near the back of the crowd at the edge of the parking area, the more able to flee if challenged for being too young. Other than the campers who called the Jump home for the week and who lounged comfortably in lawn chairs or on sleeping bags behind or to the right of the stage, most people there for the entertainment were adults who found a good spot either near the stage or around the beer tent in the masses, rather than huddling along the fence to the parking lot away from the entrance.

A couple of the boys had been quarreling about who was going to pay for the next beer, one of them arguing loud enough for everyone near the beer tent to hear his secret that he was not old enough to buy the next round. Streeter guesstimated them to be no older than sixteen, and judging by their style, maybe even younger than that. A small scuffle began to erupt between a boy who looked to be nearly adult and a scrawny boy with yellow-tipped hair who was obviously barely in his teens.

Streeter saw Chomp snap his fingers and motion to two men wearing black leather jackets and rockers indicating they were only prospects for the Inferno Force. The two quickly grabbed their beers and meandered toward the scuffle, one standing on either side of the den of boys. Convincingly, they pretended to focus entirely on the band roadies packing up the equipment in preparation for the next show.

There was no question in Streeter's mind as to what would come next. Something bad. And he trained his thoughts on Bly's numero uno rule: no matter what Streeter saw, he should never blow his cover. Bly insisted that countless undercover cops and federal agents were attending these functions and interspersed throughout Sturgis, and he, Streeter, should let them do their job and resist playing cop. It was difficult as he watched the prospects positioning themselves to flank these lame-brained boys.

Streeter pegged the prospect on the right flank to be in his late twenties, his long reddish-blond wavy hair pulled back in several staged rubber bands from the nape of his neck to the small of his back. His black baseball cap, worn backward on his head, sported the familiar Inferno Force red, orange, yellow, and white wing of an angel above the bill. The second prospect on the left flank appeared to be in his early thirties and sported a black tube domer with the words "Inferno Force" embroidered in small letters across the front and the back. He appeared to be the stronger of the two, but the prospect on the right had such a wiry tension about him that Streeter imagined him doing more damage somehow. Not the least bit angelic.

Just as Streeter was about to ask Bly if they should step away, he was rooted to the ground as one of the boys pushed another into Prospect Left, the older domer. Beneath his long, droopy black mustache he sprouted a frown as he stared down at the sloshing beer in his hand.

The boys had stopped their horseplay long enough to hear Prospect Left say, "You spilled my beer."

One of the boys' eyes went wide with fright, anticipating the prospects' next moves, the others unaware of their fate. Within minutes all four boys were lying cold on the ground, knocked unconscious by the two prospects as Chomp and three other members looked on. The prospects picked through the boys' pockets and stripped them clean of all their cash. Not only would these boys wake up with a headache like a freight train blazing a new trail through their tender brains, they would also wake up totally broke.

As the crowd ebbed around the small heap of boys, pointing and cackling at how one of them looked dead, Streeter heard Chomp once again snap his fingers, never leaving his post at the entrance of the beer tent. The two prospects obediently followed the signal, headed straight for him, and laid the cash picked from the boys' wallets and pockets in Chomp's palm. Chomp nodded once and the prospects disappeared behind the tent.

Streeter saw the wink of a cigarette glowing in Chomp's other hand as he stuffed the bills in the front pocket of his jeans. He lifted the cigarette to his lips and sucked, just as a couple of what Streeter presumed to be plainclothes cops huddled over the unconscious boys. He heard one of them say, "They're fine. Just going to have one heck of a headache in the morning. Let's get them out of here and let them sleep it off in the county jail. Safest place for these babies, anyway."

Things hadn't changed all that much after all.

A roar rose from the crowd, and Streeter looked up just in time to see seven women, nearly naked, marching across the stage and starting their various dance routines. The "dances" consisted mainly of stripping to the music and thus teasing the audience of mostly middle-aged men. As all eyes were riveted on the stage, Streeter studied the crowd instead. At that moment, Mully emerged from the crowd with three other men from an area on the right that attracted both attendees and campers, the beer tent acting as the draw for temporary as well as permanent guests.

Elbowing Bly, who was watching a particularly flexible young woman wearing nothing but a G-string do a cartwheel, Streeter said, "It's Mully."

Mully barely noticed either agent as he passed them with his entourage, not even acknowledging their presence as Serpents. They had been wrong in expecting him to gravitate to the beer tent and lucky to have spotted him anyway as he headed toward the parking area.

"They're leaving," Bly said. "Let's go."

Streeter and Bly followed behind the four Lucifer's Lot members, lagging far enough behind so that they couldn't be spotted if any of them turned to look. The crowd was expanding, filling in between the bikes parked beyond the stage area. Bly and Streeter stood by their bikes, hanging back just long enough to see Mully and crew head over to the far parking lot. They mounted their bikes and slowly drove through the lot, waiting for the Lucifer's Lot to find their bikes. Streeter stopped to let a small crowd of what looked like teenage girls cross their path, using the obstruction as an excuse to allow Mully to mount his bike. As the girls passed, Streeter resisted the urge to tell them to go home, that they were in danger and they were far too young and artless to get mixed up in all this.

Bly said, "There."

Streeter saw the foursome don their colors and mount their bikes. They were pulling out of their spaces straight toward them before turning toward the entrance. Just as Mully, in the lead, turned his bike to head toward the highway, Streeter saw it, high on the left side of the jacket.

"Purple wings. All of them," Bly said, speaking Streeter's thought aloud. "What do you want to do, boss? Bring him in for questioning?"

Streeter waited a long moment as Mully eased out onto the highway, placing a growing distance between them. He slipped on his leather jacket with the Serpent emblem and Bly did the same. He knew that all they could do was bring Mully in for questioning and hope he would break under the pressure. He didn't fool himself for a moment that there was any hope in that. The only hope they had was that one of his gang members might choose to break the silence, also against astronomical odds. The culmination of everything they had worked for over the past ten hours had harvested little in the way of evidence.

Despite the opinions of Shank, Sheriff Leonard, and Eddie Schilling, and despite the fact that Mully was indeed wearing what appeared to be new purple wings, Streeter still didn't buy the theory that Mully killed Michelle. He would have to make a mighty leap in his mind to believe that Michelle had voluntarily hopped on the back of his bike. And if she had gone by force, she would have sustained more damage—bruises, lacerations, some kind of sign she'd been forced. In that split second of analysis, his intuition told him they were after the wrong guy, but for some instinctual reason, and likely because somehow Liv Bergen was tangled up in all this Mully mess, Streeter desperately wanted to talk with this man.

Streeter nodded. "Let's follow them for now. Get some backup and we'll pick him up at the Lazy S. I don't want you blowing your cover on this. We'll have only twenty-four hours from when we nab him and I'm going to need every minute."

They rode at a safe distance behind the six bikes and were surprised when the four, including Mully, merged onto the Interstate headed toward Rapid City, not up Vanocker Canyon toward Nemo as he expected. Streeter glanced at his watch, noting it was nearly eleven thirty, and wondered where Mully was headed. He also wondered if he'd done the right thing by waiting to arrest Mully until they were safely contained at the Lazy S, knowing these four could easily outmaneuver him on bikes.

Within twenty-five minutes, the bikes pulled onto Jackson Boulevard in Rapid City. On this Tuesday night, with most locals fast asleep, the streets were fairly deserted, making it quite difficult for Bly and Streeter to follow the Lucifer's Lot without being spotted. Bly motioned Streeter off the road into a corner convenience store when Mully led his pack onto a side street up ahead, turning left.

"Shit, that's where Jens Bergen's house is," Bly shouted to Streeter, their Harleys still rumbling. "What's this about?"

Before Streeter could answer, he saw Jens Bergen's pickup pull out from the same street and head down Jackson Boulevard toward them. As the two-toned blue pickup drew near, Streeter was surprised to see Liv

Bergen behind the wheel, punching in numbers on her cell phone, totally oblivious to the four motorcyclists who had emerged from Teepee Street, hanging back without their headlights on but definitely following her.

"Oh no," Streeter said under his breath, watching Mully and his posse trailing behind Liv. Calling to Bly after the bikers passed, Streeter said, "Change of plans. Let's roll."

CHAPTER 26

AT FIRST, I WAS a little perturbed that my sister Ida left Jens alone in the bar, but once I found out she had left him under Gilbert's care, I got over it. Gilbert was his best friend since childhood and he wouldn't let Jens down. Besides, at least Ida would be safe from the tentacles of Mully tonight. Only Jens and Elizabeth to worry about, and Elizabeth was still on the road. I still had time to collect Jens and warn him about the Lucifer's Lot members who had taken a liking to me.

I hadn't seen the Firehouse Brewing Company this packed before, especially on a Tuesday night. Normally I was home in bed by this time of night, so who was I to compare? The jovial laughter, loud conversations, and clinking of glasses told me I might be missing out on something in my life and that maybe I'd become a little bit too content to watch the early news in my pajamas and go to bed. I decided to turn a new leaf. But not tonight. I was tired and wanted to find Jens. There was so much to explain.

And I needed to tell him about finding Char and taking her home, and what I had learned from her about Michelle's childhood predator. When I left Char on the Freeburg couch, bewildered, I prayed Frank and Arlene would have more sympathy and tenderness for this girl than I felt was possible from the two of them. I left a long message with a nice woman named

Sue at the FBI whom I'd hung up on earlier, telling her that Charlene Freeburg was back at home and shared some insight on my story about Mully and the other Lucifer Lot's gang members from Monday. I left off the fact that I'd been followed twice by the motorcycle gang because I didn't see it working toward the solution, only adding to the problem. I gave explicit instructions to the nice woman named Sue to give all the information to Agent Stewart Blysdorf or Agent Streeter Pierce as soon as possible.

She assured me she would.

I spotted Jens with his best friend since childhood, Gilbert Muth, and waded through the sea of people to get to them. Unfortunately, the happy patrons were not parting the way as if I were Moses, so I had to offer "excuse me" and "sorry" a lot as I bumped and elbowed my way through the crowd.

I can see why Ida left Jens here.

"Fire Jumper," I heard Jens say as I approached him.

He and Gilbert were sitting at the long U-shaped bar on the end closest to the kitchen and near the back door that led to the alley. Mental note. Easier to make a quick and effortless exit using the alley exit than fighting my way back through this crowd like a defeated salmon.

"Fire Jumper?" Gilbert asked, sitting on the stool beside him.

"A stout beer," Jens said with a smile. "Try one. You'll like it. They brew it themselves here."

"Well, I know that, Jens. We practically live here. What I meant was what's up with you ordering a Fire Jumper? You never order those unless we're with Liv."

I heard Jens say, "Just drink. A salute to her willingness to help me."

I weaved my way between the last dozen people wedged in the small space between the bar and the large plate glass wall to my right, behind which stood the brewpub's huge stainless steel vats and piping leading to the second floor, where more tanks and vats stood in willing servitude to the patrons.

"One for me, too," I motioned to the bartender, who had seen me coming.

From the ceiling of the bar hung authentic firefighting equipment:

wagons and hoses, helmets, and axes. Along the walls were dozens of black-and-white photos of firemen fighting fires, posing near their trucks, working on their equipment, and at ease in the firehouse. I was glad to see that the Firehouse—Rapid City's first fire station, dedicated in 1915 and closed in 1975—was no longer a ghostly, vacant building, but rather a reminder of the heroes who served the city for six decades. South Dakota's first brewpub filled the space with life and celebration and had been decorated with authentic firefighting equipment, as it should be.

"To Liv, wherever she is." Jens swallowed the first cool drink of his stout beer, as did Gilbert. They still didn't see me coming. And hadn't noticed the third beer the bartender placed on the bar, giving me a nod as he did.

"Now that is good beer," Gilbert said, swallowing nearly half of what was in his glass. "Way better than the wheat beer. Why don't we ever order this?"

"Because we get full before we get drunk."

"Finally, I made it to you," I said, wrapping my arms around Jens's neck from behind. "Gilbert, how are you?"

Gilbert tipped his glass toward me by way of salutation then drained the contents, starting in on the third beer, which the bartender had brought for me. "Oh, so you knew she was coming?"

Jens shook his head, sipping his beer. "Nope."

I sidled up next to where Jens sat and said, "How long have you been here?"

Jens looked at his watch. "Since about five thirty," he said. "Since I finished with the agents. Ida and I ate dinner here."

I didn't detect the slightest slur or hesitation in his speech—the tone of "drunk" that would inevitably come after seven hours of constant drinking. Instead, I detected something much worse. Vapidity, lifelessness. Jens had surrendered and was merely nursing the beers along with his emotional wounds.

I glanced at Gilbert. "And how long have you been here?"

"About three beers ago," he said with a grin, which he lost quickly after seeing my reaction to it. I pierced him with my best evil eye. He was supposed to be taking care of Jens, not getting drunk with him. Cowed by my unspoken cross-examination and condemnation, Gilbert set his beer mug back on the bar and restated his answer. "Two hours or so. I showed up just as Jens and Ida were ordering dessert."

Returning my attention to my brother, I said, "Jens, I found Char. She's alive and has been staying with a friend here in town."

He blinked once at me, straightening as he heard the news. Based on his alertness and quick response, I could tell Jens was totally sober, validating my assumption that he'd been sipping, not guzzling, beers all night. He motioned to the bartender and ordered a round of coffee for me, Gilbert, and himself. The roar of the crowd was so deafening, and their demands for drinks so overwhelming, I was surprised how quickly the bartender brought three steaming cups exactly as Jens had ordered.

I shouted over the crowd, "I found out what Char and Michelle were arguing about, Jens. I left her with the Freeburgs and they're breaking the news to her as we speak. At least I hope so."

He nodded, a sadness encircling his eyes.

"I think I know who might have killed Michelle."

"Who?" Jens asked, looking more intense than I'd seen him since yesterday morning, which seemed like eons ago.

"It's just speculation. I have to make one more trip to be sure, then I'll know if—"

The bar erupted in a roar, all heads turning toward the waiter who had dropped a tray of dishes in a clattering heap.

"Well, if it isn't Danica Bergen," the velvet voice said, so close to my ear I thought hot buttered rum had spilled down the nape of my neck.

Intrigued, I turned to see who owned the voice—hadn't I heard it somewhere recently and marveled at its seductive power?—and the gentle hand that cupped my left elbow. I was sure Jens and Gilbert were oblivious to the man who had approached me, considering his stealth and how densely packed the bar was. I myself wasn't so upset by the interruption until I saw the face of the man who owned that pleasing tone.

Mully.

Startled, I dropped my coffee cup, spilling some hot liquid down Jens's leg. Burned, Jens jumped to his feet, knocking Gilbert's coffee from his hand. Both ceramic mugs shattered as they hit the floor. One, two. Screams erupted and pandemonium ensued. I wasn't sure what was happening, although I did distinctly hear someone yell, "Gun!"

I grabbed for the Browning I had carried earlier, thinking it was still in my waistband, only to find it wasn't there. I had left the gun in the loader, forgetting to retrieve it when Tommy Jasper dropped me off after dinner. Before I could react, Mully gripped my left wrist and wrapped his other strong arm around my waist, leaning in to whisper something to me over the din.

I'm pretty sure he said, "I'll get you out of here, Princess. You'll be safe with me."

His breath smelled like peppermint.

As Jens and Gilbert fussed over their burns and coffee stains, seemingly unconcerned that I had been swallowed by a riptide, I was swept through the crowd. In seconds, Mully ushered me beyond the bar, past the kitchen, and toward the back door amid the chaos, yet more patrons panicking and scrambling as they heard that someone had a gun.

Mully didn't appear to have his gun, since I could easily account for both of his hands, so I quickly assessed that the two popping sounds had indeed been the clatter of our coffee cups. I was the cause of the chaos and the reason everyone concluded a gun had been fired. Unless, of course, one of Mully's goons was wielding a gun, in which case Jens and Gilbert especially were still not safe, considering the men in black leathers were all clustered behind me.

Stealing a glance over my shoulder to see if Jens was okay, I saw a man in jeans and a black T-shirt jump onto the bar near the front door, whip himself around the fire pole at the corner of it one handed, and run the length of the bar toward me. He had short white hair, his left eye was swollen, and his neck was an angry red, as though he'd been seriously clotheslined. He looked an awful lot like an NFL quarterback after a bad game by the linemen, only he wasn't holding a football. He was holding a gun, and pointing it directly at Mully. He also looked eerily similar—a hoodlum version of—Agent Adonis himself, Streeter Pierce.

"Yikes!" I screeched, ripping free from Mully's grip and diving beneath the nearest table, knocking my skull against the pedestal. Little yellow birdies circled my head as I tried to claw my way through a sea of legs and away from the depths of unconsciousness.

As my head spun and my world dimmed, I heard the large plate glass walls that shielded the beer vats shatter, the thunder of people stampeding through the bar, and patrons in varying degrees of intoxication screaming to high heaven. Above the fray I heard someone yell "FBI!" and the distinct words, "Freeze! All of you. Clear this area. Now!"

I felt the forest of legs around me disappear. Suddenly, it was like I was lying in the middle of a meadow, the birds floating around my head, chirping away. The next thing I knew, someone was cradling the back of my neck, holding a cool hand to my forehead, feeling for a pulse in my neck. I pretended I was Snow White and this was my Prince Charming, finding me in the forest after too many days with those silly midgets, and I laughed.

"Boots?" I heard Jens's voice.

After several tries, I opened my eyes and saw my brother's welcome face, and looking over his shoulder was Agent Adonis staring down at me.

My eyes fluttered shut and I heard Streeter Pierce's familiar voice say, "Bly, stay with her. Carl Muldando, you're under arrest for the murder of Michelle Freeburg. Anything you say can and will be held against you. Get him out of here."

Then, coming nearer to me, he asked Jens, "How is she?"

"What in the hell are you doing, Agent Adonis? I had the situation under control," I mumbled, pushing his hand away from me even though I really wanted him to stay. My voice sounded like I was storing a hundred marbles in my mouth.

I heard Agent Blysdorf say, "Probably a concussion."

"Stay with her until the EMTs arrive, then meet me down at headquarters."

"Right. Did she just call you Agent Adonis?"

I tried to protest and managed only to pass out again.

I woke up in the back of an ambulance parked in the alley behind the Firehouse, the EMTs insisting I take a ride with them to the hospital for further observation, based on the goose egg that had arisen on my forehead. I lied and told them I was married to a doctor and that he would take care of me tonight. They didn't believe me, but when I stepped out of the ambulance, my head pounding, I clutched Gilbert's arm and said, "This is my husband, Dr. Gilbert Muth."

Dumbfounded, Gilbert stuck out his hand and shook the EMT's latex-gloved hand as if we were at a Chamber of Commerce "After Hours" party. I was glad Gilbert didn't protest and even happier he didn't share that his doctorate was in mechanical engineering, not medicine. Gilbert had been Jens's friend long enough to know how to roll with the punches. I was so pleased with his performance that if I had had a bag of Scooby snacks, I'd be popping them in his smug mouth right about now.

I said a polite "thank you" as all of the emergency crew packed up to leave, and I was relieved when their taillights disappeared down the alleyway.

"Academy Award winner, you are!" I said to Gilbert with a slap on the back.

"Thanks," he said acidly.

Jens stared down at me, the color rising to his cheeks. "What in the hell was that all about? You could have been killed."

"They wouldn't have killed me, just taken me to the hospital and hooked me up to all those noisy machines again," I bantered.

"Not the EMTs, Boots. The Lucifer's Lot," Jens protested. "And this isn't funny."

"I know," I said, realizing Jens's emotional state was probably too fragile to take joking at a time like this. Our family always used humor in times of tragedy to stave off pain, to avoid the seriousness of life. But in this situation, I should have known Jens would have none of it. "I'm sorry. I should have told you."

"Was that the guy who killed Michelle?" he said, staring at me. "They said he was under arrest for the murder of Michelle Freeburg. He's the guy who was asking Michelle to go to the rally with him Sunday night. The guy who enraged Roy, the reason we exchanged words. Is that what you were trying to tell me, Boots?"

In that single moment between truth and dare, I was faced with a serious dilemma. Jens always knew when I was lying, yet if I told him the truth, I would never be able to make my last stop before confirming who I suspected was Michelle's killer. I had to think fast.

And not lie.

"Bob Shankley, the FBI director, and the Lawrence County Sheriff believe that the man they just arrested killed Michelle," I said, serious as a heart attack.

He studied my eyes, my face, every twitching muscle, and determined I was telling the truth. "Why were these guys here tonight, looking for you?"

Again, I had to tell the truth or my chances of making one more road trip were out the door. "Remember when you and Travis took off to that job site?"

His brows netted. "In Sturgis? What does that have to do with Lucifer's Lot?"

"While I was waiting for you, they showed up. They were messing around with a teenage girl, who ended up dying, and I witnessed the whole thing. It didn't have anything to do with Michelle. Just wrong place, wrong time as far as I was concerned."

"A witness? To a murder?"

The muscles around Jens's eyes and jaws slacked. I didn't want pity. Not now. Not ever. Even Gilbert looked like he was going to grab me and tell me what an unlucky wretch I was. And how much he loved me, glad I was alive to hear his proclamation.

I headed off the emotional tidal wave by dodging. "Not exactly murder. Look, I told the FBI everything. Even sent pictures. The lead guy, Mully, just happened to see me crouching in your truck, spying on him through the back window, just as the emergency response team arrived. I was the one who called it in." I averted Jens's eyes so I wouldn't have to lie about waiting until earlier tonight to call it in.

Gilbert hugged me and I went rigid.

"I didn't know," Jens said. "You should have told me."

"That's why I left all those messages for you tonight, and with Ida, pleading with you not to go home, to stay with her and instead head up to Mom's."

"Neither one of us recognized the phone number, so we ignored the calls."

"Tommy Jasper lent me his phone," I said.

"Who's Tommy Jasper?"

I didn't have time to explain. "I was calling because I was worried about you. And I wanted you to be safe, just in case Mully came back again to your house."

"Again?" Jens looked as if he was going to throw up. "Boots, you are such a—"

I interrupted, "Oh, and did I tell you Elizabeth called? She's on her way and wants to stay with us tonight. I told her you wouldn't mind. Reminded her where you hide the key. Should be here in an hour or so."

I offered a weak smile.

I knew he'd be angry, but I also knew he'd understand why I would want to protect him from all of this. Gilbert gave me a squeeze and I broke free of him. It brought Mully's comforting embrace to mind. Comforting until I realized who it was. Only, on reflection, I got the sense he was being genuine with his concern when we all thought gunshots were being fired. Just like at the quarry, when I would have sworn he was flirting with me, not trying to kill me. I must have really hit my head hard.

"By the way, I heard glass shatter. What happened?"

Gilbert's voice became animated. "That was so cool! That FBI agent came flying down off the end of the bar and tackled that Muldando guy while the other guy behind the FBI guy, who looked more like a biker, launched himself over our heads, his arms out like he was doing a swan dive or something, and wrapped up the other three bikers, all flying through the glass and banging their heads against the beer vats. All three bikers out cold in an instant."

Worried that the second FBI agent might be Blysdorf, I asked, "Was the guy hurt? The one who launched himself off the bar at those three?"

"Yeah, his head was bleeding some, but the EMTs bandaged him up and as soon as he knew you were okay, he took off," Gilbert said. Then he elbowed Jens, adding, "I think he kind of likes you, Liv."

"Who?" I wondered if he meant Agent Blysdorf or Mully.

"That FBI agent," Gilbert said.

"Agent Blysdorf?" I asked, relieved that Mully's flirtation was all in my imagination.

"Who?"

"The Flying Wallenda who tackled those other three guys near you," I clarified.

"No, the other guy."

My stomach went into free fall.

"The one who arrested Carl Muldando. He was barking orders to everyone to stand guard over you, made sure you had the best care possible, stayed with you as long as he could. But he kind of had his hands full with three unconscious bikers and that Carl Muldando character. Lucifer's Lot. Holy crap!"

"Oh," was all I managed. Agent Adonis. Streeter Pierce. My hero. He had an interest in me? In your dreams, Liv. Not after the way you treated him.

My head throbbed, and I wrote this entire conversation off to the rising lump on my forehead. Confusion, that's all this was. I tried to focus on the task at hand, remembering I had to verify one more lead before I was absolutely sure that Mully was not responsible for Michelle's murder—and my prime suspect was.

I pointed at Jens's cell phone.

"Your cell phone's missing its memory stick, by the way. You'll find it at your house by your laptop. It's what I used to get photos of Mully and the other Lucifer's Lot bikers they just arrested."

I glanced at my watch. Half past midnight. And I needed to make a quick stop at Jens's house first.

"Listen, Gilbert. I need you to give Jens a ride home. No point in making matters worse by adding a DUI to the night," I said, knowing Jens was sober enough to drive if he wanted to, but I needed the excuse of taking his truck for a little bit longer. "Plus, Elizabeth is going to be there soon. She shouldn't come home to an empty house. She's kind of upset."

"Elizabeth's upset? Right now I don't have enough energy to comfort one more grieving family member. I haven't even had time to wrestle with my own grief," Jens said, exasperated.

I touched his elbow gently. "Ernif Hanson died. Helma called Elizabeth. She's coming for Helma's sake, as well as yours."

Now it was Jens's turn to say, "Oh."

I offered him a crooked smile. "You can wrestle with your grief together. Only separately."

"Just when you think you're the only one suffering . . ."

I finished Jens's thought, our mother's motto. "There's always someone else worse off. I know, Jens. But your hurt is real all the same. And your grief deserves a little mat time, so go home and wrestle with it. Alone."

He started to protest.

I pointed a finger at him and warned, "No arguments. I need a little time alone, too, and I'll meet you at home later."

Surprisingly, both Jens and Gilbert yielded to my orders and left me to my final drive of the night.

CHAPTER 27

"WE CHECKED THE DATABASES and made lists of every psychiatrist and psychologist in the city. Even some of the smaller surrounding communities. None of them has ever treated Michelle Freeburg," Shank was saying, keeping pace with Streeter and Bly as they marched toward the interrogation room. Waving a beefy hand toward their battered faces, he added, "By the way, what the hell happened to you two?"

Bly smirked.

Streeter could tell Shank's bravado was disingenuous. His hands shook, his face was pasty white, his upper lip was dotted heavily with perspiration, and an odd odor emanated from beneath his brown suit coat. Streeter recognized the smell. Fear, the adrenaline that arose from a cornered, wounded animal.

"Are you sure?" Streeter asked.

"We've e-mailed Michelle's photo and a bio to all the psychiatrists, psychologists, and counselors in town," Shank continued, "asking if any of them had ever worked with her as a patient."

"You checked under what name?"

"Michelle Freeburg, Michelle Arlene Freeburg, Arlene Freeburg, M. A. Freeburg," Shank recounted.

Streeter had a lot to do in the next twenty-four hours and needed Shank busy with other tasks rather than being underfoot and complaining about every step he and Bly would take.

"Even if none of this pans out, Streeter, Michelle Freeburg didn't have to be a wacko split personality to get herself killed by Mully," Shank added, sweat now dripping from his hairline.

"How sensitive of you," Streeter scowled.

"Go to hell," Shank mumbled. "You're so damned sure of yourself that Mully is an angel. Let me remind you that even if you're right and Mully didn't kill Michelle Freeburg, he's still my lead suspect on the Crooked Man case. We should throw his ass in jail for killing Ernif Hanson."

"One step at a time, Shank," Streeter warned.

"It's all been theory and conjecture anyway," Bly reminded them both. In response to their quizzical looks, he added, "Not about Mully being the Crooked Man. About why Michelle got tangled up with Mully to begin with, if she did. All we have is their chance meeting in a grocery store Sunday night."

"And her dead body found Monday morning near his tent," Shank growled.

Streeter was glad to be wearing his street clothes again—his white long-sleeved shirt (to cover the temporary ink tattoos he'd gladly scrub off later) and khaki slacks—but the time he had taken to shed his biker threads (after he had made sure Liv Bergen was in the care of the EMTs) had allowed Shank to direct others to interrogate Mully, rather than wait for Streeter.

"You going in?" Streeter asked Shank as he stopped at the door to the interrogation room.

Shank cleared his throat and stammered, "Ah no, no, I'll be in observation. I decided to let Karski and Greenborough cut their teeth on this one."

It was almost as if Streeter could hear the beads of sweat popping out of every pore along Shank's upper lip. Although the reason for this entire Keystone Cop routine eluded Streeter, the one thing he knew for sure was that Shank was truly afraid of Mully and did not want to be associated with him in any way. For a brief instant, Streeter actually felt some sympathy for Shank, realizing how debilitating it would be to allow fear to interfere with his work.

Shifting gears, Streeter opened the door to the room to the left of the interrogation room and suggested, "Let's see how they're doing so far."

The three stepped into the small, dark space and sat in the chairs facing the large plate glass window. Through the one-way mirrored glass, they could see Mully's profile at the far left end of the table, the guard standing on the right end of the small room by the only door, and the two federal agents sitting at the table with Mully, one with his back to them and one facing them.

Over the speakers, they heard the federal agents asking Mully question after question without getting any answers, only a few nearly imperceptible nods and a hint of a smile from time to time.

As he studied Mully's expressions, Streeter believed the biker was enjoying this.

"So you're not denying you knew Liv Bergen before tonight?" Davidson asked.

Mully grinned. "Of course not. We go way back, Barney."

Streeter remembered hearing that Karski's first name was Tyler, and was momentarily baffled. Then he recognized the significance. Mully's reference was presumably to Barney Fife, the incapable, bumbling sheriff's deputy of fictional Mayberry. Streeter was tiring of this cat-and-mouse game, particularly as it was becoming more obvious as time passed that the cat was a bad-luck black one.

Before retreating from his observation post, Streeter stood and instructed Bly, "Under no circumstances will you allow Mully to see you here. You did a great job staying low during the Firehouse scuffle. We had the presence of mind to shed our leathers and turn our T-shirts inside out just before you tackled three members of Lucifer's Lot and knocked them out cold. So I don't want you to blow your cover now."

Within seconds, Streeter was on the other side of the glass, establishing uncomfortably direct eye contact with Mully the instant he came through the door. By way of introduction, he spoke into the tape recorder, "Special Agent Streeter Pierce joining the interview in progress at 12:40 am."

Karski and Greenborough said nothing, opting to watch the Denver agent as he rounded the table and stood dominantly over Mully.

"How do you know her?" Streeter asked with no lead-in, no explanation. Mully grinned. Streeter grabbed the front of the biker's black tee and squeezed it in his fists, closing it around Mully's neck. "What do you mean you go way back? Way back to when?"

Mully's expression went prosaic as he studied Streeter's face, felt his intensity. "Way back to yesterday. With the dead girl."

Streeter released him and walked away. At least he had started him talking.

"Who is she?" Streeter asked.

Mully's eyes flashed, never leaving Streeter's, his mouth involuntarily opening slightly before he pressed his lips tightly together again.

Streeter sat on the edge of the table and leaned his face down toward Mully's, repeating, "I said, 'Who. Is. She?'"

Mully smiled wryly. Streeter recognized in his face the obvious.

"You don't even know who she was, do you?"

No answer.

"You keep quiet and you will be the one who gets time for this," Streeter warned. "I know all too well that the likelihood of you being this girl's killer is slim. I suspect if you are involved, you had one of your prospects do it as an initiation. Am I right?"

Mully stared back, his eyes hardening with contempt. Streeter locked his fiery eyes on Mully like hot pokers.

"Prospects are expendable, Mully," Streeter said. "Are you? Because one thing that agents Karski and Greenborough failed to mention to you is that we have proof of your involvement."

Streeter thought he saw Mully's cold eyes flicker just a bit. He definitely repositioned his weight in the hard folding chair.

"We saw your new wings," Streeter said. "Purple."

"That isn't proof," Mully spat, relaxing and slumping down in his chair, folding his arms across his chest. "Lots of guys wear purple wings."

"You're right. It isn't proof. But it sure will be helpful when we explain all this to the jury." Streeter stared down once more at Mully and matched his pose by folding his arms across his chest. "We call that circumstantial evidence, something criminals like you love to disprove. But the way I figure it, simply explaining what those little purple wings indicate that you do for fun would disgust the jury so much, we wouldn't really need too much hard evidence to convict you."

Mully's lip curled ever so slightly.

Streeter pushed himself from the table and started pacing, the noise unsettling. He walked behind Mully and stopped. Mully did not move from his casual position in his chair, acting as if this was no big deal. His eyes shifted nervously to the corners, however, as he tried to catch a peripheral glance of the agent.

When the silence became too much, Mully adjusted his body slightly in his chair. Streeter paced around and sat on the other corner of the table directly above Mully.

"The other evidence would have to be compelling, too," Streeter described. "Something much more incriminating, pointing to you specifically. Now what could that be?"

Streeter drummed his fingers against his chin. Mully's burning eyes focused on the closed door across the room.

"Didn't you used to wear an FTW pin on your lapel, Mully?"

Mully's hand shot up to where the pin used to be on his leather jacket, his eyes widening when his fingers felt nothing but leather.

"That's the pin I was talking about," Streeter said. A slight buckle in Mully's jagged brow preceded a lick of his dry lips. "Want some water, Mully?"

Mully pushed himself into an upright sitting position and said, "Yes, get me some water." Then he looked directly at Streeter and added, "Please."

He was all business now. Streeter knew he was ready to talk.

Tyler Karski knocked, and the bolt slid open from the other side. Greenborough stepped out of the room, presumably to retrieve the water for Mully. Instead, Streeter knew he slipped into the observation room with Bly and Shank, waiting for a sign to return as the good cop with refreshments.

Streeter said, "Early in the weekend, Mully, you were looking good. You know how I know that?"

For the first time since Streeter had circled, Mully looked up at him, his eyes narrowing.

Streeter continued. "Because we have an excellent close-up photo of you from one of our high-powered cameras. Date stamped, of course."

Mully said nothing, staring back at Streeter.

"You know how these camera junkies are," Streeter said, crossing his arms loosely across his chest and smirking. "Always trying to capture every detail like they're photographing the winning catch at a Super Bowl game or something and need every bead of sweat, right? Hundreds of shots, from all different angles and distances. Can you imagine?"

Streeter moved over to lean against the wall facing Mully, wondering if the faint twitch of his left eye was a give.

"A particularly interesting photo," Streeter explained, "shows a very clear picture of the FTW pin in the right collar of your jacket. Really cool how they can digitally close in on that pin with the computer. The detail is so clear it shows the two gouges in the pin, millimeters apart from one another on the upper corner of the 'F'. Amazing."

Streeter was thankful he had sent the photos and pin down to Jack Linwood. He knew Shank was behind the glass, elated that Streeter had found more evidence to nail Mully but cursing under his breath that Streeter had kept these details from him. For a split second, Streeter hoped the news of the physical evidence brought color back into Shank's cheeks.

"What's your point?" Mully demanded after a few uncomfortable moments of silence. "And where's my water?"

Streeter nearly whispered, "No need to get angry, Mr. Muldando. Let me remind you this interview is being taped, and your water is on the way. Agent Greenborough went to get you some."

Sulking, Mully slouched a bit in his chair, stomping his feet on the ground as he adjusted his legs.

Streeter stared down at him. "I don't mean to bore you with all this, Mr. Muldando, but my point is, a pin with the exact same gouges in the upper 'F' happened to be found embedded in the palm of, as you call her, the 'dead girl.' What are the odds of that? And that pin has your DNA all over it."

He lifted his hands palm skyward in an animated shrug, watching Mully's expression carefully as he did. Genuine alarm registered after this last remark.

"That's impossible," Mully said, careful to control his tone, facial expressions, and body language, an effort that was apparently difficult for him. "She was already dead."

Streeter fought back a triumphant smile. Mully had finally admitted to being in the proximity of the body, or at least having knowledge about it.

"Already dead?" Streeter repeated. "Then, you didn't kill her?"

"No," Mully answered in a quiet mumble.

"Who did?"

"Nobody," Mully answered confidently. "Check your records."

"What are you talking about?" Streeter asked, genuinely not understanding where Mully was going with this.

"The autopsy report."

"I have," Streeter explained. "And if you're going to try implying that the girl committed suicide, don't waste any of our time. It would be hard to claim suicide when her skull was smashed from behind. So maybe you can tell me, how can you say nobody killed her?"

"Smashed skull? What are you talking about?" Mully snapped, bolting to his feet. The guard and Karski moved toward Mully instantly, but Streeter remained where he was, leaning against the wall, his feet crossed at the ankle. He knew Mully wasn't getting violent. It would be the last thing he would do. This was simply a scare tactic and Streeter wasn't biting.

Just before the guard and Karski reached him, Mully hissed at Streeter, "I swear, if you're lying to me, I'll—"

"You'll what? Kill me? Like you did the girl?"

"She dropped dead before I ever got there, and her skull was not bashed in."

"Explain the pin," Streeter said.

"Somebody's setting me up," Mully said, staring at nothing but seeing something. His eyes were fierce, the muscles in his jaw bulging.

There was no doubt in Streeter's mind that Mully believed what he was saying.

"If you had nothing to do with her death, why'd you dump her body by the creek?" Streeter asked.

"What? What creek?" Mully responded, confused by the information.

"How'd you convince her to get on your bike so you could kill her near the creek where she was found?"

"You're full of it," Mully answered, offering nothing more in the way of explanation.

Incredibly, Streeter believed Mully when he implied that he came upon the body after she was dead. The part Streeter didn't understand was the fine, but critical, difference in Mully's insistence on her having died rather than being killed.

"Did you earn your purple wings from her?"

Mully stared at Streeter, squinted at him suspiciously. "It's no crime. I didn't kill her and the autopsy would show that. You got nothing on me, even if you had all the evidence in the world that I tongued that bitch."

Streeter didn't understand this.

The autopsy clearly showed there was no sexual violation, no DNA whatsoever, on Michelle. This wasn't adding up.

"If someone is trying to set you up, Mully, we'd like to know who that is," Streeter concluded honestly.

He was interrupted by a knock, the bolt sliding free. Agent Greenborough reappeared with a bottle of water for Mully and said, "Agent Pierce? There are some gentlemen who would like to talk with you."

Streeter heaved a sigh and followed the agent out the door. Greenborough pointed to the observation room next door and ducked back into the interrogation room with Mully. Streeter found himself behind the glass with Bly and Shank again, plus a woman with short blonde hair standing near the back.

Bly said, "Streeter, he's telling the truth. Liv Bergen witnessed the whole scene in Sturgis. Mully's talking about the Jane Doe in Sturgis, not about Michelle Freeburg."

"What?" Streeter said. "Is this about the e-mail the Sturgis PD received from Bergen Construction you told us about, Shank?"

"Read it," Bly said shoving an e-mail and a stack of photos into Streeter's hand.

When he had finished reading the text and flipping through the photos, Streeter mumbled, "She's crazy."

"There's more. Streeter, meet Sue," Bly said, finally introducing the woman near the back wall.

After Sue told the agents about Liv Bergen's phone call and recited the message Liv had left for them, Streeter believed more than ever Mully's claim that someone was trying to set him up.

His mind raced through the names of those who would have access to Mully's FTW pin, to the campground, to the size ten-and-a-half riding boots, and to Michelle. He thought about Liv finding Char and taking her to the Freeburgs. Streeter realized they were running down a blind alley, and the way to light the path was held firmly in the hands of Charlene Freeburg. He needed to talk with her immediately.

And to Liv.

As he hurried back to the interrogation room for his final questions, barely noticing the sickly shade of green Shank had turned, Streeter called to Bly, "Get a car ready. We need to visit the Freeburgs. See if you can locate Liv Bergen. We need to talk with her, too. She might still be at the hospital for observation. She might be at her brother's house. Call him. If she's not there, get a cell phone number where Liv can be reached. And Shank, whatever you do, keep Mully here until I come back."

Shank responded with a grunt, collapsing into a chair in the corner.

Returning to the interrogation room, Streeter asked Mully, "What size boots do you wear?"

"Ten and a half," Mully said. "But you probably already knew that."

"Mind if we take a print?"

"Help yourself," said the biker, kicking off his boots. "Do your job well, man. Check very carefully." His sarcasm was duly noted.

Streeter was pleased to see that the brand and sole pattern were the same as the prints lifted from the scene, according to the report by the crime scene techs.

"Anyone but you have access to these boots, just in case this doesn't bode well for you?" Streeter asked.

Mully frowned, contemplating the thought. His eyes narrowed and he shook his head. Streeter knew his mind had landed on someone, but Mully wasn't about to share a name with the feds.

Leaning against the table near Mully, Streeter said, "You earned your purple wings off the young lady at Sturgis, the one who voluntarily wanted to pull a train with you, the one Cheetah picked up on Main Street. Right?"

"How do you know . . ." Mully stopped mid question. Then he shook his head in obvious confusion. He straightened, his demeanor changing.

Streeter speculated this was a turning point for Mully. He had made a decision to cooperate, to violate a code and talk. At least a little bit. "Look, we didn't kill her. And I don't know about any FTW pin in her palm or about her body being left in a creek somewhere. We left her in the street. The EMTs will tell you that. And she was dead before I got there, so how the hell did my pin end up in her palm? And how did she end up by the creek?"

Streeter made a decision to cooperate too. "Not her palm. Another dead woman's palm. The one found three-quarters of a mile from your campground."

Streeter watched Mully's face harden, genuine alarm registering with a man who was rarely surprised. He growled, "What other dead woman? You said I was under arrest for the murder of Michelle Freeburg. The girl at Sturgis, right?"

Streeter shook his head. "Didn't you see the tents pitched near the Lazy S? All those cars and FBI personnel, the emergency vehicles that have been in that meadow up the creek from you since yesterday morning?"

"Yeah, but I didn't know about any dead girl. I was told it was probably some old bones dug up at the quarry."

Again, Streeter believed him. "And who told you that?"

Mully opened his mouth to speak then pursed his lips in a tight line, the muscles of his jaw bulging. No doubt in Streeter's mind that the person who fabricated the story was Eddie Schilling. Streeter had to ask himself why Schilling would lie about that.

"To be clear, you are under arrest for the murder of Michelle Freeburg. The woman you were talking to at the grocery store Sunday night. The one who helped you find the needles, the thread, and the fishing wire that you used to sew those purple wings onto your black leather. The one who helped you find alcohol for God knows what."

For a second time, Mully's face registered utter surprise.

"Tattoos," Mully answered. His chest heaved in anger. He squeezed his eyes shut. "Michelle. She was all right. She was nice."

"Nice and dead," Streeter said.

"Some fucker is setting me up," Mully spat, his eyes snapping open and boring into Streeter's. "You're sure that was Michelle from the grocery store?"

"Maybe someone in your own club?" Streeter prodded.

"She didn't deserve that." Mully's eyes were distant, angry. "Somebody's going to pay for that."

Streeter took advantage of the moment to protect Liv by adding, "And just so you know, the woman you targeted tonight? Liv Bergen?"

Mully's eyes slid to Streeter.

"The one you attacked in the bar?"

"I did not attack that woman," Mully argued, his eyes like a shark's. "I was protecting her. You were the one who attacked her."

It was Streeter's turn to be surprised, become defensive. "I was after you, not Liv."

The two had sparred to a standoff.

Streeter saw a genuine smile touch Mully's lips when he added, "She's something. I just wanted to talk with her. She'd been following me all over the Hills, and I wanted to know why. That's all."

"Another nice woman," Streeter growled.

"Yeah, I figured that." The smile this time touched Mully's lifeless eyes, and for a moment, Streeter glimpsed what this man's life might have been like if he hadn't chosen the Lucifer's Lot. "She's a spunky one."

"And she's your only witness who can testify that you're telling us the truth about the young lady in Sturgis. She told us everything. She told us you didn't kill the woman. She even took pictures to prove it." Streeter leaned in close to Mully's ear and whispered, "So. Leave. Her. Alone."

CHAPTER 28

BLY SNAPPED HIS CELL phone shut and turned onto the familiar street.

"Jens said Liv's not home yet," he told Streeter. "He said she refused to go to the hospital for observation and convinced the EMTs that her husband was a doctor and he would keep a close eye on her through the night."

The boulder that crashed through Streeter's gut was unexpected and clearly tipped over the edge by the word "husband."

"Funny thing is," Bly added, "Liv's not even married, and the guy she said was her husband has a doctorate in engineering, not medicine."

Streeter felt a stir of emotions, a dangerous cocktail of frustration, anger, joy, and pride. He knew there was a reason he liked Liv Bergen. Spunky. Mully was right about that. She lived on the edge.

"What is she up to?" Streeter asked.

Bly parked the car in front of the Freeburg house and turned off the engine. "Jens said she asked for time alone, not to worry, that she'd be home later."

"How long ago was that?"

"Twenty minutes," Bly answered. "He said he'd have her call us the minute she arrived or called in. Said she borrowed Tommy Jasper's cell phone and that he didn't know the number."

"Did we get Jasper's cell phone number today when we talked with him?" Bly shook his head.

"She's up to something. I can feel it," Streeter said.

"You're probably right. Jens said before the ruckus in the bar started, Liv told him she knew who killed Michelle and she wanted to make sure the last piece of the puzzle fit before she talked with him about it," Bly repeated. Both men exchanged a glance. "Let's hope she meant Mully."

"How'd she get mixed up in all this, anyway?"

"Jens said it was his fault. He asked Liv to find Char and figure out who killed Michelle because he was afraid we wouldn't."

"Some vote of confidence," Streeter grumbled.

"Or out of self-defense. Remember, Bob Shankley told Jens he was a person of interest first thing this morning, right after he had identified the body of the woman he planned to marry. He would have been in total shock, I'd imagine." Looking at the clock, Bly corrected himself, "Or yesterday morning, technically. Before you arrived."

"It has been a very long day," Streeter agreed.

The night air was clear and crisp, reminding Streeter of the fresh air in Conifer compared to downtown Denver. He had forgotten how nature, unexplored, felt in South Dakota, a place few had discovered, unlike Colorado, where so many flocked for the experience of it.

Lights were still on behind the curtains in the living room at the Freeburgs, and Bly was rewarded quickly with his knock. Frank answered, and the agents could see that both he and Arlene were dressed in bathrobes and wearing slippers, neither looking comfortable nor rested. An old man Streeter didn't recognize was sitting on the couch.

"Now what," Frank grumbled. "It's almost one o'clock in the morning."

Streeter said, "We won't stay long. We want to talk to Charlene."

"She's in the shower," Frank said holding the door in such a way that his arm made a barricade to keep the agents out.

"We need to talk with her," Streeter said, filling the door with his impressive presence. "Now."

"I said she's in the shower, you pervert," Frank argued, sticking his chest out in a way only a protective father could.

The old man pushed himself from the couch and hobbled over toward them using a cane. He extended his hand to Streeter.

"I'm Dr. Lowell Morgan."

"Special Agent Streeter Pierce."

Bly came around from behind Streeter and shook the man's hand. "Special Agent Stewart Blysdorf. Why are you here at this hour? Is Char ill?"

Dr. Morgan chuckled. "No, nothing like that. The Freeburgs asked me to come over to be on hand when they break the news about Michelle."

Arlene said, "She's been at her friend's house the entire time. No adults around, so all they've been doing is listening to music, watching movies."

Bly said, "What about their social networking?"

"Apparently Hope's parents have the computer locked down when they're gone."

Dr. Morgan defended the Freeburgs. "They've handled everything well so far as I can tell. They've made Char tell them where she's been all this time and why she left, made her eat a bit, and sent her to take a shower so I'd have time to come over."

"Are you a psychiatrist?" Streeter asked, wondering what would possess the Freeburgs to ask a doctor to show up at one o'clock in the morning.

"An old family friend. Used to have a family practice. Have known Char all her life."

Streeter exchanged a glance with Bly and asked, "You wouldn't happen to be with the Black Hills Medical Clinic, would you?"

"Founder. But I don't do much of the family practice any longer. Mostly care for the elderly. Hospice patients, really. I've found it gives me pleasure to help good people find peace in that final mile they walk alone."

Behind Frank and down the hall, Streeter saw a teenage girl emerge from a room. She was wearing a bathrobe and had a towel wrapped around her head.

"Then you're the perfect person to be here tonight," Streeter said to Dr. Morgan. Calling to the teenager, Streeter asked, "Charlene, can we talk to you for a minute, please?"

Char looked puzzled. She came down the hall quickly and ducked under Frank's arm. "What's this about?"

Streeter met Frank's eyes as Arlene looked away. Char turned to them and scanned the faces of the three men.

"Who are all these guys?"

"You remember Dr. Morgan, honey. He's the one I took you to for shots when you were little," Arlene said.

"Kinda." She seemed to grow even younger, smaller somehow.

Dr. Morgan shook her hand, a gentle smile spread across his face. He pointed toward the couch and suggested she sit beside him there.

"And these two?"

Streeter sat down across from Char, forgoing the handshake. "We're with the Federal Bureau of Investigation. I'm Agent Pierce. This is Agent Blysdorf."

"Mom? Daddy? What's going on?" Neither answered their daughter, who sat in the dim light from a single lamp that was near Frank's chair. She looked more like a child than a teenager. "I thought you said Michelle moved out?"

"Moved out?" Bly said with disgust. "That's what you told her?"

Frank's lips puckered. Standing next to his favorite easy chair, Arlene clung to her husband's shoulder as though she were an oversized budgie and said, "We were waiting until morning. No point in ruining another night of sleep."

"You people are unbelievable," Bly said, taking off his baseball cap, which freed his curly hair to spill down his back. He beat the hat against his leg as if to knock off dust after being thrown from a bull ride, but Streeter knew he was about to lose his temper and he was doing everything he could to calm himself.

"Told me what?" Char asked, turning to her father.

The dim light from the television screen, which was muted on an old *Jeffersons* rerun, offered a ghostly glow in which Dr. Morgan was silhouetted.

Frank melted further into his recliner as if he were hoping to disappear from the inevitable confrontation altogether. Arlene stood firm at her perch.

"Tell me what's happened. Where's Michelle?" Char said in an eerily calm and direct voice.

"She's dead," Frank said simply.

Char folded like a rag doll. Dr. Morgan patted her back. The racked sobs and guttural moans that rose from her were raw. This was real. If Streeter ever had had a suspicion that Char had anything to do with or knew about Michelle's murder, he was convinced now that it was unfounded. He also dispelled any notion of the little sister secretly loathing the big sister. There was nothing but sheer remorse, grief, and love in the sorrow Charlene Freeburg was displaying.

As she clutched her knees, the towel on her head fell to the floor at her feet, revealing long wavy locks of jet-black hair that tumbled midway down her shins. Streeter studied her and the Freeburgs, wondering what would possess a couple not to share this news with their youngest child, thinking a good night's sleep was more important. Denial was all he could conclude. But the fact that the Freeburgs had called Dr. Morgan over at this hour suggested they cared deeply for Char, which was encouraging to Streeter.

Streeter saw Char reach for the towel at her feet and press it to her face. Still bent, she sat there rocking gently to and fro.

Streeter tried to reconcile the images of the Char that her parents and others had described and the devastated child who sat before him. "I know how hard this must be for you, but we need to ask you some questions about your sister. We're the ones in charge of investigating Michelle's death. She's been murdered."

"Murdered? Oh God, please, no," Char mumbled into the towel, her thin body again racked with sobs.

Streeter noticed how haggard Arlene appeared as she stood stoically by her husband's side. And Frank looked resigned, hollow, the huff and puff of indignation completely spent. His eyes sagged.

Dr. Morgan rubbed the palm of his hand in circles between Char's shoulder blades.

She recounted her story. "We got in a fight Sunday night. Over my boyfriend. I was mad. I ran away and called my friend. I've been staying at Hope's house just to hang out for a few days, get away from everything.

And I wanted to think about everything Michelle had told me. I've never seen her that mad. And I wanted her to miss me."

"What happened Sunday night?"

Char shook her head, the black curls brushing her shinbones. She wiped her face in the towel again and drew a deep breath between sniffles.

"I went to her work. She lectured me about dating older guys. I begged her not to tell Mom and Daddy. She was worried about me. Followed us after he picked me up at home."

"Here?" Arlene said incredulously, totally clueless. "I never saw anyone Sunday night."

"Down the block," Char said, her words muffled.

"What?" her mother asked.

Char wiped away the snot and tears and said more clearly, "Michelle followed us. We were hanging out. Michelle pulled me out of the car. She was so upset she dropped the flashlight, snatched me by my arm, and ran. I've never seen her so upset. Never. She told me the guy was poison. To stay away from him. That I had no idea what I was doing. That he was evil. I told her I liked him. She was so angry. Now my sister is dead. Murdered. What have I done?" Char wailed.

Streeter noted the genuine remorse and agony Char displayed. He also noted that Arlene and Frank had also begun to sob.

"She was found near Nemo," Bly offered. "At Broken Peaks."

Char stopped sobbing long enough to ask, "When?"

"Monday morning," he answered.

She clutched her knees again, rocking. "Oh no. This is my fault. It's all my fault."

"Why is this your fault?" Streeter asked.

"Near the Lazy S, right?" she asked in a muffled voice.

"How did you know that?" Bly asked.

"Who is this man, Char?" Streeter asked, although he already knew the answer. The pieces were all sliding neatly into place for him. He knew this must have been the issue Michelle was referring to Sunday night when she told Jens. What she needed to end, once and for all.

"It wasn't my fault. She never told me until Sunday night."

"Told you what?" Streeter coaxed.

"That the guy I was dating was someone she knew. He raped my sister. She was even younger than me when it happened."

Arlene Freeburg gasped. Frank swore. Dr. Morgan clutched his chest. Michelle's deep, dark secret. Out.

"I didn't know I was betraying her," Char moaned, noting the reaction of her elders.

"You didn't know," Streeter reassured her, "and these three didn't know that's how she got pregnant. Am I right?"

"Pregnant?" Char said, sitting up briefly.

The Freeburgs and Dr. Morgan shook their heads. Dr. Morgan answered, "Michelle never told us how she found herself in the family way. We just assumed it was a boy at school."

"It wasn't," Streeter said, "and you delivered the baby, Dr. Morgan? Kept the adoption quiet? Faked the mono?"

Dr. Morgan nodded. The Freeburgs nodded too.

"What baby?" Char bellowed. "Oh Michelle. What did I do? What have I done?"

Streeter turned to Frank and Arlene. "And you two took the baby in. As your own."

They nodded again, and both silently began to weep fresh tears, Arlene uncontrollably, Frank stoically.

Streeter nodded his appreciation to them. Although he didn't condone their resentful parenting of the girls, he knew on some level they had loved Michelle and Charlene the best they knew how, willing to take Char in as their own, never knowing who had fathered the child or the circumstances, only that it was Michelle's baby. There were sacrifices they must have made, Streeter thought. And at the risk of being judgmental, he wondered why they hadn't been straightforward with her all this time.

Bewildered, Char asked her parents, "What baby? Oh my word, no. *I'm* the baby? Michelle was my *mother*?"

Their guilty expressions were affirmation enough to set off another flood of tears and wailing.

Streeter was growing impatient, his instinct keenly tuned to a clock with little time left. "What's his name?"

"He'll kill me," she howled and crumpled again, sobbing into the towel at her knees. "Like he killed Michelle. I just know it. He's evil."

"Do you know that for a fact? That he killed Michelle?" Streeter insisted.

"I didn't even know Michelle was dead until just now," she shouted, eyes wide with concern. "I didn't know anything about all this. Oh, what am I going to do without her? He will kill me, for sure."

"Not if you tell us who he is. Then we can protect you," Streeter said. When nothing but muffled sobs came from the towel in her lap, he added, "Char, this is important. What is the name of the man you were with Sunday night?"

She lifted her head and sighed, weighing the idea. "If he's going to be mad at me or do something to me for telling, I guess I'm already in trouble since I told Jens's sister. So why not tell you?"

"What did you say?" Streeter asked with urgency, his throat tight and dry.

"I said why shouldn't I tell you?" Char repeated.

"No, before that. You already told who?" Streeter's stomach cramped.

"Jens's sister. Jens Bergen was dating Michelle. He has a bunch of sisters. This was one I hadn't met before."

The towel she had been pressing against her tear stained, snot-streaked face dropped to Char's lap, her eyes were wide and childlike. He had seen those features before, recognized the eyes, the mischievous smile, the black tousled curls that she kept brushing off her forehead. The similarities did not belong to Michelle, but to someone else he recognized, someone he'd recently encountered. Streeter stood and snapped on a panel of lights to get a better view, to confirm his suspicions. Bly straightened when he recognized what Streeter saw in Char's face.

"Liv? Was the sister's name Liv?" Streeter asked, worried now that Liv had also seen what he had in Char's familiar face.

"Yeah. When she found me and dropped me off here at home," she said, her red-rimmed eyes spilling again. "She asked me the same questions. Who was I with Sunday night?"

"And what did you tell her?"

"She convinced me it was a matter of life and death." Char whined, searching their eyes for confirmation.

"It is," Streeter said, only this time it was Liv who was in danger.

Char looked from Bly to Streeter, confused by the sudden urgency in Streeter's voice. "I was with Coach Schilling."

CHAPTER 29

"THAT EXPLAINS A LOT," Bly said, whipping around the corners of the highway leading to Nemo. "She looks just like him."

"Still no word from Jens or Liv?"

"Nope," Bly said, holding up his cell phone and checking for missed calls and the inbox for text messages.

"Damn it!" Streeter swore, something he rarely did.

He struggled to prepare his mind for what might lie ahead for Liv and immediately chased the thoughts from his tortured mind. He willed himself to be battle ready by focusing on Coach Schilling. Imagining Shank's face when he learned about his poker buddy's sexual conquests with underage girls and possible involvement in Michelle's death, Streeter's mind drifted to the idiotic neighbor stating things like "but he was always so quiet, so normal" to the reporter about the deranged murderer living next door. Maybe Shank already knew. Maybe that's why he was orchestrating the rush to judgment against Mully, someone no one would care about putting away. Maybe that's why Shank looked so ill.

Bly quipped, "A regular all-American couple. She a former cheerleader and kindergarten teacher, he the college all-star jock and pedophile."

"Do you suppose he knew that Char was his own daughter? A child conceived with a girl he took by force fourteen years earlier?" Streeter asked rhetorically, a shiver running down his spine.

"Or had Michelle kept the secret so well that he never knew? Eddie Schilling attracted to Char because she looked so much like the narcissistic bastard he is?"

Streeter laid his head back and imagined what poor Michelle must have seen that night. Char with her long black curls falling across her childlike face, her lips glossed and face painted in an attempt to mask her age, smiling mischievously with her inviting lips and dancing eyes. Eddie with his tanned, toned body writhing beside her, his hair mussed, a mischievous smile hiding the fact of his aged face. A black curl or two spilling onto his forehead. Michelle must have felt like she was having an out-of-body experience, watching the nightmare she'd lived through repeating itself.

Fourteen years later.

The adrenaline that must have coursed through Michelle's veins as she shone the light on Char's and Schilling's faces that night, horrified that history was repeating itself. With the one person in the world she loved and protected the most. Her baby. That Schilling was the man who raped her, a truth she had never shared before until she confided in Jens, and then only because Roy Barker called her out on the long-kept secret.

That dark secret had turned into the worst of all nightmares, unfolding right before Michelle's eyes. Certainly she had to fix things, once and for all. Her life of secrecy and unintended worries about her baby's safety had caught up with her as the monstrosity it was.

As the engine revved, Bly driving and braking expertly around the corners, they found themselves just beyond a new subdivision, at least ten miles from the Lazy S. He lifted his cell phone again as they slowed around a sharp corner. "Probably won't get reception from here, Streeter. Maybe at King Road. It's a high spot."

"Jens said Liv told him she had one more lead to follow up. Let's hope that meant she was heading to the library or somewhere other than heading toward the Lazy S, based on the same conclusion we just made," Streeter growled.

"Assuming Eddie had killed Michelle, whether intentionally, accidentally, or in self-defense, it would make sense that he would try to frame the Lucifer's Lot, and it would explain why he was so eager to point a finger their way. Kill two birds with one stone."

"But if he missed with the stone, he must have known his life would be in danger. So he rallied support and offered evidence to his friends, his poker buddies."

"Sheriff Leonard, Bob Shankley, Ken Vincent. Convenient."

"And he imposed himself in this investigation early on and was persistent on staying abreast of the latest developments." Streeter wrestled with a new thought. "Unless some or all of his poker buddies already knew about Schilling's secret."

"Not Mayor Vincent," Bly said.

"I'd agree."

"But it would explain why Shank imposed himself in the investigation, pinning you with blame for arresting Mully, but forcing you to focus only on him."

"And why he blew up when we went on interviews without him," Streeter added. "If he wasn't there, he couldn't help cover for Schilling."

"Shank did exhibit a lot of paranoia throughout this investigation," Bly agreed.

"Schilling had access to the creek, which is close to the campground, and to the secluded wooded area where he could easily hide and where they found the footprints. He had admitted to asking Shank to help him get out from under the Lucifer's Lot thumb of always having to offer the campground exclusively to them each year during the rally. He probably had plans to sell the campground, abandoning the only reminder and tie he would have to his crime. He would have access to little trinkets left behind by the bikers each day, probably the FTW pin placed intentionally in Michelle's hand. He would have the most to lose both personally and professionally if he allowed Michelle to live and tell her story of his attraction to the teenage girls on his sports teams."

"And a whale of a tale if she threatened to tell everyone how he nearly committed incest with his fourteen-year-old illegitimate daughter," Bly speculated. "It would make perfect sense why he would have killed

Michelle and tried to pin the blame on the Lucifer's Lot leader. Stupid and risky, but it makes sense coming from a desperate man."

Streeter stared out the window at trees rushing by in the dark sliced by the sweeping high beams on each corner. He clearly understood why Michelle would have gone ballistic once she saw Schilling as Char told it. She probably didn't appreciate seeing her baby in the exact same position she had been a decade and a half earlier with the guy.

He imagined Michelle driving out to the campground to confront Schilling, threatening to turn him in to the authorities if he didn't leave Char alone, if he didn't stay completely away from her. Maybe she even broke the news for the first time that Char was his child. He imagined Schilling denying it, infuriating Michelle and antagonizing her to a point of a violent rage. It would have been easy for Schilling to overpower her, hitting her on the head with a flashlight when she got out of control, maybe the same flashlight Michelle had dropped on Skyline Drive when she first saw the couple in the car on Dinosaur Hill.

Once Schilling realized Michelle was serious, he couldn't just let her go and risk having her tell the authorities. He probably convinced her or forced her to walk the distance to the creek, then smashed her on the back of her skull. He had to finish her off.

Streeter understood now why Mully seemed to have no clue about Michelle Freeburg, angered by the thought that someone was setting him up as the fall guy for her murder. He was set up.

As if Bly was reading Streeter's mind, he said, "That would explain why Schilling got so nervous when you asked why he thought Mully killed Michelle. Remember that? He said the room might be bugged."

"He knew that Mully would kill him if he found out Schilling fingered him, let alone set him up for the murder."

In an urgent voice Streeter asked, "Do we have word on the search warrants yet?"

"Let me check. I'll need to pull over, though, before we lose this signal completely," Bly said.

"Hurry," was all Streeter said, running through the story that was unfolding in his mind.

They were at the King Road intersection, the peak in Nemo Road, and cell phone coverage was spotty at best. Streeter thought about the latest turn of events and wondered what Liv had done in response to what she had learned from Char. The best Streeter could hope for was that, if Liv did act on impulse and head to the Lazy S to confront Eddie Schilling, she found the place teeming with Lucifer's Lot members pulling up stakes and heading to Colorado, causing her to delay the confrontation with Eddie until morning.

After punching a few buttons on his phone's mini-keyboard, Bly reported, "I got a text from Sue that the papers are on their way to Judge Usher's house now. He will approve the search warrant."

"Good," Streeter said. "Let's move. Quickly!"

Hesitating, Bly shot him a look and added, "And I got a text that Shank released Mully."

"What?!" Streeter snatched the phone from Bly's hand. "How long ago was that?"

The slender woman in the tight slacks and an even tighter blouse looked around the quiet office. The courthouse wouldn't open for hours; at this hour it was completely empty except for the custodians who were busy mopping the hall. She patted her brunette hair, securing the knot she had hurriedly fashioned after being roused from sleep. She turned on her computer, the soft glow illuminating the otherwise dark office. She didn't want to bother messing with the timer for the lights, the device intentionally complicated to discourage county employees from working overtime. Her fingers flew across the keyboard as she scanned the sketchy information she'd hastily jotted down on a napkin. Within minutes, the whir of the printer signified that the final drafts were ready.

She lifted the receiver and hit number one in her speed-dial list. "Judge Usher? I'm finished with the search warrants. Can I stop by in fifteen minutes to notarize your signature? In triplicate, right."

She replaced the receiver, clacked the keyboard, and generated two more copies. As the printer once more whirred its reply, she lifted the receiver a second time and punched in a familiar number.

"Mully? It's me."

She rolled her eyes as she listened to his admonishment.

"I know this is your cell phone number and that I'm not supposed to call you on it. That's why I said, 'It's me.' I didn't have time to call you from a payphone. Listen, this is important. I just typed up a search warrant you might be interested in." She thought about him in front of her—beneath her—daring her to tantalize him, a provocative curve to her lips softening her otherwise prim face. "For the Lazy S Campground."

She straightened the pile of papers, tidied up the top of her desk, and twisted her wrist to check the time.

"Not for you. Edward Schilling. The office and his car."

Flicking off the computer, she acknowledged, "I thought you'd appreciate it. Forgive me for breaking your rules? Later, baby."

CHAPTER 30

I PULLED UP TO the campground, thankful that the lights were still on in the building and the rest of the campground was quiet. The tents, a camper, and two vans were still there, but no motorcycles. And no Mully. I knew I would lose my resolve if he showed up, so I was thankful there was no sign of him. Probably still being questioned by the agents, but he would be hopping mad once he was released. And if he wasn't, the other three who got tackled through the thick glass and smashed into the stainless steel vats would be. I intended to be in and out of here before any more excitement clouded my judgment.

I flicked my lights off before pulling into the campground, wishing I still had Jens's Browning tucked in my jeans. I thought about going up the road a piece and retrieving it from the loader, but worried that if Schilling saw my lights out there in the pitch-black valley, he might call the police. Or worse, disappear altogether, and I'd lose my chance of ambushing him with the information I had unearthed.

I backed in near the front door just in case I needed to make a hasty retreat for some reason. I waited for a minute, debating again if I should go retrieve the pistol from the loader. When the thought of delaying my departure from here made my knees tremble, I decided to take my chances.

I double-checked the Dictaphone I'd strapped to my ribs with duct tape, just under my left breast, to make sure it was secure. I'd found the miniature device at Jens's house and loaded it with fresh batteries and a seventy-minute tape. I needed to make sure this wasn't just for my ears only, and I was desperate to help Jens move beyond his grief by learning the whole truth and nothing but the truth about Michelle.

I pulled the key from the ignition and dropped from the driver's seat onto the gravel. As the crunch beneath my feet sounded in the still night, I wondered if the crushed stone had come from our quarry or if it was from one of our competitors. If I could think about making a buck at a time like this, I knew I was comfortable about confronting one or both of the Schillings. As solid a decision as the rock beneath my feet. My dad's favorite biblical passage came to mind, Luke telling me to look to the rock from which I was hewn, the quarry from which I had been dug. And to gather strength, I stole a quick glance over my left shoulder toward Nemo Quarry, toward the discarded Browning that I knew was in the black beyond.

Even without the Browning as security. I just prayed they were both here, hoping Schilling's wife would buffer me from any ill will Eddie Schilling wished on me as I confronted him about his seedy past.

Swinging the door wide open, before my eyes adjusted to the lights, Samantha and Eddie Schilling emerged from the back bedroom, rumpled with sleep and not pleased to see me. My eyes rolled skyward in silent thanksgiving for prayers answered.

"Howdy, folks," I said, waggling my fingers.

Unimpressed, Mr. Schilling asked, "What the hell are you doing here again, Liv? Do you know what time it is, for chrissake?"

Mrs. Schilling eyed the lump on my forehead, but Mr. Schilling was totally oblivious and nonobservant. I tried on my best lie, in my best Columbo impersonation. "Well, to be honest, I couldn't sleep. I was thinking about something you said that just didn't make sense, and I thought you might clear it up for me."

Mr. Schilling checked his watch. "At one thirty in the morning? What, are you accustomed to having your loyal subjects attend to your every whim at all hours?"

Ignoring the obvious dig about my family's success, I dug deep for the right tone of humility. "Forgive me. Really, I am so sorry about waking you. I really didn't think it through. Lord knows, I've read enough articles about you to know all the reporters agree you accomplish so much in your life that you must never sleep."

His demeanor changed. I had successfully turned the tables on him, making myself his loyal subject. I nodded meekly, and was thankful when Mrs. Schilling piped in with, "Oh, this ought to be good." I was glad she was here to hear all of this; she'd be a kind of protective shield. I wouldn't need my gun after all.

I stole a glance in her direction. In contrast to her husband's mussed-up hair, her blonde locks were pulled back in an attractive ponytail. And I thought she looked better without makeup. More real.

"You said you didn't know Char Freeburg that well, yet you were spot on about her being at Hope Smith's house," I said, hoping I was approaching this correctly. "How is it that you were so accurate?"

"Good guess?" he said, shrugging his shoulders and looking at his wife for support. "That's what was keeping you awake? Take a sleeping pill next time, will you?"

"Eighteen girls on the team. Another twenty or so underclassmen. You have a vague recollection of who Charlene is, yet you knew exactly who she'd be staying with since Sunday night," I said, making sure I had moved over close enough to him to catch everything he said on tape, yet not get too close for him to grab me.

"Hey, like I said. Lucky guess." He offered his signature grin.

"I think it was more than luck. And do you know what she had to say about Sunday night?" I hoped Mr. Schilling would be so nervous about what Char had revealed that he would confess to his wife, that he would make it easier on her by telling the truth rather than have her hear about it from me or from the authorities.

The color in his face drained, his grin slacked. "I don't know what you're talking about."

"Oh, yes, you do. Do you want to tell her or should I?" I motioned to Mrs. Schilling, who sat with her arms crossed over her faded sweatshirt, her eyes boring into her husband.

"She's lying," he said to his wife. "You know how it is. Everyone trying to make me look bad. They're jealous, that's all."

"I haven't even told the story yet. How do you know I'm lying or that it's bad?" I said, measuring my words carefully.

Samantha Schilling never took her eyes off her husband. I watched as his shoulders sagged and he flopped into a chair at the second table, far from his wife. He couldn't—or wouldn't—look at her.

"I knew Char, if that's what you're getting at," he admitted.

"And tell your wife how well you knew Char," I demanded. "And how well you knew Michelle."

His wife sat up in her chair, tapping her foot, waiting for her husband to answer my questions.

"You know how it is, Samantha. I love you," he said, almost apologetically.

"Twenty-four years, Eddie," she said, containing her simmering anger quite well.

"Samantha, come on," he said, finally looking over at her.

"You could never keep your pecker in your pants, Eddie. Not even when we were dating."

His eyes followed her as she rose and slipped on dainty little tennis shoes, then walked over to the door and slipped hiking boots on over them. I was intent on the fact that she was about to leave and I wasn't through extracting her husband's confession, so I didn't even consider the absurdity of her actions. Until much later.

I blurted, "You killed Michelle, didn't you? She came up here to tell you to leave Char alone, to warn you that if you didn't, she'd tell everyone that you were Char's father, and you killed her."

Mrs. Schilling pulled up short. "What did you say?"

"Killed her? Sunday night? Me?" he said, his jowls drooping even further in horror.

A stronger, more confident Mrs. Schilling turned back toward me at the door, a serene expression washing over her face.

"That's right," I said, willing her to sit back down and listen as I accused her husband. "You raped Michelle when she was only thirteen. Messed with her for a year until she finally had enough. She had your illegitimate child. How many other girls in between? Until you started seducing Char? Your own flesh and blood."

"I never knew," he said, all the color in his face drained away. "My child?"

"Michelle came up here Sunday night to warn you to leave Char alone, didn't she? And you killed her."

He looked at his wife, his eyebrows furrowed. "But I wasn't here Sunday night—"

The rumble of Harleys sounded down the highway, cutting off Mr. Schilling's sentence. His face blanched even whiter. His wife stepped out the door and looked in the direction of the noise, motioning for me to follow her.

"It's them. Eddie, you have to deal with Mully and the Lot. They can't know Liv is here. Come on!" she shouted at me, grabbing a flashlight and tugging my hand as though I were a small child. Within seconds, together we sprinted through the parking lot, hopped the barbed wire fence, and splayed ourselves in the deep meadow grass just as the bikers' headlights swept across us and into the campground. If the creek had been any farther from the fence or if either of us had not been as fit, surely they would have caught us like deer in their headlights. I had discovered a newfound respect for the woman lying next to me. She was strong and quick-witted, not a dullard like her husband.

I was trembling, trying to process in my mind what was unfolding before me. I could see the flurry of activity as a dozen, maybe two dozen, Lucifer's Lot gang members dismounted their bikes and scurried about the campground. The tents collapsed quickly, flashlights and headlights darting about with the movement. Women were packing pots, pans, and other belongings into the vans as the rest of the bikers made short work of tearing down camp. I could see Mr. Schilling standing in the doorway, the light giving his silhouette a halo effect, none of the bikers stopping to answer his questions. "Fellas, what's wrong? What's happening?"

I heard the rumble of more Harleys coming from town, and I knew before I saw them that it would be more of the Lucifer's Lot. That it would be Mully.

Sure enough, the lead biker was none other than Mully. The agents had released him.

A groan escaped my lips and Samantha pushed my head into the grass and hissed, "Stay down!"

I did as I was told, hearing but not seeing her husband as he shouted, "Mully, what's wrong?"

Samantha yanked on my hand again and said, "Come on. Now!"

I scrambled to my feet as she pulled me through the rest of the meadow, across the creek, and up the other side of the bank. We scurried across another short stretch of meadow before we reached the trees. The woods were dark. Still holding fast to Samantha with my left hand, I warded off the thwack of tree limbs against my face with my right. My feet were scrabbling over rocks and branches, but she easily found purchase on the path through the woods, and I was thankful for her familiarity with this route. My breathing was heavy and ragged by the time she finally pulled up short and turned to look back at the Lazy S. I paused with my hands on my knees, doubled over to catch my breath for a minute or so, before I went over and stood beside her. We were looking down at the campground from a distance well beyond the Broken Peaks lodge and cabins.

We were on a hill—maybe half a mile from the Lazy S—just off our Nemo Quarry fence line, but not quite to the big rock. The lights that danced around the otherwise inky black campground were not unlike a well-orchestrated ballet, with the headlights of motorcycles, campers, and vans all falling into line and merging onto the highway in the direction of Nemo. The plume of dust left behind hung above the campground and eventually settled, as did my breathing.

One biker lagged behind, slowing as he came from behind the building and neared my truck. I squinted to make out his features, his movements. It was Mully. He just sat there, staring. Eddie approached him, and Mully gripped him with one hand around his neck, shouting something. Demanding something. In the still of the night, I thought I heard Mully speak my name. Eddie was pleading, pointing toward the woods into which Samantha and I had disappeared, shouting, "She ran off! She ran away!"

Mully stared off into the darkness and I shuddered, thankful I was closer to the loader than he was to me. Just as I was about to tell her my plan of retrieving the Browning as protection and hightailing it back to the campground before Mully killed her husband, a car in the distance, its headlights on high beam, stitched its way along the ribbon of Nemo Road. Mully released his grip on Eddie, gave him a shove, and took off after his pack, headlights on his bike turned off until he was well down the highway.

The car's headlights dotted the blanket of night as I watched Mully barrel down the road in the other direction, his lights disappearing in the line of trees. The car that had spooked Mully rolled past the entrance of the campground and on into the night, unaware of the commotion it had caused, a life it had saved.

The only sound that could be heard above the pounding in my chest was Mr. Schilling calling occasionally to his wife. "Samantha, they're gone now. Packed up early. You can come back. Samantha!"

I thought she would flick on her flashlight to signal him and then lead me back to the campground. But she just stood there, still as death.

"Shouldn't we—"

"Shh," she said, staring at the campground.

I wondered what in the hell was happening, just as I began to wonder how she could possibly know Mully had been after me all day long. Who was she protecting me from? Did she know her husband was a killer? Thought he might kill me next? I stood silently beside her and watched as her husband disappeared and reappeared in the doorway several more times before emerging from the building a final time, walking around back, and taking off in his red sports car. He was headed toward Rapid City.

His decision to leave the campground rather than pursue us in the woods made me realize she had indeed been keeping me away from her husband, using the excuse of the Lucifer's Lot to hide me from him. As I watched the taillights of his car disappear, I said simply, "Hey, thanks."

"No problem," she said in equal simplicity, staring long after her husband had gone.

I moved up beside her, thinking she had remained stationary in order to catch her breath. "Are you okay?"

"Not really," she said, sitting on the hard ground and lowering her head onto her knees.

"I'm sorry about all that back there, but that story had to be told. I hope you understand." I sat nearby and took a moment to reflect on what just happened and if I got what I needed on the tape.

For a long moment, neither of us said a word.

Breaking the silence, she asked me, "How'd you figure it out? About Michelle?"

Her question took me off guard, and I stammered an answer, thinking of Tommy's words to me earlier this evening. "Char was the key."

She nodded and added with a heavy sigh, "I knew it was only a matter of time before somebody would."

"You knew Charlene Freeburg was with your husband? And that she was his child?"

A throaty laugh erupted from her before she replied. "No, not that. I didn't know the name of his latest conquest until you told me tonight. And neither of us knew he had sired a child."

I was confused. "Then what do you mean? Before someone figured out what?"

"That Eddie has a thing for teenage girls," she said with a scoff. She stood up and dusted off her sweatpants. I followed suit. Once more she motioned for me to follow her. "Come on."

She was heading toward the Nemo Quarry haul road, farther from the Lazy S and closer to Nemo.

"But we're heading in the wrong direction."

Barely acknowledging me, she explained, "We came the hard way, so I could see what the Lucifer's Lot were up to and they couldn't see us. I'm taking you back down the easy way. Down your road. Come on. We'll hop the fence."

I watched as she led the way, flashlight beam dancing ahead of her, her hiking boots trudging across the rocks and dirt. I sloshed along behind her, the water not yet drained from my boots from having crossed the creek. I could see her boot prints in the moonlight, and although they were muddy, I realized what I was looking at. The distinct, yet misleading, prints of a man's hike through the woods, not of a woman who used man-size boots as overshoes. Then it dawned on me. The last thing Eddie Schilling said before we heard the motorcycles approaching. He started to say he wasn't at the Lazy S Sunday night. And the only other person who stayed at the campground when Eddie didn't was Samantha Schilling.

My heart raced. I glanced ahead and judged the distance between me and the loader, wondering if I could slip away quickly, eluding her long enough to retrieve the Browning that was near the lift and tilt levers.

Before she killed me.

CHAPTER 31

STILL PERCHED IN THE dark on the shoulder of the road like a blind buzzard, Bly waited for him to finish his call, afraid that continuing into the Hills would cause a lost signal. Streeter imagined Shank cowering in his office, his flabby body reeking of fear, his wavy red hair damp with sweat and looking like undercooked bacon.

"When?" Streeter growled.

"About an hour ago," Shank answered, his breathing unnaturally labored.

"In other words, just after we left," snarled Streeter. "We had until tomorrow, Shank. I distinctly told you not to release Mully. Under any condition."

Streeter was thankful this conversation was not in person because he knew he would not have resisted the urge to smash the man's face with his fist.

"I, I . . . We already got everything we needed from him, Streeter," Shank argued. "You heard what Liv Bergen said. He didn't kill the girl in Sturgis. And you said yourself you thought someone was setting him up on the Freeburg case. He didn't even know she was dead. I thought Mully was off the hook and we would start focusing on the real suspect."

"We were going to arrange for a lineup. For Roy Barker and Jens Bergen to identify him as the man at Barker's Market Sunday night. You said he was your lead suspect on the Crooked Man case," Streeter barked, cutting his eyes toward Bly to keep himself from saying more. He'd already spewed a line of bunk as long as his arm.

"Streeter, I was only trying to—"

"To what? Get someone killed?" Streeter shouted. He tried to regain his composure, his fury beyond the boiling point. "What favor are you trying to repay Schilling?"

"Wha. . . who told you I that?"

"What did Schilling do for you that you owe him a favor?"

"I don't know what you're—"

"Damn it, Shank! You're playing me and I don't appreciate it. But worse, you told Schilling you'd repay him a favor by getting rid of Mully for him." Streeter could hear Shank's labored breathing. He yelled, "What. Was. The. Favor."

After a long silence, Shank mumbled, "He changed a couple of grades. For my kid, my boy, so he'd be eligible for football."

In the glow of the dashboard lights, Bly slid his eyes toward Streeter. Streeter took in a long breath. "You piece of dirt. You have no idea what you've done, do you?"

Silence.

"I had more to tell Mr. Muldando and more to gain from him. If you had listened to me for once and followed my instructions, we wouldn't have to be worried about the Lucifer's Lot mobilizing. They may be setting up an ambush for us as we speak. Now, get people moving from Sturgis and Deadwood toward the Lazy S so Mully doesn't slip through our net and so that we don't walk into a trap with just the two of us."

"But we don't have any charges—"

"Do it," Streeter bellowed. "And do it now."

Shank added meekly, "The fastest way would be to call Sheriff Leonard, but at this hour . . . well, I don't know if I can reach him."

Streeter's eyes narrowed with a rage so intense he knew they must be glowing like a viper's. He snarled into the phone, "You have his home number, Shank. Tell him to get over to the Lazy S now or you two will have to find a replacement for this Friday night's poker game."

The dead space that followed was soon filled by a stammering Bob Shankley. "Wha, wha, what are you talking about?"

"I'm talking about Eddie Schilling. You let Mully go and he'll head straight to the Lazy S to kill Eddie. Don't you get it?"

"Eddie?" Shank said in a small voice.

"All for a couple of phony grades for a crooked football star. Your friend's blood will be on your hands if you don't get someone over there now!" Streeter warned. "Bly and I are still ten minutes away. Get Leonard mobilized!"

"Okay. Give me a minute."

Streeter stared out the front windshield, knowing they would be the first to arrive at the campground and knowing valuable time was ticking as he waited for Shank to return to the phone. The seconds dragged. Two emergency vehicles drove by with lights flashing, sirens wailing in the night. Ahead, he saw the Doty Volunteer Fire Department trucks turning onto Nemo Road, too, heading toward Nemo.

"Shit," Bly said. "Want to follow?"

Just as Streeter was about to snap the phone shut, Shank's voice said, "Leonard's on his way. He lives a few minutes from there. He's not happy about it, but he called on four deputies and agreed to make the arrest as long as some of our guys took the lead. I caught Karski and Greenborough here before they left. They're on their way to the Lazy S, too. They should be there within thirty minutes."

"This isn't over, Shank," Streeter warned, ending the call.

Bly shook his head. "I feel a little like Custer heading into the Battle of the Bighorn."

A niggling thought tugged at Streeter. A thought that had enough substance it would require some analysis, dissection later.

"Completely outnumbered," Bly added, speeding off toward the Lazy S Campground in the wake of the emergency vehicles that had just passed.

Streeter marveled at Bly's ability to corner blindly in the dark on this windy road.

"By the way, Streeter, the autopsy on the Sturgis Jane Doe is complete.

The text I got said the girl was a teenager, and she had traces of narcotics in her system. But the official cause of death was heat exhaustion. These girls aren't into safety first."

Just before Steamboat Rock, an S-curve that crossed the Boxelder two miles short of the Lazy S Campground, the lights of squad cars and ambulances flashed and danced on the right side of the road as though a carnival was in town.

"What in the name of . . ." Streeter said as Bly slowed down to a crawl. Streeter leaned forward in his seat and peered out the windshield into the otherwise dark night. "What's going on?"

Easing the car onto the right shoulder, Bly came to a complete stop behind the mob of emergency response vehicles. The area had not yet been cordoned off with yellow tape, and Streeter imagined there would be no need to, given the isolation of this area and the late hour. The smashed car had crossed lanes and sailed off the road, landing down in the meadow just along the Boxelder Creek bank.

As Streeter and Bly approached, they saw a woman kneel down and point the lens of her camera over the crumpled driver's side door and snap several flash photos. On the passenger side of the vehicle, two men stood posed in the attack mode: one held a long stick with a retractable metal cable hoop, the kind dog catchers often use to subdue a biting animal, and the other held a burlap sack. The man with the stick and hoop had just snagged something in the car and was holding it up in the lights.

"Got him!" he yelled, pulling the stick from the car, an ensnared snake dangling from the tightened hoop. He carefully held it out to the man with the burlap sack, who examined its mottled earth tones before opening the bag, into which the first man deposited the snake.

"Copperhead," the second man announced to the anxious emergency responders.

"Copperhead? They don't live this far north," Streeter commented to Bly.

"They do if someone brings one along for a visit," Bly answered dryly.

"A booby trap?"

A body had been tossed forward in the driver's seat, splayed lifelessly across the steering wheel of the cherry red Mustang.

"A deadly one, and we're too late," was all Bly could say. "Booby traps are typical for many Lucifer's Lot hits."

"I figured as much," Streeter said solemnly. "Come on."

Before they climbed back into Bly's car, Sheriff Leonard pulled up, his bubble lights flashing, wheels squealing. He jumped from the car and held his hands to his head, not believing what he was seeing. His friend, Eddie Schilling, lying dead in the front seat of the Mustang.

Streeter approached. "You got here fast."

"Well, I just live a ways down. On old Drew Stevens's place on Chipmunk Road. Once I got the call about Shank, my adrenaline was already spinning out of control."

"About Shank? You mean from Shank," Streeter corrected, glancing at Bly.

"He called, yes, but about two minutes after that, while I was getting dressed, I got a call from Sue at FBI headquarters asking where Shank's wife was staying this week. She's out of town and they didn't know where to find her."

Streeter watched as Sheriff Leonard tucked his shirttail in, the laces of his boots still undone. He had clearly left home in a rush.

"Sue said Shank was being taken to Rapid City Regional. He was having a heart attack."

Streeter hung his head. Bly gripped his shoulder.

"Now I have to notify Samantha about Eddie," Leonard said, clawing at his temples. "Things couldn't get any worse."

"Let us do that for you, Leonard," Streeter offered. "Do you know where she is?"

"My man there said he saw her Volvo at the campground. She must have a visitor because there was a pickup truck he didn't recognize."

For the second time tonight, Streeter's throat felt as though he had swallowed an orange. Whole.

"What color is the pickup?" Streeter asked.

Leonard made a sharp whistle and called his deputy over.

"What color was the truck you saw at the Lazy S a few minutes ago on your way here?" Leonard asked.

"Blue. Two-toned," the young man answered. "Why?"

Streeter bolted to the car, Bly scrambling behind him.

"Liv?" Bly asked.

Streeter didn't bother answering.

Bly drove the rest of the way to the Lazy S Campground in silence. News of Shank's heart attack made Streeter's sinking feeling nearly bottomless. He was struggling with his own conscience for having contributed both to Eddie's death and Shank's reaction to the possibility of it at Mully's hands. After all, he had been harsh with Shank. He had agreed with Mully that someone had tried to frame him, explaining how the striations in photos matched those in the FTW pin found in Michelle's dead palm. But worst of all, Streeter worried about Liv, praying it was not her brother's pickup truck that Sheriff Leonard's man had seen at the Lazy S.

As Bly pulled into the campground, Streeter's stomach flipped when he saw the truck, the one he and Bly had seen Liv driving a few hours earlier, backed into a spot near the building's entrance. The tents were gone, the vans were gone, the bikes were gone. The Lucifer's Lot had vanished. He hoped that he hadn't screwed this up as well, his warning to Mully to leave Liv alone nothing more than another rule for him to break, a child's dare for him to take.

Before the wheels of the Pontiac stopped turning, Streeter bounded out the door, gun drawn, and entered the building. Empty. He found a note on one of the tables, scribbled hurriedly by Eddie. It read: "Going to town to see Shank. Couldn't wait for you and Liv to get back. Bikers gone now. E."

Come back? Where had they gone? The truck Liv had been driving was abandoned. He canvassed the parking lot and circled around to the back of the building. The Volvo was empty, too. He assumed the "you" Eddie referred to in his note was his wife, Samantha.

Bly came around the corner; unable to see anything in the dark at the rear of the building, he whispered, "Streeter?"

Feeling defeated, Streeter stepped out of the darkness and held up his hands. "No one."

"Shit," Bly swore.

Streeter was about to call out for Samantha Schilling or for Liv Bergen when he saw a small light bouncing through the trees in the distance across the creek. Running, he called back to Bly, "Call for backup. Someone's heading toward the place where Michelle was killed. Hurry!"

CHAPTER 32

"**YOU KILLED MICHELLE, DIDN'T** you, Samantha?" I said, readying myself for any sudden movement from her.

Hesitating briefly, she simply kept walking, but I noticed she had slipped her hand into her pocket. In the starlight, I scanned the nearby trees, hoping I could race between them toward the loader. If I had to, I'd ram into her if she moved suddenly. I believed I would do what I had to at this moment to survive. If I had to grab a rock or a tree limb to defend myself, I would. I wondered if I could muster enough strength to tackle her to the ground and wrestle what might be a gun from her pocket, pull that trigger, and take a human life. I imagined my strength growing with every passing millisecond, along with my anger that this woman hurt my brother and took an angel from us.

I imagined Samantha Schilling being reduced not to a pile of salt if she turned back to look at me, but rather to a stringless marionette that, with one mighty swing, would crumple to the ground.

Samantha didn't look back as Lot's wife had against God's warning. And she hadn't pulled a gun from her pocket. Instead, she shook out a cigarette from a half-filled pack, jammed it between her lips, and reached into her pocket again for a lighter. The flashlight's beam danced ahead of her, and I watched as she took several long drags on her cigarette.

"That girl was always trouble. I told Eddie that when I found out about her."

"You mean Char?"

"No, Michelle."

"You knew all along that Eddie was molesting her?" I asked, thinking of the digital recorder, which I felt humming against my left rib cage. When I realized Schilling was involved in Michelle's death, I had stopped by Jens' house to grab the recording device I'd seen in his desk drawer earlier, in case I extracted a confession from Eddie. The digital device was really the only reason I had decided not to hop the barbed wire fence we were walking along and make a run for it already. I knew this quarry ground as well as anyone and could easily reach the loader before my adversary caught up with me. As long as she didn't pull out a gun and shoot me in the back first. But I wanted this confession. It might be the last chance for Jens to know the truth.

The night was quiet, other than the squish of our wet boots against the rocky path; she blew a stream of smoke skyward. "Not all along, but most of the time. He was never very discreet about his . . . exploits."

"Plural? Like a lot of women?"

"Women?" she scoffed. "They were all babies."

"There were others besides Michelle?" I asked.

"Ha," she laughed mockingly. "So many I lost count."

"Were they all as young as Michelle and Char?"

Her hand started twitching nervously, making the flashlight jitter on the path ahead. She glanced over her shoulder at me and took another long draw on her cigarette.

"He was good to me when we first married, fawning over me like I was the most beautiful thing in the world." She looked up at the stars, lost in her memories. "Did you also find out we had to get married? Rusty was born seven months after our wedding. Stillborn. I couldn't conceive after that. I was twenty-three and childless. Except for Eddie, of course. He's nothing but a child in a man's body."

She laughed, then, but choked on the smoke of her cigarette. She dried her weepy eyes with the sleeve of the sweatshirt before continuing. "I think that was about the time he started becoming interested in other 'women,' as you so delicately call them. When we learned I couldn't bear him any children."

She trudged up the path, a path that clearly was leading to the big rock, not to the haul road, and not doubling back on Nemo Road as promised. I dropped back a few paces, not so many that the recorder couldn't pick up her words, but enough to give me a head start if I bolted over the barbed wire. I realized why she felt the need to wear so much makeup, why she found it difficult to see her own natural beauty. I realized that when I had seen her earlier today it wasn't the harshness of daylight that illuminated her sour disposition, but rather her disgust in him.

"The first one was nineteen, old enough to know better. But quickly he went to younger and younger girls. Too young to argue with him." I could hear the intake as she drew hard on her cigarette. "The last time was two years ago. We were on a road trip with his volleyball team. I went out to shop for a bit and forgot my purse. Eddie wouldn't let me in our hotel room. I forced my way in. There was a girl hiding in our closet. Naked. She was fourteen."

What a monster!

Poor Michelle, to have to live with that burden for all this time. Plus the guilt of not turning him into authorities years ago, possibly sparing others from his treacherous hand and lecherous heart.

I heard her sniffle. I couldn't help feeling sorry for Samantha, also a victim in all this, along with loathing her for allowing her husband to abuse so many girls and then taking the life of one of his victims.

"I tried everything I could to stop him. He is a very sick bastard. I threatened to leave him, to expose him, to have him arrested. I even threatened to kill him."

These last words were accompanied by the twitching of her hand again, the arc of the flashlight jerking about in the path ahead. I understood that she was not as tough as she would have liked me to believe.

"Only thing I can't seem to do is stop loving him." She wiped her nose again with her sleeve, took a drag on the cigarette, and blew out a long stream of smoke. "God knows I've tried. So, what does that say about the sick person I am?"

"Tell me about Michelle," I encouraged her. I looked up ahead to my left, and in the pale moonlight, I could make out the shape of the big rock. She was taking me back to where she had killed Michelle. The loader was about ten yards farther beyond the rock to the right. And I was running short of time for her to finish the story.

"Michelle was a handful, not stupid like so many other bimbos Eddie picked. The volunteers, I call them," Samantha said glancing around at the woods, her eyes settling on the creek bank to our left.

I'd heard stories of Mr. Schilling's coaching abilities, his wins, his teams' successes, but never in my years of knowing him had I heard he had lost a child. I could see why Samantha had resented Mr. Schilling's applause taking precedent over their family tragedy. But that wasn't reason enough to kill.

"Sunday night was the first time I had seen her in years," she said, lighting a new cigarette after crushing out the old with the toe of her hiking boot. "She marched right up to the door that night, pounding until I answered. It was nearly midnight. Eddie was supposedly at the campground, and I was left at home in Rapid City, alone as usual."

"But Mr. Schilling said he wasn't here Sunday night," I stammered, wondering what I was missing.

"He was supposed to be at the campground. But lucky for me, he was out cruising for chicks as usual. I didn't find that out until later. Until Michelle told me about finding Eddie parked up on Dinosaur Hill with her little sister." She made air quotes on the last words, her cigarette and bobbing flashlight like sparklers in the night.

She tapped the ashes onto the ground, the amber glow coming to life quickly before going out. I stepped on the embers as I passed, just to make sure we weren't aiding and abetting the pine beetles devastation. "Anyway, Michelle came to our house. I tried to close the door on Michelle so she'd go away. Really, I did. But she was persistent. She demanded to know where Eddie was and if he was with some girl named Char. I had no idea who Char was and I told her so."

After a long pause, Samantha Schilling—idolized kindergarten teacher, former cheerleader, and wife of a renowned coach—continued her sordid story. "That really pissed her off. She was in my face, shouting at me, telling me what a coward I was for hiding my husband's weakness for little girls. That pissed me off. I told her she should leave, but she refused, insisted she be allowed inside to wait for his return. So I decided to take her to him. Arrange for a front row seat to her ripping my husband's head off right."

Samantha's footsteps were starting to slow, and I could tell we were within a yard or two of where she had killed Michelle. She hadn't turned around yet, but I still kept my distance, praying she'd finish telling me the story of what happened to Michelle before she killed me, which I had no doubt she was planning to do.

"Eddie had been through counseling. He promised there would be no more young girls. I believed him. When Michelle told me about Eddie and the newest volunteer, their *child*, something snapped. I wanted Eddie dead."

The conviction with which she delivered this admission made my skin crawl. The sound of wet boots against the rocks was like fingernails on a chalkboard, sending chills along my spine. Her voice broke into the dead of night.

"We couldn't have children. But this annoying bitch carried his baby? And he was off scoring with his own child, for God's sake. A child he didn't even know he had. Do you know how that made me feel?"

"I can't imagine." The lifelessness in my own voice startled me.

"No, of course you can't."

"So you drove with her in her car?"

Samantha shook her head. "No. I told her I would take her to Eddie under one condition and it was that I would drive her there. At first, she refused. But she was so desperate, the poor fool. She told me it was time to end all of this, once and for all. I figured, after hearing about how Michelle had caught Eddie with Char, that he'd hightail it back to the campground, not home. So that's where I took Michelle."

"So Michelle suggested she drive her car back to the grocery store where she worked and you two would leave from there?"

"No, I told her she couldn't leave her car at my house in case Eddie showed up. She told me she'd leave her car at work, and I followed."

"What happened once you got to the campground?"

Finally turning to face me, as if facing her accuser eye to eye, she answered, "It's all Michelle's fault, you know. If she hadn't told me Char was her daughter, was Eddie's daughter from when he raped her at thirteen, I probably would have let it all go. I always have. Like water off a duck's back. Men will be men, right?"

The night was still again. I could hear my own ragged breaths.

"I had a change of heart when I realized he wasn't here to deal with the problem. I thought about how this transgression of Eddie's, above all others, would ruin my reputation. It wouldn't be fair to me after everything I'd been through. Michelle was threatening to go to the authorities with her story unless she found out where her sister—her daughter—Char had run away to and was hiding. I believed her. She was ready to face the consequences no matter what the outcome. I could tell from her cold eyes, her determined tone. She had crossed over."

"Crossed over?" I asked, gauging in my peripheral vision where to jump the fence and calculating how long it would take me to reach the loader.

"Eddie had been lucky up until Sunday night," Samantha explained, pacing back and forth along the creek bank. "I was never willing to cross over and suffer the consequences by leaving him. None of the girls he molested or seduced were willing to cross over and turn his sorry ass in to the authorities, even after years of being convinced, or forced, to have sex with him. We were all willing to keep silent, our secrets safe, allowing him the freedom to continue his prowling.

"I was the biggest idiot of all, though, believing it was all in his past. If Michelle hadn't come along, I would probably still be in denial. She had crossed over, which gave me the courage to cross over. I was suddenly willing to take matters into my own hands."

She stopped pacing and made her way back toward me, a move I hadn't anticipated. I should be running, but she was so close to telling me the truth. "I killed her. Just as you said. Eddie didn't know anything about his illegitimate daughter. Until you spoke up tonight. No one did except me and Michelle. And now you."

In the thin moonlight, I could see her eyes wildly fixed on me, her mind working on this last revelation. I knew this would seal my fate. I prepared to spring into action, to launch myself over the fence and dart toward the loader for the gun.

"Eddie really believes Mully killed Michelle," she added softly.

She turned and smoked the last of her second cigarette, anxious to finish her story. I watched as she once again began to pace back and forth, back and forth, along the creek. "Eddie's too weak. He'll probably puke his guts out if he ever hears about this," she said with a wave of her hand. "Anyway, my plan worked perfectly. With Eddie gone and knowing Mully and his crew would be at the rally, I had the Lazy S to myself. No one would see me there. I grabbed a flashlight that one the bikers left behind in the building, and told Michelle that Eddie and Char had been hiding in the woods this whole time, camping."

She sucked hard on her cigarette, her lips trembling.

"She was so trusting. What a fool. A bigger fool than me. She followed me into the woods. I know them well because I hike the area all summer long. I knew exactly where to take her, where someone would find her body and start poking around at the Lazy S."

Her hands trembled as she flicked the lighter on and off, on and off.

"You wanted them to arrest you?"

She barked a laugh. "Not me. I wanted Eddie to shit bricks. And I wanted Mully and his filth gone. If Mully was arrested for Michelle's murder, so what? He deserved it. If Eddie was arrested, I would be free. Either way, I would win."

I stood perfectly still so the recorder would pick up on every single incriminating word.

She stood staring in the darkness at the creek bed below. "It was easy, you know. I told her to cross the creek and look up the meadow and she'd see the light in their tent. When she stepped to the other side of the bank, I followed. She bent down to get a better view, and I hit her on the back of her head with the flashlight. Unfortunately, the light broke when I did that. I couldn't see a thing. I felt for her body and undressed her. She wasn't dead yet, but the pulse was so light I knew she'd be dead by morning."

"I grabbed the pieces of the flashlight I could find and crept back to the office. I drew a map of where her body could be found. I walked over to one of the biker bitches' campers and threw the flashlight and Michelle's clothes in the back of a small compartment. A little insurance policy, I suppose. If the police found it, they'd believe me over the Lucifer's Lot, right?

"I pinned a note I had hurriedly scribbled, along with the map, to the inside of one of the Lucifer's Lot tents, the one I'd seen a prospect using. I was thinking the prospect would be tempted to violate the dead body, leave DNA that would point to them. I had signed the note "Eddie" so I had a little insurance against him as well. But as I was in the tent, I found an FTW pin, decided against leaving the note, and returned to the creek to put the pin in Michelle's hand.

"Eddie collects little trinkets left behind in the garbage of those slimy bikers. And I made sure to tell one of the prospects earlier this week that Eddie had found an FTW pin. A lie, but I considered it a little insurance I'd keep tucked away in the back of my mind for someday when I needed to have Eddie walk the line. If Mully ever found out, he might just find a reason to kill him. Of course, I'm in complete control of all that. And for now, I think I'll keep all that to myself. Eddie enjoys the fact that these bikers are bad. He's bad and gets away with it, just like them. Or so he thinks. I let him think that all those years. Then, when Michelle came knocking, it was over. I wanted him to pay. I crossed over."

"You shouldn't have killed Michelle. She was innocent in all this," I growled.

Samantha stopped pacing and approached me, standing within an arm's length of me. Sweat slid down my sides, back, and arms. I met her eyes in the pale moonlight, her back to the creek where Michelle was killed only two nights earlier. By this woman. This poor, pathetic excuse for a woman. Michelle didn't deserve this. And neither did I.

"Innocent?" Samantha Schilling repeated. "Don't you get it? All these years I thought Eddie was the reason I couldn't have a child. I thought it was his sperm that was deficient. After all, none of the hundreds of girls he bedded over the years had ever gotten pregnant. Never."

She took a step closer to me. I held my breath and my position.

"Then Michelle storms up here and tells me Eddie has a daughter. He fathered a child." She leaned in and shrieked, "Do you know how that made me feel? The one thing I could cling to, the only reason I didn't get washed down the storm drains of my gutter life, was that he was impotent. Not me. Not me!"

A twisted grin spread across her face just before she whipped the flashlight above her head with lightning speed.

I bolted to my right to avoid the crushing blow meant for my skull, feeling the wind rush against my face and neck as the flashlight narrowly missed its mark. After a few steps, I leapt over the barbed wire fence, snagging my jeans and crashing hard to the ground on the other side. I felt Samantha's strong hand on my boot, hung up on the top wire, and my pant leg rip as she smashed the flashlight against my leg. An animalistic noise escaped my mouth and I kicked at her, yanking my foot hard and ripping my jeans free of the barbs as I scrabbled away on my hands and knees.

I heard the wires creak as Samantha squeezed the top wires with her strong hands and stepped over the fence.

She would close the distance in no time, her being in such good shape and me with a bruised calf.

I pushed myself off the ground and began taking awkward steps toward the loader as quickly as I could. I tripped on a rock and ended up in a heap instead. Hearing my adversary's footsteps pounding into a dead run, I pushed myself up a second time and crabbed across the rocky ground on my hands and knees until I was running again toward the loader, thankful I would have the advantage if I retrieved the loaded Browning before she reached me. My mind raced back in time to earlier that day, and I tried to recall if I'd clicked the safety back into place before dropping the pistol near the levers, knowing every millisecond would count. Samantha clearly didn't have a gun of her own or I'd have been shot in the back already, an easy target in the thin but adequate starlight.

Just as I pulled my way up the loader ladder and hurled my heavy feet onto the platform, I felt this evil woman's hand reach around the heel of my boot. I yanked the door open and dove across the seat, my fingertips landing on the butt of the gun just as she gripped my ankle. I wrapped my fingers tight around the gun as she pulled me off the seat and back again onto the platform, my elbows and legs scraping across the metal grids.

I tried to ignore the searing pain that shot through me as she tugged at my limbs from her purchase on the ladder.

I knew if I didn't hold tight to the gun, I was dead.

I flipped over onto my back, my legs twisting awkwardly as she gripped my ankles tight, and I leveled my gun at her. She gave a swift yank and we both dropped like rocks off the platform onto the rocky ground below, the breath knocked completely from me and the pistol knocked from my hand.

She regained control more quickly than I had, but I flopped over onto my belly and crawled to within reach of the gun. When I turned over onto my back, her twisted face was directly above me, the flashlight gripped in her raised arm, ready to strike.

I tried to level the pistol on her stomach in time to protect myself. I heard gunfire and felt the flashlight glance against my skull before Samantha's body landed on top of me.

And then my world dimmed.

CHAPTER 33

I WAS REALLY STARTING to hate the sounds of emergency vehicles.
The steady wail of sirens, the beeps of monitors alerting emergency response teams, and the squawking radios.

My head felt like a little minion was inside my skull working overtime with a jackhammer, lighting off an occasional stick of dynamite just for variety. My mind raced to find the cause, and I saw De Milo's face as he knelt over me, sticking me with a needle, filling my veins and brain with something wicked. Then I smelled the barroom floor—spilled beer and dirty feet—as my head banged against a table pedestal, legs wriggling around me like undulating bars in a twisted Stephen King jail. Finally, I landed on an image of Samantha Schilling's contorted face just before she clocked me with a flashlight.

I wasn't in Poudre Hospital. Or Rapid City Regional. Thank God! I was in the back of an ambulance again for the second time today. Well, technically it was yesterday when the emergency response team attended to my concussion at the Firehouse.

I lifted my hands and saw that my palms were bandaged. I pulled back the sheet, only to discover that my jeans had been cut into shorts and my knees were both bandaged as well. I remembered scrabbling across the iron ore on my hands and knees trying to get to the loader and then being yanked across the catwalk of the loader platform like Colby cheese against a sharpened grater. I wiggled my fingers, and lifted my arms and both legs to make sure everything was working. The back of my left calf was sore, but no bones were broken. I remembered the pain I'd felt as Samantha gave her best wood chop to that leg when I was hung up on the fence.

All in all, I was in great shape. Considering.

I tried to sit up, and a wave of nausea rose in my throat. I rested my head back on the flat pillow and willed the fluorescent lights inside the back of the ambulance to dim. But they didn't. I was startled by the noise that rose in my throat, a raspy groan that gargled up when I tried to roll over. I felt a warm hand on my forehead and forced my eyelids open.

At first, I wondered if I was staring at Michael, the Archangel.

But it was Agent Adonis. He was staring down at me, dressed in white, his head covered with short white hair and his face sporting a sexy five o'clock shadow. His throat had been slit and his left jaw was black and blue. I reached up to touch his face, unsure if he was real. He smiled at me. I liked his sea green eyes. And his smile. And the touch of his fingers against my forehead.

I liked having my own angel. A cool angel.

"Streeter," I said, my fingers lingering against his stubbled cheek.

He smiled.

Another face appeared over his shoulder.

I croaked, "Agent Stewart Blysdorf."

He grinned. "You know me?"

I nodded, the pain in my head sending tidal waves of nausea through my stomach once again. I lay still and tried to smile up at him.

"What'd you do to your eye?" I managed.

His grin was crooked. "Nothing much. You did good, Liv."

"And to your neck?" I dropped my hand from Streeter's cheek.

"It's nothing," he whispered.

"Samantha Schilling?"

"Dead."

"Did I shoot her? 'Cause I can't remember firing my gun."

Both men shook their heads.

I remembered Samantha's story and was worried for Char Freeburg's safety, wanting to warn her about Mr. Schilling.

My lips cracked when I spoke. "You have to find Eddie Schilling."

"He's dead, too," Bly said. "Before Mully and the Lucifer's Lot pulled up stakes, they left a little present for Eddie in his car. A copperhead. They probably knew that Eddie would eventually leave the campground in his car and speed off toward some refuge. The snake was probably coiled on the floorboard or on the passenger seat of the convertible."

"Nice guys," I said, trying to decide if I felt sorry for Mr. Schilling or if I felt vindication. All the young girls Eddie Schilling had hurt during his authoritative reign of terror could now rest, knowing he would never hurt them or another again.

Bly added, "One bite is all it takes to disable a driver. He crossed two lanes and ended up in the creek."

I closed my eyes and imagined Mr. Schilling's terror as the copperhead latched onto his arm, releasing its deadly poison. He would have been horrified, panicked, dead within minutes.

"Roy Barker?"

Streeter never said a word, content to hold my hand.

"He stole Michelle's book from her locker," Bly explained. "Didn't want the police to think he had anything to do with her murder if they found it, so he put it in Jens's bedroom."

"Mully didn't kill Michelle," my mouth worked to form the words that were racing through my head.

Streeter pressed his finger gently against my lips and said, "Shh, we know."

Bly held up the recorder I had taped to my ribs before confronting the Schillings. "We heard all about it. Digitally. You're a genius, Liv Bergen."

I tried to sit up again, this time successfully.

Streeter said, "Are you sure you want to move?"

I nodded.

Agent Blysdorf sighed. "They want you to go to the hospital for observation. To make sure you don't have a serious concussion."

"Yeah, that's not going to happen," I said, sliding off the bed and out of the ambulance into the fresh air.

Streeter held my arm and steadied me as I warded off the initial dizziness. He brushed a strand of hair from my bandaged forehead and said, "You're lucky that Samantha Schilling was shot before your skull was smashed. You escaped with only a concussion."

"It feels like I cracked some serious corn," I agreed. "I have a killer headache."

"They say you'll be fine," Bly said with a smile. "You take care of yourself and heal fast, okay?"

"Agent Blysdorf?" I called after him as he went about his business with the other emergency personnel.

He stopped and turned, grinning.

"If I didn't shoot Samantha Schilling, then I need to thank you for saving my life," I said, my heart filled with gratitude.

He shook his head, his gray and black ringlets dancing against his shoulders. "Don't thank me. That would be my partner."

He nodded toward Streeter, my human crutch. Streeter's smile was crooked, endearing. I noticed for the first time his hand was braced.

"What did you do?"

"I broke it in a beer brawl at Sturgis earlier tonight. Long story. Kind of messed it up a little bit more when I tackled you and Mully at the Firehouse."

My mind flashed to the image of him running down the length of the bar at the Firehouse Brewing Company, saving me from Mully's grasp. The same man I saw in my dreams. Michael, the Archangel.

"Yeah, about that," I said, straightening a bit and releasing my grip on him. "I was fine, you know. I could have handled that situation by myself and without earning a concussion."

Streeter grinned.

"So where do I send the bill for all the medication I'm going to need for my massive headache?"

Bly answered for Streeter. "Mail it to the Denver bureau, because unless they talk him into temporarily running this Rapid City one and solving the Crooked Man case, he'll be heading back home later this morning."

"I thought Agent Shankley ran the Rapid City office."

"He used to. If he lives, I bet his ass will be fired for his involvement in covering up Eddie Schilling's extracurricular activities," Bly answered.

"Too much information, partner," Streeter said.

Bly ignored him and said to me, "So this guy is leaving on a jet plane unless you can convince him to stay."

Giving me a wink, Bly took off to talk with the rest of the emergency response team near the Nemo Quarry office building.

"You're really leaving?" I asked Streeter.

He just stared at me. "Are you okay now, Liv? You really should go to the hospital."

"I've had my fill of hospitals." With him staring at me, face to face, I struggled to find the right words. "Thank you for saving my life tonight. And from De Milo. I owe you."

I felt so stupid. I had thought hundreds of times about what I'd say to Streeter Pierce when I first met him, when I thanked him for saving me. And never had it come out so . . . stupid.

"You don't owe me. In fact, I owe you. An apology," he said, taking a step back from me and releasing me from his paralyzing stare.

Those green eyes were absolutely trance inducing. I blamed my ditzy thoughts on the two blows to the head.

"Apology for what? I'm the one who owes you an apology for how I treated you at my brother's house."

He chuckled. "Well, I won't argue with you. But let me go first. You were right. And I apologize. I shouldn't have assumed you needed my help with Mully," he said, walking behind the door of the ambulance bed and out of sight. He returned with a leash in his hand, a big red bloodhound close at his heels. "And as a peace offering, I wanted to introduce you to Beulah."

The big red dog with long ears and saggy jowls walked right up to me, wagging her long tail, and started licking my shin. She must have weighed ninety pounds. I dropped to my scabby knees and hugged her neck. She groaned as I wrapped her in my arms. Her fur was warm and silky.

I pulled back and scratched her ears. "Nice to meet you, Beulah. How long have you had her?"

"About a month," Streeter said.

"She's gorgeous. I love bloodhounds. They're great pets."

"Good, because she's yours."

"Mine?"

"Like I said, she's my peace offering to you since we started off on the wrong foot," Streeter said, handing me Beulah's lead. "A gift."

I was overwhelmed by the gesture.

My heart flipped.

I loved dogs and I had always wanted a bloodhound. I couldn't believe Agent Pierce had bought me a dog. How did he know how often I'd lain awake this past month worrying about how I'd feel going back into that house? My house. In Fort Collins. The house where my friend Lisa Henry had been murdered.

I turned back toward Streeter, my grin wide.

"Beulah was Special Agent Lisa Henry's dog."

My grin faded. It wasn't a dog he had bought for me. It was a dog he was palming off on me. But after a moment of thought and shaking off what I thought was a fairy tale ending, I realized that just made it even better. Lisa's dog would keep me company.

"Beulah's been staying with me ever since . . . well, for the past month or so. Beulah's a professional, a trained dog."

"Trained for what?" I asked, wondering what this heap of lovable cuddle could possibly be trained to do well other than slumber and drool.

"Beulah's a trailing dog," he explained, kneeling beside her and roughing her loose skin with a friendly pat. "She tracks humans. Escaping criminals, lost kids, even finds cadavers."

It was hard to imagine this dog's accomplishments or energy as I watched her amble up from her sitting position to stand between us. She laid her nose on my thigh and nudged my hand. I stroked Beulah's head and scratched her ears as she stared at me with her sad, droopy eyes.

"Beulah," I said, "you're a beauty."

"Come on. We'll take you home so you can both get some sleep," Streeter said, rising to his feet.

"Home? So, she's really mine to keep? She's retired?"

Agent Pierce's impish grin reappeared as he walked the dog to the car and coaxed her into the backseat, waving to someone and saying, "Thanks for bringing her up." He turned to me and by way of explanation added, "The agent who had brought Beulah up here tonight."

"At your insistence," I guessed.

"Precisely."

"And you knew I'd accept this responsibility? Just like that?"

"She's a peace offering. And, yes, I was hoping you would."

We stood staring at one another for a long moment. I wondered how long I'd been out of it to allow Streeter time to call someone, retrieve a dog, and drive her up to me. From the corner of my eye, I saw Agent Blysdorf padding back from the office and toward Jens's truck. He flashed me a smile and a wink and slid behind the wheel.

"What's he doing?"

"I told you. We're taking you home. He's driving the truck. And I'm driving you."

Before I could even think about it, the words tumbled from me, "I'm sorry about earlier. I didn't mean to kick you out of Jens's house. I was just—"

He touched my lips with his finger and time froze. The acceptance of my apology was offered in a twinkle of his eyes and he pulled away from me far too abruptly.

"She's not retired," Streeter explained, pulling a book and file from the dashboard of the car and handing it to me. "She needs a new handler. Everything you need to know is in there."

"But I don't know how to train a dog to track," I argued, not fully grasping the change from owning a new pet that I already loved to caring for a professional working dog in a world I knew nothing about.

"We're not worried about you training her," he said, heading for the door again. "We're worried about how well Beulah's going to train you."

My mouth slacked open.

Streeter laughed. "There's been a lot of talk at the bureau over the past month. Beulah is an important part of the FBI family. And she meant the world to Agent Henry, who was an even more important part of our family."

Streeter fell in behind the wheel of the Pontiac, waiting for me to climb in on the passenger's side.

"So why me?" I said walking around the car.

Agent Blysdorf had the window of Jens's pickup rolled down. His smile softened. "Because Special Agent Streeter Pierce thought you would be the best one in the world to care for Beulah."

I felt myself sliding into an emotional avalanche.

"But I don't deserve her," I managed to say before my voice cracked.

"Streeter thought you did. He went to bat for you to become her handler, despite the bureau's opposition. Nothing against you, Liv, just that you're not bureau. But Streeter argued that you solved the De Milo case, and after last night, who could argue with him?"

A lump filled my throat, tears burned in my eyes. "Thank you!"

"Don't thank me. Thank Streeter," he said, giving me a wave and rolling up his window.

I made my way to the passenger seat of the Pontiac, unable to hold back a few tears that leaked from the corner of my eyes.

"Are you okay?" Streeter asked, concern etched in his face.

"Happy tears."

Happy that I was alive. Happy to own a bloodhound. Happy to know somewhere Lisa was smiling down at me, thankful that I was Beulah's new housemate. Happy that I wasn't going home alone to my house in Fort Collins. Happy that Streeter thought enough of me to give me the gift of Beulah.

Happy that Streeter believes in me.

THE END